THE GENTLE ART OF FORGETTING

Part of The Snow Trilogy

For everyone we lost too soon.

The Vivid Press

Hello & Goodbye.

First, since there are billions of lonely books waiting to be read in the world, the fact you've chosen this one has just given it a purpose. So on its behalf and mine, thank you.

*

"The Gentle Art Of Forgetting" is part of The Snow Trilogy, along with *"The General Theory Of Haunting"* and *"The Littel* Tale Of Delivering"*.

   * Yes, it is "Littel".

Although the three stories can be read independently and in any *order you choose*, they are connected.

Seemingly minor references in one become major themes in another. Ideas set up in one story are given further explanations elsewhere. Themes recur in all three, but in different contexts.

If you still have questions after one book, I hope you'll find the answers in another. But don't expect this to be a prequel *to* nor sequel *of* the others in the trilogy, *"…Haunting"* & *"… Delivering"*.

Because it is, as you'll discover, *both* and *neither*.

I know that's cryptic, but I can't say any more because this is no longer my tale. I'm just here to make a formal introduction.

Normally I stick around, right to the last word. That is my job, after all. But here's where we must part and I leave you with another narrator.

It's OK. They know what they're doing.

So this is goodbye. We'll meet again in stories to come, but for now, I'm gone.

I'm interested to see what happens.

Please say hello to a friend of mine.

Richard Easter, September 2019.

Introduction; I Am Context.

Hello, welcome, make yourself comfortable. I hope you're ready and warm, because these pages are about to get *cold*.

So before things freeze over, and since we're going to be spending a lot of time in each other's company, I really should introduce myself. My name is… well, that's the question isn't it? What is my name? I suppose for the moment you can call me…hm, Context.

Why not?

Context. Yes. It suits me.

Some "Narrators" can be unreliable, but I won't give you false perspectives or red herrings. You can trust me. I'll stick to the facts.

We have much to cover, and while I have all the time there'll ever be, sadly, you are somewhat limited in that department. So, since I don't know your "Best Before" date, we really should get to business, quick sharp. With some *context*, I think.

*

Books are often arranged in convenient chapters, which helpfully follow each other to develop plot-lines and characters. This one is the same. But here's my problem. Real life is *not* neatly laid out in chapters.

Unlike books, your life's supporting cast and storylines change, apparently at random. Sometimes people and plots are introduced, assume massive importance, then disappear, as if they'd never existed.

So in hindsight, I've decided *life's* more like a collection of loosely related stories which often don't fit together neatly.

Some can be entire novels, others, a few throwaway paragraphs. Then, there are odd little narratives that don't seem to tie in with the rest at all. Oh, but they always do, and often a life only reveals its many connections at the very end.

So it will be with this story.

*

This is a tale of love, loss, memory and mortality which concerns a lost woman named Jane Dawn.

To understand who Jane is and why she's become lost, we must jump and slide through her life together.

So as your guide, I should give you a gentle warning - in the beginning, this may feel like a bumpy ride, but that's just how things are.

I promise to help you hang on, and guarantee this, too; when you reach the very last sentence, I'll tell you my name. You might already suspect I'm Death, Fate, Irony, Time, The Blue Fairy, Rumplestiltskin, Spring Heeled Jack, or whoever, but you're wrong. I am Context, and that will do, for the moment.

*

Here we go, then. We shouldn't keep these pages waiting any longer. After all, this is their job. They've been patiently waiting for somebody to sit down and read them.

And look, here you are.

But where should we begin?

Well, if *your* life was a book, which scene would you open with?

Let me think. Ah, yes. I know the place we should go - it isn't really the beginning of Jane's story, but it is a start.

Perhaps all that is beautiful, unbearable, magical and terrible in Jane Dawn's curious life flowed from here. Then again, perhaps not.

However, for what it's worth, I can categorically say this brief moment *is* a start.

Hello, Jane.

A Start, Of Sorts / Jane Dawn, Bow, East London / February 4th, 2003

Jane Dawn stood in the hallway of her tiny terraced East End home, stared into the mirror, then shut her eyes for a moment and sighed.

She was about to leave for work, and that was never a good thing, because once there, Jane became other people.

Soon, she might be a platinum blonde, sulky brunette or black bobbed, icy European dominatrix. There was always the possibility of a suit and tie, twinset and pearls or maybe just jogging gear.

She sighed again and opened her eyes. *Bloody hell, my schizo profession. Haven't I done well? My careers officer would be* so *proud.*

The hallway clock ticked on, with what sounded like a disappointed tut-tut-tut-tutting.

Yeah, OK, don't rub it in, clock. Smug doesn't suit you. We've both ticked out the same moves for years *now, going no-where.*

She raised an eyebrow at her reflection, which responded in kind. Jane tried a smile, which looked like she mainly felt. False.

Oh, please, you drama queen, she admonished herself. *It's just a job. It's not the end of the world, is it?*

Mirror-Jane stared back, with no opinion one way or the other.

She shrugged, resigned to the fact that no work meant no pay, fastened the buttons of her big black coat and opened the front door.

The cold rushed in and turned her breath to fog.

It was Jane's kind of day. Frost-kissed and ice-chilled. She stood on her doorstep, looked out at East London, smiled, and breathed in the frozen air. Her smile faltered.

No, stop, whoah, wait. What? This feels different, somehow, it's…what? Important? Why is that? What just happened? Déjà vu? No, not déjà vu, more like a memory I didn't quite grab.

She waited for an answer to focus, but couldn't find one, so stepped from her home and thought;

OK, today. I'm ready for you. Here I go again.
Let's see what happens.

*

So yes, that brief moment in Jane's hallway was a start, but beginnings and endings are illusory, anyway. Like chapters, we bolt them onto stories to give us the hollow comfort of order, when the world rarely arranges itself so helpfully.

She had the right idea, though. Life's chaotic, and often there really is nothing else to think, except *let's see what happens.*

*

Once upon a time, I was told everyone has a story and the best we can do for them is to tell it well. I made a promise to do just that, and for Jane it's a vow I intend to keep.

But you must forgive me now, because I must push you straight in at the deep end. Other books might let you dip your toes into the narrative for a while, but not this one.

You're about to get very lost, very deep and very cold, very quickly.

Like Jane Dawn, at first you may struggle to orient yourself, but trust me, I have you. I'll *always* have you, from this moment to the very last.

No matter how strange things might become, I promise I'll have you.

And *remember*. That's all I ask. *Remember.*

Very well, then.

Take my hand, fill your lungs, hold on tight.

Here we go, down, down, let's plunge together.

You, Jane and I, into the deep end.

/ **BOOK ONE /** *HERE* **AND** *THERE*

1/ *Jane Is Lost - Minute 1*

Listen.

For a moment, there was something that sounded like a kettle boiling. Then a thirty year old woman called Jane Dawn awoke.

She came to, blinked, and slowly her eyes focussed.

It took an effort to see, as everything seemed blurred and white. Then she realised everything *was* blurred and white, because her vision was filled with thick snow.

Her mind was blurred too. Thought itself was an effort.

Distantly, Jane knew she was now *somewhere different*. She faced a window, *somewhere else*, and eventually managed to think, *now where am I?* But putting those words together in the correct order proved difficult.

Wherever she now found herself, it was completely silent. No background rumble of traffic, nor aircraft droned overhead. No ticking of clocks, or conversation in another room. Just Jane, this wood-framed window and the deepest of silences. Against it, even her shallow breathing seemed a cacophony.

She looked through the window and saw a dense line of trees in the distance. Their branches drooped under a thick layer of snow.

There was an empty clearing between wherever she sat and the tree-line. No green shoots, saplings or rocks peeked from that smooth, frozen landscape.

Jane was drawn to the snow that fell outside. She couldn't pull her eyes from it.

In the sky above this frozen clearing, a green Aurora performed aerial origami, folded into shapes; a wave, a sand dune, a sheet drying in a brisk wind. Then it dispersed, like ink in water. The Aurora diluted, faded and was gone.

Jane never saw it.

But with every flake that fell past her eyes, she felt strangely comforted, as if the snow wasn't just erasing the ground, but *her* too, like chalk from a blackboard, ready for the next lesson.

Jane was inexplicably calm, because other than her name, she couldn't remember anything. Her memory, like the ground outside, had whited out, become smooth and featureless.

So she watched as both the snow and her mind drifted.

She had no desire to look away from this window. Jane knew there was something she *should* think, but it was just out of reach, a lifebelt that floated one way while the drowner chose to flail in the other.

*What should I. Be thinking? I don't. Know. I am…*and then, oh-so slowly, words came with difficulty, fetched from part of her mind she no longer knew.

I am numb. Dumb. I am.

Strung.

Out. Inert.

Yes.

She reached up and placed her hand flat on the window.

It was solid.

Aha, oh, take note, Jane.

This is.

Solid.

That was important. The window was solid. The window was real. So it followed that all this was real, too.

Outside, the snow chased its shadows to ground, thicker and thicker.

Part of her, inside - only a small part, a tiny, sensible, aware Jane, many hundreds of miles away, shouted, ran in circles and tried to attract her attention.

Listen! What's happening? This tiny Jane deep in her mind screamed. *What is happening to you? What is happening? What is happening Jane? What is happening you were not* here *you were somewhere else not here* before*, ask yourself what is happening?* Ask ask *ask.*

Oh be quiet, she thought, still oddly tranquil, in emotional slow motion. *I'm just Watching The Snow.*

And even as Jane thought that phrase, she realised the words had gained capitals, like a heading in an instruction manual. *I am Watching The Snow,* she thought again, and there they were, the capitals, **W.T.S.** Watching The Snow, in bold, capitalised in her mind. Odd.

*You don't give a capital to a word...*she tried to remember. *Oh no, you do NOT give capitals to words...unless...the beginning...sentence of a noun...proper noun?* She stopped, confused, and stared back at the flakes.

"I think that's enough, Jane," someone spoke from behind her, and she felt a rough, dry hand gently touch her face and pull it softly away from the window.

2 / Jane / Between Thoughts

As Jane's face was tenderly drawn from that unfamiliar, worryingly solid window, other memories flickered. She tried to hold onto them, but they raced into the distance.

Remember, please remember, you are Jane, *remember who you are, quick, before all your memories are gone. You can feel them fade. Yes. You are Jane, you are* Jane, *you are…*

Where?

London? Am I from London?

It was cold. It was cold and then I met someone. Who?

A garden and roses.

I had promises to keep, a job to do, but now I am…where?

I became other people. Wait. What? How?

There was a typewriter. Was it a typewriter?

No, it was my…Companion. What?

Wait.

Grapes and chilli sauce.

Grapes and chilli sauce?

I am sure I was just with someone, someone very old, but they are not with me any more.

That old someone led me here.

There was a dare. A dare? I was given a dare. What dare? I don't usually accept dares, so why this one? Who gave me a dare?

I time travelled. No, no, that can't be right. But I was out of time. It was one year outside and another inside.

Someone dancing. No, someone tap *dancing. Tap dancing? Me? No.*

She fumbled at the images and feelings as they passed, but they were too quick for her, or she too slow for them. She tried to focus on what felt like the most important questions.

Who was I with? Where was I? Who am I?

But even the questions grew indistinct. Everything that once mattered ceased to. Her memory melted, like snow.

3 / *Jane Is Lost / Minutes 2-5*

I'm aware this hasn't been the easiest of starts. But although there are many ways to recount Jane's tale, after much consideration, I think this particular one is the best. I did warn you we'd drown together, didn't I?

I'm also aware that's not the most comforting of statements.

So far, we are just sixty seconds into this story. A lot can happen in one minute and much more can happen in even less, as you will discover.

You and I must meet throughout these pages, because not every moment of Jane's life is known to her, which may sound counter intuitive, but I'll explain why in time. I'm here to help you understand, and while I'm not going to give you *all* the answers, I won't leave you wondering. The threads will be neatly tied. That's what I'm here for.

We must move on - sorry if this is such a brief re-acquainting, but this isn't about me, now, and we have many places to visit and so much to know about Jane, you and I.

Fill your lungs again.

I told you this would be the deep end.

*

"I think that's enough, Jane," somebody said. Listlessly she turned her head from the wood-framed window and allowed that weather-beaten hand to guide her gaze from the snow.

She slowly looked about her new surroundings. They were made of;

One room.

Wooden walls.

A cupboard.

Candles.

A wooden chair.

A desk with a little box on it and next to that, an old typewriter.

A man.

A small oven, attached to a tubular black metal chimney that ran up and through the high ceiling.

The turned-down bed on which she now sat, cross-legged.

A small sink and tap.

A window on each plain wooden wall.

Only a few moments before, a tiny, rational Jane had ran around frantically inside her mind, and shouted at her to look away from this snow and ask the only question that mattered.

But she continued to ignore that inner voice, for now.

I am drowning in this, she thought dimly, still bafflingly calm. *I'm lost. My memory is.*

Gone, I don't.

Know.

Where I am, or.

Who I am.

But I'm - what? Accepting. It. Why?

Hold on. Stop. Oh. Man*? Wait. There's a* man*?*

The man leaned against the cupboard with a mug in his hand. He looked at Jane with a smile on his lips and in his eyes.

She stared back and blinked like someone caught in a spotlight.

How did she miss him? He was, after all, an actual man.

Somewhere far away, Jane's little voice, lost inside her, still screamed. *Whoever he is, ask him the question! The* only *question! Ask it!*

The man in the corner raised his mug in greeting and then tapped it.

"Oh, bugger." He brought it up to his face, squinted at the mug and turned down his lips. "It's cracked. Oh dear. When did that happen? Seems OK, though, *fit for purpose*," he added in a silly posh voice. "But *yoo knoh-oh*, it's the cracks you can't see that get you. Always do. There are…" He put on the posh voice again. "…cracks in the *nate-uuuure* of things."

The man frowned as he turned the cup this way and that.

The silence fell again. Jane looked down at herself. She wore a green blouse, a short black skirt and flat shoes. Without thought, she reached up to her neck and felt something there, a tiny silver snowflake which hung from a thin necklace.

She looked down at her short skirt and glanced back out of the window at the icy clearing.

I'm not dressed for snow am I? But I was never dressed for snow, was I?

But she had no idea what that statement meant.

"Coffee?" asked the man. "Tea? Something weaker? Stronger?"

Jane stared at him. *Did he really just ask if I wanted tea or coffee?* She wondered, but her voice replied automatically. "Tea please," and although this seemed the most normal thing in the world, that small voice from the edge of space shouted again, *You're talking to this stranger in this weird... hut...and asking for* tea? *Hello? Where are your memories? Your memories? Who* are *you? Hello? Can you hear me? Ask!*

"Yes, tea, I should have known, of course." The man opened the cupboard/larder. "English Breakfast." It wasn't a question.

He dropped a teabag into a pot of boiling water on the stove.

"Sorry - no kettles Here." He apologised, and somehow, Jane heard he'd pronounced *Here* with a capital H.

"Why. No. Kettles?" She asked, but her lips still struggled to form words. It was a ridiculous question, but she went with it, because what else could she do?

The man shrugged. "I don't think it's an...anti-kettle thing. It's just... there's no, er, what is it? Oh yes, electricity, see. Hence..."

He gestured to the little typewriter on the desk and the candles, "Don't blame me. I just work Here." He shook his head and laughed quietly to himself.

"Who are. You?" Jane asked. Her tongue engaged, failed, and she knew *who are you?* wasn't the real question.

"Who am I? Well..."

She took him in as he considered his response.

He was over six feet tall and wore a bright yellow oilskin. A cable knit woollen jumper poked from under the collar and above that, a spotted red neckerchief. He had a dark beard speckled with snow-white patches at the sides and was aged somewhere between forty five to sixty, it was difficult to tell. Black hair tufted out from the sides of his hat and the man's eyebrows grew upwards and outwards, untamed. His eyes were blue and kind, but scrunched up as if he stared into a wind, despite being indoors.

It was easy to trust those eyes.

He's like Captain Birdseye. She wasn't exactly sure who Captain Birdseye was, but in those microseconds, words, images and feelings flashed into her mind…

Captainbirdseyeeattastedinnertimehallfishbreadchipssmellcookinghall mumgrandadsboatdadsfavouritechairbottleofbeerthameschoolsnowwhowh ojanefindusplatecookingbeefcrispypancakestomatosauce

…and then they were gone.

"Who are you?" Jane asked again, still dimly aware that it remained the wrong question.

The man yawned, stretched, and put his hands into the small of his back. "Well…" He puffed out his cheeks. "I'm, well, you know, I'm your…what's that word…*"handler"*? Ugh, horrible word, but that's the one they use, don't they? You can call me The Man." He gave a little bow and she realised he'd given the words, 'The' and, 'Man,' capitals, too.

He took another sip of his drink then fetched another mug from the cupboard.

"Jane Dawn. Yes, oh, beg my pardon, how rude. Hello, welcome… we're ready for you, of course. Hoping we wouldn't have to be, but there you are. Everything is present and correct. English Breakfast, white, one sugar. Hmm? You don't remember much at all, do you?" He stirred the tea. "That's why you shouldn't Watch The Snow too long. The right memories will come back, the wrong ones won't. You'll get used to it. Bit like knowing how much to drink before you fall over, sort of."

Jane stared at this strange Man, empty, no idea what to say.

"It's odd, I know. If you Watch The Snow too long, you'll get wiped. Memory gone, kaputt. It happens. Some get lost in the Snow and never find themselves again. But I'm getting ahead of myself. You have many questions, that's obvious. Here…" He offered Jane the mug.

She took it from his hand and sipped like a sleepwalker.

For a moment, she allowed herself to believe she was just a woman, drinking tea. But then, a voice leapt into her mind with full clarity. It was her own voice again, but twisted.

That voice formed words with no problems. Oh no, *that* voice knew exactly what it wanted to say.

You have killed. It whispered. *Killed again and again. You don't remember, but you* know. *You have killed people, Jane.*

She shook her head and tried to clear that cracked, tiny voice, but it hissed again, *Jane, pay attention. You have killed. And that is why you are here.* Then fell silent.

The words were vicious, but meant nothing to her. No memories were attached to them.

She sat and waited for who-knows-what. No ticking clock, traffic, birdsong or jets overhead. As far as she knew, there might be nothing behind that frozen tree line, just infinite emptiness. Snow, forever and after.

"Alright. Let's start with the basics. What do you know?" The Man asked, kindly.

Jane thought. She knew her name, and there were flickers and shimmers that bounced about her mind, but other than that, nothing. She simply shook her head.

"I know... I am Jane. Jane. Dawn. Yes." Her tongue still couldn't form words naturally.

"You are." He nodded and smiled. "Good. You are Jane. Jane Dawn. That's all you need to know, for now. Are you scared?"

She searched inside herself and was surprised by the answer.

"No," she whispered.

"Good, that's good. It's working." He took a sip of his tea, leaned back against the larder and waited. Jane tried to think of something, anything to say.

So, without thought, the only real question came out.

"Where am I?"

The Man smiled. "Well, you're Here, of course."

Here. Of course. So now Jane had one answer, however vague. She was sat in a place called, simply, *Here.* Capital H.

4 / Jane, Lost, Minutes 5-8

On a single bed, in a hut, in a silent, frozen clearing, a lost woman called Jane with no memory thought about this Man's response for a moment.

"OK, very good, where am I? I ask and. You say, whoever. You. Are…" She sighed and took in his response sluggishly. "I am Here. Here I am. Ha ha. *Goooood* answer."

As she said the words, she'd also somehow recognised the capital 'H' of 'Here,' but didn't know why.

I should be panicking and yet I'm not, why is that? Jane remained unfathomably rational inside, although her thoughts still juddered and slipped.

Why aren't I screaming? Why. Aren't I running. For. The door?
Where was I before this? Who was I?

And again;

What is happening? I'm not. Dreaming.
No, this is. Not a dream.
I'm wide awake and. I'm calm. So am I drugged?
No. Yes. I feel drugged, but not. I feel
anaesthetised, but totally
conscious.
This Snow is like….

She searched her mind for the right description.

Like…icy morphine. Like.
Codeine blizzard.
I am not panicking because the snow is.
Like. Snowman methadone.
The snow has frozen my fear, chilled my confusion. Like.
Heroin Glacier.
But I can feel it, the fear, the confusion, beneath the ice.
Waiting

Despite herself, Jane smiled at the shape and feel of the words.

Words, she thought. *What is it about words? About me? About me and words? And a companion?*

"Wait. You knew what tea I… like." She realised something important. "Ooooh, Oh, oooh, you knew. You knew my. *Name*," she whispered as fear tiptoed toward her. "Do I know you? Did I know you? Before…?"

"Everyone knows me, well everyone *Here* knows me." He looked up at the low ceiling of the Hut and wiped away some dust that Jane couldn't see.

"Please," she sighed, softly. "Don't treat me like some kind of…" She had the right word for a moment, fumbled, grabbed it again. "Like an ingenue."

"But you are. That's exactly what you are right now. Everybody is, at this point. Accept it, and we can move on. Right. Any questions?"

He said it dismissively, like there couldn't possibly be any questions.

"Well, only. Every. Question. Ever." Jane still wondered distantly why she hadn't hollered the walls down. But then, speech was still difficult. "Please. Where am I? And don't say 'Here' again, it's not helping."

The Man looked slightly deflated.

She took a deep breath, then steadied herself like a drunk person who just needed to say *this one thing*.

"I get it. I am Here. Here I am." She struggled for the right word and hooked it. "Mm, semantically, it's. Correct, but. Factually. It. Tells me nothing. I don't. *Remember*. Anything. I don't know where I was, before…Why don't I know? Why can't I remember? So…" She looked back at The Man and tried to fix him with a stare. "Where am I?"

He suddenly shouted, which took her by surprise. "AHA! YES! Yes! Told!" He bellowed. "With a capital T! You must be Told!!"

"Told? Told? Yes. You know, I heard. It. Told with a capital *T*. I heard. It." Jane's mouth was still not working properly. "You have capital letters - upper case letters for things *Here* where there shouldn't. Be. Any. But… Told? Told what?"

"That's what's happening now. You're being Told. About Here. About what it's for. What this place does. That's my job. I do the Telling." The Man answered, proudly. She couldn't be completely sure, but he seemed to puff his chest out, like a pigeon in an oilskin.

"You know…ah, I really should have a notebook. Even a blackboard. Right. Right. You ask - where is *Here*? I suppose it won't floor you to discover it's not on any maps. Here is….er, "restricted". Redacted? Isn't that what they say?"

Jane stared dully back at him. She had no answers.

"Sorry. I'm really not helping am I? But not everywhere has a map reference, you know."

"No. No. That's not. Right."

A tiny part of her, that small but shrill voice of reason, screeched again. *Why are you so calm when this is so frighteningly insane? You're in a tiny room who-knows-where with a man who is who-knows-who and you're just sitting here, on this bed? Talking like it's some kind of mad tea party? How have you been re-programmed? Hypnotised? Re-wired? What drugs have you been given exactly?*

But the Jane on the bed over-rode that internal voice again and pushed on. She couldn't afford to surrender to panic, had to try and keep herself centred. The alternative was insanity.

"Everywhere. does have. A. Map reference." She stuttered on, belligerently. "Even if it's. The. Middle of. No-where. Everywhere still. Has. A map reference."

"No, it doesn't. Not everywhere's on a map. For example, I met my wife at a party. She introduced herself! Just walked straight over as if she'd known me forever." He shook his head and chuckled. "Most unusual. I was a bit taken aback, but she was *so* beautiful. I forgave her instantly." He smiled, and Jane mirrored it, as one does when caught in the middle of someone else's happiness.

I'm getting his life story, she wondered, *but I don't have a clue about. My. Own. Why. Is he. Telling me this and why. Don't I tell. Him to stop?* Inside, however, she felt it was something important. But what, she had no idea.

The Man carried on, lost in his reverie, "Oh, the way she looked at me. That first second, that very moment, I knew I was going to marry her. But of course, I had to go through the whole 'proper' routine, you know. I'd have married her on the spot, but there were no shotgun weddings, not those days."

"When were… Those. Days?" Jane forced the words out and surrendered to whatever this was. She was weak, confused, had no fight.

"Oh, *somewhen* else." She realised he'd avoided yet another question. "So we did it properly. We went for tea, and tea led to a dinner, dinner led to a dance, then, well, everything."

The smile disappeared from his face.

"She was, is, and always will be, the loveliest thing I have ever seen, or ever will."

Jane didn't want to ask, but her heart got there before her head. She spoke without thought.

"What happened?"

The Man looked away, empty. He folded his hands primly and replied, "what always happens."

The only sound was their breathing.

Then The Man came back to life like a wind up toy, clicked back into movement. "Sometimes you don't have to accept '*what always happens,*' though. The point is, the place we met doesn't exist any more. They pulled it down, turned it into a school. So where I met my wife is no-where, now. See? So where are *you* now? Well, you've been, er, "relocated". For your own good, I should add."

None of this helped Jane, who felt she was being deliberately mis-directed. But now she felt fear grow inside her. The bizarre calming morphia of the snow had faded.

This fear wouldn't pass by. Jane felt it rush toward her. The storm was about to hit.

"Please," she began to shiver. "Please. No. I can't…Am I? No. No. Please. Tell me. No. Please. Am…? *Am*…?… Am…I?"

An impossible question had formed in her mind. But she couldn't, wouldn't say it loud. Not yet.

The Man hadn't seen Jane's fear.

"You see," he smiled. "You have to forget the usual rules, *Here.*"

She crumbled. Until this moment, her expression had been confused, yet stoic. But now it collapsed, and any remnants of strength melted from her face.

"Jane?" He reached for her again.

She backed away from his hand. Jane didn't want to ask - the question itself was madness - but then, wasn't everything skewed in this new, strange place? She closed her eyes and took a deep breath.

*

You'll find out what that question was soon enough.

Take my hands, it's OK, let me pull you up to the surface. You and Jane have floundered enough. Come, I'll take you from these depths to somewhere more familiar. Everything will be explained. There are no riddles, not really, only perspectives. Breathe.

BOOK TWO/ 1979

5 / Jane's Early Life / Some Family History

If you want to make sense of *now*, you have to understand *then*.

So in order to do that, let's travel together, many miles and years, back to *then*.

Come with me to the nineteen seventies, specifically, 1973. Oh, the seventies. I was there, of course. But then again, I've been *everywhere*.

If you weren't present, it doesn't matter. The seventies were essentially identical to the decades that preceded and would follow. There are only so many variations of the same story, whether global or personal, and the relative good or bad of a time depends on who's experiencing it.

For example, 1973 defined David Bowie, while it destroyed Richard Nixon. He really should have stayed away from all that bugging. Nixon, not Bowie.

But more importantly for our purposes, it was the year Jane arrived.

*

Jane Dawn was born in The London Hospital on the 27th September, 1973, and grew up in Bow, a district of the capital's East End. Her mother Irene worked in a Bethnal Green curtain factory, while father Dave was a street cleaner.

Dave knew that way back in history, one distant branch of the Dawn family tree was considered *very* upper class and had amassed a fortune. He "enjoyed" the irony of that most mornings as he picked up litter for £4.20 an hour, a life he'd vowed to save his own daughter from. Dave didn't have his faraway ancestors wealth, but was blessed with a quick mind and an impressive memory, and they can't be bought.

Outside the Curtain Factory, Jane's mother Irene earned a little money on the side as an artist. She'd received no formal training, but real talent isn't learned, only nurtured. Irene's paintings of pets, children and families could be found hanging in many homes across the East End.

Unlike Dave, who would happily talk for England, Irene spoke little. She chose her words very carefully, but on canvasses, never held back. Irene's paid commissions were almost always copies from photographs, but in private she favoured an untamed style. Her paintings hung on nearly every wall of their small terraced family home - layers and shades, luminescent greens and blues. Little Jane would often lose herself in them, finding shapes in the colours, as one does when watching clouds.

While Irene was happiest with her brushes, David's passion was reading. He consumed books like he consumed beer, which is to say, with great enjoyment and as much and often as he possibly could. He piled them up in little towers next to his favourite chair, with a West Ham United mug of tea, or more likely, a can of lager at their side. Consequently, Dave could conjure up insights and lessons on pretty much everything, which meant every day, without even realising, Jane received extra education from her father.

She grew up with the best of both Irene and Dave; Jane had been gifted patience, kindness, a love and respect for words, a voracious need to learn, to fill her memory, *to see what happened.*

Later in life, after she'd heard about some of her friends' upbringings, Jane realised how lucky she'd been. Her early years were uneventfully, wonderfully, normal. Mum and Dad had made childhood seem effortless, although money was tight.

Nowadays, the Dawns would be considered a family on the edge of poverty, but it hadn't felt like that, not once. Jane's clothes were often hand-me-downs, although she never knew. Her toys were mainly from charity shops, but when you're a child, provenance is unimportant.

Food was always on the table, books were read at night-time. She received all the attention and love any child could want from their Mum & Dad, and while that's priceless, it costs nothing.

Of course her parents argued, but the disagreements were rare and took place after Jane was in bed. Like distant retorts on a battlefield, they were bad, but too far away to hurt you.

Then, for a few terrible days in December 1979, everything changed.

6 / December, 1979

By '79, at six years old, Jane had already turned her back on doll's houses and plastic babies, preferring to play inside her mind. After lights out at bedtime, Mum and Dad often heard her muttering away in a variety of voices, telling herself stories. Like all children, she didn't really know the difference between tales and truth. Perhaps the only real difference is who's listening.

As with every child, Jane had plenty of questions that needed answers.

"Where does snow come from?" She'd asked her Dad one teatime.

"It's just frozen rain, really." Dave answered. "You knew that, though, didn't you?"

"Mm, so, like ice?"

"*Like* ice, but, well, fluffier. That's why it's white, instead of glassy, like ice."

"Why's it fluffier?"

"Well, you've made cut-out snowflakes at school. You've seen how they're all spindly and spiky. So there's spaces between them. Ice is solid, like a brick, snow is…" He searched for the right description. "…Kind of knitted, like a jumper."

"*Knitted?*"

"Now you've done it," muttered Irene from the sink.

"Snow is knitted?" Jane went to the window, no doubt to see if a blizzard of cardigans had started.

"No, it's similar. Lots of *bits* that thread together to make one bigger bit. You can't see the smaller bits, but eventually, they make a snowflake, and that's the big part you do see."

Jane continued to peer out, then looked up to the highest high of the sky.

"Will it snow soon?"

"Well, it's winter, so somewhere up there…" Dave joined his daughter at the window and put an arm around her tiny shoulder. "Snow's getting ready for its holiday."

"*Holiday?*"

"Uh-huh. It spends most of the year as water up there, comes down for a bit, then evaporates. But once it's snow, it can stay longer, to play. Become snowballs and snowmen. Have a holiday down here on Earth."

Irene turned from the sink then smiled round at her little family.

"When I was tiny, I thought Father Christmas threw the snow out of the back of his sleigh," she laughed. "That's why it only came around Christmas time."

"I like that," mused David. "Talking of which, you know, if only everyone stuck to Father Christmas' one rule, the world would be much better."

"What's Father Christmas' rule?" Jane asked, and craned her neck to look up at him because surely her Dad was as tall as the house.

"Oh come on, you know! It's only two words. What's Father Christmas' one and only rule? Two words?"

Jane thought. "Oh. I know. Yes. Be nice."

"Exactly. Be nice. And it's so easy to do. Nice takes no effort, naughty is exhausting."

Jane nodded in agreement, very seriously. "I'm going to try and always be nice. Really try." But there was still one question she needed to ask again. For Jane, it was the only question, really.

"When will it snow again?"

Snow came once more in 1979.

*

Take heed. Here's a truth we'll revisit many times in this story; *seemingly insignificant decisions change lives.*

For example - and forgive me for making assumptions - if you've ever fallen in love, I'll bet it happened after, yes, some *seemingly insignificant decisions.*

Maybe you took *this* route rather than *that* route, or went out one night when you were supposed to stay in. Perhaps you tried a different bar to your usual, chose an earlier train, or went for one job over another.

My point is, tiny choices can have huge consequences that only reveal themselves in retrospect.

And sometimes retrospect is all we have.

*

So, in December '79, the *seemingly insignificant decision* that would lead to so much was as quick as this;

IRENE: Shall we go to the playground or the park?

JANE: Park!

It was a white-canopied London Saturday and Jane knew if snow were to fall, Victoria Park was the place to be. "OK, park then," said Irene, and that was that.

Jane lived in a two bedroom terraced house in Bow, with window boxes full of dead flowers in lieu of a garden, so wide open spaces were a very good thing. Trees to climb were even better.

Hand in hand, mother and daughter headed out into that chilly London afternoon, on their way to keep an appointment they hadn't even known they'd made.

Quickly, Jane spotted a likely candidate for climbing, an alder set in the middle of a patch of grass. She rushed up to it, then had to decide which branch to start from.

This thick one with all the little branches?

Or this long, strong one like a pirates' gangplank?

She plumped for the long strong one.

And so the next decision was made.

Huge events can take seconds, and their outcomes are sometimes decided by inches.

Jane was only about one foot above the ground when snow began to wheel lazily in the air.

She saw the flakes and was distracted.

Oh, snow, she thought, and fell.

Had Jane fallen two inches to the right, her temple would have struck earth and grass, but she dropped two inches to the *left* and hit the edge of a stone, stood straight up, like it had always been there, waiting for its cameo.

Her head struck the stone, and Irene rushed forward, arms outstretched to instinctively catch her, but was too late. Jane lay on the grass, and a paper-cut worth of blood appeared on her forehead. Irene dropped to her knees next to her little girl, and shouted, *"help, help!"*

Jane lay silent. Irene didn't know what to do - there were no mobile phones in 1973, no Help Points, no Office First Aiders, no computer-guided GPS tracked ambulances, just a mother and her unconscious daughter. As Irene yelled, the first flakes of snow started to rest on Jane's white face.

That fall was to have consequences that would ripple outward and onward for a very long time.

7 / After A Fall / Jane Wakes / 22nd December 1979 / 21:02 P.M.

Let's jump forward a little now, because we can. The unconscious Jane was taken to The London Hospital, where she was watched by her helpless parents and monitored by doctors and nurses. Tests were performed, 'experts' came to examine, medical students trooped in as if Jane were an exhibit, and all the while, this six year old girl remained elsewhere. No-one had any answers, nor offered any solutions.

Jane slept deeper and longer than any person should. But then, a few days later, with no fanfare, she came to, on December 22nd, 1979, at 21:02 p.m.

As consciousness returned, images flashed through her brain.

Was I in a park? Did I see snow? There was a tree. A park, yes. Lots of trees. Snow.

But then the pictures disappeared.

As she opened her eyes, six year old Jane thought, *now where am I?* She couldn't remember where she'd been *then*, and didn't know where she was *now*.

The first thing she saw were three people, a *lady*, a *friendly looking bloke* and *another man*. The *lady* put her hands over her mouth, eyes wide, as if shocked or excited, maybe both. The *friendly looking bloke* simply looked at her, with wet eyes and a big smile. The *other man* wore a white coat and no expression.

"Oh," said the lady.

Jane looked at the man in the white coat and slowly thought, *oh, he's a Doctor. A proper Doctor.* Then she took in the room.

It was made of;

Bed.

Hospitally thing which goes bleep.

Desky table thing.

Typewritery thingy.

Sink.
Man.
Other Man (nicer).
Lady Who Says,"oh".
Poster saying "WASH YOUR HANDS."
Window, dark outside.
Clock, saying two minutes past nine.

At night? She thought. *What? How is it night so quick? Wasn't it just day? No, wait, was it? It was very bright, wasn't it? No, it was bright then very dark. I walked towards the trees and then it all went dark. How?*

Jane decided to leave that question for later. There were other more important things to deal with.

"Don't say anything, please," the other man said to the lady and friendly looking man, and yes, that *other man* was Definitely A Doctor because he wore one of those listeney-things round his neck.

"Is she actually…?" The lady kept her eyes on Jane.

But Definitely A Doctor ignored her and said, "hello."

Jane knew she should say something back, but - *ooh that's funny* - couldn't remember how.

"Can you say hello?" Definitely A Doctor said, but then held up a stern hand to the lady and the man.

Ooh, he doesn't want them two to talk, thought Jane. *That's what the teacher does when she doesn't want us to talk.*

But then Jane realised she couldn't remember what her teacher actually looked like.

It was all very confusing, this suddenly-waking-up-here thing. This not-knowing-where-she-was thing. This not-remembering-things-thing.

"Can you? Hm? Say hello?"

Mmm, she thought. *I can say hello, I know I can.*

"One of the after effects," said Definitely A Doctor, "one of the after effects is disorientation, confusion - now, we know she hasn't had a stroke, so that's not a factor."

Disoryoryastation? Jane turned over the new word in her mind.

"And for a while it may be that. For a while, er, she might not be able to move parts of her body."

Not move? thought little Jane. She tried to pick up her hand and wave, and Definitely A Doctor had lied, because - look! - she *could* move her hand, so *ner*.

"Oh," said the lady, who seemed to say, "oh," a lot.

"She's moved her hand!" The friendly looking man smiled, relieved. "Can you…?"

But the other man held up his hand again. "We need to find out exactly how confused she is. Hello. Let's try this. Can you say, 'mmmmmm?'"

Of course I can say 'mmmmmm', thought six year old Jane. *I'm not a baby. That's a silly question. This man must be a bit thick in the head.* But just to prove it, she tried. "Mmmmmm."

"Oh," said the lady, "She said 'mmmmm'."

Blimey, thought Jane. S*he's a bit thick in the head too, everyone knew I just said 'mmmmmm', why did she say that? Are they all a bit thick in the head? Am I in a hospital for people who are thick in the head?*

"That's good. She can hear, she comprehends, her brain is telling her mouth and larynx to form the sound, that's very good. It's like the brain is switching itself on, bit by bit. Like lights in a house, room by room."

Why's he talking about the lights now? What lights? Didn't I just see lights? Jane's eyes went between the lady, who stared at her very hard, and the friendly man, who still smiled and nodded her way.

The Doctor had that not-real-puppet-smile back on his face. "Now - let's try it. Can you say hello?"

Jane knew this time she really could. "Hello." But her voice sounded sounded scratchy, old and dried out.

"Oh," said the lady, again.

"Why…do…you…keep…saying…'oh'?" asked Jane, but the other man held up his hand again.

"Have some water. Your throat's very dry, you see." He leaned over and put a glass of water to Jane's lips, which was the nicest thing he'd done so far.

It was then she noticed there were a lot of wires on, *no, ugh,* in *me,* and she must have done her Confused Face, since The Doctor looked at her, then at the wires.

"Yes, ah. You've been…asleep."

Durrrr, thought Jane. *No I haven't. He's a* rubbish *doctor.*

"And since you couldn't eat or drink asleep, we gave you food and water through the tubes, you see."

"Oh."

"Can I ask you a question or two?"

"Aha."

"What is your name?"

"Well...that's a silly question," said Jane. The lady giggled, and that was nice, because Jane preferred the lady giggling to saying, "oh," all the time. She was nice when she giggled.

"It may sound like a silly question," The Doctor looked a bit cross. "But can you tell me your name?"

Jane said nothing. Now that really was funny, because she couldn't remember her own name. That was *weird.* That was *odd.* That was *peculiar.* That was *strange.* She could remember lots of words, so many words, but her name? "Hmmm…" She said out loud, and realised the lady had stopped giggling and the friendly looking man was no longer smiling.

"My name is…" Jane singsonged and stalled for time. It was there in her brain, she knew it.

"Hold on." Inside her mind, a tiny Jane ran around, opened cupboards and drawers, and tried to find her name. All sorts of things fell out. It was very untidy in there.

christmastreefinduspancakesspecialdollysarahfromnumber12crayonsn aughtypeterfromthebackofclasssnowbluepetermarymungoandmidgeplaysc hoolhousepartyradioonetonyblackburndavidbowiealvinstardustcomfybedr edshoesfavouriteshoeshereagainfinduspancakesinthelardersnowgrandadin bootspussinbootswesthamunitedlagerricekrispiesitsfrothymanboomboomb oomboomessobluema-ah-ah-agpie

The tiny Jane threw out memories all over the place and made a *right mess* in there.

*easteregghackneywickliverpoolstreethooppubaxepubflyingscudpathpub
fishandchipspieandmashsouthendonseacinderellapeterpansnowhitebigted
pathlittletedjemimamacocatoosnowvaleriesingeltonsallywalkerfromnumbe
r22pathpencilsetforbirthday?*

"Hold on," Jane scrunched up her face in concentration as the tiny girl
inside her found the right drawer.

*johnjanetjanicejennyjeremyjuliajaninejenniferjessicajeanjosephinejoan
najoan*

"Joan! No, that's not right."

Judithjilljackiejuliettejanjanjanjanjan

"Jan. Janet? No. Jane. I'm Jane."

"Oh," said the lady, back on *that* again, and the friendly looking man
put his head in his hands and seemed like he was going to cry.

"Excellent," said the Doctor. "Now. How old are you?"

Off went tiny Jane to another drawer in her mind.

1234567891011121110987...

"Six and a quarter."

"Good, good," this time his smile looked real. "Now try this. Do you
know who these two people are?"

Well, thought Jane. *They're the lady who says, 'oh' and the friendly
looking man, I know that, dur, but who* are *they?*

The lady and man looked worried now. And sad.

I do know them, thought Jane, and sent her tiny self to scurry off again,
since it seemed to be quite good at that kind of thing.

*mrwatsonfromthebakeryronniefromthebarmrsclarkfromthecoopsimonth
egardenermrbelljonsonthelollipopmanjansenmrbenwhodressesupasaspace
manmissparkerfromschooltheladyinthewindowmfishermanspacemanwhom
anmrdunnetheheadmaster*

There were a lot of names and faces in there, but she couldn't quite get
these two people. And that was weird because she felt she knew them. She
felt she knew them very well.

They could be my Mummy and Daddy, she thought. *But I'd know* them
wouldn't I? She didn't want to say that out loud in case they weren't, and
her real Mummy and Daddy found out and got sad about it. So the tiny
Jane rummaged on.

mrclarkfromthebutchersyumwiththeslicesofhamhegivesmefornothingjill thebarmaidgrandadwithhislagermisslawsonfromgamesmarkgriffithsfromth eshopmrwhitetheoldmanwholivesattheendandhiswifediedmrhannet

But then Jane noticed something else. How had she missed it?

Snow had begun to fall outside. White flecks whirled on the dark frame of the night.

It was enough to stop the tiny Jane in her head looking through the drawers of her mind.

Snow, thought Jane, distracted, then spoke out loud. "Oh. Look. Snow. Again."

The snow was an old friend. The people in the room were strangers.

8 / After A Fall / Going Home

The following day, David and Irene sat in an office somewhere in The London Hospital.

Pale faced, adrift, they waited for answers.

The Doctor shuffled papers and tried to sound like he had them.

His name was Doctor Perry and was just as lost as the parents opposite him.

"Well, yes. Right. Yes. Mr and Mrs Dawn - obviously this is upsetting, so we need to go through what we know. Your daughter displayed the usual symptoms on coming to from an unconscious state over a sustained period of time. Firstly there was no motor control, no ability to vocalise, disorientation. All distressing for the patient and family, but perfectly normal. But it was the *speed* at which she reverted that was abnormal. She regained full motor control and speech within literally a few minutes - I'd guess at no longer than three."

"Why is that abnormal?" David jumped in.

"It was more like she'd woken from a deep sleep than an unconscious state. I would expect the usual symptoms to continue for some time - possibly days - but not in Jane's case. As you heard, I often compare this period to switching on the house lights one by one. But that didn't happen with your daughter. She was back - *bang!* - with very little lag. I've never seen that before, not ever."

"So why doesn't she remember us?" Asked Irene. "She remembers so much else, but not us. Why?"

Dr Perry spread his hands wide.

"Well, think back, when she came to, she looked blank. Not confused. She just…took you in, I suppose. There wasn't any, '*they're* not my Mum and Dad!' Histrionics, or anything like that. She was - I suppose it's the wrong word, but she was, ah, analysing you. Her expression was like someone who'd been given a problem, and was taking it in, dealing with it."

"Is her brain damaged, then?" Dave asked weakly, not wanting an answer.

"She's fine physically. Yes, from a physical point of view, there's no damage to her brain. That we can see or measure, I should add. Things can occur on a microscopic level though, so when it comes to the brain, it's never black and white. Just because we can't see damage, that doesn't mean it's not there."

"Double negative," whispered David, almost to himself. "Uh-huh. It's the damage you don't see that really does the damage. You can spot a flat tyre, but if you can't see the crack in the chassis, it's the crack that gets you."

"Yes, er, exactly. " Doctor Perry looked round at Dave with concern. "But I simply can't understand this strange... localised... amnesia, regarding you and your husband. So yesterday I got in touch with a Psychologist friend of mine, Dr Peter Marryman - he's excellent - to see see if he has any thoughts from that direction."

"Psychologist?" Dave grabbed the word as Irene knew he would. "She has a psychological problem?"

"I don't know, is the most simple and, er, most truthful answer. And believe me that's not an admission I or any Doctor wants to make. But, ah, Peter wrote me a note, here's what he said…"

Dr Perry put on his glasses, blinked a little and picked up a piece of paper from his desk.

"He says, 'First of all, the girl's calm reaction to her parents shows that subconsciously she knows there's no threat. That the memory loss is surface, rather than as a result of any neurological damage. That's your field.'"

Dr Perry raised his eyes to Dave and Irene. "True, but…" he said apologetically. "It's a field that's still mostly unexplored." He read on.

"Peter says, 'You mentioned 'selective amnesia,' and yes, there have been cases where patients have, I suppose the best description is, "chosen to forget." The brain can protect itself very well if needs to. There's a theory that we don't remember our birth, not just because we were too young, but because the brain chooses to erase the trauma of it. Just a theory, though. There have been plenty of cases where a conscious - or should I say unconscious, to be correct - an unconscious decision has been made to wipe the slate clean, as it were.'"

"Someone chooses to forget?" Dave asked, incredulously.

"Mm. Peter goes on to say, 'There's a phrase we use with alcohol - 'I drink to forget,' - which is an example of *choosing* to wipe your memory. Alcohol inhibits the production and retention of memories. So, if an external agency can do it, then the brain can do the same easily, if it puts its mind to it, pardon the pun. There's a memory impairment condition called Korsakoff's syndrome related to alcohol, but of course your little girl wouldn't have that."

Dave grunted. "Hardly."

"Well, yes," agreed Dr Perry. "But he qualifies that statement. 'People with Alzheimers often forget things that are closest to them while retaining stuff and nonsense. Perhaps, in some odd way, she has a form of highly localised Alzheimers. But I doubt that's even possible.' I concur with him. She has no damage to the hippocampus or the fornix, which I would associate with Alzheimers, but even so, the chances of it occurring in a child are astronomical."

"What do we do? What can we do?" Asked Irene.

"Wait. That's all. Be with her as much as you can. Just remind, re-enforce, remind, re-enforce. Repetition is the key. I'd say use the same techniques as we'd recommend for emotional and psychological trauma - stick to a daily routine, find activities that she really enjoys, listen to her, be patient. But you know, here's what I think. One day, one moment, it'll all come back. Just like that. And you know, I'll wager she won't even remember she forgot."

*

The following day, after Jane had been checked over, and further help put into place in the form of health visitors and arrangements for further examinations, Dr Perry decided that home was probably the best medicine.

There was a knock on the door, and Jane entered with the Ward Sister.

"Hello Jane," Dr Perry said with a big smile. "Are you ready to go home with your Mummy and Daddy now?"

Jane slowly took them in again.

In those seconds, they hoped she'd suddenly smile, run, hug them and say, "Mummy! Daddy!"

But their heartbeats raced in vain, as Jane simply said, "hello," with a friendly enough smile but the same expression she might use for a vague acquaintance.

"Are you ready to go home with *Mummy and Daddy* now?" Dr Perry repeated, with extra emphasis.

They each held out a hand, which the little girl took. A little girl who trusted herself to strangers because she was told to by a Doctor, and Doctors Don't Lie.

And so they walked down the hospital corridor, on their way to who-knew-what.

Dave looked down at his daughter and made a vow.

I won't let her go, no, not ever again.

9 / December 1979 / Jane Returns Home

Dave, Irene and Jane were given a lift back home to their home in Bow by a neighbour.

Snow turned lazily in the air. It started to fall the moment Jane fell, and since then, had lightly dusted London every day.

"Do you like the the snow?" Irene asked.

"Yes," replied Jane. "And it likes me."

"Does it?"

"I think so." Jane watched it spin from the back seat. "Whenever I look out of the window, it starts falling. When I stop, it stops too."

"Well, that does sound like it likes you."

There was silence as Jane intently followed the progress of snow to ground. They pulled up at the terraced family home in Grace Street, E3. Dave and Irene looked at Jane and hoped for recognition, but she simply asked, "are we here?"

"Yes darling, we're here. This is your home," said Irene. "Do you remember?"

"Not...really. Not this one. I remember houses that look like that. But they all look like that, don't they?"

Jane stepped out of the car, but didn't make any move toward number nine.

She was clearly about to say something, but her expression - which Dave and Irene recognised immediately - suggested she thought it might not Be The Right Thing To Say.

"I shouldn't talk to strangers, should I?"

She looked from the house to her parents and back again.

"My Mummy and Daddy - well, *you're* my Mummy and Daddy, but, my Mummy and Daddy - well, *you're* my Mummy and Daddy, they - you - said 'don't talk to strangers,' well, Doctor Perry said *you're* my Mummy and Daddy..."

Irene went down on her haunches to Jane's height and stroked her hair. Jane didn't shy away.

"Ssh, ssh. You're right. You're absolutely right, Jane. Don't talk to strangers. That's very good. Very good. Isn't she good, Daddy?"

Dave nodded and over compensated. "Yes, excellent. Brilliant. Stupendous! Immaculate!Wonderful! Amazing!"

Irene shot him a look and he stopped. She reached into her purse.

"We showed you this, didn't we, darling?" For the umpteenth time she pulled out a photograph of Jane, Dave and herself on the beach at Southend On Sea earlier that year, 1979.

Jane looked at the photo, and by now, of course, recognised the two people who *said* they were Mummy and Daddy, simply because she'd already seen the picture so many times in the hospital. But she just couldn't - didn't - remember them.

"If we were strangers, then why would we be with you, here on the beach? See?"

Irene held up the photograph. Jane had a bucket and waved, Irene wore a one piece and Dave looked over his right shoulder at something, which meant he'd missed the moment when the shutter clicked, with no chance of deleting and trying again. What you took was what you got in the Seventies.

Jane looked hard. "I know. And I do remember bits of the beach. There was that long…long... pier. And an ice cream van with a clown on the top. The pier had a train! And there was a pirate ship next to it! Ooooh!"

Dave and Irene looked at each other and both thought their own version of, *please let her remember us when she steps through the door.*

Irene unlocked the door and they stepped inside, Dave was first, and turned hopefully to watch Jane's expression.

*

She stopped and looked at a painting that hung just before the stairway, a burst of green and blue that shimmered on a black canvas.

"I remember that," she pointed at the painting.

"Do you, Darling? Do you really?"

"Yes. I have definitely seen that before, definitely. It's very pretty, who did it?"

"I did," said Irene. "I like to paint."

"So do I."

"I know. Would you like to see some of your paintings, Jane?"

"I think I sort-of sort-of remember them actually." Jane's eyes went wide. "Wait. My bedroom is up there!" She gestured up the stairs. "It is, isn't it?"

Dave looked like he may faint, and steadied himself on the bannister. "Yes it is," he confirmed, then added nonchalantly, as if the question didn't really matter, "so if you remember your room, do you remember..."

Jane anticipated the question and diplomatically answered, "I definitely remember my bedroom."

"So can you describe the house for us, Jane?" asked Irene.

"Right, aha," Jane replied, as some of the dominoes of her memory stood up. "Through there," she pointed to a door on the right of the hallway, "through there is the front room, with the telly, then there's a door next to the telly and that goes to the kitchen, and the cooker is... there...Upstairs, there's a bathroom and two bedrooms."

"Anything else? A Garden?"

"No garden. That's why I have to go and play in the Park." She stopped.

Jane tilted her head to one side, thinking. "I don't think I like the Park, actually," she frowned. "It's cold and there are too many trees. Too many, all round you. Nowhere to go."

"That's very very good Jane, you remembered," said Irene.

"And now you've remembered the house..." began Dave.

"Yes I remember the house." Once again, Jane answered a question Dave hadn't even asked. "I definitely remember the house."

Dave and Irene didn't look at each other. They couldn't, scared to see what their own despair looked like.

10/ Christmas Day, 1979 / 14:00 P.M.

Jane had been taken to a place she didn't remember, with people she didn't know.

Irene looked at her little girl, sat in flowery pyjamas in front of the TV.

She is in a strange house, with strangers on Christmas Day, she thought, and the hairline cracks in her heart which had appeared that awful afternoon spread a little further. *As far as she knows, as far as she remembers, my daughter is with strangers on Christmas Day.*

Jane had come home from hospital after two days, once the specialist and consultants were absolutely convinced there was nothing physically wrong with her.

Now the family of three celebrated the Big Day.

Inside their tiny terraced house stood a tiny tree. Under the tiny tree was a big box, Jane's big present. She didn't remember, but in this house, it was traditional to have one big present, centre stage.

Jane sat in front of the tree with the two people who *said* they were her parents.

She still didn't remember her Mummy and Daddy.

Sometimes they'd catch her as she regarded them like she might follow the path of an insect on a window - interested, but with no further emotional connection. She often smiled their way, but the smile remained unfinished.

At first, Mum and Dad thought they'd lost her, but it was the other way round; she'd lost them.

He looks so tired, Irene thought, and saw past the smile on Dave's face.

The wine and beer today, yesterday, and all the days before hadn't helped, but it was more than the bags under his eyes and pasty skin. It was a tiredness that seemed to surround him. Like the fog of a cigarette, his fatigue filled the room. He looked at the big box under the tree, and he hoped.

The tree itself had seen better days - but then again, so had everything in this house. Once a year, Dave would climb a rickety ladder to the loft and pass the tree down to Irene, who always handled it gently, like a relic. It was made of shabby white plastic fronds that stuck out from thin metal branches. It may have been cheap and falling apart, but it was made of memories and they have no price tag.

Jane, however, wasn't interested in the bulbs, tinsel strips and fake snow. The last thing she remembered before she woke up in hospital was snow falling. It was not an altogether happy memory. No, she only had eyes for the big box. Dave and Irene saw her stare, and hoped.

This years' big box was Dave's idea, which he'd had even before Jane fell.

It was mainly a gift for her, of course, but partly a gift for them, to see what it might unlock in Jane, who loved to tell stories.

Today, though, they hoped the big box might contain their daughter.

Outside, the snow still fell. It tumbled and watched through the front window.

"Go on then, Jane," said Dave. "Go on, open the big one."

Jane knelt down in front of the Christmas tree and put her hands on the big box. She looked back at the people who said they were her parents and smiled that imperfect smile again.

"This big one is for me?"

"Yes, and you'll need this." Dave picked up a piece of paper. Jane looked at it, confused, then gently opened the wrapping, which revealed another box, a plain cardboard one.

"Go on, love," Dave egged her on. Irene said nothing. She didn't need to.

Jane opened the lid of the box and looked in.

"Ooooh!" she gasped. Dave and Irene glanced at each other. "Is this for me?"

"Do you remember?" Dave asked. "Do you remember you said you wanted to tell your own stories, instead of being told other peoples'?"

In Jane's mind, a flash;

enidblytonroalddahlcinderellagoldilockspenguinbooksbluepeterannual daddysbooksmybooksbooksbooksmybooksstoriestellstories tell

my

stories

My
Story

She reached in and - it was heavy so took some effort - pulled out a typewriter. A beautiful, second hand typewriter, which had suddenly been *just there* in the pawn shop window one day in early December.

Dave had walked past, done a double take, then stepped back to examine it. The typewriter sat in the window and examined him back. They'd considered each other for a moment before Dave made up his mind. He had no idea why it fascinated him, but he'd brought it home, cleaned, oiled, and boxed it up.

"Oooh," Jane delicately touched the keys. Don't confuse a child of the Seventies with a child of today. Don't confuse Jane with anyone else. To her, this typewriter was a magical object. Dave knelt down next to his daughter with the paper.

"You put it in like this," he slid it into the machine. "Turn this wheel here, see?" Jane turned it, and the paper rolled. As the snow fell past the window, Dave gently said, "you just find the letter and press. And it comes out on the paper. You can write whatever you like, whenever you like."

Jane may have only been six, but she was Dave and Irene's daughter, so even at that age could still write better than any of her friends. She just had to get used to doing it with this wonderful machine. She sat and looked at the keys. Something about them wasn't right.

"They don't go from A to Z. They should go from A to Z."

"No, because if they did, it would make it harder to type. Sometimes it's better not to go from A to Z, start to finish. Sometimes it helps if you start in the middle. Or even the end. Trust me."

Jane thought that statement made no sense, but part of her understood completely.

Jane looked at the paper, then out of the window. The snow had stopped. She watched the last few flakes fall to ground. She stared out, and shook her head, as if to clear a thought.

She began to type, slowly.

Tap
Tap

Tap

"my name is jane," she wrote.
London's snowfall was over, for now.
Jane thought for a moment. She gave a tiny nod, put her hands to her temples and shook her head.
She looked up at the ceiling, back down to the Christmas tree and round to the window again.
Jane closed her eyes for a moment and frowned.
She opened her eyes, then looked over her shoulder at her Mum and Dad and smiled. The smile was different. It was real. It was for them.

"my mummy is called ireen and my daddy is called dave"

Tap
Tap
Tap

Jane remembered her parents again, she came back, on Christmas Day, 1979, on a 1941 Royal Companion Typewriter.

BOOK THREE / HERE, REVEALED

11 / The First Minutes Jane Arrived Here / Minutes 8-15

Goodbye to 1979, for now. But let me tell you, the past is never really gone, but filed and accessible, if you know where and how to look. By the end of the story, I'll have taught you that trick.

It's a good one.

But now, at this particular moment, a woman called Jane had come to in a strange, frozen place simply called, *Here* only - by your terms - fifteen minutes previously.

She sat upon a single bed, in a tiny wooden hut, while a Man dressed for an Arctic sea stood before her.

One terrible, impossible thought had grown in her mind ever since she'd become conscious.

Jane didn't want to ask - the question itself was madness - but then, wasn't everything skewed in this new place? She closed her eyes and took a deep breath.

"Am. Am. Am. I...am I *dead*?" She asked, quietly. Deep in a dark corner of Jane's mind, part of her asked, *did you* seriously *just put those three words together?*

The Man, whoever he was, looked back at Jane with an expression somewhere between impatience - and, for the first time, a hint of anger.

"Really? I never had you down for the dramatic type," he huffed. "'Am I dead?' she asks! Would you like some limelight on you? Shall I strike up the orchestra, Lily Langtree?" He snorted again, went up a register, and sarcastically approximated Jane's voice. "'*Am I dead?*' What do you think? Dead? Honestly? Ah, I thought you were smarter than that, you of all people, Jane." He shook his head.

Jane splintered then, as she'd always known she would, from the moment she'd opened her eyes with no memories.

The storm hit. Jane tumbled at its centre.

"Enough!" She reacted to his anger and raised it. She felt that weird, warm anaesthesia fade, as the muffled cotton wool hug was pulled from her. "Enough, enough, no, no, no, fucking no!" There it was, finally, the confusion and whirling bedlam within her broke out. That tiny, rational Jane inside was astounded it had taken this long.

"Stop! No, I've failed your test, or whatever it is!" Her voice raised in pitch, dangerously close to total hysteria. "Enough! Stop! It's just...it's just...help." She stabbed a finger at the window of the Hut. "Please help me, I can't...stop, help, please, stop...this...where? Who? ...are...am?... No, this is insane. I can't. Help. *Please*."

She felt hyperventilation approach. Her lungs began to demand more oxygen. The Man cocked his head to one side, raised an eyebrow oh so slightly, and distantly, Jane thought,

No-one has spoken to him like this ever.

But she carried on, unable to check on the incoming panic. "What did you give me? What? Morphine? I was drugged, wasn't I? You drugged me, somewhere, you took me...somewhere...you drugged me, you fucking *drugged* me and kept me calm. But now it's gone. Please, why? Help. Please. The drugs don't work."

The drugs don't work? repeated in her mind, but she wasn't interested in its provenance.

Her breaths came faster. She gasped for air and one hand went reflexively to her chest.

Jane stood up, unsteady but defiant, shoulders back. She weaved a little, put out a hand to steady herself, faced him, but then made no move to run for the door. She didn't know why that was.

Why don't I run? Why won't *I run?* flashed through her mind, but her voice hollered out loud, "so where am I? Why did you take me? Who are you? What did you do? What do you want?"

Part of her wanted to attack him, but she had no strength. Mainly, fear kept her rooted to the spot.

No no, no, no, stop, this isn't right. Just stop and listen, part of her begged, but she ignored it again, as she'd done so many times before.

Jane felt she might faint, but then where might she wake up? "What? This place, *Here*, with its...snow...and *you* and I don't know who I am or how I got here, so please..." she pleaded, anger replaced by desperation. "Please, I...Please."

She slumped back onto the bed, barely able to sit up straight. Jane looked at The Man and realised he looked angry, surprised and sorry.

"Please. Please help me." Without thought, she held out a hand to him, so he could pull her out of the dark well she'd tumbled into. She stared down at the floor and breathed hard. "Please. Help me. Because I don't know anything, and this is all I have and I don't know why I'm asking it but it's all I have. Am. I. Dead?'"

She hung her head and hair fell over her eyes. Not much of a barrier, but it had to do.

"I'm sorry," he said, gently. "I am. That wasn't supposed to happen. I understand the question. Anger, fear, Here? No, no. So shall I ask you a question in return that may clear things up in that respect? Do you feel dead?"

Jane sighed and shuddered, but didn't raise her eyes from that wooden floor. "Since I don't know what feeling dead feels like… I don't… really… know, do I?"

"Are you conscious of external stimuli? Are you breathing? Can you hear your heart, Jane? Can you?"

Jane waited another second, checked. "You know I can."

"I can almost hear it myself, it's pumping so hard. Calm down. I mean, really." He pointed back at the window. "If you think that's 'Heaven', well, your expectations are frighteningly low, aren't they? A few huts in a bleak forest? Where is the choir invisible? Are you telling me The Creator made this the perfect afterlife destination, did he, and no-one bothered to turn up, apart from you?"

"Yes, but you, you're Here, too." Jane tried to sound strong.

"Yes, yes, you and I are Here." He sighed, softly. "And do you think I want to be Here? I'm called Here when someone arrives. That is, as they say, "the deal." I don't have a choice either. I'd rather not, but that's that. So. *Here* we both are. And before you wonder or ask, since this place is neither Heaven nor Hell, it follows I am not God or the Devil - because you are *not dead*. Neither is it purgatory, Oz, Narnia, or any fiction. You are not a ghost, nor a memory. This is not - what do they call it? - "Virtually Reality"? This *is* reality and you are alive, fully alive, fully aware, which is why you are *Here*. So that's the first thing you need to understand. This is real. This is happening. It is no dream, or fairy tale. If you think you're dead - and some have - then you are lost. You are alive, Jane. Feel it, know it…"

The Man reached forward and gently stroked her hair. That made her think, *Daddy?*

"You are *alive*, and remember that, because it is important. And I'm not your father, get away from that thought, right now."

The Man was so gentle that Jane couldn't help her eyes run to tears.

yesyou'renotmydaddyIknowthat

"No crying ah, ah," said The Man. "Don't cry because you are alive."

"I'm crying because I'm *not dead*," she retorted, and still could not believe she thought in those terms. "That would have been an... explanation, and now I don't have one. Being dead would have made sense of the …senseless."

"No it wouldn't, not Here." She could tell he trod carefully. "Which is why I am here for you, now, because you must be Told. So - again - do you have any questions?"

Jane looked up at the low ceiling in exasperation. No help there. Her heart clattered on.

"I told you, I have all the questions in the world, wherever in the world I am."

"Still fixating on the where? Please. No! That is the wrong question. You know where you are. You've just forgotten. Wrong question, Jane."

"But I don't know what the right question is, help me," she begged. Jane felt utter terror circle, here in the eye of her own storm, one she didn't think she could weather any more.

"You do," said The Man. "You just haven't asked it yet. You need to work it out. If I have to tell you everything, then you won't understand. Come on, Jane. It's just one word. One word."

Jane put her head into her hands and stared down at her bare legs, in that inappropriate short black skirt. She moaned softly. "I don't know."

She was untethered now, dangerously close to falling for good. Her fingertips hung on, but she was losing purchase.

The Man stood up again, looked around the tiny room and appeared to make a decision. His shoulders raised as if a weight had been lifted.

"Alright, my dear. What is the one word that has kept humanity moving forward? One word. The second most powerful word in any language. The word that empowers you?"

Jane thought, hard.

whowhatwhywherewhen

Those words that led to any question ever asked, or ever would be asked.

whowhatwhywherewhen

Yes.

But not all of those words, just…

Why.

"Why?" Jane asked so softly she may not have even said it at all.

The Man rotated his fingers as if to say, *carry on, you've nearly got it.*

"Why am I Here?"

"BINGO!" yelled The Man. "FULL HOUSE! TOP PRIZE!" he roared, pointed at her like a game show host and really smiled for the first time in what seemed ages.

"Exactly, Jane! *WHY AM I HERE?* That's the question! Not who, when, where, what, not 'to be or not to be,' but WHY. Why am I Here? That's it Jane, now we're getting somewhere. Now we can move on, get busy, get going! Now you can be Told!"

"Oh. Good," replied Jane, but gently, without sarcasm. She was so tired, and had started to feel the pull of the window, but the sky remained Snow free.

"Yes!" said The Man. "We are moving along now, good, excellent, marvellous!"

"Marvellous," Jane agreed, wearily.

"Right," said The Man, again, and it felt like he'd metaphorically rolled up his sleeves, ready to tackle the job at hand.

'Why are you here?' His expression changed and he looked down at the floor. "I'm so sorry. You're not going to like it."

12 / The First Minutes Jane Arrived Here / Minutes 15-21

Jane waited in that tiny strange Hut, in a lost, frozen clearing. She felt she could wait forever for what The Man was about to say.

"Why are you Here?" The Man took a deep, sad, breath. "That's the question. I've got this bit sorted out in my head, no problems. Don't need any notes. I'm "across this", isn't that what they say?"

"They do, some of them," agreed Jane, and tried to prepare herself for what was coming.

Strap in, she thought. *Somehow, I know this is going to be a bumpy ride.*

The Man gathered himself, then changed gears, quite dramatically. You could almost hear those gears crunch.

Without looking up, he turned Jane's world topsy turvy one more time, as if it couldn't get any topsier or turvier.

"Something terrible has happened, Jane, and you have done something terrible, too. We need to fix both. I am so very sorry," he said, softly, sadly, carefully.

Jane looked at him sharply, but he didn't return the gaze, just stared at the floor, unable to connect with her eyes. "What happened?" she asked, voice dry as kindling.

"Something terrible. If you break a leg, do you walk on it?" His verbal gears crunched again.

"What? If I? What? Break a leg?"

"If you break a leg, do you walk on it?"

"No."

"Of course you don't. You put no weight on it because it cannot support you. You need to rest, put it in a cast, until it's healed and you can put weight on it again. Correct?"

"Yes," Jane replied, more confused now, if that were even possible. "But I don't…"

"And when the bone has set, and the cast is removed, you still take it one step at a time, until you know your leg can handle that weight, correct?"

"Yes," she agreed, because what else could she say?

"You see, *Here* is a cast. Not for your body, but for your mind, making it strong again, until you are ready to start anew. And it does this not with plaster of paris, but by making you forget what has happened to you, what you have done. Forget until you're strong enough to remember."

Jane nodded. Part of her understood the analogy completely, but the other part was on a loop;

Impossibleimpossibleimpossibleimpossible

"It is not impossible," continued The Man. "It is Here, and this, er, *'facility'* is here to save you. When the Snow falls, it covers up what you cannot accept, what you *must not* remember, until it is Time to do so, when you are capable of deciding what happens next. At this moment, if you were to remember these terrible things, you will fall, break and the Kings Men will never put Jane together again. Right now, your memories are your enemy. Let them through the gates and they will ransack you. But one day you will be ready to deal with them. And then you'll no longer need to be Here. You can leave. Do you understand?"

The Man took her hand and stared into her eyes, unblinking.

"No. Of course I don't."

"You do, you just can't deal with it right now, but that's…usual. You will."

"I'm here to forget?" she asked, while that little voice inside chittered away, *why is the senseless making sense? Why won't you question the unquestionable? Why is this impossibility possible to you, Jane? Do you know more about this place than you remember?*

"Yes, good. Ignore your inner self, it's not helping. You forget and keep forgetting until you are ready to face what has put you Here. It is a gentle art, forgetting, and one you must master. To forget, you Watch The Snow. Every flake covers up part of those memories. It's like…targeted radiotherapy, wiping away the tumours in your memory. Snow attacks what threatens you - reduces those memories until you can deal with them in a fair fight. The Snow knows. You just have to be careful not to wipe yourself too much. It happens. Some become husks, empty. I've seen it. Wiped so much they lose everything they once were. Perhaps they do it on purpose, use The Snow as an emergency exit. Or like jumping from a collapsing building. Either option is untenable, is it not? Suicide of the soul. But you're smart, Jane. You'll find your level. Watch The Snow. Forget. Become strong again, then you can move on."

"I Watch The Snow," she replied. "Because it is...medicine? An... antibiotic for the memory?"

The Man nodded, pleased.

"The Snow wipes away what could..." Jane grasped for the idea, but it seemed too dramatic even as she said it, "...destroy me?"

"Yes, and that word isn't too dramatic, it is correct. Do not underestimate the time bomb you have in here," He pointed at her forehead. "You don't have the tools to defuse that bomb, not yet. So you must forget it is there. Because Here, what you don't know really *can't* hurt you."

"The Snow wipes me for my own good?" Jane offered, and The Man nodded.

"Excellent. You volunteer to lose your memories, in the same way people volunteer to lose a limb to save the rest of their body. But the good news is, you're not losing them forever. Just until you're ready. This isn't amputation, this is treatment."

"What happened to me? Who was I? What did I do?" Jane asked again, but knew he wouldn't tell her. Because that was *kind-of-the-whole-point-of*-Here. The not knowing. So she waited a second and tried something else.

"Why the typewriter?"

"Oh, that." He idly pressed a few of the keys, and the tap *Tap* TAP threatened to uncover something deadly, already hidden by the snow.

"Everyone who comes Here has something that is...a walking stick, if you like. As I said, when you break your leg, you need a stick to take the weight until you're strong enough to walk unaided. This typewriter is your way of testing the weight, seeing if you're ready to walk again, properly."

"A typewriter?"

"Jane," sighed The Man."You of all people will use this typewriter. Don't ask me why. It's here for you to sit at, write, and through writing, you'll let parts of your memory back, to test the weight, to see if you can walk again. The words, Jane, for you, the words are what you are. Try them out for size on this. It's a 1941 Royal Companion." He looked at her pointedly, as if that name was important, but it wasn't, not at that moment.

"Write when you feel like it. Test the weight. See if the words mean anything. Some come Here and have...a teddy bear, or item of clothing, or book. The walking stick takes many forms, but for you, it's this old typewriter. Use it. Write. See how ready you are to remember. Test the weight on your...metaphorical... broken leg."

Jane leaned forward and *tap* tap *tapped*. She smiled.

"What about paper?" she asked, but The Man just waved away the question.

"And that?" She pointed at The Larder/Cupboard/Thing.

"It's a larder, cupboard, thing." The Man opened its doors again. "You have to eat, don't you?"

"I do." Jane concurred.

"And, all these…" He swept his hands over the contents like the magician's assistant, to show that, no, there are no hidden doors, and yes, this is magic.

"Look! I'll bet these are things you liked, maybe loved as a child. Comfort food. The cabinet remembers for you. Frosties! Heinz Beans! Tinned Hot Dogs, Rice Krispies, ooh Vesta Curry! Vesta Chow Mein! Ready salted crisps! Fray Bentos Pie In A Tin, Marmite! Such modern wonders! I'm carbon dating these to the 1970s, right?"

"I think so."

"I know so. All your favourites, present and correct."

Despite herself, Jane smiled, but then stopped.

"Apart from the Marmite. I can't stand Marmite - I remember that. It must be hardwired. I hate Marmite, that's a definite."

"Hm," grunted The Man and picked up the pot. "Well, that's odd. There'll be a reason it's Here, though, always is."

"Maybe Marmite is the terrible thing that happened to me," Jane attempted levity for the first time, but The Man didn't smile. "It isn't," he muttered, then shuffled over to the oven and his gears ground once more.

"The oven, yes. Right. It's for cooking, but more importantly, mainly, burning."

"For cooking, but mainly burning?" Jane tried to keep up.

"The Oven is here to Burn you."

The tiny black oven stood next to a basket of wood. There was room for one pan on top, and a little door on the front. Jane didn't bother to ask where she'd get the wood from.

"The oven burns me? Oh, well, that's nicely counter intuitive."

"Suddenly waspish, aren't we? Lesson Two; You use this…" He pointed back at the cute little 1941 Royal Companion typewriter, "…to write, test the weight, see how you feel when the memories start crowding back. If you don't feel you're ready, you take what you've written, and Burn it. In the oven. You Burn any memories that threaten you. Then you watch the Snow, wipe those memories, and start again. Tap, tap, tap, Burn, Burn, Burn, watch, watch, watch. Repeat."

"Burn what I write? Why?"

"If you feel scared by what you write, on the edge, or trapped, you Burn. Memories are your enemy for now. If they manifest themselves in any way through what you write, and you don't want them in your head, you Burn them, then Watch The Snow, re-set, start again. Mm?"

The Man waited.

"I write to test how ready I am to remember," Jane said, the good student. Crazily, somehow, this all made sense. Minutes ago, she'd been whirling in hysteria, but now - inexplicably - calmness and acceptance had fallen over her. It almost felt like the strange comfort of deja vu, when new surroundings are not as unfamiliar as they should be. She didn't think about that too hard. Jane felt she'd have plenty of time to think. A glance out of the window told her she was going no-where.

"If I'm not ready, I burn what I write in the oven, I Watch The Snow, I forget, I start again. I say this with the caveat I'm accepting it despite knowing it's impossible, because right now I have no choice. Do I pass?"

"You pass," nodded The Man. "Some never do, you know. They can't even get past all this," he waved his hands round the Hut. "Many forget, and never remember ever again. The cast stays on even when the leg has mended, if you like. But you, I know you will heal. You will write, Burn, forget and you will heal."

"And then what? When I'm ready, when I remember, what do I do then?"

"One step at a time, Jane," said The Man, and the question seemed to make him sad again. "For now, let me show you around. Give you the guided tour."

13 / Between Thoughts

Here, in a hut, in a frozen clearing, memories still waited at the doorway of Jane's mind. They peered round the frame, and some gingerly stepped forward, but always scuttled back outside.

A coffin, Jane stared inside herself. *Whose coffin? Not mine, I know that. I'm alive, but someone else is dead. The coffin changes everything. For good or bad?*

A tapping sound. From the coffin? No, I don't think so.

It makes me smile, this tapping sound.

Drinks, now. I don't think I drink much, so why drinks, no, why stupid *drinks? Stupid drinks? When is a stupid drink not stupid?*

Then, like an out of control vehicle, another memory crunched into her;

I stand. People look round at me and part, to let me pass. Then I fly. I fly, above these people, looking down. I have killed them. At this moment, I have killed them. I know that. It is a fact. I fly, they fall. Yes.

The glitching memories drifted from her door. She watched them go, fade into the darkness. She did not mourn their departure. They frightened her.

14 / Jane, Selected Diary Entries, '87 - '92

Let us leave Jane in that frozen place called Here, for now, and return - because we can - to her linear life, the one where time always marches forward.

We've already seen her as a child in the late '70s, when she fell and forgot, typed and remembered, but now I'll let Jane introduce herself as a teenager.

In 1987, Jane was fourteen, a tricky age for anyone.

The fourteen year old can feel adulthood so close, but their parents are terrified at how quickly those two out of control horses, Time and Life, have galloped away from them.

It used to be so easy. Once, they could ride those horses, but now their child is fourteen and it feels like they've dropped the reins. So they grasp them ever tighter. To protect their child, of course, but to protect themselves, too. Because if their son or daughter can be fourteen with so little effort, then they can become old, older, oldest, and after that, well, what always happens.

That fear creates the grinding tension of the teenage experience - the belief you are old enough, set against the rest of the world's opinion that you are *not*.

Very well. Since you've been cast as the voyeur in this tale, you should see some entries from Jane's teenage diary. They won't scrape away enough to reveal the full picture of her past, but they may reveal enough of what was there originally.

Know this; history is just an instruction manual for the present. And if you don't read the instructions, the best outcome is that things don't work. The worst is they break, and history doesn't offer refunds.

*

18th March 1987

I hate maths and I hate fractals and I really hate logarithms. They're so unbelievably stupid. I got into trouble with Mrs McKenzie because I said logarithms were stupid, no actually, I said they were pointless. I told Dad and he said "not everything has a point, it's all about the learning" or something and how "you only know what a lesson really means when it's all over." I said that didn't make sense and he changed the subject and said he can TAP DANCE. TAP DANCE. YES. MY DAD CAN TAP DANCE. He said he learned it for the sake of learning it because "anything new is good." Apparently, he saw a poster one night when he was 15, or something, and he had nothing to do, so went in and just signed up. He said he'd done about two months of lessons. I asked him to do it but he said it wasn't the time. I asked when it would be time to tap dance and he said "I'll know when I know and it will be a VERY BIG DEAL." And he said VERY BIG DEAL in capital letters, which is why I've used the same. Mum said she'd seen him do it once and it looked like he was having a penny dreadful of a fit so maybe I'll do without. One day, I'll catch him off guard and get him to do it. DAD TAP DANCES!! Not sure if that's cool or not. *Not*, probably. TAP DANCING DAD!? Will wonders never cease?

23rd July 1989

End of term party last night at Dave Leaman's. Not sure how I feel. Thought about it a lot since. All signed each other's shirts, but Paul K signed my chest and winked at me while he did it.

Ended up in the spare room with him. So that's that then. The deed is done. Don't know how I feel. Didn't use anything. Very stupid. HONESTY? Yes, it was- what was it? Fun? I don't know, no-one tells you how to feel in biology lessons they just tell you the mechanics. It's how you feel after isn't it, I suppose? That's how you really feel, not during. After is when it means something. If a feeling melts away, like a snowflake, then obviously it didn't mean anything. If it freezes your heart, it did. This feeling melted. Mum knows, I'm sure of it. But she won't say anything unless I need her to, as usual. HONESTY? I feel a little lost.

13th August 1989

Biology C Maths D (as expected) Physics C Chemistry C oh dear oh dear BUT History A, English Lit A English Language A HOORAY.

Dad opened a bottle of fizzy wine, Mum let off a party popper. Very un-Mum, which is what made it hysterical.

THE PLAN
Sixth Form College
University
Become a writer
Become a VERY SUCCESSFUL WRITER
Buy us all a new house.
Retire.

Possibly fall in love, get married, have babies, but one step at a time. Maybe not even in that order. Actually, I've decided doing things in the "right" order is boring.

14th September 1991

I'm now the oldest person in the Sixth Form. Hooray for me. Everyone else has left to go to work or Uni, and I'm still here, where I'll spend the next five terms trying to get an A in Classics and more than a D in Biology. Fun fun fun!

The Classics Course sounds good but doing bloody Biology again is going to ruin me.

My friends are all gone and I'm here, look at me now, the coolest person in the Sixth Form since all the other years look up to me because I'm nearly EIGHTEEN but that's like looking up to a runner because he nearly won a race but wasn't good enough so CONGRATULATIONS WELL DONE he's still going round and round and round the track FOREVER.

March 9th 1992

We've been 5 months together! October 9th - March 9th. A new
GUINNESS RECORD. Call Norris McWhirter. Or Ross. The one that
didn't die, anyway.

This is officially my longest, so what does that mean?

Does it mean that perhaps I am actually in love? Lower case? Go on,
give it some reverence, give it the bloody caps, Jane - LOVE?

I think of him and he's not like any of the others - of course he's not, if
he was I wouldn't be with him!

OH DEAR. I'm using exclamation marks! LIKE I'M THIRTEEN
AGAIN! Grow up, Jane. 18 and yeah, why don't you draw a floppy eared
dog on the cover, since you're so mature?

But but but. He's funny, he's sweet, KIND, gorgeous (that helps, and
yes, that's scarily shallow, but it's true), smart and yes, I admit, I AM now
writing like my 13 year old self. That's not an altogether bad thing.

So honestly, am I in love? Actual love?

Think about that carefully, now. Whatever you write will stay in these
pages forever. Yes, I turn my back on you, Tippex.

OK. Thought about it. Yes! Yes! YES! He told me he loved me on
December 2nd and I told him back. FIVE MONTHS. THAT'S
VIRTUALLY MARRIED. TOO MANY CAPS, JANE.

But if I have to ASK myself if I really love him, then do I really love
him really?

Just read that back. So glad I got my 'A' Level English.

Dad is trying too hard to be his mate but I can tell he's jealous because
I am after all, always was, always will be, his girl, but he's so good with
him, so charming, so clever. I catch Dad looking at him sideways and I
know he's happy for me. I just cross my fingers he doesn't turn into Lager
Dad with him. The one who snaps at people. I do wish he wouldn't be
Lager Dad.

Mum's opinion is harder to guess.

She said, "I was pretty sure Dad was the love of my life, but until you
know someone you don't know them" - her exact words. And then she

smiled that smile she always does when Mum knows she's said something deeply wise that I'll only understand years later.

I'm not going to use his name, so in years to come I'll know if I was truly in love with him.

Because I've had an idea. I'll only remember what really counts. If a memory won't hang around, it wasn't supposed to. So if he matters, I'll remember his name, and if he doesn't, he'll just become a blur.

But maybe - AH AH *DEFINITELY* - we'll still be together as old people and I'll show him this and he'll laugh. Yes, that's how it will be.

But whatever happens, DO TRY TO EASE BACK ON THE CAPS, JANE. IT'S LIKE THE PAGE IS SHOUTING.

May 11th 1992

I couldn't write about it until now. I'm still not sure I can, but I must make sure I remember this feeling and never allow anyone to make me feel like it ever again.

Mum said, "if you've never had your heart broken how will you know when someone's fixed it?" But that doesn't help me this moment.

There was no sign that it was going to happen.

XXXX took me for breakfast at our place, and he told me, and that was that. Should I have known? Was I an idiot for the last five months? YES JANE, OH YES YOU WERE.

He'd been quiet for a while but that was because his dog had died (he said but he lied).

I thought, I assumed that he needed to deal with the grief of his not-dead-dog. People talk about dealing with it, as if grief *can* be dealt with, negotiated with, like a person who's being unreasonable.

Ha, like you can "*calm grief down,*" get it to see your side of things if it would just listen, but grief won't listen. It just keeps taking from you, reminding you what you've lost.

I know now that I was never really in love with him, this LITTLE STUPID BOY, but thought I was very close, closer than I've ever been before, maybe too close to get a perspective on it. I fooled myself. Turns out I was rather good at it.

And I also know that I am grieving, not for him, but for what could have been. I had it all mapped out, and now it's lost. So is that what grief really is, after all? An overwhelming sense of something stolen? Not just missing, or lost, but *stolen*?

I am putting this into words because I want to remember the shape of grief, so I can recognise it next time, because there will be a next time.

This is mine, for me, I will NOT waste it on him. I'll feel this and learn from it, ride it, let it take me and I know this is only about a stupid lying so-called boyfriend and that's true, but this feeling isn't stupid, is it? It's real and it's mine.

If I thought I loved this time, what will happen when it really takes me?

And then, what about this grief? I'm sensible enough to know it's just passing through and, yes, perhaps I'm wallowing in it a little too much. I don't think it's self pity, though. It's true enough. But if this is only a taste, what's grief like when it is truly let loose?

What does that do to you?

I never, ever want to know. I must remember this, and be careful. I don't know if I could outrun real grief if it decided to really hunt me.

Mum held me for a long time. I wish I could forget any of this happened. Just clean my memory out, paint him away forever, whitewash him. No. He doesn't deserve this many words.

Dad has a phrase - one of many, actually, "lesson learned, experience earned".

So I've had my lesson, and I've learned.

I'll find another boy. And this *other* boy will be THE one and he'll never lie or leave me. I'll be with him forever, I just know.

Or rather, I hope.

I'm beginning to think all those fairy stories Mum used to read at bedtime have given me totally unreasonable expectations. I've just met Dopey and eaten the poisoned apple, so surely my prince should be riding out of the woods any time now. Quick sharp, prince. I'm not about to climb into a glass coffin and wait for you. And your tights.

15 / The First Minutes Jane Arrived Here / Minutes 21-33 / The Guided Tour

Twenty minutes had passed since thirty-year-old Jane first woke in a wooden hut, in a strange frozen clearing.

At this point, The Man, her Handler, Point Of Contact, Instructor, Duty Manager, her *whoever-the-hell-he-was* had offered a guided tour.

She was still awed and confused by her puzzling calmness in the face of this total shift in reality. But had somehow accepted the shift, gone along with it. If she hadn't, Jane knew she'd dissolve into an eternal hysteria and never return.

*

"Guided Tour? *Guided Tour?*" Jane looked at the door properly for the first time, struck by such an ordinary phrase in such an extraordinary place.

The door was wood, like everything else. It had a simple metal catch, but no lock or keyhole.

"Wait. There's no lock. What if I want some privacy?" She asked, aware it was another ridiculous question.

"Privacy? Here? Take a look." He waved at the window and the cold, empty clearing outside. "Not exactly Charing Cross, is it? Not really thronged with revellers, unless they're hiding."

"But you were suddenly in here."

The Man raised his hands in frustration. "I work Here!" He spluttered. "If I hadn't been 'suddenly in here' you would have wiped yourself totally by Watching The Snow, forgotten everything - and then where would we be?"

"I don't know. I don't know anything, actually. Where would we be?"

"We, well *you*, you would be in trouble," he replied, sternly. "Once totally wiped, you're gone. No more Jane, ever. So…"

"Well, thanks," she found sarcasm again. "But if this is what you say it is and I don't believe…I don't just want you walking in on me. I may be…indisposed."

Despite herself, she gave a little moue and reached up to her neck again, to rub the little silver snowflake that hung there, unaware she'd even done so.

"Hmph. Well, the next time you see me…" but then he stopped and changed the subject, a manoeuvre he was rather good at. "Anyway. It's part of being Told, getting the guided tour. You have to know what's out there."

"Out there? Out *there*?"

"Where else? A promenade at the seaside? A trip up the pier? What?"

"But look at it!" Jane almost wailed. "It must be minus something horrible. You may be dressed right, but look at me." She surprised herself with a twirl. "This blouse is cotton. Bloody cotton! Scott never wore a cotton blouse! Look, short skirt! Flats!" She did really wail that time. "Flats for god's sake!"

The Man shrugged. "Better than heels, I suppose."

Jane looked at him, hard. "I'll die. I will catch hypothermia, I *will* catch hypothermia and I *will* die and it will be *your* fault."

"Oh stop being such a baby. It's just a bit of Cold."

"Please. If I don't talk normally, I will start screaming. Please."

"Complain as much as you like, we're going out. Because if you don't, what could happen will be worse than dying."

"Worse than dying?" Part of Jane still believed she would wake up any moment. That part had watched all this unfold with a distant, detached interest. "Well, that's raised the bar, hasn't it? 'Worse than dying'? Oh, real drama. 'Worse than dying?'"

But while Jane ranted, The Man had gone over to the door and thrown it open.

The Cold smashed into her like frozen plate glass. Jane felt she'd run directly into a wall of frigidity. She took a step back, and held up her hands to ward it off, but even as she did, felt her fingers ice up and face burn, as a million particles of frost rushed into her trachea and caused her lungs to expand as they froze.

"Aaaaah," was all she managed. Jane looked wildly at The Man, who stood by the door and waited.

"Aaah." She fell backwards onto the bed, as her bare legs froze.

"A...a...a....a..." she chattered, but now her blood was icier than water in winter pipes. Thought became incoherent but she managed, *colder than dark side of coldest galaxy* before words failed her.

In just microseconds, frostbite had taken hold, in a few more her heart would surely stop.

The Man left the door open.

"Give it a moment," he said with all the urgency of a fell walker.

Jane's hands and feet battered against the bed and the floor. He body attempted to generate heat through motion, but was losing the battle.

And then the frozen waterfall that had engulfed her began to subside.

The body-lock started to release. Feeling returned, finger by finger, toe by toe. Numbness gave way to control.

The Cold had introduced itself, and passed by.

Hello, Jane, goodbye. For now.

Jane lay on the bed like a stone, physically able to move, but mentally still iced up.

"What...happened?" She managed to ask between deep breaths.

"The Cold happened." Replied The Man. "And then it didn't happen any more."

"Could...have...warned...Aw, *fuck*."

"Language, dear. Warned you? What good would that do? The Cold, like The Forest, protects Here. It's our guard dog if you like. It comes and sniffs you out, checks you're supposed to be Here. Yes, it bites, but it lets go. Well, most of the time."

"The Cold is alive?" Jane asked, while part of her thought, *of course the Cold is alive, that's why it's The Cold, not just the cold. Of* course *it is*.

"No. How can The Cold be alive? It's The Cold. But it has a job to do, just like me. Like everything Here. Sometimes people come who shouldn't. Who knows how they find this place, but they do. Not often, but it happens. The Cold makes sure they don't stay."

"It kills them?" Jane asked, horrified. That put a spin on things.

"No, goodness, no, it freezes them, sends them back. It's The Cold, what else can it do? It guards everyone that lives Here. Never forget, lies find a way into even the truest of hearts. Come on." He smiled and offered her a big hand. "Tripple trapple, up you get. You'll still feel the cold, but it will only be cold, not *The* Cold. You'll cope with it. I promise."

Jane, despite herself, did as she was told and stepped out of the Hut.

The Snow was deep, and almost came up to her knees. But - another strange thing - although it was very cold, it wasn't freezing or unpleasant. If anything, it was almost refreshing.

Jane looked down at her feet, lost in the white field that made up Here.

"My toes should be dropping off," she said in wonder. "Why aren't they?"

"Mm, good isn't it? All the fun of the snow, but none of the frostbite, or hypothermia. The Snow knows, you know. It keeps you from harm. Quick, jump a foot to the left."

So she did, and then, yes, *oh yes*, the Snow was beyond freezing.

Minus Something Horrible, as predicted. But instantaneously, the freeze went away, and became just bearably...cold.

"You took The Snow by surprise. But then it realised where you were, and warmed up accordingly. I told you, nothing can hurt you, Here. This way." He pointed to a spot a few feet away from the Hut.

A couple of feet ahead, The Man held up his hand. Jane stopped.

As he looked over his shoulder, his eyes gleamed and a broad smile burst through his beard like sun through storm clouds.

"Now look behind you."

Jane did.

Her footprints were gone.

"Wait. Hold on. What?"

"The Snow wipes your memories, and wipes all physical traces of you, too. You can leave nothing of yourself behind, Here. In case..."

"In case what?" Jane stared at the flat white surface behind her. She saw but didn't comprehend.

"In case," said The Man, and that was that, clearly.

They'd reached a spot that could be called the centre of Here, the middle of the clearing it occupied.

Circled around them stood the Forest. The trees were of a fairly uniform height, about fifteen feet tall. Above them, only sky. The Snow clouds were gone, replaced by a vibrant clear blue.

Jane looked up and couldn't stop the grin that spread across her face.

My god, that is the bluest blue I have ever seen.

There was nothing else to see. Just Snow, Huts, Forest, sky. Not much for a guided tour.

"So, Ladies and Gentlemen, or rather, Lady, singular," The Man put on a peculiar 'Tour Guide' voice. "Today, we have three Huts."

And there they were, identical, arranged at random intervals in the Snow.

"*Today* we have three?" Jane repeated.

"Tomorrow there may be more. Or less," shrugged The Man.

"Hold on, what, you pull them down? You build more?"

"I don't do anything. They're Here, or they're not Here. No more complicated than that."

"Right," said Jane uncertainly. "That is complicated, actually. Is there anyone in those Huts? Should we knock on and say hello?"

"No!" Barked The Man, forcefully. "No, No, No. Never."

"Why? It might be nice to have some company, you know, compare notes?"

"No." Case closed. "You are here to Forget. Think of this as a patient/ doctor relationship. You cannot see the files of other patients, can you? You can't just go up to other people in the ward and ask what they're doing there, can you? No. No."

"But what if people do want to talk?"

"Maybe…" he offered. "But I'm not saying these Huts even have anyone in them. Sometimes they are made ready and no-one arrives. So they are taken away again. Sometimes they wait, just in case. But poking about, peering through windows, talking to someone else about Here, about who they are, or what they are is not a good idea. You may force memories to return before they are ready. They may push a switch in your mind that turns your unwelcome past back on, in glorious, awful technicolour. And that must not happen, or any good that could come from being Here will be undone in moments. Do you understand?"

"Right," said Jane and internally admitted, *I'll just keep going with this until something cracks. Here, or me.*

"Come on." The Man walked about twenty feet to his left. Jane followed, and watched over her shoulder as The Snow popped back up and filled in her footsteps with a light crunching sound. It was a hypnotic effect.

"What time do you think it is?"

Jane tried to feel her internal clock. Inside, it felt like the evening. *Yes, it feels like evening, but the brightness of the day gives a lie to that.*

She looked up and tried to get a fix on where the sun was on its East-West journey.

Jane looked again.

"There's no sun," she gasped, and there they were, three more words that couldn't possibly be thought, let alone said.

The Man laughed. "Of course there's a sun."

"Well, I'm looking and there isn't one. Unless I'm missing something, you know, sun-y."

The Man looked back up and shrugged. "It's hiding behind the sky."

"Hiding behind the sky? The sun is hiding behind the sky?"

"Doesn't every sun hide behind the sky?" He knelt down and rolled a small snowball in his hands.

"Not really. Not in my experience. The sun doesn't really hide behind the sky. It gets hidden behind clouds, yes, the Earth turns and we lose sight of it, yes, but it doesn't…for *christ's* sake…hide…behind the sky."

"Well, it does Here," The Man rolled his snowball in the fallen Snow. "So I ask again - what time is it?"

Jane decided to let a sentient childish sun that played hide and seek with planets go for a moment. She had no choice if she wanted to keep a grip on what she now laughingly considered her sanity.

"It feels like, er, eight in the evening."

"Then it's eight in the evening."

His snowball was now double its previous size. "There are no clocks Here, so you decide the time. It's arbitrary anyway, time. If you want it to be eight, it'll be eight. Eight in the evening when? What season?"

Jane felt it inside her. "Eight in the evening, winter."

"Aha. Your wish is *Here's* command. Watch." The Man began to roll another snowball in his hands.

Above, from one corner of the sky, the bright blue began to darken.

Electric Blue gave way to Maya, to Azure, darkened and spread, the line between the darkness and the day as precise as an architects' plans.

Azure to Royal, then Denim to Yale, the night closed over Here, almost mechanically, like the dome of an observatory shutting. It slid from Prussian to Midnight Blue and settled.

All this took no more than a couple of minutes as Jane watched, dumbfounded.

That didn't happen, she thought, open mouthed. *None of this is happening, oh, but it is*, she realised. *It is, it really is.*

The Man didn't even bother to look up. He'd rolled his next snowball to the size of a watermelon and slowly placed it on top of the larger ball. "If you do decide you'd like it to be day again, just, you know, say the word. Well, you don't have to say anything, but you know what I mean. Time has no place Here. Forget free time, Here, we are time free."

"Mm. You've worked on that one, haven't you? The 'time free' bit? Very clever."

"Everyone's a critic," he sighed, and stood back from his SnowMan.

If that comes to life and starts talking, thought Jane, *I will scream and keep screaming until I have screamed my reason away forever.*

"Watch this." The Man stepped back.

Slowly his SnowMan began to deconstruct. The flakes rolled off, back down to the ground, then made their way to the exact spot they'd first come from. Flake by flake, crystal by crystal, like a stream of white ants that poured down the surface, the Snow went back to where it had started and settled there.

Parlour trick done, The Man went back to business.

Despite the darkness, Jane could still see him perfectly. He got serious. The Man pointed, first one way then the other.

"North," he said, then turned. "South. You asked what happens after you've been Here. Well, you leave, of course. This isn't a prison. You leave by North, or South. Come." He trudged towards the edge of The

Forest. Jane followed, as the snow crackled behind them, and erased their journey.

The Man stopped at the trees and pointed down at the ground. "North. There are two paths out of Here, one North, one South. This is the North Path. The South looks just the same."

Jane looked. Some bright yellow stones formed a path (*no, a Path, capital P,* she knew) no more than three feet wide.

The stones gleamed, placed so close together you could hardly see the joins. But after just a few feet, they faded into darkness. The Forest wasn't dense, but the Path simply disappeared as it led between the trees.

"Does it stop?" Jane went to put a foot on it.

The Man grabbed her arm. "NO!"

When she looked at him expecting anger, instead she saw only fear. "You can leave by a Path only when it is time. Please, I beg you, do not step onto a Path until you are ready."

"But I can't even see it after a few feet. Is it still there?" Jane chose to ask another question rather than confront that fear.

The expression on The Man's face scared her.

"It is there. But you cannot see it until your Aurora comes. Your Aurora comes when you are ready to leave, and lights the Pathways so you can see them. Please, please do not try to step onto the Paths unless your Aurora lights the way. It is one of the most important things you need to be Told."

"Aurora? My Aurora?" asked Jane, knowing he wouldn't elaborate. But she needed to address his alarm. "Why do I need it lit?"

"These two Paths are the only ways to leave Here. If you try to step into the Forest, you'll find the trees are much closer together than they appear."

Jane looked at the trees, which stood only a few feet apart, surely enough room to get between.

But oh no, she thought. *Oh no, if I were to try, that Forest would be much denser than it looks. I'm sure I'd be caught in those branches, unable to move. Yes, that Forest would be impenetrable if I tried. I don't know how I know this, but it is fact. Those trees would not let me leave.*

The Man spoke on. "The Aurora comes when people arrive and it dances when they leave. It was Here when you arrived. *Aurora Janaris*, if you like. It lights these Paths, North and South, so you can find your way safely. Without your Aurora, you will be lost within feet. Lost and Forgotten. Never to find your way back to…Here, There, Everywhere or…anywhere."

Jane looked at the North Path. She saw how quickly it faded from view, and just knew that if she stepped onto it without light, she'd take a wrong turn in seconds.

"What happens without the light? My Aurora, I mean? What happens to the people who try to walk into the Forest without it?"

The Man looked stricken.

"It happens, sometimes. For whatever reason, some feel they must leave before they are ready. They think they can negotiate the Path, get through The Forest. But they are wrong. They are all wrong. They walk onto the Path, and by the time they have taken their second step, they are lost in the Forest. Forever. Out there."

He waved his hand at the Forest, but, Jane noticed, he didn't get any nearer. Like it would bite.

"One step without your Aurora is all it takes. An eternity of wandering in the dark, not even knowing your name, or how you came to be in that eternal Forest. No breadcrumbs or snow white pebbles for those Hansels and Gretls, no moonlight to shine their way. Just gone. I beg you, Jane, do not step onto a Path until your Aurora comes. Promise me."

Jane looked into that Forest and saw in her minds eye (and was it really her imagination?) those lost, forgotten people, who walked in circles, trapped in a wooden Möbius strip, round and round for eternity, not knowing who or where they were.

"I promise." She shivered, but not from the cold.

The Man pulled her back a little from The North Path, like a relieved policeman pulling a jumper from the edge of a building.

"Without The Aurora, you will lose yourself forever," he repeated, quietly, but the message had already got through, loud and clear.

Jane thought for a moment. There were many questions, but she knew as far as The Man was concerned, she'd been been Told.

But she still asked one more.

"When will my Aurora come?"

"Your Aurora comes next time we meet, Jane. You'll know it is is yours. There may be others, but they are not for you. Wait for yours. It will come when you are ready to leave. I will be with you. And then you must decide. North Or South."

"What's the difference?" Jane knew she wouldn't get anything else, but tried nonetheless.

"North or South," he sighed sadly, looked left and right, between the two Paths. "Depends on love."

BOOK FOUR / IRENE

16 / 1993 / Mother Stands For Comfort

Here we are again together, you, me and Jane, into another year.

You've already seen parts of her diary, and I'm pleased to say, after a few false starts and a prolonged, painful period in the Sixth Form, Jane managed to achieve the results she needed for a place at University.

Why she was so bothered about attending University rather than Polytechnic came down to the simple fact that one sounded way better than the other, even if the courses were the same. These seemingly unimportant little details and choices all add up to make a life.

To her surprise, Jane landed a few hundred miles from home, up the M6, at Manchester University.

She'd hoped for a place nearer the East End, where her friends and family lived. It was, after all, Jane's first proper move away from Mum and Dad, and although smart and independent she was also a little scared, as you all are, of the unknown.

The thought Mum and Dad weren't on tap to put their arms round her shoulders and say it was *all going to be alright* had made Jane uncomfortable. Should she fall, the safety net was a long, long way down South.

But she never fell. If anything, she flew.

She was homesick, yes , but that was numbed a little by the out of control cultural train called Manchester. Once there, Jane went for it - she tried out bars, boys and *being* and liked it all, very much.

Alongside life, she'd also found time to study English, Lit and Lang, with the intention of becoming a professional writer.

She knew a degree wouldn't necessarily help in that direction, but it would give her the tools she'd need. Just as a mechanic must know how a vehicle is welded together, she saw her degree as a lesson in the mechanics of writing, no more.

Then, when it came to her first summer holiday, Jane smiled all the way back home.

Dull Euston Station always looked wonderful when she stepped onto the concourse and breathed in London again. St Pancras might look like a Victorian Lady made stone, and Waterloo had its sunset, but Euston was the gateway back home, and nothing could compete with that.

But for Jane, the summer of 1993 became one to forget, wipe away, burn down until nothing remained, not even ashes.

*

Irene still made curtains in an East End factory, but as you know, Jane's mother was really an Artist.

The walls of the family home were hung with her canvasses. Look there - it's a blue and green dragonfly, no wait, it's a humming bird, no, hold on, a wave, a dress. Irene's pictures shifted, danced and Jane never grew tired of them.

But while her daughter had been away, Mum had tried something new. Propped up in the kitchen were several small pictures of roses that burst from their canvasses.

Irene hadn't given up the impressionistic side of her art entirely (*"it's still life, yes, but it's still me,"* she'd explained) because these roses existed outside of their three dimensions. Their colours left traces behind, like after-images from looking into a bright light. They were roses both here in the world, but apart from it. The flowers appeared to strain and shift, to occupy different places and times simultaneously.

They were beautiful.

Sometimes, a beautiful object can transform its surroundings. Irene's roses bent and shaped the kitchen around them, until Jane couldn't see the room, just the flowers. She simply stopped and stared, literally open mouthed.

"Mum." She managed after a few moments. "Are these yours?"

Irene put down her handbag and raised an eyebrow. "No, they're your father's. Of course they're mine. Do you like them?"

Jane's mother didn't often make jokes, so that alone should have been a distant alarm that something was not right. But some alarms are so distant they can't possibly be for us. Let someone else deal with that far-off siren, let *them* call the emergency services.

"I love them, I really do. They're like nothing you've done before. Well, they're still in your style, but - I'm not saying I don't like your other paintings, I do, I love them too, but these...these are...Mum, these are..."

Her Mother waited patiently.

"I don't know *what* these are."

"So glad that English language degree is paying off," Irene giggled. Two jokes in one conversation. Like the roses, that had come from somewhere else.

"Why roses? You've never been so...specific before."

"Oh, I just..." Jane saw her mother's mind wander. "I just started thinking of roses. One day, roses. Big, red, living roses growing and not stopping. I wanted to show a rose that didn't want to stop growing, ever. So that's why the colours go beyond the borders of the flower - it's impatient to grow. It won't be held back."

For Irene, whose use of language was the definition of brevity, that was a very long statement to make. Another unusual marker, but one that remained unseen, for now.

*

It is said that history repeats itself, first as tragedy, then as comedy. For Jane, the comedy came first but the laughter dried up very quickly.

A few days after coming home, Jane had gone to put a Fray Bentos pie in the oven.

That proved to be slightly difficult because there was a bunch of bananas in there.

Jane looked at the bananas for a while to confirm that *yes*, we have some bananas, and *yes*, they are in the oven rather than the larder. Bananas *per se* were also strange. Irene never bought them because there was something about the skin she didn't like. "It's the texture, ooh, *penny dreadful* it is," was as far as she'd ever explain.

"Mum?" Jane called through to the living room, where Irene sat and read a magazine. "Mum? There are bananas in the oven."

No reply.

"Mum?" Jane tried again. "Why are there bananas in the oven?"

Silence.

Jane sighed and walked the full four feet to the door of the living room, where Irene sat, glasses on, head down in a copy of Woman's Own.

"Didn't you hear me just then?"

"Hear a what a what-what?" replied Irene, distantly.

"Me. I said there are bananas in the oven. It's not a euphemism."

Her mother gazed back slightly scornfully. "No there aren't." She returned to her magazine.

Jane took it out of Irene's hands and pulled her up. "There are. Look."

They went into the kitchen where the oven stood open. It looked guilty, as if caught in the act of eating forbidden fruit.

"See? Why are there bananas in there?"

"Why did you put them there?" Irene looked confused.

"I didn't. You did. They weren't in there an hour ago. You went out, you came back, you must have bought some bananas and put them in the oven."

"I don't even like bananas," replied Irene, outraged. "Why would I buy them and why would I put bananas in the oven? Bananas, I ask you."

"Can we just stop saying bananas? You're clearly going a bit doolally in your old age."

"Well I never put bananas in the oven." Irene turned to go back to her seat.

"Stop saying bananas!" Jane laughed. "You've gone crackers this time."

*

Jane had told Dad about it over tea that night, and they'd had a good laugh. Even Irene had managed a slightly embarrassed chuckle, but more for politeness sake, as she'd genuinely not remembered putting the fruit there.

The Banana Incident, as it became to be known both first humorously and then tragically, was the first definable moment in a series of incidents that overtook them all that summer, then gathered them in their wake.

The next was another a simple moment, unrecognised as it happened, but in hindsight (and isn't *that* a wonderful thing, as they say) marked the last spot where Jane and Dave had a chance, not to avert the already written, but maybe to delay it.

*

On her return, Jane had been "debriefed" by her parents who'd wanted to know about everything and everyone that had happened in the last few months.

So she'd gone back through her diary, told them about University days and Manchester nights, parties in digs, and gigs in digs, gigs at the Ritz, and parties at the Hacienda, dancing at the Twisted Wheel, drinking at The Star & Garter, boys, girls and occasionally, even a bit of genuine learning, *who would have thought?*

*

A few days after The Banana Incident, Jane sat with Mum at breakfast, as Dave was on his early shift, where he cleared up litter left by the even earlier shift that had poured out of pubs and clubs in the early hours. That shift left a trail behind them to follow should they wish to return, like drunken Hansels and Gretels.

Breakfast without Dave was usually a quiet affair, a time to prepare for the day ahead.

But today, again uncharacteristically, Irene wanted to talk.

"Jane," she'd waved a piece of toast to get her attention. "When are you going to tell me about Manchester?"

Jane picked up her own toast to wave back. "Hello?" She shook it, like bready semaphore. "Hello over there? I seem to remember an entire evening dedicated to every detail of my last few months in Manchester. A whole night, with every single question that was possible to ask, for about three whole hours. I didn't realise you wanted it written up too."

Irene looked a little hurt.

"Well, you didn't tell me. You must have told your father. I'd like to know, too."

"You were there!" Jane laughed. "You were there!"

But Irene just looked blank. "I wasn't." She said slowly. "Or I would have remembered, wouldn't I? And unless I'm losing my memory, which I know I'm not, you never told me."

For a moment, Irene looked - not scared, no - but unsettled. Scared would come soon enough.

Jane put down her toast, laughter gone.

It's possible, perhaps, that Mum's forgotten some of the detail - but all *of it? She didn't even recall being there? That's odd. I must tell Dad about it.*

Dementia? Fireworked in her mind for a second, followed by a burst of *Alzheimers?*

But she didn't want to watch that particular display and turned from it.

There's an explanation. Mum may have just been tired. Or dozing. Or not listening. Or perhaps she's going a bit mutton, that would do it. But another part of her said;

Shedoesn'trememberbeingthere

Shedoesn'trememberbeingthere

Shedoesn'trememberbeingthere

Over and over.

There'd been other things. Tiny moments that by themselves meant nothing, but laid end to end would eventually form a huge arrow that pointed to the inevitable.

Irene sometimes zoned out, gone somewhere else, but hadn't snapped back like a daydreamer, but rather, *slowwwlllly* re-inhabited herself.

She'd make a cup of tea, add sugar, then a few minutes later, add a few more spoonfuls, blank-faced.

She'd found a recording of Bobby McFerrin's, "Don't Worry, Be Happy", played it, rewound, played, rewound, on a loop. She sang along lustily, again and again, as if she'd forgotten the previous plays.

When Jane or Dave asked her to switch it off, she'd looked hurt and confused.

Don't be silly. I've only just put it on. Surely?

But they never put those tiny moments together to form that arrow, not until after. We all see that arrow then, don't we?

So within days of Jane's return, everything buckled and cracked.

Take my hand, again. We must hold on tight for dear life, because things will rush now, as they always do, because big events usually happen very very quickly, sometimes in seconds. So please hold tight because this road is downhill and we have no brakes.

Jane had decided to have a quiet word with her Dad about the strange forgetfulness Irene was displaying.

That word never happened.

*

She would remember this moment in all it's ghastly clarity, forever.

Jane went to the living room where Dad sat and read. Irene was upstairs.

Her plan had been to float a question at him plainly, without cause for concern, to gently ask, "have you noticed Mum forgetting things at all recently?" Something harmless like that.

Dad looked up at Jane and they'd both smiled. Those smiles would be their last genuine versions for a long time.

Then Irene appeared at the doorway. She floated there for a moment, clutched at the frame and whispered, "live some past in the grey round man night snow reason." Then vomited down herself, and the bile fell from her mouth without effort.

"Oh God," Dave jumped up. "Oh God, love, are you alright?"

It's amazing isn't it, how we always ask that question - *are you alright?* - even when we already know the answer.

We ask because it's the last hope that person will say, "yes, just something I ate." Or, "yes, no problem, I'm fine."

But when your love, the centre of yourself, whispers, "live some past in the grey round man night snow reason," then vomits and doesn't even seem to notice, *are you alright?* is already redundant.

"Mum?" was as far as Jane got before Irene croaked, "better half the man got new marmite spread box," and collapsed.

After Irene fell, Dave ran to the phone in the hall, Jane dropped to her knees but couldn't help. The ambulance drove right up to their door, the paramedics carefully put Irene on the stretcher, the vehicle battered its way through summer traffic to the London Hospital, and then things got worse. Round and round we go, don't we? The names change but the script stays almost the same.

Irene was taken away to who knows where, while Jane and Dave waited, hand in hand.

*

It's cruel, isn't it, that hospitals have The Waiting Room, the sole function of which is a holding pen for hope.

There you go, they say, *nothing you can do now, go there and you wait. And wait.*

And so you wait. Because you are in The Waiting Room and that is all you *can* do there.

Go on, try. Try to read, talk, or watch other people, it will make no difference. You'll still wait, whatever you attempt to do. Go on, hurry up and wait.

A Doctor entered The Waiting Room, looked around - and wasn't that peculiar? - didn't shout their names, or look at a chart, but went straight over to Dave and Jane.

"David," the Doctor said. "Jane," he added, and offered a hand to shake.

Jane glanced at her father for an explanation for this medical telepathy, but Dad hadn't returned the gaze. The last thing Jane needed was another mystery, but she held her tongue. Wrong time, wrong place.

"Doctor Perry," Dave replied, weakly. "You're still here."

"Yes, I'm still here." Doctor Stephen Perry spread his arms wide and sighed. "A lot older, hopefully wiser. I wish we could have met again under different circumstances. Jane, my word, look at you. How old were you when I last..?"

Jane looked at her father pointedly, but he shook his head, *later, darling, later*.

"She was six." Dave replied.

"Six, my goodness. Where does it all go?"

"What's happening to Irene?" Dave asked, small talk over, never requested.

"Come into my office," Said Dr Perry, and so they did.

And there they were again.

Father and Daughter, back in Doctor Perry's office, after fourteen years.

1979 and 1993, the times stitched together so neatly you could hardly see the join, unless you looked at the decor and, of course, the ages of the players.

Jane, naturally, didn't remember her first time in this office. Somehow, she'd covered over those few days in December 1979, when she'd had an accident, and lost her memory.

And wasn't that ironic? She'd forgot she'd forgotten.

So Jane wondered how and why this doctor already knew her name. That knowledge made a chill settle about her like the sheen of a morning frost. Dave, however, had already raced ahead and recognised a rather important fact.

"Tell me, Dr Perry, why am I sitting in a brain specialists office?"

No-one had mentioned this. Not the nurse, nor the Doctor himself. But Jane's father knew and that sent up a few more emergency flares.

What is going on? My Dad is privy to information he can't possibly know, but since he can't read minds, I have to assume he's met this brain specialist before, which begs, no, demands *the questions WHEN and WHY?*

And why is the most important question of them all, isn't it?

Dr Perry gathered himself, as he'd done over and again through the years. His job required him to offer an opinion the people on the other side of the desk were never ready for. When you trained to become a doctor, you learned how to treat the body, but no-one taught you how to suture emotions, transplant hopes. The operations were the relatively easy part. It was the telling that couldn't be truly prepared for.

So every day, every hour, it seemed, Dr Perry sat in this chair and delivered news that was unexpected and unwelcome.

In 1979, he'd been younger and stronger, he'd taken the tears and walked away from them, because he knew if he didn't, they would eventually corrode him. It's said water is the universal solvent, but tears and time are just as effective. They'll wear anything away, given the chance.

So Dr Perry gathered himself.

"David. Jane."

Father and Daughter reached for each others' hands again without even looking or thinking. The way Dr Perry said their names, without a smile, or holding up his own hands in the universal gesture of *it's OK* was enough. They'd known.

"Your wife...your Mother...Irene...she is displaying symptoms and signs that…Well, this isn't a given. This isn't definite."

"Why am I talking to a brain surgeon?" Dave asked again. The first time hadn't worked.

"She is showing signs that she...perhaps...has a brain tumour."

And there it was, *that word*, out in the open, where it couldn't be taken back. And now, no matter what happened, they couldn't catch up.

Tumour is not a word that can be misconstrued. And it is not a word one ever wants to hear from a Doctor.

Dave slumped in his chair. Jane, conversely, sat bolt upright.

"*Brain* tumour? Brain *tumour*? *Brain tumour*?" She felt she might sit there forever, as those two words looped over and over.

Dave ignored her and made a beeline for hope. "You said 'perhaps'."

"I did," said Dr Perry.

There's always a perhaps, isn't there?

Doctor's don't lie when they use *perhaps*. There's always a perhaps, always a maybe, always an, "I hope."

Perhaps there's another treatment.

Maybe you got it wrong.

I hope she'll be one of the lucky ones.

Maybe there's a new drug.

Perhaps there's an alternative therapy.

I hope there's a higher power.

Perhaps, maybe, there's Love.

Until all the perhaps and maybes have been tried and you're left with;

I hope it will be peaceful.

"Yes, as I say, this is only an initial diagnosis." But Dr Perry had known it was a brain tumour. Now he only had to confirm what kind, how big and how long there was left.

"Perhaps I am wrong."

'Perhaps' offers the possibility - however remote - of an emergency exit. Because if you can't find that exit, you just stay in the building until it burns down with you inside.

"I need to perform exploratory surgery. To get more of an idea. As soon as a theatre becomes available, I'll perform the procedure. As soon as, I promise."

"What kind of surgery?" Jane asked, which was the wrong question.

"Oh, it's routine." Dr Perry was relieved she hadn't asked the right question. "I make a small hole in the cranium, and through that, we're able to examine the tumour, hopefully, and get an idea of how we can proceed."

"But what if the tumour is inside her brain?" Jane asked, which again, was the wrong question.

"Well, we know it's not from the scan - it's surface, which is a good sign. If tumours are deep that makes it..well…trickier...but your mother's is surface, so perhaps that could work in our favour."

Dr Perry suspected more than this, but had to go through the motions.

"How long before you know?" Jane asked the wrong question again.

"We'll know straight away, pretty much. So please, let's take this one step at a time. I know you're distressed, which is ,er, an understatement, of course, but for your own sakes, just remember nothing is written in stone. People have tumours every day, which doesn't help you right now, but this is what I do. I treat them, and many of them recover. That is what I do. This could be...benign. Treatable. Today."

Jane smiled, because that's what she'd wanted to hear.

But Dave, naturally, asked the right question.

"Why are you rushing her in so quick?" He didn't look at Dr Perry and chose instead to stare out of the window. "I know how hospitals work. There are - what? - ten theatres here, if that? Every minute, the...damaged and the dying turn up here and you can fit Irene in like…that?" He snapped his fingers, angrily. "That's not how it works, is it?"

"Dad?" Jane pulled a face that said, *be nice to the Doctor.*

"I was here in 1979, and I wanted the truth about my daughter then, and now I'd like the truth about my wife. Please."

What the hell happened to me in 1979? thought Jane.

Dr Perry sighed, but not with impatience, rather the sigh of someone whose poker face had failed and they'd lost their stake.

"The truth. Yes. The truth this moment is, I really don't know until I perform the procedure. I suspect Irene has an aggressive tumour that has been growing for some time. The symptoms and signs point to that diagnosis, but until we do know, let us not posit possibilities. One step at a time. I just want to warn you that in my experience, that is the most likely diagnosis. But let us deal with it when we have to deal with it, not before. That is the truth. I swear."

But that was the edges of the truth rather than the centre. Dr Perry knew what he would find. He just had to confirm it.

"Thankyou," Dave whispered. "Thankyou, I appreciate it."

"Irene is sleeping. Of course you can go and sit with her, but as soon as I have a theatre, I'm taking her in. Is that acceptable? There will be forms, naturally."

"Naturally." Dave replied, although there was nothing natural about this situation, nothing natural at all.

Irene slept.

17 / Irene, 1993

Jane and Dave waited, again.

There, in the Waiting Room, but also in a no-man's land between knowing and not knowing.

They fetched tea for each other, and talked about nothing. But even the nothing had a subtext, because by refusing to speak about what *was* and what *might be*, they spoke of it loudly, just without words.

Finally, Jane confronted something else instead.

"Oh. How did that Doctor know you?" She flicked through a magazine, to give the impression of disinterest.

"Which Doctor?" Dave gave the same act, but with a newspaper.

"We've only seen one." Jane kept her gaze down and pretended to read an article.

"Oh, Dr Perry." Dave offered nothing else.

"Yes, Dr Perry. He knew you and he knew me, but I've never met him, so how is that possible? Was this happening before I came home? Have you been here before with Mum?"

"No. The first I knew about it was the first you did."

"She has been acting a bit out of character."

"I thought that was just her getting old, perhaps. It might still be."

"Old," snorted Jane. "Forty? OK, "getting old," yes, I suppose it might be." But they both knew it wasn't. "So, how did that Doctor know you, Dad? And me? What did he say? That I was six when he last saw me? I don't remember that, no, *noooo*, not at all."

Jane closed the magazine, reached over and shut Dave's paper. Time to talk, about this, at least. She could deal with a trip down a curious side-road. It was a welcome diversion from the coming storm.

*

At that moment, Dave had a choice. He could tell Jane how she'd once been treated by Dr Perry for a highly specific, very unusual form of memory loss following an accident.

Or he could lie.

Between you and me, I believe telling Jane might have changed her future.

Dave, unfortunately, did not have my perspective, so decided to lie.

Only a bit. Too much. Just enough. Who can say?

*

"OK, fine. You were at the park, you fell and hit your head. We brought you in for a check up. Dr Perry is a brain specialist, so naturally he took a look at you. That's it. No big mystery. No conspiracy."

Jane looked into her Dad's eyes and gauged him. He held her gaze and his stare said, *nothing to hide here, darling.*

"Ah, but that's not quite true is it?" Jane sighed.

"Yes it is. Why would I lie?"

"Mm. I don't know. But I know you, Dad, and you've never been good at lying. Neither have I because of it. Your nostrils are flaring. They always flare when you're fibbing. Like mine do."

"My nostrils are flaring because I'm trying to keep a yawn in," he lied, as his nostrils flared again.

"Ah-ah, nope. If I hit my head, why would I see a brain specialist? That seems …the nuclear option, don't you think? I hit my head in gym at school, remember, when I fell off the climbing rope. The nurse shone a light in my eyes, did a few tests and sent me back up the rope again. No need a for a brain specialist."

She opened her hands wide to him, to say *over to you.*

"Yes, I remember that, and the school were lax. They should have taken you in for a check up."

"But even if they had, Dad, I'd have gone into A&E, seen a nurse, or even a junior Doctor, and been sent home if they hadn't found anything. But I see a brain specialist? Seriously?"

"He was just around, Jane, alright? No big deal. He happened to be about and he happened to just look in on you. You got the deluxe treatment, because he was there when you came in. OK?"

Jane looked around the waiting room, as the wheels of her mind ground small, and applied themselves to the problem forensically. "That doesn't make sense," she concluded.

Dave had picked up the paper again, but put it back down, exasperated.

"Because, Dad, if he'd just been passing through, if he'd just happened to be there, I was just another kid who'd hit their head, so…why does he remember me and you from, what fourteen years ago? He walks in and straight away it's, 'hello David, oh, you must be Jane,' that's weird. What really happened, Dad?"

"I don't know why he remembers us!" Dave hissed, then immediately felt guilty. "How should I know? Shall we ask him?" Inwardly he prayed Jane wouldn't. As parents, they'd been irrationally scared that if Jane remembered that time it might happen again. So they'd kept it from their daughter, both for her protection, and theirs.

What you don't remember can't hurt you.

"OK, but why don't I remember it? I've been in hospital exactly once." She held up her index finger for emphasis. "And that was for a poxy twisted ankle we thought was broken. So since I've only been in once, you'd think I'd remember this one other time. But I don't. And that's very, very odd."

"Well, I don't know then. Perhaps…" Dave hid the lie in amongst the folds of a truth. "Perhaps you did have some amnesia. From banging your head. You fell out of a tree. Quite a distance, actually." Another lie. "Amnesia - that could have happened, amnesia, right?"

"Mmm," Jane wasn't having it, not for one moment. "Well, when Mum's feeling better, let's see what she remembers about it. See if she can shed any light, right?"

But that was never going to happen, because events were about to spin out of control, rush past with no handholds to grab, then steam on without them both.

"David? Jane?" A nurse had silently appeared by their side.

Father and daughter looked up at her. She was smiling. A good sign? Or perhaps she always smiled.

"How's my wife doing?" Dave cut straight to it.

"I'm afraid I don't know," smiled the Nurse. "I've just been asked to fetch you to Dr Perry's office."

"Oh, right, thank you." Dave and Jane both stood up. Neither wanted to.

So.

The short walk to Dr Perry's office was the last time they'd be wrapped in the protection of ignorance. They had neither good news nor bad. They walked in a liminal state, between outcomes, kept from harm for those short precious moments by wonderful obliviousness.

It was a short walk and a very long one. Perhaps part of them will always be there, safe in that walk where the future was still unwritten. David took Jane's hand and she squeezed his, three times, just as she used to as a child. Three squeezes that were code for, "I love you".

*

Dr Perry was at the door of his office. He'd just returned from drilling a hole in Irene's head to see what he could see.

There is a game all friends and relatives play when someone they love teeters between outcomes. It's a desperate, painful game called *Read The Doctor* and the rules are simple. You look at the Doctor's face, then from every subtlety in their expression, try to guess What Happens Next.

So Jane and David searched Dr Perry's face, but he'd played that game enough times to become quite the expert. He never let anyone race ahead. The situation must be controlled, because heaven knew there wasn't a lot of control to be had.

"Come in," he said, expression inscrutable, voice neutral.

They went in, sat down, held hands.

Dr Perry began. There was no stopping him, no time for Dave and Jane to even start the game.

"Irene has a butterfly tumour across the two frontal lobes of her brain. I'm sorry. It is an inoperable condition."

Inoperable condition

Another two words you never want to hear, alongside;

Irreparable damage.

Terrible cost.

And no options.

Jane and David's hands involuntarily squeezed each others'.

"I'm so sorry. We can give her steroids, which may slow the growth of the tumour, but there are no options. We can't operate, it would cause irreparable damage which could kill her there and then. Radiotherapy and chemotherapy may buy time, but at a terrible cost. She would be so ill through the treatment that any time she has left would be spent unable to function. I'm so sorry."

Jane was struck mute as the words ripped into her. Little words, big consequences. *Tumour. Inoperable. Buy Time. Terrible Cost.*

Terrible Cost.

Yes, the cost was terrible, but Dave went for it, as they always did. He started to gabble, one desperate hope after another;

Perhaps there's another treatment.

Perhaps you got it wrong.

Perhaps she'll be one of the lucky ones.

Perhaps there's a new drug.

Perhaps there's an alternative therapy.

The Doctor nodded to all but didn't agree with any. He had no choice but to let Dave exhaust the possibilities.

Dr Perry took a deep breath. The worst part was coming.

"I'm sorry, but I think… she has no more than six months."

Jane gasped, David choked. Suddenly there wasn't enough oxygen in the room, in the world, to let him breathe. Jane looked to her father (*do something Daddy*) but Dave couldn't do a thing. No-one could.

"The steroids might buy her time, radio and chemotherapy, perhaps, but…they won't change anything. This tumour is too big, too, er, aggressive. Those treatments would just give her adverse quality of life. She wouldn't be able to register the time she has left, just survive it. We can provide palliative care, of course."

Jane still didn't cry. She knew she would, and probably never stop. She spoke first. Her father blankly looked around the office, as if somewhere on a shelf might be a book, potion or pill Dr Perry had forgotten about.

"Does she know?" Jane took control.

"Yes."

Dave's eyes widened . Now he had something he could work on, to get angry about.

"You told her without us there?"

"Yes, David. The patient is my priority. I tell them first. Others do it differently, but I prefer to be one on one. If I tell them in front of an audience, then I'm having to deal with two, three, four more reactions at once. The patient is my priority. They must have this knowledge first. It is their life."

"We should have been there," whispered David, with furious sibilance. "We should have been there to…hold her hand…"

"No, Dad, I see," said Jane, gently. "Dad, it makes sense. He's only thinking of Mum."

Dave shot Jane a look, but the fight had gone out of him. He was smart enough to see the logic in Dr Perry's method. Oh yes, it was very logical.

"Can we see her?" asked Jane. "I really want to see my Mum."

"Yes, yes. You must have time alone, of course. Then we can discuss the…er….possibilities. Together."

"Yes, of course. But can I see my Mum now?"

Irene lay in a private room somewhere inside a maze of corridors Jane doubted they'd be able to negotiate again. Mum had the tiniest bandage on the top of her head and Jane thought, *that's all? The world changes and that's all?*

Jane and David simply walked in and clung to her, daughter one side, husband the other. There was nothing to say because there was nothing to say, simple as that.

You know, I hope somewhere, *somewhen*, they are still there, all three. In their time between.

Eventually, David reluctantly pulled away and looked at his wife.

"Oh darling," he whispered, but didn't cry. Not yet. He would.

"Oh darling," smiled Irene, then, to Jane. "Oh my darling, *now* where am I?"

"Mum." Jane's eyes became wet, but still held onto her tears, perhaps because she knew those eyes had a lot of work ahead, and miles to go before they slept. "Oh, Mum."

"This wasn't supposed to happen, was it?" said Irene, quietly. "What a shame."

David nodded. Jane clutched her mother again.

"What do we do?" Asked David, like a lost child. "What do we do? What can we do, Irene? What can we do? What will I do? What will I do, Irene?"

"We'll live, just as we always have done," she said, softly. "We'll see what happens. But I have you, don't I? I'm lucky. I have you."

Jane nodded, she nodded like the ferocity of her agreement could alter things.

"Yes, I have you," nodded Irene in return. "The Doctor says I have to stay for a few days. A few more tests. I think there are many tests ahead."

"We'll stay with you," said Dave. "We won't leave you. Not ever."

"How funny." A weak smile floated across Irene's face like a gentle breeze. "How funny it's the same Doctor. Older, but I recognised him. How funny. What a small world. He treated you, Jane. You fell and he treated you. Oh, years ago. But no time ago." She frowned. "No time at all. Yesterday. Tomorrow. When did you fall, darling?"

Jane said nothing.

"You got better though, Jane." Irene smiled and stroked her daughter's hair again. "Didn't she, darling? All better, thank God."

"I'm not thanking God for anything," Dave said, almost to himself.

"Ooh, don't let God hear you say that," Irene scolded, but had never been religious anyway. "God's already got it in for us, wouldn't you say?"

Jane smiled, despite herself. "Yes, he has," she said quietly, and realised she'd left the capital 'H' off 'He.' No capital "H" for he, or him, for god, not from Jane, not evermore, God became a lower case 'god' at that moment. "god has got it in for us."

"Hm," Irene closed her eyes, but didn't sleep yet, just felt her family around her. "Hm. We've got a lot to do, I think."

"We don't have to do anything," said Dave. "We do whatever you want."

"I have a lot to do," said Irene, eyes still closed. "I just didn't even know it before now. Chop. Chop chop! I have so much to do and we really don't have much time, so chop chop, I must get a move on. Chop. Chop, before the curtain drops. Remember that nursery rhyme?"

Jane didn't, but then;

herecomesachoppertochopoffyourhead

"We'll do what you want," said Dave, then put his hands over his face and tried to block it all out.

"Yes you'll do what I want. But no change there, right?" She opened her eyes, looked at them both, and a minxy smile flickered over her lips.

"No change there, Mum." Jane attempted to giggle, but choked on it.

"No change there, darling." Dave managed a laugh so thin it may as well not been there at all.

"And the first thing I want to do. The only thing I want to do is go home. We can go home, can't we? After the tests?"

"Yes, I promise." Dave took his wife's hand.

"I'm scared," said Irene. "I don't remember ever dying before. And I'm scared."

Jane and her Father were scared too, but what could they say? Their fear was nothing compared to Irene's, who was about to go somewhere else without them.

"Let's go home, Mum," was all Jane could manage.

"Yes, Home." Irene closed her eyes again. "Home."

But no-one else heard the capital letter she'd given it.

18 / Irene / Lists And Loss.

Goodbye kid, hurry back.

It's better to burn out than fade away.

I am just going outside. I may be some time.

Famous last words.

Most fading thoughts are never recorded, but Irene's last are here in Jane's story, of course. They may not be particularly poetic, but they *are* universal.

Irene's final words on this planet were, "this doesn't feel right."

Goodness. *This doesn't feel right.* Four words that sum it all up, really.

When death comes, preceding its entry with *this doesn't feel right,* is as good a farewell as any.

Death shouldn't feel right. Expected, inevitable, natural, yes, but right? No. Never.

"This doesn't feel right," she said, and no more.

But wait, I'm getting ahead of myself again. That's what happens when clocks mean nothing.

*

Irene was dying, fast, and all Dave and Jane could do was watch, helplessly.

After her diagnosis, she spent a few more days in hospital and underwent further tests before being sent home to rest. Of course, *sent home to rest,* like, *making her comfortable,* are both euphemisms for *there's nothing else we can do.*

Operating on the tumour wasn't an option. The procedure would either kill her, or leave Irene so incapacitated that the last months of her life would have been no life at all.

A hospice was offered, but father and daughter had reacted to that suggestion with horror. They never said it out loud to each other, but their thoughts were mirrored;

We *will look after her. We will be with her until she must go. She has lived in this home for the last twenty five years and when she leaves, at least she will be here, still.*

So Irene came home.

She was placed on some pretty ferocious steroids. In theory, steroids may cause a tumour to shrink, or inhibit its growth. But steroids only equal time, not cure, and as we shall see again and again in this tale, time becomes your most precious commodity - your only commodity - when it's running out.

So Irene lay on the sofa, as husband and daughter fussed around her, and no-one talked about the present or the future, but always the past.

When the present is unbearable and the future is untenable the past seems like a safe place to visit.

They fetched her tea and toast, and the occasional nip of gin and tonic, but the medication made her nauseous and the tumour left her confused.

Because this was not a drill, this was real, it was happening, and everything had moved so fast that in the gyre of it all, Jane and her father were still trying to deal with the initial symptoms, let alone diagnosis.

*

Jane massaged her Mum's feet. Irene's eyes were closed.

"Lovely," she said, softly. "I didn't know you were this good at foot massaging."

"Neither did I," said Jane, who realised she hadn't known much about anything, as it turned out.

She had so much to ask, so much still to learn. Simple questions she'd always meant to get round to, but the time was never right. It wasn't like they were that important, they could wait, right? There would always be another day.

Except they were important, they couldn't wait and the days were counting away.

Please tell me Mum, she thought, but couldn't say out loud;

What was my birth like?

What's your oldest memory?
What was I like as a child, really?
Tell me about Dad when he was young.

Tell me about your parents, your home, your Christmas Days, Holidays, rainy days, sunny days, sad days, happy days and birthdays, tell me how you fell in and out of love and how you felt when your parents passed, tell me about your favourite toy, favourite band, film and place, tell me what made you laugh, cry, angry and calm, tell me where you've been, where you wanted to go, tell me who you are tell me, tell me, tell me all the things I never thought to ask and are now the most important things in the world because all these things are you, Mum, *they are* you *and I don't even know the answers so tell me, tell me, tell me, please, tell me,* please.

But Jane said nothing, because to ask would be to start the process of finishing the story and closing the book. And we always drag out the last pages of any wonderful tale, don't we? We try to stop the threads being drawn for good, and hope the story never ends, but it always does.

*

Six Months, Doctor Perry had said.

No, clarify that; six months at the most.

Six months is nothing.

Half a year ago it was Christmas, thought Jane, shocked at how fast the days died, *and in another half a year, it will be Christmas again. Except...*

Well, there it was.

That big except.

Except it will be Christmas, but my first Christmas ever without Mum. Except...

And there it was again, another out-of-kilter *except.*

Jane thought on;

That's not quite true is it? There was *one Christmas without my Mum. I'm sure of it.*

But that's impossible. I've been with Mum and Dad every year, without exception.

So why is part of my mind saying I wasn't? There was *one year they weren't around. But when? And why? I've been with my parents every Christmas, of course I have, where else would I be?*

Jane looked around her front room, the same room she'd always known.

And there it was again, the odd feeling that at some point in her history, while she was in this room one Christmas, her parents weren't. How was that possible?

Jane wanted to ask her Mum about it, say, *Mum, was there a Christmas when you and Dad weren't around? When I was here with someone else?* But she couldn't.

Because very soon, in six months, Mum wouldn't be in this room for Christmas ever more.

My Mother has a sell by date, she thought, and the banality of the comparison horrified her. *My Mother has an expiry date. There are things in our* larder *that will last longer than my Mother.*

Oh god, she pleaded for the first time. *Oh god, let her live, let my Mum live, what has she ever done to you?*

For Jane, upper case God had become lower case god.

he'd lost his capital G when *he'd* turned his back on Irene.

Jane's relationship with god went as far as childhood trips to Church and R.E lessons, so the fact she'd opened the lines of communication again surprised her.

She mentally went through the same list her Father had already considered;

Perhaps there's another treatment. No.

Perhaps you got it wrong. No.

Perhaps she'll be one of the lucky ones. No.

Perhaps there's a new drug. No.

Perhaps there's an alternative therapy. No.

Perhaps there is *a god ?*

Why not? Why not give god a go? Jane hadn't exactly been a Saint, but was hardly a sinner. She remained open to possibilities, and they were all she had.

She started to pray, but it all came out wrong.

god, it isn't fair, she raged at the sky. *If you're real, you have eternity to sit my Mother at your side. What do a few years matter this end? Why do you need Mum* now?

Jane started to massage the soles of her mother's feet harder, as the anger manifested itself subconsciously.

You can't have her.

You can't have her. If you take her, god, I will come and find you. Take all the bad people, go on, do your job and take the bad ones. Leave the good people, like you should.

You mess with my family, I will find you.

Wherever you live. Whatever cloud, mountain, beach, or snow bound paradise you make your home, I will find you. Because I have Love, *and* Love *is more powerful than you ever will be.*

So yes, perhaps, over god, there's Love.

Love destroys god every time.

Ah, perhaps.

"Ow, not so hard, darling. Not quite the masseur I thought," murmured Irene, eyes still closed. "Don't take it up as a career, dear."

"Sorry."

"I've made The List." Irene pointed to the side of her chair, eyes still closed.

"A list?" Repeated Jane. "What kind of list?" but knew, even as she asked.

Not *a* list, *The* List.

"Oh," Irene replied, dreamily. "You know, a List of things I'd like to do, before   "

Sometimes there are no full stops.

Dave sat in his favourite chair opposite. He looked up, and Jane saw he was scared.

Oh. Of course Dad's scared. His wife has made a List because she is dying.

On a little table next to Irene's sofa sat a piece of paper. Fractured writing scuttled across it.

Jane frowned. This wasn't her mother's handwriting, but ghost script, a last weak transmission. She tried to decode the message. Anything but ask Mum for a translation.

David tried to keep his voice level, but it caught in his throat.

"What kind of list, love?"

"Oh, you know," said the fading woman, quieter yet. "Things."

"What do you want to do, love? Whatever it is, you'll do it. I promise. I promise, darling."

Irene fell silent. Jane and David looked at each other again.

No words.

"No time," Irene's voice fluttered, weakly. "There's no time. No time where I am now."

Jane held her Mother's hand tight. "There's time Mum, there's always time."

Eyes still closed, Irene placed a hand on her stomach and said;

"This doesn't feel right."

She started to sit up, but fell back onto the sofa.

*

And now we rush, as I promised we would. Irene was right. There was no time.

After she fell back onto the sofa, Jane ran to the phone, then after a wait of millennia, the ambulance drove right up to their door. The paramedics carefully put Irene on the stretcher, then the ambulance tried to batter its way through summer traffic to the London Hospital. Once there, Irene was taken away from her daughter and husband.

*

And then there they were once more, in Doctor Perry's office.

Doctor Stephen Perry, the brain specialist who appears four times in this story. This isn't quite his last.

Once again, they sat here silently, but this time hope was extinguished.

Before, Dr Perry had said, *perhaps*, *possibly*, *might* and *maybe*, as he always did with relatives who clung onto words that might keep them afloat a little longer. But now those words were obsolete.

"Irene has had an extreme reaction to the steroids," he began, then ploughed straight on again, performed the procedure as quickly as possible. "It happens, it is a risk. The steroids have caused a massive ulcer in her stomach lining. It has eaten away that lining. Irene is bleeding from within. I'm afraid…"

I'm afraid, thought Jane, *he just said* I'm afraid*, and now I'm afraid too.* She reached for her Father's hand. *I am so afraid now, because when a doctor says, 'I'm afraid' that is permission for everyone else to feel the same.*

"…I'm afraid you have a choice now."

Jane looked straight ahead at the doctor, because she couldn't look into her father's eyes.

Don't give me a choice, she thought. *Don't you* dare *give me a choice. What kind of choice are you offering? A choice preceded by the words, "I'm afraid"? What kind of choice is that? What consequences are we to face?*

"You have a choice now." Dr Perry repeated. "We can operate to try and stop the bleeding…"

"Operate then," whispered David. "Just do it."

Dr Perry waited for a second than continued. "If we operate, she may not survive. She is very weak. If we operate and Irene lives, she won't be able to move, for at the very least, six weeks, possibly more. She will be bedridden, in more pain and attempting to recover from an operation that will only buy her the smallest time - but leave her with no quality of life. If she survives."

David started to breathe faster. His body prepared for fight or flight - and neither was possible. Dr Perry carried on, relentlessly. "So this is your choice, and I am so sorry that you have to make it. If you choose to have the operation and even if it's successful, you will be left with a recovering patient with no hope of recovery. She'll be immobile. We X-rayed and the tumour has grown. At this rate of growth, she won't even know who she is or… where she is within a few weeks. Her last days will be spent afraid, confused, lost and in pain. I'm so sorry."

And Dr Perry was always genuinely sorry. What choice did he have? Being sorry was part of the job, another lesson they'd never taught at medical school.

"What's the other option?" asked David, quietly. He already knew.

"You can let the process play out naturally. Let her continue to bleed out from her stomach. Eventually, her brain will be deprived of oxygen and will shut down, along with her heart. She will fall fully unconscious before that. She will sleep. It will be painless. She will sleep, and she will slip away."

Jane's eyes ran with tears, Dave slumped in his chair. No fight, no flight.

"No choice." He wheezed. "Is there nothing? Can you fix it? The bleeding? So she'll wake up? So we can say...we can say..."

"Goodbye?" finished Jane.

"There's no way. I'm so sorry. Shall I leave you to think about it?"

He didn't need to leave. They both knew what the other thought.

Jane spoke first.

"No pain? Really no pain?"

"None. Like falling asleep. I give you my word."

"And no chance, Doctor? No chance of waking her up again? No way of stopping this without...all...the consequences?" David still attempted to catch hope. "We can be with her?"

"Of course."

"Can she even hear us?"

"Hearing is the last sense to go. It's likely, yes."

Ah, *likely,* that's another one.

"How long?" Jane asked, even though every part of her soul screamed at her to stop. It was not an answer she wanted to hear.

"Difficult to say," replied Dr Perry, even though, of course, he knew. "No longer than an hour."

"An hour?" Gulped David. "An hour?"

All those years together, those times, memories, love, all to be squared away, boxed up, finalised in one hour. Less.

*

Think of where you'll be in an hour.

Now imagine that's all you have. No putting the clock back, nor bargaining for more, the next hour is all you have, all you will ever have. The next sixty minutes.

Make them precious, because they *are* precious, the most precious minutes of your life. Never to be played out again.

Come on. Move. Don't think about it, you're just wasting your time thinking.

Next time you're on a motorway, and pass a car crumpled into a tree, surrounded by blue lights, remember; *this is now*. One hour ago, the driver had no idea their last sixty minutes on earth were counting down, waiting for that tree. If you think about it too much, you'll go insane, so perhaps it's best to stick with what Bhagavan Dass once said; *Be. Here. Now.*

Just feel now, think later.

*

Every second wasted was a second with Irene lost.

"Dad," said Jane. "We should be with Mum. Now."

"Yes. Where is she?"

Dr Perry took them.

For now, they were still a family of three, but they were on the clock. Only two of them would leave this room.

Irene lay on the bed, apparently at peace, but inside, a hole in her stomach allowed blood to drain away. She was dying by increments and no-one knew which beat of her heart would be the last. So they waited.

Just four short decades previously, Irene had taken her first breath, soon she was about to take her last. Skin as white as snow, Irene slept, yet didn't sleep. She was somewhere between.

Jane sat on Irene's left, David on her right, and watched her chest rise and fall, rise and fall. They watched as a mother and wife died a little more with every heartbeat.

"I love you Mum," whispered Jane. "I love you."

She'd never planned what the last words to her Mother would be. It's not something you rehearse. Had she known this moment would come so soon, Jane would have said so many things while Irene could still hear them. Perhaps, somewhere far away, she still could.

Jane would have told her Mother how she wanted to be *just like her*, to have an ounce of her kindness, intelligence, talent, her passion, which was less like fireworks and more like a slow burning flame. She would have thanked her for everything, for reading to her every night, nurturing a love of story, for sitting with her for endless evenings, consoling over boys, celebrating over successes, crying, laughing, educating her with the fewest of words but the greatest of import, for showing what was possible, never holding her back, for lifting her up to the world, holding, protecting, comforting, tucking her in, in life and in bed, for putting long arms round her and never letting go, for her art, for firing off in Jane a love of magicking up something that had never existed before, being the counterpoint to her Father, concentrating while he was distracted, staying silent while he gabbled because sometimes silence says more, for being her Mother, a role not everyone is born to do, but for those that are, well, they take it, embrace it, fly, reach their apotheosis and oh, how her Mother had flown.

But now she would fly, fly higher and further, into the forever.

But Jane couldn't find those words. All that mattered, all that ever matters, really, are three words that say everything.

"I love you Mum," she said. "I love you." She repeated it between every rise and fall of her Mother's chest as Irene's heart beat her life away.

*

David sat on Irene's right, and held her hand. This was his last chance to speak with his wife, and although he'd said so many words, collected and hoarded them, now they failed him. What could he possibly say? In the here and now, all he could do was wait with Irene as she shimmered out.

He desperately wanted to say something that mattered, to tell Irene how much her life meant to him, so that wherever she was going, the last thing she'd hear was how she'd left some of herself behind, and was the most important thing that had ever happened. But words and thoughts formed and fell apart. He grasped for them, but they slipped away with the seconds.

They watched, and held her hands as Irene's chest rose and fell, rose and fell. Each time it fell, they thought;

Is this the one?

Will there be another?

And Father and Daughter were suspended in time, caught in those moments between breaths. They knew one of them would be the last. So they waited for that breath, as Irene's blood flowed away. And they willed those moments between breaths to last forever, so that Irene would exist between times, neither alive nor dead, just here.

And Dave suddenly realised with absolute clarity what he must say, so Irene could leave and know that everything would be alright, that she'd be safe, wouldn't be alone. His mind and heart came together at last to give him the words.

"I love you. And I'll find you, Irene. I'll find you again, wherever you are, I'll find you again. I love you and I'll find you, Irene, I'll find you again, I promise, I love you."

But Irene's chest did not rise again. This moment, the only time when he'd truly needed them, David's words were too late, by a heart beat, no less.

"Oh, dear." David reached to touch Irene's face. "Oh. Dear."

And it was the devastating simplicity of his grief that shattered Jane's heart.

No big speech, just two words that were both statement of regret and a term of affection.

"Oh, dear." He muttered again. Nothing else came.

"Oh, my dear."

19 / After Irene / 1993

David sat in his favourite chair and stared vacantly at the unlit fireplace.

His impending eulogy to Irene had given him something real to concentrate on. Everything else was unacceptable.

The absent presence on the left of the bed, the shoes like loyal dogs that waited to be taken out onto the streets, the favourite cups and mugs that would never see *tea, one sugar very little milk*, again, the chair to his right with its foot rest, slippers beneath, where they would stay for the next ten years.

When someone passes, they leave little reminders that bite when you least expect them. It's incredible how a house can become a mausoleum without even trying.

So Dave sat with the same A4 pad and pen Irene had used to write her last wishes.

Thinking about Irene was like flicking through a randomly ordered photo album, one picture after the next with no sense of chronology or context. No such photo album existed in his family. They never owned a camera, so the few pictures they treasured were taken by others.

Some people collect stamps, records, or toys. Dave collected words. They were his hobby, but now none of them seemed good enough.

I could stand in the chapel for the rest of time, he thought, *and still not cover everything*.

So Dave looked at the paper, and the paper waited.

He'd started many times, usually managed a paragraph or two, but always gave up.

He tried to write about how they'd met one night in The Hoop & Grapes pub in Aldgate, when Irene was sat with her friends, Dave with his, and he'd looked over and - what a curious thing - suddenly, there wasn't anyone else in the pub. They'd all gone. A moment ago it had been packed, but obviously the entire clientele had nipped out, because there was only this girl sat in the corner, and she'd glanced up from her glass of lemonade, he'd looked back and - wasn't that strange, too? - it had gone quiet, the glasses no longer clinked, the conversations were over and there she was.

And Dave had thought, *oh, so it really* does *happen,* with some surprise, and then with equal shock, he'd ordered a small glass of wine, which was very unusual and very *posh.* Then, before he'd been able to stop himself, he'd taken the glass over to this beautiful girl, who'd made the grotty pub around her equally beautiful simply by virtue of being in it, and said;

"You're lovely, would you accept this drink?"

And as the words came out, unplanned, David had mentally kicked himself in the mouth for ruining it. But while the girl's friends giggled, and his mates' mouths had gone into comical O's of shock, she'd simply looked him straight in the eye and replied, "thank you. And thank you. I will."

There'd been no embarrassment, or sneering, just thank you (for the compliment *and* the wine) and an acceptance. She'd taken a massive gulp, her eyes went wide, she'd coughed, her friends slapped her on the back and then she'd spluttered, "I haven't actually tried wine before."

He'd replied, "er, you just sip it."

She'd stared hard, accusingly, at the glass, then agreed. "Aha, *sip* it, ah yes, sip it, I think I know that now."

They'd sat together that night and talked, and Irene (*Irene*! He'd never known an *Irene* before) had drunk two more glasses, stood up, staggered, said, "I feel drunkier than I've ever done before," then vomited on David's coat. In all her life, Irene was never, "drunk" just, "*drunkier*". It wasn't the most romantic of starts, and yet it was, because that very night both of them knew they were going to spend their lives together.

But they'd only managed twenty five years.

He wanted to talk about their wedding, simple but beautiful, surrounded by those they loved and who loved them in return. How they'd spent their honeymoon, the classiest holiday they'd ever had, at a gorgeous nineteenth century hall in a Dorset forest. Irene said she'd felt like *Lady Muck*. Surely that was where Jane was conceived, one night as thick snow sparkled outside.

He wanted to talk about Jane's birth, how Irene had gone into labour in Tesco by a stack of Marmite pots, and knocked them over. About how they were convinced Jane's hatred of the salty vegetable spread came from a *in utero* memory of that moment.

How she'd been rushed to the Royal London (and, he realised, how that building weaved itself through their history, for good and bad) and given birth within two short hours. "That was fast," the nurse on duty marvelled. "Not when you're lying here," Irene had panted.

David's first words to his newborn were, "welcome to the world, Jane." She'd looked up, he'd stared down into those bright new eyes and thought, without drama but utter honesty, *I would die for you.*

They'd already chosen Jane for a girl or Edward for a boy. Edward for Irene's father and Jane because Dave wanted something literary. Of course there was Ms Austen and Ms Eyre, but there was also Jane Taylor, who wrote, "Twinkle Twinkle Little Star," David's favourite nursery rhyme as a child.

He had so much to say, but the memories were jumbled and his words stuttered. The paper waited and accused him with its blankness.

But then he'd looked down at the side table where the pad and paper rested, and knew what he must say. It had been there, all along.

He stared, and he wept.

*

The service took place in a small chapel at the London Cemetery and Crematorium.

Funerals are magical thinking made real. Their physical purpose is simply, brutally, the disposal of a body. But their spiritual purpose is to finish a story, and finish it well. For good or ill, weddings, christenings and funerals always contain elements of theatre. They all have a stage of sorts, a script and an audience, who also play their part.

The coffin sat on a trestle on a raised dais.

It is always difficult to tear your eyes from that box.

Jane couldn't.

She refused to deal with the fact her Mother lay there, wanted to stand up and shout, "no! Everyone, wait, wait, this is a mistake. You have to let my Mum out, you can't keep her in that box and burn her. Let's just stop this nonsense, right now."

They'd been offered the chance to see Irene's body, but both declined. As far as her husband and daughter were concerned, she wasn't there any more. They may as well look at her clothes in the wardrobe or books on the shelf, which were more of the person than what lay in that box.

A few of Irene's friends had viewed her and had tried to persuade Jane to do the same. "Oh, you should see," they'd cried. "She looks so beautiful, she really does. Her hair is wonderful, and she's so at peace."

And Jane had wanted to scream, "she is not beautiful, she is dead, OK? And you can paint and dress her as much as you like, but she's a mannequin now, that's all, you could put her in a sack and she wouldn't care, because of *course* she is at peace. She won't worry about anything any more because she. Is. Dead." But of course, she'd said none of those things, just politely smiled and said no.

*

Dave stood up. He wore his best suit, which translated to his only suit.

He looked like a little boy who'd been forced to dress up for an occasion. Dave didn't suit suits.

Jane felt herself slide.

If Dad starts crying, I will too, and I won't stop. I'll have to be taken out of here, weeping, and she could picture it, like a memory that was yet to happen.

We have had tears, she attempted to gather herself, *and we will have many more, but I have to get Dad through this. If he goes, I must not. If he loses strength, I must find it. I must finish this for him.*

She took a deep breath and prepared for what were to be the hardest few minutes of her life.

Dave stood for a few moments and looked down at the piece of paper in his hand.

"I tried to write a speech for Irene, I really did." He glanced at the box by his side but didn't look there again.

"I sat for ages, trying to think how I could…" and his voice caught, "… Ah… Celebrate her. But it's not a celebration is it, this?" He waved his hand round at the room. "It's not a celebration. It's a goodbye. People talk about celebrating a life, but this is goodbye. Irene's life was celebration enough as she lived it. But this…this is not a celebration. Irene, my Irene, is gone. So I thought and I thought so hard, I really did. I started so many times, but it was never enough. She deserved better and I just couldn't do it."

Come on Dad, thought Jane, *for Mum, for you, come* on.

"But then, I realised I didn't have to write anything. Because I had this all along."

He held up a piece of A4 paper.

"Before she…before… Irene made a list of things she wanted to do, you know, *before*. But it was more than that. Her handwriting wasn't so good, she was weak, you see, but she did this. And I think this tells you everything you need to know about Irene, my Irene, our Irene."

He looked at Jane and she gave a tiny nod to her father, on that strangest of stages, alone, despite being stood next to his wife.

"We had to decipher it, me and Jane, sorry, I mean, Jane and I. Once we started seeing how Irene's writing had changed, and changed so fast… We put it together, didn't we love?"

Jane smiled a tiny smile and nodded again. *Go on, Dad, go on.*

"So this is Irene's list and it's more. So I'll, er, let her speak now."

David stopped again for a moment. His shoulders rose and fell and Jane saw he was building a wall against the grief. That wall only had to last for a short time, but strong enough to keep the storm away, for now.

"My List," he began, and Irene took over. "'1/ I want to visit Bruges. I've never been to Bruges but it looks like a place everyone should visit once. Once is all I have, so that's a good enough reason. 2/ I want to go ice skating. I like the idea of just gliding off, nothing holding you back, speeding away in the cold. I ice skated once but I fell. I won't fall this time. I've got wings. 3/ I want to write a book. David has all the words but I don't think he has the patience to put them down. I want to write a book about what I have done so I can talk to my husband and daughter any time they pick it up. I hope hope hope I have time.'"

David stopped, re-built, brick by brick. The wall held, but only just. He read on;

"'4/ I want David and Jane to be happy ever after. I want them to go on just as if I was there, because I am. I want them to be happy, whatever that takes, because it's all I've ever wanted and all I ever want for them.'"

David breathed in again, waited for the wall, which re-built, but more fragile than before.

"'5/ I want to buy some very high high heels and the tightest of skirts and go out dancing. I want to feel like a teenager again, like when Dave and I first met. It would be like time travelling. I want to be sixteen again for a night. 6/ I want to be cremated so I can fly.'"

The wall cracked, then, and David's voice cracked with it.

"'7/ I want to see Brief Encounter again and I want to go and see Paul McCartney play. He was always my favourite. She loves you yeah yeah yeah, Dave. 8/ I want to try food I've never tried before and drinks I've never drunk and visit places I've never been that are right next door where I've lived for so long. 9/ I want to see them again, just once wherever I go, I want to see them again just once, my man and my girl. 10/ I want to see the snow again. I saw it... '" and we can't read the next bit. But that was Irene, saying goodbye."

Dave stopped. Not because he couldn't go on, but because that's where Irene's list ended. He breathed deeply again. "There. That was my Irene, our Irene. And we love her forever and after. Thank you for coming."

He stepped off the dais, went to his daughter and they held each other.

*

Later, when the sandwiches were reduced to crusts, memories shared, words spoken and the mourners had drifted away, guiltily in some cases, back to their *living* loved ones, David and Jane sat together in their tiny front room, in their tiny terraced house in Bow. Dave was in Irene's chair, still wearing his suit. Jane sat on the floor between his legs, like she used to when she was a child.

Dave absently stroked her hair, just as he'd done years before, and alternated his attention between a glass of whisky and the few photographs they owned of the family together.

"I just want to step into these." He stared at each photo in turn. "Wouldn't that be a thing, to step into one? Go and visit yourself, hold her again?"

"It would be lovely," Jane agreed. "Not a photo, a door."

"Mm, a door. That's what these are, aren't they? Doors. But they won't open, you can just look through them. I wish they'd open. I'd give anything to walk into one. Find her again, now we've lost her."

Jane thought for a while. *Lost.* That was an interesting word.

"I have lost my wife" "I have lost my mother" "I have lost my keys" "I have lost my shoes". Lost. A word that can be applied to both the incredibly important or completely trivial.

"Lost?" she wondered out loud.

"Mm?"

"Think about it. Lost - the word, I mean, if you lose something, it's implied in the word, isn't it? If you lose something there's a chance you can find it again."

"I suppose so," Dave shrugged. Jane knew she was trying to comfort them both with semantics, but for some reason, this was important.

It had weight.

"Yes." she was bizarrely energised. "If you lose something, you can find it again. Lost doesn't mean gone forever. 'Gone forever' means gone forever. Why do we use the word 'lost' for death?"

"Because it sounds less final," sighed her Dad.

"No. That word has been chosen. We chose that word. It's deliberate. We chose it because we know, somewhere deep, that we will find them again."

And Jane remembered her Dad's final words to Irene on her death bed, the ones she missed by one heart beat.

"I love you. And I'll find you, Irene. I'll find you again, wherever you are, I'll find you again. I love you and I'll find you, Irene, I'll find you again, I promise, I love you."

"Perhaps, perhaps," he managed.

Jane picked up one of the photographs. It showed her tiny family in 1979, on a beach in Southend On Sea, Essex. Jane played with a bucket and spade, Irene looked directly at the camera and David stared over his shoulder at something.

"Who took this?" she asked. Dave took the photo, turned it over in his hands, and saw where Irene had written *'S-O-S 1979'* on the back. "Can't remember. We borrowed the camera from our neighbour. He had a few left on the film, so let us take it. Don't know who took it though. Probably just someone passing. I'd love to step into that, sit on the beach with us all, enjoy the sun. Wouldn't you?"

"Yes. Build a sandcastle with myself. What are you looking at?"

In the photo, Dave had craned his head round, and looked over his right shoulder. No chance of deleting and trying again in 1979. You got the photo you took, no refunds, no exchanges, no trash bin.

Dave frowned. "Not a clue. There's a lot going on in Southend. Could be a donkey ride or an ice cream van! Could be anything. We should go again, to Southend, you know. I loved it there."

But as Dave spoke, his nostrils flared, a sure sign he was lying.

Jane knew her Dad well, and the flaring nostrils were always a giveaway. She did it herself - it took one to know one.

He's lying, she thought, *he knows* exactly *what or who he was looking at, so why won't he tell me? He remembers, so what's so bad, what needs to be kept from me, lied about even after all this time? At a random moment on a beach in Southend On Sea, what did he see that he has to lie now?*

"Are you sure you don't remember?"

Dave turned to his daughter, sighed, and looked her in the eye.

"You could ask me from now to forever and I still wouldn't know what I was looking at," he said firmly, and his expression added, *so leave it, because there's nothing else to say,* with clear, but unspoken words.

She looked at the photo again, but whatever her father stared at was outside the frame. She tried to read what she could see of his expression, but couldn't tell if it was confusion or recognition on his face.

But this was not the time to push him. So - as we all do when the subject is something we can't change - she changed the subject.

I'll ask him again when it feels right, she thought, but never did. The time was never right and things got in the way.

"Dad," she said, as he stroked her hair. "I've never told you this, but you're the smartest person I've ever known."

He smiled and looked down at his daughter sat on the floor, as she'd done as a child.

"Thank you," he said quietly. "I wish I was smarter." He picked up the photo, stroked it.

"Dad, you're…you taught me everything, more than any teacher. You're so smart, I just don't know why…" She faltered.

Jane knew what her Dad saw; a little girl under an adult's face, so tired, so heartbroken, so gone, but she was all he had now.

As always, he was ahead of her.

"You want to know why I picked up litter for a living? Why do you think?"

Jane picked up a book from his table. He put his arm round her shoulder.

"You could have written that. You could write anything you like. A novel, a biography, anything." Then she felt herself run, because Mum was gone but Dad was still here, and she had to make him see that *now, now* was *now was now,* there was nothing in the universe other than *now.*

She realised she was trying to give him direction because he had no maps anymore.

"Ah," he replied."So you want to know why I didn't write? Do that novel everyone has in them, apparently? Go on, you tell me - why do you think I didn't?"

"I don't know," Jane answered truthfully. "I never really thought about it until now."

"I cleaned streets because of you. Because yes, I could have got a job that paid more, and asked more of me and more of my time, but why would I want to? Time is precious and you, you're my novel."

David gazed down at the floor. He'd waited a long time to say this, but she'd never asked, so now the words rushed from him.

"Don't confuse what I do with who I am. Your living isn't what makes you live. I chose my job so I could spend as much time here with you - I could see you to school, walk you home. I didn't want to miss a moment of you growing up. Street cleaning came up - it was shift work, fitted in with your Mum's job and meant I could be near to you. See? What I am, what I really am…" He stopped and smiled. "Is your Dad. That's it. That's all I was ever going to be, I know that now. That's all I need to be. First I loved your Mother and I still do, forever, but then you came along, and I knew that moment that I had two people I would die for, literally die for. Irene died, but not for us, because of a tumour, but I know she would have jumped in front of a bullet for us, as I would, as you would, because there is only us, there has always been just us, and I swept the streets because I wanted to know my daughter, see her grow up and not miss a moment. I swept the streets because I love you."

Jane stood up from the same carpet she'd played on as a child, held her father and he held her back.

They both wished Irene could be there too. And somewhere, somewhen, she was.

BOOK FIVE / SIX SHORT SCENES THAT ARE LINKED

Stop.

Pause.

Freeze frame, if you like.

I've already informed you telling Jane's story would involve vaulting and sliding about her life with a quite vulgar disregard for time and space, so, now, as promised, we must visit some destinations, events, people and perspectives that are relevant.

Jane knows some of them, but not all.

You, however, must be made aware of these pieces, as they will eventually fit and lock together, I promise.

I wish I could promise Jane more.

You see, for Jane, time is a bear hunt. She can't go over or under it, she has to go through it.

You and I, however, are not so constrained.

So think of these next fragments as scenes that seem unconnected.

In time, however, they'll be revealed not as separate stories, but disparate chapters of Jane's life, some hidden from her, but all with their part to play.

We'll start with Jane, as she writes on her Royal Companion typewriter, in a strange, new, frozen place called *Here*.

Sometime *after*.

20 / Jane Types A Diary, Of Sorts / Here

Tap, Tap, Tap.

I am Jane.

I am Jane. Yes.

I AM Jane, and I'm typing in a Hut, in a snow-covered place called Here.

That's right.

I can see trees dressed in white, snow on the ground - naturally - and a sky which is a beautiful vivid blue. It's what I see every day, if there even ARE days, Here.

I can't feel time. Even as a write that, I know how screwed it sounds. I can't feel time. I never thought of time as something tangible, other than when trapped by clocks, but now I miss it.

So.

I worked out what's really scaring me about all this.

The fact that I'm NOT scared.

That I'm totally accepting this worries me, because it means I must know more than I know.

And if I know more than I know, then what does THAT mean?

I just read that back.

Wow, Jane, you were clearly never a copywriter.

Uh-huh. This is so fucked up.

I was Told to write, and so, I do. It's part of my...treatment. Yes.

OK. Roll up metaphorical sleeves, let's get this down.

"Here" is a facility to make you forget what could hurt you. But despite that, apparently, I am to gently call my memories back to me. This I do with paper and rolls of ink.

So I'm typing to see what I might conjure from my memory. But if I remember too much, and those memories scare me, The Man said I should burn the paper. I may have already done so, many times.

I was Told the rules and purpose of this place a long time past, I think. Or was it only yesterday when I first arrived?

Or an hour?

Forever ago?

How long have I been Here?

I can't tell. Perhaps if you broke time down into ever decreasing amounts, incrementally smaller and smaller, eventually, you'd be in a place between those tiny ticks and tocks where there was almost no time anymore, and perhaps that place is Here.

I admit that is a big "perhaps".

But time is crucial to what's happening to me. Or has happened, or will happen.

HAS much happened since I arrived?

Maybe. If it has, I have watched the Snow and forgotten, by choice. Funny, I never forget the rules of Here, but everything else blurs and fades when I Watch The Snow.

Somehow (hypnosis? Drugs? Something unknown?) the Snow covers any memories that may be relevant. So I watch, I forget, then, I type to coax anything back, well, anything that won't bite, I suppose.

Tap, tap tap. On this 1941 Royal Companion. Why so specific a make of typewriter? I don't know, like so much else.

All I know is one day I woke up Here.

I know that much is true.

Stop, no, wait- I know that much is true? - that sounds familiar.

Did I just make that up, or remember it?

The snow isn't falling right now. I think it only comes when I really need to forget.

So what do I remember? Or rather, what do I believe I remember?

That's the thing; you can't trust your memory. Any witness in court will know that.

Memory is a palimpsest. You keep scratching new stories over it, until the old ones become fragments that can just about be seen, ghostly, broken tales you may not be reading right.

Palimpsest. Now that's a word, Jane.

OK, I think I'm in my 30s.

I think I'm from London.

Ah, shit.

This idea keeps coming;

I think I may have killed people.

Yes. That thought won't leave me.

I think I may have killed lots of people. And before I did, they were scared of me.

Was I in a car crash, or was it a war? Or was I swept away in a hopeless, romantic , epic, doomed love affair? Did I use a gun, or a bomb? Ah. Or was that all little white lies like, "I was there."

But whatever, death is with me. I can feel it. Many people died and I was responsible. How?

Here seems to have a scattershot approach to wiping memory.

Big things - like my Parents - are hidden, but then little things like, "I know that much is true," seem to have resonance, but I don't know why.

Equally - and just as inexplicably, the following phrases have just flashed into my head, uninvited;

Don't you want me?

The Reflex.

Darkness.

Are friends electric?

Tears are not enough.

What is love?

We are so fragile.

Tainted love.

What are they? A poem? Songs? It feels like they're connected, and when I read them, they seem to be, but how?

I'd love to know why The Reflex (with capital letters again) is an only child, though.

But - oh - when I think of "The Reflex", I smile, and a ghost passes through this room. A ghost who doesn't even know who he's haunting. Or perhaps I'm haunting him. I haunt ghosts. What a thought.

Wait. "He"?

A he from my past? An important he? My hand just went up automatically to the necklace I wear. Why? Rather appropriately, considering my current location, it's a tiny silver snowflake. Is this necklace like some kind of identity badge? Are you given it on arrival, or was I already wearing it before?

Alright, try this.

Perhaps there is another possibility, one I don't think I've addressed yet because it scares me senseless. The overwhelming probability is that Here cannot exist. But... if Here does not exist, then how can I see it, experience it?

Because.

Go on, just type it.

I may be completely mad.

Everything points to me being insane.

But then again - hooray, good news - if this Alice In Wonderland Rabbit Hole only exists in my mind, then I can get better.

I can leave Here, because Here is a mental condition. Here is treatable.

But then...maybe the Wonderland Alice may have simply been a girl lost at the outer limits of derangement. While her mind sat with Hatters and Dormice, Alice's body might have been in a Victorian asylum, dribbling.

That would mean one of our most beloved literary characters was actually demented. That thought's so bleak it made me laugh out loud, which is not the action of a sane person, is it?

I am either mad and none of this exists, or I am sane and this is all solid matter as real as I am.

Either possibility is terrifying, if I am honest.

I just tapped this table, which was hard, and then felt the little whorls and grain of the wood. It's real. It's solid. I breathe and I feel the crisp air in my nose. It's real. Shit shit shit it's real.

Oh, god, it's real.

I'm truly scared now, so I must burn this writing. It's one of the rules.

No-one will read it, anyway, maybe not even the old, old man who also lives Here.

Yes, along with The Man, there was someone else Here when I first arrived, but is he still a resident?

I don't know. I haven't seen him since. Or if I have, I have forgotten. I am sure he still lives Here, in one of those other Huts.

He's a very old man and his name is Janssen, or wait, is it Johnson?

I don't know, I can't remember. Janssen or Johnson was way older than The Man and he WAS Here.

Yes.

We sat together at my window, we Watched The Snow, and talked as it fell.

Yes, that happened, I can almost grasp it.

I remember I was crying, yes. Why? Because I was scared and confused. Who can blame me? Wait, yes. He offered me a handkerchief.

Keep going.

What did we speak of?

Bees.

Bees?

Why did Janssen or Johnson talk of bees?

Wait, yes, he spoke of regret. The snow fell and he warned me about regret. He compared the snow to...what?

I forced the memory back. But it scares me. I don't like it in my head.

Cotton wool balls, yes, he compared the snow to cotton wool balls and said he was originally from Norway? Yes, that's right, Norway.

Is Janssen or Johnson still Here?

He's been Here the longest, I think; he has a feel for things. I should talk to Janssen/Johnson, really. He could probably help me get an idea of wheres and whys. He knows more than he lets on, that I'm sure of.

We talked of the Snow, and of what it could mean, and I think I remember parts of Janssen or Johnson's life because he told me, didn't he?

But who is Janssen, or Johnson?

I must speak to him again, so at least I'm not going insane alone, Here.

Janssen, or Johnson, is real and he is (was?) Here.

I hope.

21 / Cracks

Quick, come this way. Let's leave Jane at her desk, in her Hut, in that strange frozen clearing for now. You must see all these fragments or you won't recognise the full picture when it is finally revealed. Come with me, to this other place, Spring Bridge Road, Ealing, in London. Another name to note and remember.

Let me show you something.

Look, past the Arcadia Shopping Centre, round the back.

In here, come on, don't worry, nothing will hurt you.

Dirty, isn't it?

It's the kind of place that will always be slightly dark, no matter how much light you throw at it. The darkness crowds the corners like cobwebs, it can't be lit away.

In the middle, see? There, another character of sorts, waiting for the show, which happens in 2003.

Twenty-five years old, by my reckoning. I'm no expert, but I do know the effects of time. Yes, twenty-five years old, maybe even more.

And over there, see those two guys?

They've done their job, but they haven't seen. They haven't seen, and because of it, they are killers. This place is a killer, these two are accessories before the fact, but have no idea.

The terrible crime hasn't happened yet. When it does, they won't even know. They might *suspect*, but won't dare speak of it out loud, not even to each other.

These two men will go to their graves having re-tooled and retrofitted their memories to believe they weren't responsible. How could they be? This terrible thing could have happened any time.

But it didn't .

It happened in 2003 and it happened because, remember this, too, *it's the cracks you don't see that get you.*

22 / Context / The Ridiculous Story Of Paul Jiggens

We have so much to see, so many people to meet and they all have a purpose.

Context is my name and context is my job. Being dislocated in space and time can be fun, I suppose, but when you're looking at everything at once, from every angle, one needs to take a deep breath and ask *where the penny dreadful am I?*

I now know no-one is truly in control of their lives. The sad - or liberating - truth is, you are leaves in the wind. Unlike leaves, of course, you have a degree of self determination, but after that, you're held aloft, or thrown down by other forces. Some of those forces are known to you - friends, lovers, family, career, even enemies - but others remain totally hidden, influence felt, origin unknown.

Events that happen in other places - even other times - can collide with lives in ways you can't even begin to imagine. I won't use the butterfly effect analogy - it's not true, I've checked.

Jane's life, like yours, was not immune to these hidden forces.

But one of the most seismic shifts was down to one man's action - or should I say, *inaction.*

*

Let's travel to a flat in Cricklewood, London. It belongs to a twenty-two year old named Paul Jiggens.

On a late weekend night in 2003, Paul Jiggens was approximately nine hours from the inaction that would change Jane's life.

Stood in front of Paul was his twenty-four year old girlfriend, Julie Markham. Things had clearly not been going well. Julie's eyeliner had spilled down her cheeks and she waved a glass of something flammable at him.

"You were never a footballer!" she wailed, which seemed a very random statement to make, but only because we have joined their story at the end. "You weren't ever going to be Chelsea."

Forgive Julie her syntax, it's not one of her priorities.

Julie and Paul were in the bitter closing moments of their short relationship.

A few months ago, they'd met on the internet, which was a relatively new dating destination in 2003.

Paul had simply been looking online for a good time.

Julie was looking for a footballer.

Julie, who'd lived her entire life jealous of others, had hoped to become a footballer's girlfriend, or Holy of Holies, wife. She'd been working on that project for a while.

She'd imagined herself with a country house and sports car, hanging out at exclusive bars talking with exclusive people. Through the internet, she'd found Paul Jiggens, an up and coming player, or so he'd said.

Except Paul's online dating profile wasn't completely based on facts.

Yes, at nineteen he had tried out for Chelsea (failed) then spent six months with Leyton Orient (contract not renewed) but then used those slim truths to manufacture an online scenario where he was about to hit the footballing big time.

In truth, he was employed as an Engineer, a fancy name for someone who fixed and reloaded machines. Paul had managed to keep up his footballing pretence with Julie for a while, but wasn't that good an actor and the facts were against him.

So on that cold December night in 2003, a Bacardi-enlightened Julie Markham had finally enjoyed perhaps her one and only important insight into the internet world, which was;

What people say *they are isn't always what they* really *are.*

*

"I did play for Leyton," stammered Paul, equally drunk.

"Shut up," Julie slurred. "I would never, ever have even…" She wove, then pointed at one corner of the room. "I should have known - you don't even have a *big* flatscreen TV! Ha!"

"It's a 42 inch," Paul offered, with a strange need to defend his television size.

"You wish," screeched Julie, slammed her drink down on his black ash table and wiped her lips. "You were *never* Chelsea."

This was important to her, she'd told all her friends. "You never played for Chelsea." She sobbed again and burst into defeated, put-upon tears.

We don't need to stay too long in this room. We all know how these situations disintegrate. No-one survives these kinds of exchanges, where words are said that can never be apologised for, accusations made that can never be taken back. We all know how the ground of a relationship can become so blasted that nothing will ever grow there again.

Julie Markham stormed out.

After a few minutes staring around his living room - possibly to check his TV size, possibly to check his grasp of reality, we can never be sure - Paul Jiggens also stormed out. For that we must tip our hats to him, because the ability to storm out of *your own flat* is quite a talent by anyone's standards.

He then proceeded to get extremely plastered from an all night Off Licence.

Paul eventually crawled back home from Who-Knows Where at Who Knows When O'Clock.

The following morning, he was supposed to be at work, where he fixed and loaded machines, but didn't really surface until after mid-day, after his mobile phone buzzed angrily with further abusive texts from Julie Markham and missed calls from his employer.

Paul Jiggens didn't go to work that day, and, since he was already on a written warning, for the days and weeks after.

*

So there it was. The ridiculous story of Paul Jiggens.

Jane never met him or even knew of his existence.

23 / Tap

You're confused. I feel it. *Where is all this going*, you ask. I asked the same thing, over and over, when I looked down on Jane's life from so many angles. All I can do is repeat my promise; *there will be no loose ends*. Once you have the context, the entire picture will slam into focus.

Look over here, now. Just a tiny thing. Just a huge thing. Somewhere in London, there was once a tap.

At some point in 2003, this tap started to drip but no-one realised.Then, the old and tired rubber washer inside failed completely.

At that point, the tap flowed fully into a sink beneath it.

But here's the problem; the plug was in place. Without it, the water would have flowed into the drain, and away, as it should. But no, the plug was in place, so the sink began to fill.

Then it overflowed onto the floor of a kitchen, where it pooled.

No permanent damage was done. Well, not to the *kitchen*. The floor was tiled.

But damage was done.

The kitchen became unusable.

And because that kitchen was closed, other events took place.

How ridiculous that a dripping tap changed lives forever.

Drip, drip, drip, went the tap.

How I wish it hadn't.

*

Let's now study another piece of writing from the icy clearing called *Here*. I don't use the word study lightly. This is a document with weight.

We must now return to the old man Jane spoke of, called *Johnson* (or *Janssen*) because he is so very important. Trust me. Let's see what *he* has typed. You already know so very much of what is to happen - you may not be aware how, but you now have most of the pieces in your possession.

This is what *Johnson or Janssen* tapped out, *Here*.

24 / An Old, Old Man Called Janssen (or Johnson) Also Types, Here

Let me try this, it may work. I write, I write to remember.

Remember, please try to remember.

Who am I? I am... Janssen (or is it Johnson?) I am <u>so</u> old now and I am Here, in this frozen place where apparently I have come by my own volition, although I do not remember giving such a permission.

But remembering is not encouraged, Here, is it?

Johnson, or Janssen. I'm not quite sure. How peculiar that I don't even remember my name. Johnson, a good English name, or Janssen, a good Scandinavian name?

Stop.

I'm not sure how long this diary will last in one piece. It may burn. It probably will. I think it usually does.

I keep having to stop. This isn't working.

Try again. What would I say? What would I say to Jane?

Yes, think about JANE. I don't think there was much said when we first met. No, that's right, few if any words. Why so quiet?

This is the first time I have used this typewriter. I wonder if all the huts have one. Jane has one. But I know I must use my oven to destroy whatever was written if it does not help me.

When paper burns, the charcoal rises from the chimney like angry bees who have collected bad pollen. That's the image that leaps into my mind, unwanted. Bad bees, yes, there were bad bees, chimneys, yes. Why do I remember that?

Remember. Go back.

But everything is unfocused.

Yes. Try. Become. Be.

I am Janssen OR POSSIBLY Johnson.

I know I shouldn't, but I think I would like to watch the moment pages are destroyed.

Watching someone's memories go up in smoke stirs something. I'm not sure it's a good stirring.

Stirring. That's something. I can feel something important about stirring. Soup? This is lacherlich. Why do I even know such a word? Lacherlich? I must be German, then, so why do I think of Norway?

What <u>do</u> I remember about when we first met? Jane and I, we met in this place, yes, this place is where we met.

Try.

I remember...an old old face and a young woman's face, Jane's face, reflected in the window, sitting together in this tiny space. Snow on the window. We watched the snow.

There was talk of Norway? Yes Norway.

The War. Which War? The only War, yes.

We talked of father, and soup.

Bad Bees? There it is again. Bad Bees and Chimneys.

I should stop.

No. Continue.

I should remember where, when and why and who. It's important.

Here, there are other huts and other people, I am sure of it, but I'll stay with me. What do you know? What do you remember?

I must burn these pages. Every word I write takes me a little closer to something and I don't wish to go near that something. But I don't know if I can, or should. Perhaps I should keep them as - what? - insurance?

Ach! Yes, that is my sound, Ach! I <u>am</u> Johnson or Janssen. We write, we burn, we write again. Smoke. Why is smoke billowing in my memory? I believe I have been Here the longest, I have a feel for things, but that is only because of my reflection. What did I say? "How my molten reflection scolds me"! Yes, but where was that said?

I may wish and I may burn and I may type and I may not. I should stop this because it doesn't help and I am wasting my time. This is an exercise in memory but it is not working.

Let me pretend I know.

Is my name Johnson? Or Janssen? My memory is faulty, Here.

But whether that is a first or surname is also unknown. The name is Johnson or Janssen and the reflection in that window before says I am old. How old? The reflection won't say. There I am, in the window. in this place. The young girl's face and the old man's face.

Reflected. Twisted. There, in the reflection is Johnson. Or Janssen.

That may be vague but it is what I know. I have at least pared the possibilities of a name down to two. That is a victory, Here.

Ah, this isn't good? Why am I writing this? Why am I fixating about whether my name is Johnson or Janssen? Maybe I shouldn't bother. Put it away, hide it away, stick to who I really am, whoever that is.

25 / Context / Mark Griffiths

Another jump, another place, another face, our cast of characters expands, one by one.

Jane is centre stage, of course, but let's recap. So far, in these side-stories, we've seen whatever waited in Spring Bridge Road, Ealing.

 Met the online faker, Paul Jiggens.

Saw the tap that dripped and then, heard the old, old man called Janssen (or Johnson) who also sits *Here* and types to find himself.

So - onto our stage, no applause please, for another player who'll appear but twice again in this story.

As such, his *temporal* presence here is small, but his effect will be seismic.

This man is named Mark Griffiths. Store that name too, you'll need it. We won't see the full picture without him.

*

Here we are at the door of a bedsit on a cold December morning in 2003.

Mark Griffiths, the occupant of this room, has lived a life no-one would envy, unless they were a masochist.

As one of four children, little Mark and all his siblings just seemed to *get in the way*.

Mark was the eldest, so received the full force of his parents' resentment. You'd have thought after their first child proved to be such a *fucking chore*, Mr and Mrs Griffiths would have realised they weren't suited to having kids, and stopped.

But no.

Unless you can step out of any negative patterns you were born into, you'll keep repeating them, and so, like their *own* parents, Mr & Mrs Griffiths kept having more children. It wasn't their fault, but it was their choice.

Mark's parents treated him and his siblings as the source of all their ills. Those *fucking kids* were the reason they had no money, time, room, happiness. This too was pre-programmed. Some threads are stitched so deep that unpicking them is almost impossible.

The results were pitifully inevitable.

As the the Griffiths children grew up, they followed their Mum and Dad s into becoming bullies. It was all they'd ever known, the only option available. Round and round and round.

Mark's parents never realised the simple maxim - *you get the children you deserve.* And if you treat them with no worth, then they'll go on to consider everything else worthless.

Over their children's formative years, Mr & Mrs Griffiths weaponised their offspring. As he grew up, Mark's skin bloomed with black and blue flowers, which would grow into quite a crop.

As a child, he was in a continual state of emergency, never knowing when the next crisis would come.

He was kicked out of school for good at fourteen, finally expelled after he attacked a boy for his trainers.

At that point, he had a choice - take responsibility or abrogate it.

No choice, really.

Into adulthood, Mark attempted to hold down a series of jobs, all of which he hated. Having to work seemed very unfair.

He worked in a garage, but stole from the till. Got a job in a nightclub, but fought with a punter. Tended a bar but threw a glass at his manager. Mark bounced from job to job, and although he came close, never committed a crime that deserved incarceration. Things would have turned out very differently if he had.

*

So, cursed from birth, Mark Griffiths now lives in this bedsit, a jail he'd constructed for himself. He believed the world built these walls, but over the years, he'd put them up, brick by brick. He was the architect of his own prison, but never saw his own name on the plans.

He sat on the old mattress on the dirty floor and listened to the steady beat of music from above. Day or night, those beats never stopped, a steam hammer in his head to add to all the other noise.

Mark wanted to do something about it, but the man above was *connected*. In his mind, Mark was a big man, but in a gang of one. The man upstairs flooded the entire house with his personality simply because he could. He was effectively in every room through the *thud, thud, thud-thud, thud, thud, thud-thud.*

Mark did not question his role in all this. It was clearly the fault of all those bosses who'd given him the sack, the fault of the council, government, foreigners, blacks, Pakis, Jews, lezzers and queers, immigrants, the people who were *not him.* It was - and in this at least he was absolutely correct - the fault of his parents.

Any time Mark lashed out, he attacked his Mother and Father - the victims may have had other faces, names, nationalities, *whatever*, but in the end, they were always his parents, telling him what to do, screwing up his life, telling him to *get out of the way.*

Mark sat in this tiny room and felt the fury rise again, the one that came every time he opened his eyes on another rolling, sickening morning.

He heard footsteps on the stairs. There was always a blend of shouting, swearing and crying out there. Never laughter.

Mark Griffiths had never really left his childhood home. He'd been locked in this one house all his life, but what chance did he ever have? He was never given a key, nor shown a door. In fact, he didn't know there was a door, so how could Mark find an exit?

Mark Griffiths was still seven, he remained eleven, stayed at eighteen, existed at twenty-five and lived forever in the house of his parents.

The law called Mark a perpetrator. It may have helped if they'd also recognised him as a victim.

He was always going to intersect with this story. His choices and the paths of the people within it were destined to cross at one exact moment.

For you, that moment has yet to come.

For Mark, however, that moment was today, in 2003.

Right now was where he would *always* be.

Mark Griffiths sat in his bedsit.

Soon, he would act.

Mark will act, because no-one ever showed him the respect he deserved. Not his parents, employers, not the girls he takes, not the man upstairs, none of them.

Everyone else, like he once was as a child, is simply *in the way*.

*

You have so many of the pieces now. Just a few more need to be put in place. Jane's script is almost complete. You simply need to discover the right way to read it.

You will.

BOOK SIX / FORWARD / HERE / THERE / THE 90'S / THE '00'S

26 / Jane Types Again, Here

Tap, tap, tap.

My name is Jane and I live - or rather, I <u>now</u> live in a place called Here.

I live and I type and I wait for something, anything to form on these pages that will lead me out of Here.

I know this because a long time ago - or was it only weeks, days, seconds? - I was Told so, by The Man.

There, those are the - ha ha - <u>facts</u>, so obviously a good start for today's typewriter therapy session.

Or, rather, I suspect it's another start.

Because I've started before, haven't I? Oh yes, I think I've started many times. That's the whole point. I keep writing, re-starting myself, over and over until I'm ready to face the real why I'm Here.

OK.

I Burned some of my words last night. I Burned, then Watched The Snow and forgot.

I don't remember doing it, of course, but there's charcoal round the oven, and a few scorched pieces intact on the floor.

On one it says, "tap tap tap" and because it had the cheek not to burn, it's made a re-appearance here. So;

Tap, tap, tap.

I wonder what I Burned? Well, I can only guess I must have been getting a little too close to whatever I've forgotten.

Clearly, I'm not ready to face whatever led me Here.

*

So how should I start - I assume - again?

Well, I've found a box. Or rather, I've found The Box. T. B., capitals, as always. Here loves its capitals.

It was under my bed.

I must have looked under there before, sometime.

In a Hut with almost nothing inside, I must have checked every inch, but clearly, no.

Because there was suddenly The Box, under my bed.

Maybe The Box was placed there as I slept - but by who? - I can't imagine it was The Man sneaking in.

Or does it belong to the old man, Janssen (or Johnson) and he's been tiptoeing around in here? That thought creeps me out.

But there it was, under the bed, The Box, pushed up against the far wall of the hut, lurking.

Lurking? Is that right?

Yes, lurking.

It felt like The Box was waiting for something, or someone. I let out a little, "oh," of surprise when I saw it.

Why? Well, Here is uniform. It's predictable - or rather it's as predictable as an impossible place can be - and generally, there aren't many surprises.

And as I write that sentence, "generally there aren't many surprises" I realise that's inappropriate, but what I'm trying to say is; Here, things are always where you expect them to be.

I reached out under the bed and was a little scared to touch it. Why? Because.

Is it mine? Did I put it there? And if I did, why did I choose to forget it?

I don't feel like it's mine.

Because if it was, I would have put it pride of place where it now stands on my desk.

So I didn't touch it for a while. Strange how inanimate objects can have personalities.

The Box, it seemed to be

*

I needed to think about that for a bit.

I thought, 'coiled,' but that's too dramatic, 'watchful,' but that's too gothic. 'Haughty,' is too female, so I've ended up with, 'mindful'. The Box seems mindful. It seems to, 'keep its counsel', seems like, no, not a warning sign, but certainly a whisper to be careful.

So I was careful. I slid it out.

And now it sits in front of me now, mindful.

The Box is just over a foot long and just under a foot wide, and about five inches deep. It's a deep coloured wood that's shiny and reflective. Mahogany? I don't know, so clearly I wasn't a carpenter. It has two little brass hinges on the lid, and one tiny brass keyhole. Naturally, of course, there was no key in the hole. Where would be the fun in that? But the key, wherever it may be, must be dinky.

I suppose I could just about get a knife in between the lid and try to force it open. But the fact there are no scratches seems proof I've never tried to do that, which also suggests I've never seen The Box before.

So I think I should leave well alone. I looked through the whole of the hut (which took all of a few minutes) in case I missed a secret draw, or something behind the larder which may hide a key, but no.

The Box doesn't weigh much. When I shake it, I can hear, feel, a little movement inside, a shush shush of something sliding, but beyond that, I don't know.

A mystery then. Because that's just what I need Here. Another mystery.

Hooray.

This place was sorely lacking in questions wasn't it? It just didn't have enough enigma for me. Thank Heavens for The Box, to inject some much needed riddle into the proceedings.

So it sits there, like someone in the corner of a party who you keep catching staring your way, expressionless, creeping you out.

But to hide The Box away would be worse, because then I would know it really was lurking. Now I prefer to know exactly where it is. So I can keep an eye on it.

I remember this, at least - I was so scared when I first arrived, and now, for what I must assume to be only the second time, Here, I am dreadfully afraid again.

Whatever is inside The Box should <u>stay</u> inside.

If it gets out, well, I think there will be hell to pay.

27 / Jane's Diary / Selected Entries, 1993 - 2003

SEPTEMBER 21st 1993

I miss Mum so much. No, no, it's more than just "missing", it's a physical need, like breathing. I'm gasping for air every day.

I keep bumping into her, if that's even the right expression, but it feels that way. Clothes in the wardrobe, books on the shelf that she won't read again, even food in the freezer.

I keep looking at a box of pies she once bought and wonder if I should eat them, or should they stay there, like relics? Every morning I come downstairs and assume she'll be stood in the kitchen, listening to Radio 2, sipping her tea, and smiling hello. It's still a surprise she isn't, and breaks me to know that she won't be - not tomorrow, not ever.

This is the first time I've actually written about Mum. I've tried before, but no. The pen wouldn't move. It's still refusing to, but I'm pushing. This is difficult enough.

Dad has started going back to work. I think he needs to get out of the house, really. We both do, but trips out together tend to end with long silences followed by unspoken decisions to just come home.

I've been looking through this diary and a long time ago - well, only last year, but it feels a lifetime away now - I wrote about grief.

I was grieving for a *boyfriend*, ha. What did I know?

I read those words and the 1992 me seems so…what? Immature?

No, that's unfair..

Immature's not the right word. Blissfully ignorant, perhaps? No, I think it's more like my perspective was limited and my priorities were different. I didn't know that last year, of course.

1992 Jane thought her perspectives and priorities were perfectly correct.

I want to reach through the page and tell myself I knew nothing. But I suppose in the future, when I look back on today, September 21st, 1993, I'll realise I knew nothing, *again*.

Ah, retrospect is shit. I want futurespect.

But one thing I got right; I wrote that grief can't be negotiated with, and had no idea how spot on that was.

I should be back at University now, but I'm not going. Dad pleaded with me, said that's what Mum would have wanted. But I also know this; Mum didn't want Dad to be alone. She would have put that above all. And more to the point, I don't want Dad alone here and me alone in Manchester, either. I can go back to Uni anytime, be a *mature* student, but right now, we need to be together, Dad and I. We're all we have. Love you, Mum.

NOVEMBER 13th 1993

I don't write in here as much as I once did. It feels odd and unfair, documenting life going on. Oh god, I hate that phrase, "life goes on".

A couple of old dears round here have collared me, pulled the right expressions, then imparted that "wisdom" like a panacea. "Life goes on", they croaked.

Yes, well spotted, it does. That's life. It goes on. I know they are trying to help, but I want to scream, "how is *that* possibly supposed to make a difference? Look at you, you're 150 years old, YOU go on. On and on and on. But my Mum doesn't, does she?" I don't, of course. I just pull a similar expression and agree.

There are stages of grief, as everyone knows. I've been at anger for a while now. I'm feeding off it, I think. Anger feels better than depression, or bargaining. I still do those occasionally, but I hate the way they make me feel diminished, disempowered. Anger works just fine.

Yes, life goes on, ha. A year ago I was at University, and now look at me. What did I leave Uni with? Cigs. I went there a non-smoker and left as a nicotine addict. No degree, just £1.60 a day on 20 B&H. Well, that's some kind of achievement, I suppose.

Now one month into my first 'proper' job. Debbie, Karen, Tracey and all the others are probably out dancing in The Hac right now, and here I am, back in the bedroom I grew up in - *am* growing up in, I should say. I wouldn't have it any other way though. I want to be here with Dad, where

Mum's still present. The mortgage doesn't pay itself, so hi ho, it's off to work. Oh god, I hate it. *Life goes on.*

NOTE TO FUTURE JANE. Hello future Jane, this is 1993 Jane calling. Should your memory be impaired and you look back on your first job fondly, DON'T. It's rubbish. Don't let yourself get fooled by rose tinted glasses. Time does that to you. For starters, I think we all have this odd yearning to go back to just before our own birth, as if everything suddenly went to hell the moment we took our first breath.

For example, born in 1973, I'm convinced the '60s must have been a glorious Paradise Lost, when everybody loved each other and there were only Beatles and Astronauts.

That's what I call my *Fuck! I Only Just Missed The Good Bit By Moments* theory. Looking at older people, I also realised they tend to consider the period of their teens/twenties as what I've named the *It Was So Much Better Then Than It Is Now* period. Avoid these mistakes, Jane. Memory is selective and tends to blur out the bad bits while highlighting the good.

So, for the purposes of derailing any warm, fuzzy nostalgia, here's what you did, Future Jane.

You worked in a video hire shop which meant you got in at 9:30 (WHY? NOBODY HIRES VIDEOS AT 9:30 IN THE MORNING) checked video tapes out, checked them in, then put them back in the relevant section. But mainly you rewound tapes all day long, which sounds like it should be a metaphor for something, but I haven't worked out what yet. If you still have Video Hire Shops, Future Jane, your world is stupidly static.

I need to get a Proper, PROPER job. I need to get paid for writing. Future Jane, if you ever invent a Time Machine, DO NOT go back to November 1993. Do NOT start smoking. Although I do enjoy it.

And Jane - if nothing else, use this diary to remind your Future Self of any mistakes you may have made in the hope you won't make them again. Some chance. Farewell, Future Jane. Life goes on. Ha. Message ends.

MARCH 5th 1994

Today, I am an actual, *published* author! Well, not an author as such, but a published writer, at least, in Cosmo Magazine, no less. Next to me I have a cheque for £90, which is great, but just annoyingly short of the full ton. £90 is good, but £100 just sounds better, doesn't it, even though it's only a tenner difference.

When I was little, ONE HUNDRED POUNDS was a magical, impossible amount of money. I thought I'd never, ever, earn that much in one go. And guess what, I still haven't. Ah well, it gives me something I can aspire to. Don't let anyone say you haven't set your bar high, Jane.

The actual article isn't that special, just a fluttery thing about How Your Hair Defines Your Personality, much of which I made up, but they went for it. They don't take 'unsolicited articles,' but I was smart. I saw the Editor had written a piece about how her hair makes her feel different depending on the style. So I spotted the opening, got some quotes from the library (IE; Jim Morrison, "some of the worst mistakes of my life were haircuts") and of course, that appealed to the Editor's ego, and bingo. That's how to get on in life, then, bite the bullet and flatter complete strangers. I should do more of it.

Mum would be so proud. I sat in the front room by myself and read the article out loud, as if she was there. I hope she was.

JULY 22nd 1994

Well, that was a waste of time, wasn't it? I won't even write his name. Me and men. I never learn. Maybe I should be a lesbian, but then I'd have to sleep with girls. *Bit* of a stumbling block for me, that. I've met and loved plenty of beautiful, funny, attractive girls, but *vive la différence* and all that.

I look back through this diary and see a grand parade of losers, with me at the front, twirling my baton. Oh yes, I am the majorette at the front of that ghastly parade, but I keep bloody joining it, don't I, twirling my stupid glittery stick. *He* had a nice flat though, shame to leave it, but I'm not going to sleep with someone just because they have a tidy bedroom. Well, to be honest, it does help.

I must pick and choose more carefully. Dad doesn't say much about these - ha - *paramours*. I know he doesn't approve, and hasn't approved of any boyfriend, really.

Note to Future Jane; if you're reading this and happily married, you have my permission to smile knowingly and nod your head sagely.

Something else to remember. I started writing a(nother) book today.

No, not a 'book,' a novel, aha, oh yes, a *novel,* would you please. I shall move to Haworth at this rate. It's about snow. Difficult to write when it's boiling outside, but I'm channeling my inner Hemingway.

Whenever I think of winter, I think of Mum. I suppose because I miss her more that time of year. I've started writing books before, but managed not to finish any of them. So if I have it done by the Millennium I shall consider myself quite prolific. Watch out Brontës, I'm onto you.

DECEMBER 21st 1994

So here it is, Merry Christmas, CHEQUE FOR £120! Thankyou, Cosmopolitan Magazine! YES. £120! A full score over the ton! I've officially made it.

"How To Avoid Office Christmas Party Horrors." YESSSS! My second published piece in a year, surely I'm a professional writer now.

The irony being we've never had a Christmas Party at Supervids Video Hire Shop. I can't believe I'm still there, stocking, rewinding, spotting guys who come in for Bad Porno, pretend to look at the family films, then casually pick up, "*Laundromat Girls*", as if it were a spur-of-the-moment decision. I tell them it's a good choice, although I recommend, "*Laundromat Girls 2 - Dirty, Dirty Linen*", but only because I prefer the plot and cinematography.

Last week, a greasy guy hired one and then asked me out for a drink. Well, that made me feel like a princess, didn't it? I'm such a catch that pervy Adult Vid Customers ask me out in moments. Of course I went for that drink and we're now married. Joke. Although I was tempted for about four seconds, which is a terrible indication of how shit things have got, men-wise.

Back with Dad again, but can't be helped, couldn't raise the rent on the Roman Road flat. Money in, straight out again. Dad remains my most patient landlord and charges nothing.

Christmas always hard. I've had some of the family photos framed. Dad will like that. Love you, Mum.

FEBRUARY 9th 1995

My new favourite band are Oasis. Sorry Duran Duran, I've moved on. They're no-where near as immaculate looking as DD, in fact, they dress like builders, but there's something of the Bit Of Rough about Liam. 'Definitely Maybe,' getting me through hideous days at work.

Note to Future Jane; if you think that leaving Supervids for The Royal fucking Bank Of fucking Scotland was a great idea, it wasn't. At least at Supervids you could watch films all day - without that job, you would have never seen 'Super Mario Brothers- The Movie'!! Imagine that. So there are plus points in everything.

But now I just sit and file, and file and file and file and file. It pays more, but what price money when you lose your soul? OK, bit much, but I also have to wear an A-line, white shirt and heels, so I look like an Air Hostess but with none of the fun of feeling like I'm going anywhere.

AUGUST 11th 1995

Back home, *again*. Good work, Jane, lasted all of 5 months with Hideous Flat Mate Who Shall Not Be Named. Every night was a soundtrack of ecstatic/pained moaning from Debbie Does Deptford in the next room. She sounded like a sentient apple being cored. Well, *semi* sentient.

My favourite moan; "there. There. THERE. THERE! THERRRRRRE!" She sounded quite adamant that something should be put 'there.' I can only assume he was moving furniture, but the *feng shui* wasn't happening. Or she was just having *really* bad sex.

She also won my trophy for "World's Most Neurotic Female" which, considering the competition, is quite an achievement. The slightest wobble and she'd totally flip, which meant it was like living with a game of Buckaroo. I'm well out, but of course that also means I'm back in with Dad.

On a much more/less important note, Blur or Oasis?

It's a very important decision this week. I'm guessing in a couple of years no-one will even remember the Battle Of Britpop, but it's like we've finally been given our own '60s, apparently.

I have to say, I'm rather enjoying it. I didn't think things could get any better after Manchester, but now London is also the place to be. I've started wearing DM's again and had my hair cut like a cross between Justine from Elastica and Sonya from Echobelly, which looks far better than it sounds.

I am tentatively (very tentatively) seeing another boy (no names, let's see if he deserves his name being in here first) who sings in a band called - wait for it, drum roll - '*Muswell Hill*'. I can but dream I'll see them on Top Of The Pops soon. But 'Muswell Hill,' I mean, really. 'Muswell Hill'? They may as well be called 'Apples & Pears' or 'Jellied Eels.' He's already asked me to move in with him, probably so both he and I don't have to commute for *rudies* as Mum called The Act Of Love and I'm happy to do the same. I'm predicting that A/ I won't move in and B/ This one isn't going to last beyond next week. There, I said it. Ta ta, Muswell Hill.

My book is coming on. Still not happy with the main character's name, Peter Hope. Dull, and a bad aptonym, too. Need a better one but nothing happening, still, only three years to get to six chapters. I'm a machine!

Oh, Future Jane - on the question of Oasis or Blur, it was neither. Try to forget both "Country House" and "Roll With It" ever happened. It will stave off cold-sweat nightmares.

NOVEMBER 4th 1996

Annoyed Dad today. I asked if he would ever see anyone else and he looked so furious I thought he was going to throw his plate at me. He'd been drinking. He was Lager Dad, the shirty version of himself. I should have known.

He said, "who could ever replace Mum? And why would I even want to look?" Then went back to dinner. Message understood, I won't be asking that again. But I worry. I don't want him to replace Mum, I just don't want him to be alone. He's not that old. He keeps telling me to get my own place, but I can't. I *can't* leave him here by himself, with his books, lagers and memories. I wouldn't want to. He hates me smoking, and I know why. Cigs equal bad and that's that. I will stop.

I know me rebounding back to Dad seems weird to people. god, yes, last year Nameless Boyfriend from 'Muswell Hill' even said it out loud, which, along with his Marmite breath, was the final nail, but I can't leave Dad right now. It would feel like the only other girl in his life had gone too. I'm happy here. I love him, and I love you, Mum. Also, emotion aside, I can't afford to. London's not getting any cheaper.

MAY 2nd 1997

"WHOO-HOO" as Damon says. YES, after 250 years of Conservative Dominion, Labour are in. Tony Blair is one of us. He plays guitar! He knows who today's bands are! He's younger than my Dad!

Dad and Mum always voted Labour, of course, so I asked Dad how happy he was today, but he just said, "moderately happy, but you know what Roger Daltrey said, the new boss is the same as the old boss and all that."

So, a quote from The Who says it all for Dad. Let's see. Stopped the fags for 6 days. Had a drink, started again. Well done, Jane. You seem rather determined to make an appointment with lung cancer.

OCTOBER 24th 1998

Good news/bad news. So often the way. The good news is Autumn's finally decided to pull its finger out and make a move.

It's a windy day, so gusts caught the oaks and suddenly the air was full of tree-snow. I never realised how much falling leaves look like giant tumbly gold snowflakes. I watched the flurries for a while, and caught myself smiling, which was nice. I'm amazed it's taken me this long to see how trees undressing themselves is like nature rehearsing snowfall.

I can almost imagine it's December out there, if I swap the ochre for white. I see people with spades and brushes clearing their drives, tree-snow drifts and lonely little swirls now and again.

It's lovely.

But now, the bad news. Ended it with XXX last night. Which, I suppose, is also good news.

I keep doing it, don't I? I keep forgetting Mum's 5 Dating Rules. Why? They're not difficult and I know them by heart.

1/ Don't Date anyone shorter than yourself.

2/ Don't Date anyone who doesn't drink.

3/ Don't Date anyone who has substantially <u>more</u> money or substantially <u>less</u> money than you.

4/ Don't Date anyone you work with.

5/ Don't Date anyone who calls you a "bird."

I can see the rules from here, *still* sat on my dressing table where she put them after I'd split up with XXXX back in '92. So why do I keep ignoring them? Sorry, Mum.

I managed to break 4 of the above rules with XXX XXXXXX from work, the smug shortarse (there goes rule 1/).

I kept rule 2/, as he's not a teetotaller, but he does drink - a LOT and when he drinks, he gets all laddy and oiky (5/) - it's OK to be a 'Lad' nowadays, god help us all, and I fell for it.

I had to be drunkier than him even to sit at the same table after a while. I should have known. He got on my tits almost immediately, then permanently set up residence there. I think he now pays council tax on them.

He's my Manager (so that's 3/ AND 4/) and I got fooled by the *barra boy* patter. Remember this one Jane, you lasted two months and even moved in with the idiot for a whopping two weeks. I hope you look back on this diary because I'm WARNING YOU, DON'T DO THIS AGAIN. We had NOTHING in common except our place of work and now the Royal fucking Bank Of fucking Scotland is an unhappy place to be. Or should I say, even unhappier than it was, which is an achievement. What a waster. By which I mean him *and* me.

DECEMBER 31st 1999

Here they come then, the Naughties! Ooh, stop! Me and Dad are off to The Hoop, which will be fun. Apparently at the stroke of midnight, all civilisation will collapse thanks to the 'Millennium Bug,' which will throw us all back to the Stone Age when computers turn on humanity because they don't understand a very basic linear calendar system, or *something*. Quite a big design fault, in my opinion. But that'll serve us all right for relying on them too much. Computers will be the death of us, says Nostradamus here.

So by 12:01 tonight, I expect the apocalypse to have started. This may be my last message. Note to Future Jane; please know that these last few hours of civilisation were joyous and fun and we were happy. My New Years' Resolution, after surviving technological armageddon, is to leave the Royal fucking Bank Of fucking Scotland. I think I'd prefer armageddon to another year at TRFBOFS actually. At least post-apocalyptic survival might be interesting. Other resolution; stop the cigs. Please Jane, stop them.

JANUARY 1st 2000

Still here, then. The apocalypse has been put on hold for now, pheee-eew. So next stop, walk out of the TRFBOFS, laughing and throwing ring binders in the air behind me.

Dad suggested we take the train to Southend On Sea, like we used to, and walk the pier. So I write this on the Fenchurch Street Line, rushing toward SOS. It may be a bit cold to go walking down The Longest Pleasure Pier In The World, but we haven't been to Essex for a while (about 4 years I think) and Dad loves it because it reminds him of when he was courting with Mum. People don't court anymore do they? The world would be better with a bit of courting.

5 p.m. Nice day, but freezing on pier, as predicted. Dad upset me by asking if I would scatter his ashes from the end. I don't want to think about that and told him so. He said, "nothing lasts forever," and I know, but I don't want to think about a forever without him. So this year, my resolution is to leave The RFBOFS. Life's too short for banking, and a girl can't wear A-line forever. So, then, Southend, done for today. Last time I visited was in the '80s, what a thought. The '80s! Did it ever exist?

SEPTEMBER 11th, 2001

Jesus. I can't process what I've seen, what I'm still seeing. There are no precedents. Today is new.

It's 4:30 p.m. the twin towers have fallen, the Pentagon's gone, and who knows what else is going on? This is our Kennedy Moment. Even as today's happening, I know it. Kennedy Moments are not good things. If your generation has one, then it's time to strap in and hold on tight, because Kennedy Moments don't stop. There will be repercussions, forever - we're going to live these few hours over and over again.

I'm scared. We all woke up this morning on one planet and now that world's gone, forever. I didn't think it was possible for one world to end in moments, but it clearly can. That terrifies me.

MARCH 15th, 2002

So, I had a think today and realised since I left university, almost a decade ago, I have been gainfully (ha) employed as;

Human Filing Machine for Royal fucking Bank Of fucking Scotland.

Human Filling Machine at Pie and Mash Shop - nice people, but really?

Free Local Paper Deliverer (yes, I finally got my paper round).

Receptionist at Dentists (worst of the lot, Dentist had arse-seeking missiles for hands).

Pretend Author With Almost Finished Book Nobody Wants.

To be fair, I haven't really tried to sell it/don't know how to sell it. It will be my posthumous mark of genius at this rate. Maybe I'll be Bow's equivalent of Sylvia Plath, although I don't intend to stick my head in an oven. Well, not until I see how the new job goes. Stand by, oven, I may need you.

I still keep starting to write other books, but now never get past the first chapter or two before realising they're not working. I write articles, but no-one accepts them. I just checked and I've made exactly £210 from writing. Then there's the poetry, which is usually terrible once I've sobered up. Case in point - I started a poem with, "writers are just actors who take to the page rather than the stage," and then, incredibly, *didn't* ram the pen into my eyes as punishment. So my un-published book and this diary, yes, you, my friend, are the sum total of my Creative Writing and no-one will ever read it. Pah. On an unrelated subject, Tony Blair is not the man I thought he was, which is the story of my love life, now I come to think about it. So many broken promises, so many false smiles, so many disappointments in the bedroom. Yes Tony Blair, I'm talking about you. Ha. I'm here all week.

Tomorrow I have an interview for working as a waitress in a cocktail bar, which sounds like a joke, but isn't. They call it 'duty manager' but that's just a fancy name for waitress, effectively. The only bonus is that I may end up as the subject of a Human League song in real life.

Dad ordered me to move out, again. The move last year didn't work though, did it - wrong boy, wrong flat, wrong everything for a bloody change - so what can a girl do? Broke in finances, broke in love. Broke, broken, full stop. Boo fucking hoo me.

FEBRUARY 4th 2003

Odd day today. Very odd. <u>Good</u> odd, but still…

A day to work on. I don't think I've finished with 4th February 2003 yet. I hope I haven't.

I smile as I write this and I can't help myself. Fingers crossed this smile isn't a wasted one.

28 / Garden Of Remembrance / Tuesday, February 4th, 2003

So what happened to Jane on the 4th February 2003? I won't keep you waiting.

Some more context, then. After all, I do it so well.

We're now into a decade called the 'Naughties,' but the naughtiness involved really wasn't much fun.

2000 started at the stroke of midnight with fireworks, was followed by a yet more spectacular display on September 11th, 2001, then continued to be defined by people playing with explosives. Perhaps the Millennium was informed by its birthing moments; those bangs and cracks never stopped.

It started with the world looking up to the skies and ended with the planet looking down at their phone screens. That should sum up the progression of the human race quite nicely.

Here we are, then.

*

On February the 4th, 2003, Jane sat in a garden at the London Cemetery And Crematorium.

Half an hour earlier, she'd stared into the tiny mirror in the tiny hallway of her tiny terraced house, and thought, *OK, today. I'm ready for you. let's see what happens.*

You already saw her there, way back at the 'start' of our story, if, indeed - as I pointed out all that time ago - any story really has a 'start'.

So. Quiet, now. Let's stand here together and watch. That's all we can do, after all.

Jane liked to visit this place when she could, sit in the garden and remember. February was her favourite time, when the lawn was still dusted with frost, and roses slept between the trestles that ran along the borders. They were yet to flower, of course, but the promise was there.

The roses always reminded her of Mum.

Irene's spot was marked by a small cross, just a few inches high. Jane had added flowers, placed pictures and left messages, but the awful fact remained that her mother now occupied an eternal resting place compressed into less than one foot square.

It was 11:30 a.m. and the garden was quiet. Jane breathed in the chill air. Winter made her sparkle, while summer made her sluggish and irritable. Given a choice, she would have preferred to live in perpetual cold.

She stubbed out a cigarette on the arm of the bench, then threw it into a nearby bin.

Jane looked around at the various plaques, crosses and stones. She chose one at random; Helen Piper, born, 1864, died, 1907.

"Helen Piper. Hello, Helen Piper."

Jane liked to say the names of the long dead out loud, to let them inhabit the world again, if only for a moment. Piper. A good name. Jane filed it away.

She hoped that one day in the future, someone might pull *her* name from the vast army of the forgotten, to bring her back, just for the time it took to say, "Jane Dawn."

In her peripheral vision, she saw a figure with a wheelbarrow approaching. She didn't look round, but then the *whoever* stopped right next to her.

*

We both need to stop, you and I, right here, right now. Take another deep breath, orient ourselves.

We must pay attention, open our eyes wide. Let's give the following minutes the respect they deserve. From here in, everything will flow from this apparently trivial event.

Jane didn't know that at the time, of course. But eventually, as the fulcrum of her life revealed itself, she was almost able to trace it back to here, like playing a film in reverse and watching dominoes right themselves.

*

"Don't mind me," the figure said. Jane finally looked round and up, then itemised him in microseconds.

Nice blue eyes - tick.

Shaggy dark hair - tick.

Taller than me, but not a beanpole - tick.

Ooh, pouty big mouth - tick.

V necked jumper under cool coat - tick.

DM's, blue jeans, bit 1995, mm - tick.

About my age - tick.

Oh, tick tick tick tick tick.

He's either in a relationship or gay, she added, miserably.

He wore gardening gloves and held pruning shears. He sized up the dormant roses behind Jane's bench, worked out a plan of attack, then began.

Say something, Jane, her mind urged.

So she did, but perhaps should have thought about it a little more.

"Are you the gardener?" Jane asked, then mentally smacked herself in the forehead.

This man pointedly looked at his shears, down to the wheelbarrow, then back up.

"No," and then, in a stage whisper, "but for God's sake, act normal. I'm an undercover policeman. This is an extremely elaborate cover."

They looked at each other and both raised their eyebrows.

But then he smiled.

"Yes, OK, I asked for that," she giggled.

"Yeah, you did, really."

He stuck out the tip of his tongue out in concentration, and carried on cutting at the roses.

Jane pretended not to watch him.

For a while that's all there was, the clip, clip, clip of shears and the crack of stems.

"It always feels barbaric," he sighed. "Hacking away at them like this. But sometimes you have to cut things down to build them up again, I suppose."

She noticed he had the shadow of a Scottish accent, but had managed to cover it up with a London twang. He'd pronounced, "build" as, "*beld*."

"They're lovely," Jane meant it. "Well, they will be lovely. It's one of the reasons I like this place so much. It just gets on with being beautiful without making a song and dance about it."

"I know what you mean," he agreed, but still concentrated on the pruning. "Beauty without ego. The best kind." And then he looked at her again, just for a moment.

He continued to work in silence while Jane desperately tried to think of something else to say that didn't make her sound insane. "So…Why gardening?" slipped out. Not great, but certainly workable.

"My Dad." *Clip, clip, clip.* "He passed on six years ago."

"I'm sorry."

"It's OK, you didn't do it," he smiled round at her. "Dad was one of the reasons I came here, to do this. I volunteered at first, but they insisted on paying me after a while. Getting paid to do something you enjoy. Best kind of work."

"It is," she agreed, and they fell silent again.

I should keep him talking, Jane thought, surprised at how quickly she'd found herself interested in this man. *I should keep him here a while, pass the time.*

So she took a deep breath, both mentally and physically.

"Well. You do a lovely job. Your gardens are…magical."

"Magical?" He tried the word out. "Yes, they are magical, aren't they? Thank you, but I can't take credit for them. For that you'd have to thank God, or evolution, whichever you prefer."

"Well, not god, evolution," Jane hoped she'd picked correctly.

"Yeah. But then, if I were a far-right Christian, I'd just say God invented evolution and therefore, bingo, it was all part of his plan. I never get why they don't do that, why they deny evolution rather than just co-opt it?" He grinned at her, a proper toothy one. "But each to their own, eh?"

"Each to their own," Jane nodded. "I haven't seen you here before."

Oh please, her inner voice chided. *That's the idiot cousin of, 'do you come here often?' 'I haven't seen you here before,'* echoed sarcastically in her mind. *Why not ask him if he's* single *while you're at it, since you seem to be so eager to cut straight to the chase?*

But he hadn't seemed to hear the inference.

"Well, I could say the same about you," he replied, but that was a lie, this whole *act* was a lie. "But I suppose it's a big place and I'm only here three times a week. So…"

Mm, Jane thought, *he's* noticed *that he's never* noticed *me before. That's a good thing isn't it?* But another part of her mind simultaneously wondered, *what's the end result of this chat, Jane? What are you hoping for?* But she ignored herself and just carried on talking.

"How long have you been a gardener?"

He used a little spade to dig away at the base of the roses, then pulled up weeds. If there was a particularly testy one, he grabbed a knife and hacked it away.

"A gardener? Oh, I'm not."

"Oh yes, you're an undercover Policeman, I forgot."

"No, that was actually a terrible falsehood." He grinned up at her again. "Hard though it is to believe, what I really am is a mature student. Psychology." And he'd said, *'mature student,'* in a silly posh voice, like Dave Dawn would if he hadn't taken something too seriously.

Jane had only spoken to The Gardener for a few minutes, but could see that he definitely warranted further investigation.

"I aim to pull the weeds out of people's minds," he added with a flourish of his hands, then waved his knife like a wand.

Jane decided that caution should go windward so turned the flirt dial up a notch.

Why not? She thought, *what's to lose?*

"Ooh, nice knife, nicer metaphor," she laughed.

"Thanks. I have been working on it for a while. The metaphor, not the knife. Glad you spotted it. How about you? What do you do?"

Jane sighed. Now she'd done it. She'd asked, and since it had just boomeranged right back in her face, decided to deflect the question.

"Well, what I want to do is write. I've written since, god, I was six. That's what I want to be, a writer."

"A writer. Nice. I like writing. Well, good writing. Aha. What kind of stuff?"

She noticed he seemed to have spent a lot of time on the same patch.

"Oh, I've done magazine articles." Jane opted not to mention she'd had precisely two published. "Fiction, really. That's what I love. Making stuff out of nothing."

"Bit like gardening."

"Ha, yeah."

They went silent again, and he turned his attention to another plant.

Phew, thought Jane, *I got away with that one.*

But unfortunately, The Gardener wasn't finished.

"You said what you want to do is write, so what is it you *do* do?"

Damn, thought Jane, *now I have to tell him.* She toyed with lying, but didn't want to - what? - *start the relationship with a lie?* And her eyes went wide that she'd even considered the word *relationship.*

She thought;

You know nothing about this man and you're already thinking, 'relationship'? Bloody hell, girl, foot off the accelerator, you're not that desperate.

But after all this time, she was that desperate, actually.

So Jane just came out with it.

"I work as a waitress in a cocktail bar," she sighed, and gritted her teeth.

"You don't!" His head snapped round and he beamed. "*Nooo!* Tell me you don't! As in, 'Don't You Want Me?' Really? You work as a waitress in a cocktail bar?"

Jane started to gabble. She felt herself doing it, but couldn't stop.

"I do, well, I'm technically a manager, but I don't manage at all well. I am the manager who just can't manage. It's The Reflex in Hoxton. Do you know it? Of course you don't, nobody does. It's an '80s bar. We have to dress up in '80s gear, and it's '80s music all day, all night. Even '80s food on the menu. We do omelettes called, "Beat It." An all day buffet breakfast called, "Just Can't Get Enough." Really. A bit of me dies every time I write down a food order. I became a teenager in the '80s. I didn't really want to take employment back there, but it's better than stacking shelves, I suppose."

"Really? I have always wanted to meet someone who worked as a waitress in a cocktail bar." He wasn't kidding. "Did you say it's called The Reflex? As in Duran Duran?"

"I did." And she gave the song a go, her querulous singing voice out of place as her breath plumed into the air. "'The reflex, la la la la, *fl-fl-fl*-flex, la la la la...*" He looked confused, so Jane attempted to justify this weird outburst. "Remember? 'The Reflex'? Big '80s anthem. I hear it at least three times a day and despite that, I still think it's one of their best."

"Nah. Sorry, but no." He shook his head. "'The Chauffeur'. Off, 'Rio'. Bloody great track. 'The Reflex' - ha, sounds right up my street. Hitting my teens in the '80s and all that. Mind you, I only really, properly, discovered '80s music in the '90s. Still, better late than never, and all that."

"These days I'm on the side of never. It's grim," she groaned. "I want to kill Lionel Richie. Honestly, the ways I've planned to kill Lionel Richie. I've got a whole slasher film in my head. 'Hello', Lionel, goodbye, Lionel. I've got his head, like in the video, except it's not made of clay, it's his *actual head*. If he knew the depths of my hatred, he wouldn't leave his house."

Jane realised that could have sounded psychotic, but this man had cackled loudly throughout. It was a laugh like Mutley from Wacky Races, a *tsk tsk tsk, hee hee hee,* that would have sounded ridiculous from anyone else, but from him sounded stupidly attractive.

"An actual waitress who works in an actual cocktail bar," he wondered aloud, then looked at his watch. "Would you mind if I sat down? It's almost lunch."

Would I mind? thought Jane, *I've been waiting for you to ask since you first appeared, and isn't that peculiar?*

He went to his barrow, picked up a lunchbox and flask.

Oh my god, he has a lunchbox, thought Jane. *That is impossibly cute.*

He sat down and opened the box. Inside were sandwiches, an apple and Mars Bar. He unwrapped the sandwiches as Jane looked on, delighted.

This is a man who has a Tupperwear lunchbox, and I never believed that anyone could make a Tupperwear lunchbox look sexy, but you've just pulled it off, Mr Who-Ever-You-Are.

"It's cold. Would you like a cup of tea?"

"Yes please." Even though she didn't, not really, but her internal response was, *oh god he offered me a cup of tea!*

"English Breakfast OK?" He asked, and of course it was.

"The Reflex, wow." He shook his head and chuckled. "What do you wear? Please don't say Debbie Gibson."

He poured some tea and handed it over.

"Nooo, no. Rah-rah skirts weren't funny first time round. No, it changes," she grimaced. "Sometimes hard and teutonic, sometimes the classic frilly shirt, asymmetric hair and pointy boots. I get some looks on the bus."

"I bet you do." He looked into her eyes, and that made Jane feel ever-so-slightly like a teenager again. "They actually make you bring your own costumes?"

"No, no, imagine how sad that would be," she laughed. "They have a box round the back. Honestly, it's the only job I've ever done where they have a dressing up room for the employees. I'm a different person every night. That's something, I suppose."

"Well, at least your work uniform changes every day. OK, then, since we're on the subject, you're clearly the expert, I'm on a break, and if you don't mind…"

She didn't.

"A question. The only musical question of the '80s, really. Duran Duran or Spandau Ballet?"

"Oh god, easy. Duran Duran every time. Even when I was twelve, I had an unfeasibly massive crush on John Taylor. I think I still do."

"Who didn't? Duran were just…better, weren't they? 'Through The Barricades'? Jesus. I still can't believe that was written by the same guy who wrote, 'To Cut A Long Story Short'. Truthfully, even I fancied John Taylor, and I'm straight."

Phew, tick, thought Jane.

"Alright - er…Soft Cell?"

"Well, 'Tainted Love', could never be played again until the end of time and that would be too soon, but other than that, yeah. One of the better straight man/camp man synthesiser duos, you know, out of the hundreds in the '80s."

"Uh-huh. Agreed. 'Non-Stop Erotic Cabaret' is a terribly under-rated album. Shake my hand," he stuck his out. They solemnly shook as Jane thought, *we're actually having the 'what music do you like?' conversation. Already. Oh my word,* she wondered, *this is like a date. If we were sat in a bar over some drinks, this would definitely be a date. But he's eating egg sandwiches from a Tupperwear box and we're sat in a Crematorium Garden. Ah well, can't say it's not different.*

"OK, everyone's favourite '80s synthesiser band - Human League?"

"Aha, that was one of the perks. Thanks to The Reflex, I finally discovered The Human League properly. I have 'Reproduction' and 'Travelogue', but I never got 'Dare'."

"What you never 'got' 'Dare' or never bought it?" He raised his eyebrows in mock surprise.

"Never bought it. As someone who actually works as a waitress in a cocktail bar, I'm one of the few people qualified to say, 'Don't You Want Me' is so…not the case. No-one's ever just walked in, picked me up, turned me round and made me into something new. Every time I hear it I cringe. And I hear it a *lot*. Sorry, just my opinion."

"Don't apologise for opinions. Opinions…" he went on in a grand voice, "…are what we decorate our personalities with."

"Oh, that's good," Jane flirted. "I think I'll nick that and claim it as my own."

"Go ahead. I stole it off my Dad in the first place. But you really should get 'Dare'. It's brilliant."

He stopped, took a bite, nodded, satisfied, "Well, look at us. Two British people and we've managed to not talk about the weather once. Just synth pop. I'm not sure if that's better, actually."

"It is. Only just, though."

Oh dear, thought Jane, *this is all suddenly odd and a bit oddly sudden.*

"Simon," he offered his hand again. "But not Le Bon."

"Jane. But not, er, Austen." She took his hand and shook hello, as both of them pulled exaggeratedly serious faces, as if at a business meeting.

He took the cup back.

"Thanks for the tea."

"Pleasure. Ah well," he stood up again. "It's been very nice meeting you, but I have some other lovelies to attend to…"

Did he just say other *lovelies?*

"…and flowers don't prune themselves, alas."

Ask him, Jane, ask him right now, part of her mind ordered while another part answered, *but what if this was just a harmless chat? What if I look weird? I can't ask a stranger for his number, that's what strangers have done to me, and I have always, always thought them deeply disturbing.*

He stood for a second in front of her and waited. But for what?

Ask him ask him ask him Jane, her passionate mind implored, but her sensible side and, yes, her scared side won out. Because if she asked, then he screwed up his face and walked off, she might never recover. Occasionally it was best to leave some possibilities unexplored.

"See you about then, maybe." He pushed his wheelbarrow away, and the wheels squeaked to try and helpfully fill the embarrassed silence.

"Bye," she said, softly.

What are you doing *Jane?* Her passionate mind screamed, but it was too late. He walked off down the path, and away from her life.

Tiny snowflakes had started to fall.

But just before he turned the corner, he looked back and shouted. "Oh. Another important question; Oasis or Blur?"

She thought for a moment.

"Oasis!"

He raised a solemn, closed, Noel Gallagher we-shall-overcome fist back at her then walked away. Gone.

Damn.

29 / A Dare / Tuesday, February 11th, 2003

One week before, Jane had sat, smoked and remembered in - appropriately- a Garden Of Remembrance.

Seven days later, as usual, she was dressed up at her regular place of work, 'The Reflex,' an '80s themed bar in Hoxton, East London.

On that particular day, Jane wore a black peaked cap, white shirt, thin tie and pencil skirt.

She was supposed to be long lost '80s New Romantic chanteuse Ronny, but since absolutely no-one who went to The Reflex had even heard of Ronny, Jane would explain she was Steve Strange from Visage and that left everyone happy.

On February 11th, 2003, she was duty manager on the much coveted twelve - eight p.m. shift, which was relatively quiet, involved few drunks and meant a possible night out after. It was a Tuesday, quieter than usual, so Jane had time to wonder how she'd ended up back in the '80s, while the '00s passed by outside. Stuck in 1982, she looked out enviously at 2003, and wished to be there.

Since Jane was dressed as Ronny, she'd felt a little decadent, so had sneaked on the soundtrack to *'Cabaret'*. From the jukebox, Liza Minelli told the sparse clientele she'd be *through* when she was *through*, *toodle-oo*.

Jane was also gasping for a fag, but staff weren't allowed to smoke. That was a shame, as it would have really suited her outfit.

Trapped here in the '80s, between bottling up, ordering and changing the lines, Jane hadn't stopped thinking of the gardener from last week. She'd been immediately, what was the right word? Yes, *interested* in him.

Yeah, well done, you were so *interested you didn't ask for his number, did you, and he hadn't offered anyway. So in terms of phone-number-exchanging effectiveness that counts as a 100% lack of success. Good work, Jane, really excellent job.*

When things don't go your way, it's tempting, no obligatory, to analyse all your options into the ground.

For Jane, those options included;

He didn't give me his number because he didn't really care.

But… he must have been slightly *interested otherwise he wouldn't have stayed to chat.*

Then again, he might just be nice and talk to anyone.

Or… he might have just talked to me.

But however I look at it, he didn't offer me his number.

And so on, round and round. She'd tried out every possibility, gone through the positives and negatives, stood in The Reflex and probed those few minutes in the garden from every angle, like a director tries different cuts of the same scene. Some end up with a happy outcome, some don't. As director of your own life - to an extent - it depends on where you've chosen to put your camera.

But Jane had come to one conclusion.

I must, must, must, *see him again and find out one way or another. Or I'll be stood here for the rest of time, dressed as various '80s icons and also-rans, going over these possibilities. Aha, yes, I'm on the move now, I have forward momentum. I'm a car, I'm a train, I'm a shooting star, a fighter plane and I am foot down, I am Jane and I vroom, Vroom, VROOM!*

So whilst being held captive by the '80s, Jane had been working on The Plan.

Capital T, capital P.

The Plan had one purpose; to see him again, and take it from there.

So what do we have? What do we really know, Sherlock?

OK, his name is Simon. Surname unknown.

He prefers Duran Duran to Spandau Ballet, but that's not really going to help. Most people do.

He is doing a degree in Psychology. Location unknown.

He works as a Gardener at the London Crematorium And Cemetery.

And that, my friends, is our soft underbelly. Because I know one crucial thing about him.

Where.

He.

Is.

So now, I give you; Jane's Plan.

Somehow, she'd managed to work it out over several boring afternoons and evenings in The Reflex, despite Frankie telling her to *Relax* and Van Halen yelling that she might as well *Jump*.

The original plan (lower case "p") was to hang around the garden of remembrance again, and hope he'd turn up for some more pruning. That wasn't a euphemism, although, in the middle of the night, Jane had wondered.

But the evidence was against it. She'd never seen him before and clearly he hadn't seen her, so the idea of waiting around like Greyfriars Bobby until she was found dead at seventy-five on a bench didn't appeal. Therefore, more direct action had to be taken.

So The Plan (now having gained its capital 'T' & 'P') was more of a pincer movement.

She'd go to the Manager of the Crematorium and explain how she'd met The Gardener - *"what a friendly guy, a real credit to you"* - and was looking for tips on growing roses. *"I wonder possibly, if it's OK, could I leave my number so he could help, you know, if it's OK, if he has time, if it's OK?"*

The Plan was cunningly simple, and came complete with three emergency exits, which went;

If he wasn't interested, he wouldn't call.

If he was just being polite, he'd call, give her some rose growing tips, and that would be that.

But if he was very interested, he'd arrange to meet in a bar, to discuss a *good hard pruning* over a few drinks, maybe a meal.

Jane had looked at The Plan from every angle, explored all possible outcomes, and it seemed watertight. Now she just had to make it happen.

Right now.

OK, maybe tomorrow.

Thursday. Thursday feels good.

By the weekend, definitely.

"Can I have a Sloppy French Kiss please?" asked a punter who'd materialised in front of her.

Inwardly Jane groaned. She hated the stupid drinks she had to serve here. Stupid cocktails with stupid names that gave stupid idiots a chance to flirt under the disguise of making an order.

"Of course," she replied as neutrally as possible, and looked at the customer.

It was him.

Him, from the Garden.

Him, the subject of The Plan that now clearly wasn't needed.

Him, who'd filled her head for the last seven days.

Him, whom she knew almost nothing about.

Him.

She couldn't take it in. She literally couldn't speak, her mouth goldfished, her brain seized up.

He was smiling.

"Nah, not really," he added quickly. "Just a Foster's please."

Jane couldn't get to grips with it. *How was he here?* Why *is he here? How did he know I was here? If this is coincidence, then it's not coincidence at all - it's fate. He happened to walk in to this place, where I am, now. No, this is meant to be.*

Oh, she thought, *oh, my giddy aunt.*

"Hello," was all she managed.

"Hello, again."

Whitney Houston was now telling the bar she wanted to dance with someone who loved her.

"Hello, yes," Jane repeated, then remembered her job, and above all, her cool. "A Foster's? Right. Yes."

As she turned to fetch a glass, thoughts rushed past at just below light speed;

Don'tmuckthisupdon'tmuckthisupohmygodhe'sherebutitcouldbecoincide nceohgodheprobablyhasagirlfriendthismeansnothingtohimthismeansnothi ngtohimohVIENNA

"Are you dressed as *Ronny?*" he asked from behind. She looked over her shoulder, pencilled-in '80s eyebrow raised in amazement.

"Oh my god, yes, I am," she gasped, actually gasped. "You're the first person who's ever spotted that."

"It's a good look," he nodded, and his eyes took her in from waist to the top of her peaked cap. "I've got 'Blue Cabaret' somewhere. Cracking track."

"It is," agreed Jane.

Get a grip, girl, get a grip. You are dressed as Ronny *in an '80s bar, So get. A. Grip.*

"Talking of which," he reached down. "Aha, talking of cracking tracks, you need this, I think."

He pulled up a copy of The Human League's 'Dare' LP, original gatefold sleeve, all pure white and go-faster logo. Phil Oakey stared out and wondered if, perhaps, you'd like to join in with *the sound of the crowd.*

"You said you didn't have it, and that's not a statement I like to hear, so, this is for you." He put the LP down on the bar between them.

Well I never, thought Jane, then;

Ohgodohgodohgodhe'sboughtmeanalbum.

Well I never, this is incredible. *This is better than The Plan could have ever allowed for, him, here, with The Human League.*

"But I don't want you - or your, er, boyfriend - to think I'm weird or anything." As he'd said, "your boyfriend," he'd looked away, and Jane knew he'd practised for this moment.

He was fishing, and it was insufferably cute. But as Jane breathed an internal sigh of delight (*"he's single!"*) she realised he wasn't cute enough not to have one tiny bit of fun. She needed to let off all that tension.

"No, my boyfriend won't mind," she shrugged, and instantly regretted it.

He gulped. It was a micro-gulp, but Jane saw.

Because although he'd just achieved a 90% perfect job of covering up his disappointment, the other 10% was obvious to any connoisseur of disillusion, which she was by now, and hated herself for it.

Jane rushed to fill the awkward hole she'd just created. "No, uh-uh, no, my boyfriend won't mind, considering he doesn't exist. No, no boyfriend to mind. No, ha."

He smiled widely, in pure relief. All masks and bets were off.

"Oh, OK, right, good."

"Good?"

"No, not good you don't have a boyfriend, just good that I won't…er… be offending anyone. It's just 'Dare.' I don't want you to think I'm being weird or anything. But…" He started to gabble. "You mentioned you didn't have it, and I was passing a charity shop and saw it in the window…So…"

No you didn't, thought Jane, *god bless you, you went looking for this. I can see you did, bless and* love *you for it.*

"…and I remembered you said you didn't have it, and I thought, oh, look, there it is, "Dare," and only £2.50, so I thought, well, why not, so I got it…"

"Why are you even here? No, sorry, I mean, how did you know I was here?"

"You told me." He opened his palms to her, *look, nothing to hide.* "You told me you didn't have 'Dare' and said you worked at The Reflex. So when I saw this…"

He pointed at the album, began to gabble again.

"…I remembered that…er… you didn't own it, and that you worked at a place called The Reflex, and so I picked it up, and thought, oh-ho, well, next time I go that way I must pop in and see if she's there and you are, and…"

You liar, thought Jane, *you beautiful, wonderful, exquisite liar.*

"Well, it's brilliant." She smiled her biggest "Rio" smile. "Thankyou, so, so much. It's very kind of you."

"Well, er, good," he replied, picked up his drink for the first time, then took a huge gulp of relief.

"£2.00." She put one hand on her hip, held out the other, palm up, and waggled her fingers in his direction.

"Sorry?"

"It's not a bartering system. You can't give me 'Dare' and I give you a pint. I'm afraid it's two quid."

"Oh, yes, right." He pulled out a couple of pound coins.

"I'll get the next one," Jane offered, and was shocked how easily she'd just come out with it.

"The next one?" He asked, innocently, but his expression gave him away. He knew.

"I finish at eight." She turned away to the till, but still smiled. "Shall we go next door? The Fox And Eagle. Less noisy. We could talk about The Human League. Or Spandau Ballet, if we get really desperate."

She turned back to him, picked up the album, opened the gatefold sleeve and looked at the track listing.

"'Do Or Die', right?" She looked up at him and smiled.

"Yeah, do or die." He mirrored her smile.

30 / I Love 2003

And so, at 8:05 p.m. on Tuesday the eleventh of February, Jane and Simon finally met in a socially conventional way; at a pub.

Call me old fashioned, but neither awkwardly flirting in a crematorium garden, nor awkwardly flirting whilst one party's dressed as an '80s pop dominatrix count as "socially conventional".

Maybe that's just me, though.

Jane had changed out of her Ronny outfit - she'd considered keeping it on, but then realised that would have been way too weird - and tried to calmly walk into the Fox And Eagle pub.

He was there in the corner, with two pints. He looked up, smiled, and pushed his fringe out of his eyes.

She sat down and stared incredulously at the drinks.

"You bought me a pint?"

"Aha. I did. You don't look like a white wine kind of girl. You look like someone who goes for an honest pint." He pronounced, "honest pint," in an exaggerated Cockney accent, "*onist paaant.*"

He was right, which made her heart jump. At first, always a pint or two, then, once she couldn't take the bubbles any more, she'd switch to vodka. But as an opening, always beer.

"You're right, actually, *saaaaaalt* of the earth, me." She spoke the real cockney to his impression, picked up the lager and took a large swig. "Aah," she sighed. "You have no idea how much I've been looking forward to that. Mind if I smoke?"

"I can hardly say no," he shrugged.

"Do say. I know, it's disgusting. I started at University - Manchester - and never stopped. So any excuse not to, I take it."

"I don't really…" He pulled a conciliatory face. "It's just…I'm not really a fan."

"That's fine." She waved her hand in the air, *no problem.* "I'll go outside in a bit."

"No, no, it's OK. I get it. If you want one, have one."

Oh please, let's not start on the back foot, she thought, *I knew smoking was bad for me, but now I know how bad.*

"I'll stop," she said. "Promise." Then realised she'd made him an offer that assumed he'd be around in the future to enjoy it.

Interesting.

"You should. It will age you. And that wouldn't do, at all." He extended his hand, and they shook, formally, seriously, just as they had in the Garden one week before.

"Hello, properly. Simon Marryman."

"Marryman? Marry. Man. Nice. Jane Dawn."

"Dawn? The Latin for dawn is Aurora. Did you know that?"

"Er, no, I've never paid any attention to *my own name.*"

He nodded in supplication. "Sorry. Nice to meet you. Again." He sipped his pint and grew a beer foam moustache. "What were you studying in Manchester?"

And there it was, they were off, with no tip toeing round, not like bashful teenagers, certainly not relative strangers. Just two people at ease, in a fairly grotty pub in Hoxton.

"English. Lit and Lang."

"Lit and Lang? You're such an English Student. You want to write. I remember."

You never forgot, thought Jane. *Just as I haven't. Every moment of those five minutes is stored.*

"I *do* write," she said primly, and put on a Barbara Cartland voice that made him cackle into his pint glass. "It's simply that the shocking plebs don't acknowledge it."

"I'll read what you've got. Send it my way, I'll give you an honest criticism."

"Thankyou. Not too honest though, eh? And, as I recall, you're a 'mature student'."

"Oh, I am. Always sounds so grand that, 'mature student,' oh, I *say.*"

"Er…In…Psychology, yes?" She pretended not to remember.

"Correct. My Dad was a psychologist, did I tell you that? Quite the big psychological cheese in the '70s, apparently. But right now I specialise in memory, though. That's my thesis."

"Sorry, you specialise in what?"

"Memory."

"Joke."

He paused for a moment, made the connection, then laughed out loud, a genuine, throaty bellow.

"Sorry, bit slow. So, yeah, think about it, memory is all we are. For example, did you know you can store about seven things in your short term memory for about twenty seconds? Seven seconds after that, if you don't re-enforce the memory, it's gone."

"Remind me of that in twenty seconds."

"Same joke twice. Good work. Not many people could pull that off."

She winked and tipped an imaginary hat at him.

"So. Ha. Aha. Yes, OK, ah... the technical name for when you can *almost but not quite* remember a word is anomia. 'It's on the tip of my tongue,' is anomia. Oh, and, ah, yes. Insulin is not just for diabetics- it helps promote memory function in the brain too. But what I'm really interested in is how memory can be selective. You know, people can actually choose to forget. It's not always just a natural leeching of memories. Sometimes, it's deliberate."

"Really?" And she thought, *you will talk and I will listen for as long as long can be* and that surprised her again, the ease with which she'd been smitten by this man.

"Aha. In extreme trauma - not just brain injury or natural degradation, but psychological trauma too, the brain wipes out memories to protect itself. I've got plenty of documented cases, and they are fascinating. Holocaust survivors who simply don't think they were ever in the camps, victims of violence who see photos of their own injuries and can't even recognise themselves in the picture, a girl who forgot her own parents, then remembered them again. My Dad dealt with that one, actually, way back when."

"Forgot her own parents? How did that work? Did they hurt her?"

"No, no, I'm pretty sure they loved her, but she suffered a head injury and that was that. She forgot her parents. Remembered them eventually, but for a few days, they were nothing to her. Fascinating."

god, thought Jane, *I can't imagine anything worse than not knowing Mum and Dad.*

…and that was beyond ironic for reasons you already know.

At that moment, Simon *could* have told Jane more about the little girl who'd lost her Mum and Dad somewhere in her mind, and how her memories were re-fired by the appearance of a typewriter on Christmas Day, 1973, but hadn't wanted to go overboard in case the not-so-little girl in front of him got bored.

If he had, this would have been a very different story.

He moved on.

"I'll show you my thesis if you like." He stopped, then pulled a moue. "Ooh, sorry, that sounds like 'come up and see my etchings,' doesn't it? 'OooOoh, do you want to see my thesis?'"

"Oh, sir, you are a one," Jane replied in her best Barbra Windsor Carry On Flirting voice.

"It's an impressive thesis. All the girls say so."

"Send it my way, I'll give you an honest criticism."

"That sounds like a threat. So what was your thesis?" He asked and pushed the fringe out of his eyes for the umpteenth time.

"Ah, well, yes. I never finished University. My Mum fell ill, died. Horrible, absolutely fucking horrible. I stayed with my Dad, I couldn't leave him."

"I'm sorry. That must have been hard. Do you regret not finishing? Do you wonder about how different your life would have been if you had?"

Well I never, she thought, *this is not exactly a casual conversation. How wonderfully odd, and how oddly wonderful. But if I had finished Uni, I would never have met you, that I am sure of.*

"I wouldn't have made any other decision. I love my Dad and wanted to be with him. I needed to be with him. Still live with him, actually. On and off."

"Good for you. I'd probably still be living with my Dad now if he hadn't passed. People forget too quickly how parents change their lives for their children. Because they love them. So I get that."

"Your Mum?" Jane ventured. He hadn't mentioned his mother yet, which was a worry.

"Dead," he replied quietly, without drama. "When I was three. Lung Cancer. My only memories of her are feelings, really. I look at photos and…She's just a person. I hate that."

Aaah, thought Jane, *oh god, and here I am with a packet of B&H*. But he hadn't said it with any weight directed at her.

"I'm sorry."

"Thankyou."

Jane had no-where to go, so went somewhere else.

"You're not from London are you?"

"Oh, well spotted. Here's a thing. Before we carry on, you should know I was born in Glasgow. By the Clyde, no less. I am very Glasgae. I am a genuine Scottish Man, from the Scottish Marrymans. The ones without the money, it turns out. Way back when, there's a line of my family who are stupendously rich, but they don't share it with us."

"You and me both. Apparently sometime in the past, a branch of the Dawn family were a bit loaded. But none of it made our way, either."

"Then we were surely fated to meet. The poor cousins. The bumpkins. Glad tae meet ye." Simon dropped into a brogue so deep that Jane laughed, delighted, like a child surprised by a magic trick.

Oh, she thought. *I need a response.* And it came without thinking, *aha, thank you. Mel Gibson.* "I will never take your FREEDOM!" She suddenly bellowed in bad Mel Gibson-esque Scottish, and he laughed, too.

Once again, Jane realised she'd made a direct comment about a possible future together.

Incredibly interesting.

"Scottish," she wondered. "So why no accent? Or rather, why do you choose not to have an accent?"

"I don't really have a Scottish accent. Just occasional echoes. That's my Dad's voice I just did. He moved out of Glasgow after Mum died to come here, well not to this pub, I mean, but London, to practice psychology. That's why I want to do it. For him."

"Right. You should do the Scottish voice more often, it's…" She caught herself before she said, "*sexy,*" and instead tried, "distinguished."

"Och, destangweshed," he agreed, Glaswegian again. "I see we're making short work of our pints. Perhaps a wee whiskey? Or some…ah… Highland Toffee?"

"I'll get them," she rose. "I was supposed to get the first, actually."

"Same again, please."

Jane almost skipped to the bar, but stopped herself. On the way, she thought, *oh my god, this is an actual date, unplanned, in no diary, not dressed for, made up for, nothing. But this is a date. And it feels perfect. god, I hope he likes me.*

When she returned with the pints they both sat and sipped in comfortable silence, as if they'd known each other forever.

"'The Gentle Art Of Forgetting'," he said.

"The what *what* of a what *what*? Sorry, but for a moment there it sounded like you'd just said something totally random, which can't be right."

"Ah, yes, sorry, yes. I did just go weird. 'The Gentle Art Of Forgetting,' that's the name of my thesis. Remember, we just discussed it and you *pretended* to be interested."

"I was, I am interested." She threw up her hands and dismissed him. "Sorry about all the yawning."

"You were very polite." He flirted back. "Screaming 'stop for the love of God' really kept me focused."

"Sir, that was my intention," Jane whispered demurely and crossed her hands on the table, very Brontë.

"But I'm still not sure about the title. Is it a bit too… frilly… for a thesis?"

"You are talking to the Queen Of Frilly. I work in an '80s bar, I wear '80s gear, I know frilly and it's not frilly. It's good, I like it. It makes me interested to know what it's about. Is there an alternative title?"

He grimaced. "The other option is 'Directed Recall And Controlled Memory.'"

Jane slumped and put her head face down on the table.

"Hello?" he asked, mock concerned. "Wake up. Wake up."

She sat up, wide eyed. "*Now* where am I? I was just talking and suddenly somebody said something so dull I must have passed out. What happened?"

Internally Jane thought *too much*? But he went with it.

"I got rid of the dull guy." He took her hand, as if he were a doctor and she a patient, but the touch was good. "I'm here now, it's all going to be OK. I got rid of the boring bloke. It's just me and you, now."

Jane laughed, *Oh, would that be true. Let it be true. I've gone from zero to full flirt in just a pint. The pedal is right down now, we are* off.

"So what do you think?" He hadn't let go of her hand. 'The Gentle Art Of Forgetting'?… or… 'Directed Recall and Controlled Memory'?"

Jane slumped face first onto the table again.

"The Gentle Art Of Forgetting." She stayed face down. "Just for god's sake don't say the other one ever again."

"I won't."

We keep talking about a shared future, Jane thought. *Why is that?*

"So - serious question," she asked, and meant it. "Giving Human League records to girls you've just met. Is that a usual technique?"

"No," he replied, expression open. "No technique. I don't have techniques. I'm technique-less. Well, I've got New Order's 'Technique', naturally, but that's the only technique I have."

Jane sat back, smiled and raised an eyebrow. "You know, I don't think I've heard the word 'technique' so many times in one sentence. Are you going for the record?"

"Rambling, sorry," he muttered. "But I swear that's a first."

"So why, then? Why buy this?" She picked up the bag containing 'Dare' from the side of the table. "For me?"

"Well, the first bit's easy. You didn't have 'Dare'. Everyone should have 'Dare' - especially someone who likes The Human League."

"I do, yes. 'Marianne' is one of my favourite tracks, ever, by anyone."

"Exactly, yes, mint track."

"But why? Why me?"

That was the real question,wasn't it? The question everyone asks at some point, for good or ill, *why me?*

"Because…" His answer may have swung this conversation one way or another. One direction good, the other not so agreeable.

"Because you looked like someone I wanted to get to know."

And there it was, out in the open.

"When we started talking, that made me want to get to know you, that's all," he lied.

Same here, thought Jane, but had to ask once more. "Why me, though?"

"Because you were friendly, you weren't uppity, made me laugh, you were interesting. And interesting people are always worth knowing."

She smiled and jumped in. "Well, that's handy, because I thought the same."

"About me or about yourself?"

"Oh me, of course." She risked it. "I found you an inconvenience. No, of course you."

He beamed then, raised his glass, she raised hers and they chinked them together.

Now we can move on, she thought, happily, *we know where we stand, we've set out our stalls, we've put our ducks in a row.*

She'd been surprisingly relaxed before in his company, but now any lingering tension - apart from the obvious - had evaporated.

Over the evening, she found out/he found out, amongst much else;

He didn't like cats, she didn't like cats.

He liked Star Wars, she'd liked Doctor Who in the '80s, but found Star Wars fairly pointless. However, he considered her lack of enthusiasm for - at the very least - Harrison Ford - perplexing.

She liked Chinese; Sweet & Sour Chicken Balls.

He liked Chinese; Sweet & Sour King Prawn Balls.

Much innuendo- based merriment was had.

He'd "enjoyed" a variety of jobs, too, with perhaps the best/ worst working as a street cleaner. "Like my Dad!" Jane said, delighted, as she added up all these odd connections.

His favourite poem was, "Stopping By Woods On A Snowy Evening" by Robert Frost, which he knew by heart, and at that moment became Jane's favourite, too.

Her favourite lines were the last. *"The woods are lovely, dark and deep, but I have promises to keep, and miles to go before I sleep, and miles to go before I sleep."*

After a few more drinks, they told a few war stories about life on the front line with their exes. As you know, Jane had endured a few non-starter relationships.

"Right. You have this life." She waved a knowing, slightly drunk finger. "And if you mess it up by taking second best in love, then you have really messed it up. I know. Better to be wait 'til eighty and find the right someone, than put up with the wrong person and wonder what might have been. Better to just keep on trying, come what may."

They both knew that was another very loaded statement, but he let it pass.

Apropos of nothing, she confessed to loving Findus Crispy Pancakes. He nodded with gravity and said, "minced beef." She agreed, as if that was the most important choice anyone could make.

Jane then revealed that, *actually*, as long as she could remember, her favourite snack was cold baked beans spooned onto ready salted crisps.

"Seriously?"

"Bear with me. Dad came up with the, er, *recipe* one night after the pub when there was nothing in the larder and, to my knowledge, only me and Dad - sorry - Dad and I, eat it. So that's something, isn't it? Right. Here we go. The recipe for Bow oysters. That's what, me and Dad, sorry, again, Dad and I, call them. Pay attention. Take a spoon of cold baked beans, put them on a crisp, knock it back. Lovely."

Simon looked disgusted. *"Bow oysters*? I thought pie and mash was bad enough, with that green…stuff ladled all over it. What is that? Agh."

"It's liquor. Or *raaaather, paaarsley sooorce.* " She affected a ridiculous upper class voice.

"Urgh, no thanks."

Jane ramped up her East End accent to something that sounded like a language constructed without need of consonants. "Ex-cuh-use me, sun-shee-ine, tha's me cul-u-ral 'eritage yoo-err bleedin' in-sul-ing."

"Excuse me?"

"Sorry, but you'll just have to deal with Bow Oysters and liquor," she shrugged, knowing actually, he would.

Tiswas, not Swapshop.

Liam, not Damon.

John Taylor, not Martin Kemp.

It was all there. They sat and talked until last orders.

Jane moved on to vodkas and Simon to brandies. They talked of everything and nothing, but it wasn't the conversation that mattered, it was the subtext, and the subtext was time.

They talked for all the time they had. Neither of them made excuses to leave, or became bored. The talking simply extended the *time* they sent together. That was its real function.

The last bell rang.

"Oh," said Jane, who definitely felt like she'd had three pints and a few vodkas and cokes.

"Oh," Simon slurred. "That's that, then."

Neither of them made a move.

"Better get going, then."

"Yes, going. Ah, yes, better had."

"Where do you…?" she asked, and he waved his hand airily at the door. "Oh, you know… Angel. Little flat. Northern line."

"I'm in Bow, as you now know. Ooh, listen to me rhyming. *Propaah* Cockney, me."

Simon stood, grabbed imaginary braces and did a Mary Poppins knees up. "Always wanted to go out with a Cockernee," he twanged in a frankly appalling East End accent. Jane raised both eyebrows.

"Go out with a Cockney?" she repeated. "*Go out* with a Cockney?"

He looked embarrassed, but only a little.

"You know, go out. Go out for drinks and that. With a Cockney."

"Mm," she said, and thought, *no go on, you can do better than that. You know what I'm saying. Yes, it's sudden, yes, it's madness, but that's what this is, isn't it, a sudden onset of madness?*

"Did you want to go out with a Waitress Who Works In A Cocktail Bar, too?"

He looked her straight in the eyes.

"Ah-ha. Mm. Yes, I did."

"Well, perhaps you should," she whispered, leant forward and softly kissed him on the lips.

There it was.

And there they were.

31 / Jane Watches And Types, Here

Tap, tap, tap.

I have to write. I must write, right now, because an Aurora came. It appeared in the sky over Here and was so beautiful I cried.

And then, if that wasn't enough, something else followed it.

I was Told that the Aurora - well, my Aurora - lit my way Here, but I don't remember that.

I can only remember coming to in this hut - or was it waking up? No, it was neither. My arrival was more like finding a signal, slowly being focused - I seemed to go from static or blur to clarity, like being tuned in as if I were a TV or Radio.

So, no, I don't remember my Aurora, but was Told that we all have our own, and can only leave when ours returns to light the way. If I try to leave without the light of my own Aurora, then I'll become lost in The Forest, forever.

I was Told that would be worse than dying and I believe it.

So I watch and I wait for my Aurora, because when it comes, I am ready to go.

And tonight - whenever "tonight" is - an Aurora appeared, but wasn't mine.

How did I know it wasn't my Aurora? Well, in the same way you know the laugh of someone you love in a crowd, how you recognise their walk even before seeing their face.

So, an Aurora came, which meant someone was arriving, or leaving.

We're not supposed to interact with others in this place (another one of the Rules) so I was good, and didn't leave my

Hut to watch the light show outside, although I really wanted to.

Let me try to describe Here's Aurora, then;

It's like watching deja vu. Parts of it appear before they appear, which I know is nonsense, but that's how it is. Sometimes the Aurora appears in your memory first, and then it does what you remembered. That's not quite right either. Is it a reverse echo, does it arrive before it arrives?

No. Try this. You're watching several films at once and somehow, know the beginning and the end at the same time.

Nope.

That's not how it is.

The Aurora dances, seems to operate within its own choreography, moves in three dimensions and adds a few more just for fun. It danced and I didn't even realise I was crying until I felt the tears.

But did it dance? Or was it being buffeted, in and out of time? No, Jane, no, no. C minus, Must try harder.

Bloody hell, if I was a writer before Here (which I feel I was, but I'm not sure) then I can't have been very good, if I can't even begin to describe an impossible multi dimensional piece of sky that dances.

Ha, joke.

Then, as an Aurora danced above Here, suddenly, there was an actual person standing in the clearing. I was scared. I couldn't tell whether they were male or female. I didn't know if they had just arrived or were about to leave. They could have been someone else I'd never seen, who'd stayed in their Hut, with curtains closed, and minded their own business. Or they could have been saying farewell. I just don't know.

And then, suddenly, The Man was stood next to this person and they looked so little. Or perhaps they just seemed little because The Man is so big.

But that's interesting.

Question; is it always The Man, The same Man who greets us? We all have different ways of dealing with Here - mine is this Royal Companion typewriter - but are we always met by the same Man? And if so, why? Why doesn't he change according to the new arrival?

Hold on - something flickered in my mind for a moment then.

Do I know The Man? Or rather, did I know The Man before Here?

Is that why he's Here? Is he a familiar face, lost in my memory, my DNA even, yes, but hiding there, somewhere, coming Here to make me feel safe?

I don't know. I'm reaching. Perhaps I should just let things be what they are.

So this is what happened.

The Man said something to this person and then pointed North and South.

Why? What was he doing? A ritual? A speech? I don't know.

But then he bent down, and hugged that little/not so little person.

I wonder if I got that treatment when I arrived, or will receive it when I leave?

I wanted to hear what The Man was saying so much, to know who he was talking to even more.

But then, as the Aurora faded, echoed, tuned out, collapsed, imploded, exploded (and it did all those things and more) the little person walked away and then they were both suddenly gone.

I think I even heard air rush into the space they'd vacated.

Had that person relocated to a Hut, to be Told, as I was? Or had they walked into the Forest, North or South?

I don't know. All was still and dark again.

I wonder when my Aurora will come. It feels so close now.

32 / Bow, London, Saturday 3rd May, 2003

Hold on tight. In Jane's linear life things will move, for good and otherwise, so fast from here.

It's May 2003, and Jane's in love. Proper love, the kind you envy in books. She'd realised all her relationships so far had been practice runs, training wheels for the real thing.

Somehow, even from their first brief meeting in the garden of remembrance, Simon and Jane had known it really *was* the real thing.

When you've been waiting for someone forever, you don't muck about when they finally make their appearance. You make up for lost time, you run for it.

Of course, Jane had frequently wondered, *if I'd met Simon earlier, would we have got together so quickly? I think so, but… the perfection of that first meeting, its location and timing couldn't have been replicated elsewhere, elsewhen.*

Had they met somewhere, *somewhen* else, things may have taken longer, but Jane was certain it would have happened, eventually. They were supposed to meet, surely the universe demanded it. She didn't know why, but couldn't imagine any other possibility.

She was realistic enough to pull herself back from these fairy-tale scenarios before she gagged on her own tweeness. Jane knew it was just love talking. Love does that; it whispers in your ear that *you* are the centre of everything and how *no-one else in the history of all time and space has ever felt the way you do*. Love is the ultimate motivational speaker.

But damn it, Jane often thought. *Give yourself a break, all this just* works*, doesn't it?*

Simon had given Jane the album 'Dare' by The Human League - and, with a little creative interpretation, it was an appropriate gift.

Love had taken *seconds of her time*. She loved his *love action*. These were what *dreams were made of*. They *got around town*. She'd *opened her heart*. Yes, she'd had a few problems reconciling *I Am The Law* and *darkness* with their relationship, but you don't get more apposite than working as a waitress in a cocktail bar, being picked up, shaken up and turned around, turned into something new.

*

So, on the evening of Saturday 3rd of May, 2003, David fussed around the family home in preparation for the Big First Meeting With The New Fella.

He picked up ornaments, put them down again. Treated himself to a lager. Straightened and re-straightened chairs. Had a cheeky lager. Polished the mirror above the electric fireplace. Earned himself a lager.

Jane sat on their worn sofa and watched with a mix of pride and a tinge of sadness that he was filling the roles of both a Mum *and* Dad.

"Please, it's fine. It's not a state visit. Sit down, you're stressing me out."

"First impressions count," he replied, for the umpteenth time.

"I know, but he doesn't care about things like this. He's just excited to meet you."

"He'll be the first, then."

He wore a shirt, tie, neatly ironed trousers with a fresh crease, and had combed his normally wild hair down into a side parting. He looked very smart, apart from his furry blue slippers, which made him look like he'd cut the feet off a muppet and was wearing them like some weird trophy.

"That's not true. I've had boyfriends who wanted to meet you before."

"Hm," he arranged papers in the magazine rack again. "Maybe, but I never wanted to meet them. You didn't really sell them to me, did you?"

That was true. Jane hadn't really encouraged cosy get-togethers, because she'd known in her heart none of those boys were going to stick around. Dave was right; she'd always undersold them.

For your consideration, then, I give you a taster of Jane's many and varied 'Boyfriend Sells'.

Oh Peter's happily unemployed.

Well, Mike sells tubs of seafood at pubs, but that's just a stepping stone, really. To his own burger van.

Warren's so healthy he eats raw garlic every day. You know, for the blood. Or something.

U-Vox is in a band, he doesn't want to do anything else. He plays the guiro.

I'm so proud of him. Merlin barely *touches drugs any more.*

Tarquin has dreadlocks and doesn't believe in washing.

He likes people to call him "Chilly", because Graham's so chilled, Dad.

Julian was gay until seven months ago. No really, isn't that fabulous? I turned *him!*

"If I can talk freely," Dave finally sat down. "I can finally, safely say that not one of your boyfriends deserved you. Sorry."

"You would say that." She thought, *oh great,* now *he comes out with it.*

"Of course I would say that. I'm your Dad. That's my job. I know what boys are like, I was one, once."

"And I know what boys are like, too. Probably way better than you."

He shook his head. "No thanks, dear. But they didn't deserve you. This one, though…You're different when you talk about him. You shine. You're ten foot taller. I can't believe it's taken three months for him to come round."

"Yes, alright, I know. We've been through this. A lot."

That was also true.

Jane had met boys, occasionally loved them (so she thought) left home, moved in, moved out… met boys, occasionally loved them (so she thought) left home, moved in, moved out, shouted, met boys…always on a parade that never quite started and never quite finished. With every passing year, she'd felt diminished, unloved by anyone but her father. To make matters worse, she was living at home. Again.

In early March, 2003, just three weeks after Jane and Simon first met, Dad had asked to meet him. That was fast work, his fastest ever, once she'd thought about it..

It happened one teatime, whilst Jane was preparing herself for the hated 6 p.m.-2 a.m. shift at 'The Reflex,' Hoxton's premier '80s themed bar. Scrub that, Hoxton's *only* '80s themed bar.

Dave had noticed Jane's social life was suddenly much busier; she was out far more and smiled, a lot.

"OK." He'd put down his knife and fork, meaningfully.

"OK? OK what? You sound like you're about to tell me off."

"No, no. You're twenty-nine, that would be weird. I just want to ask you a question."

Jane's mobile phone had bleeped with a text.

Talk?

"Sorry," she apologised.

"Aah, not at table, love," he grunted.

"I know, just one moment…" She texted her reply;

Having dinner with dad talk in a bit. Work tonight yuck.

Dave looked at his daughter as she smiled and texted - who? - but recognised her expression. He'd worn it himself.

"Is that him?"

"Yes," Jane sighed, then realised she'd just revealed a gender. "Sorry. I was going to tell you. I mean, he's not a secret or anything, but I wanted to…see how it was going before I said anything. You know, just in case it was a non-starter."

But David knew his daughter.

This lad, whoever he was, wasn't going anywhere soon. So Dave took things very slowly and extremely carefully. When someone managed to look at a text message *tenderly*, they hadn't just fallen in love, they'd dived in headfirst.

"You don't have to tell me everything." He pretended not to care. "I'm not your…bodyguard, I'm your Dad. You tell me what you want, when you want. I trust you."

So why haven't I told Dad? Jane wondered, *I tell him everything else, all the big news, all the trivia, so why not this? Why did I feel the need to keep this for myself?*

*

Dave knew this boy meant change was finally coming, *but then again,* he thought, *Irene's father would have gone through this, too, all those years ago, when I chatted up my way into her life. You just have to accept it, I did it to another Dad, now it's happening to me. So it goes.*

The only question that ever mattered to him was this; *is my daughter happy? And if the answer is yes, then that's what everything else flows from.* Her smile was all he needed.

Move over, old geezer, he thought. *Just look at those pearly whites.*

*

"I know you trust me," she'd said. "And really, I didn't not tell you…"

"Didn't not tell me? Wow. That was a semantic car crash. Double negative, Jane, double negative."

"Oops, double negative. It wasn't like I deliberately didn't tell you. Ah, sorry, shit, sorry, another double negative. Hear those cars collide. I just wanted to see how things went."

"OK. So who is he? Where did you meet him?"

"At the Crem. He's the gardener there. But he's also studying psychology," she went on quickly, just in case a gardener wasn't high powered enough for the daughter of a street cleaner. "He's a mature student. His Dad was a psychologist. He's dead now. That's why he wanted to work at the Crem. To tend his Dad's plot."

Dave nodded again. *Yes, I get it.*

"He's really, really nice Dad, I …" And she caught herself - too soon! "I like him, a lot, and I think, I hope, you will too."

"Well, I need to meet him, then, don't I?" Dave picked up his knife and fork again, which left Jane shocked at the speed of the request. Mind you, all this had taken place at high velocity. It was still hard to believe she'd only spoken to Simon for the first time three weeks ago.

"Get him round here. Anyone who can make you…er, radiate like this needs to be given the full red carpet, I think."

Dad hadn't even asked his name. Did it matter? The name is the name, the person is the person. Names are interchangeable, a person is not.

But it had taken three more months for the Big Meeting to be arranged.

Simon hadn't resisted the idea, but was shy of it, because he knew how important Jane's Dad was. He'd been her only parent for a decade. If he couldn't get past Dad, things wouldn't be insurmountable, but they wouldn't be easy, either.

*

The date was set. 3rd of May, 2003.

Dave may have flitted about like a nervous schoolgirl, but inside, Jane was the real deal. She'd become her fourteen year old self again.

What if they don't click?

What if Dad hates him?

But, counterpoint to all the 'what if''s, another thought calmed her, even though she had no idea where it came from. And, on repeat, that thought said; *Everything will be alright, because everything will always be alright.*

Her Dad had become quite the cook since Irene passed, so he'd taken control of the big Saturday Night Meet The Boyfriend Roast.

And then, at the door;

Tap, Tap, Tap.

There it was. Curtain up. Showtime.

Dave ran the full five feet from living room to front door. Jane tried to be first to open it, greet Simon and bring him over the threshold. For a moment, it looked like a bizarre filial rugby push off, as father and daughter barged each other out of the way. Dave won, and as he opened the door, they both suddenly became the image of calm.

Hi there, all good here, just a Dad and Daughter at a door, Hi there!

Simon stood on the mat, with flowers and a gift wrapped parcel. He wore a tie and jacket, which in Jane's mind, now surpassed even his Tupperwear sandwich box as the cutest thing she'd ever seen.

And she thought, with love;

My two men, both dressing up for each other, for me.

"Hello!" As Simon extended his hand, Jane spotted he smiled a little too widely, over-compensating. "David?"

Dad shook the proffered hand. "Dave, please. Simon?"

They shook hands on the doorstep, but neither wanted to be first to break the shake, so Jane prised them apart.

"Very good, boys. You've both proved you can shake hands, come on, come in… into the, er, study." She ushered them down the hall, five feet back to the living room.

Simon stopped in front of one of Irene's paintings of roses.

Just before her death, Irene's art had leapt in quality, if that was even possible, and she'd created a series of still lives that were anything but still, roses that shimmered with colour and movement, apart from the canvas, more than the paint.

"Your mothers'?"

"Yes."

"It's beautiful." He leaned in closer to the frame. David watched him closely - *to see if he's putting this on* - Jane realised - but of course he wasn't.

"Your wife is an extraordinary artist."

Dave, a lover of language, was confused by the present tense. "Thankyou, er, on her behalf, but she's, er, no longer with us."

Simon turned to Dave. "Yes, Jane told me, I'm so sorry. But she's still an incredible artist. She is *still* that, isn't she?"

Dave nodded and smiled. "Yes, she is."

"Yes, she is." Simon turned back to the painting. "My word, yes, yes, she is."

Jane looked at her father and read him, so very clearly.

He's warming to Simon already. Dad likes him. But…Why is this not quite right yet?

They stepped into the tiny living room, made of sofa, telly, stereo, electric fireplace, two single seats, and lots of shelves loaded with books.

"It's not much," shrugged Dave.

"Ah, it's almost the same layout as me and my Dad's old place. Although we had the telly in that corner, and he kept his books in the kitchen. I don't know why. Ooh, Chess board."

Simon wandered over to the board and looked at the pieces, frozen in the middle of a long-forgotten game.

"Are they magnetic?"

"Er, No," Dave replied.

"Ah, gravitational, then."

David laughed out loud.

He spotted Jane's typewriter sitting on another shelf.

"*Very* nice. Yours?"

"Jane's," replied Dave.

She smiled and gently tapped a few of the keys. "It's my Royal Companion, 1941. Pretty much the only Christmas present I still own from when I was a kid. Been somewhat upstaged by my dull laptop, but it still gets a workout now and then. No plugs or phone lines required."

"It's lovely. A work of art, really."

Simon stared at the typewriter again, with a quizzical expression on his face like he *should* be thinking something, but wasn't. The moment passed.

"Oh, aha, to business. These are for you…" He handed Jane the flowers and kissed her on the cheek.

"And this is for you." He handed David the wrapped gift.

"Oh!" Dave took the package as if it were a mistake. "Really? Oh, thankyou. Shall I open it now?"

"Of course. It's just something little. Jane told me you read, and, er, you really do, don't you?" He waved a hand at the shelves of books.

"Oh, that's just the ones in here. Dad has more, everywhere." Jane filled the silence as her father pulled at the wrapping.

Inside was another book, of course.

It was called 'The Word Mine.' On the cover was a picture of a mineshaft, but rather than coal or diamonds, from inside the cage tumbled a haul of words.

Dave turned it over to look at the back cover.

"It's all about where words come from," Simon said. "I read it years ago. Jane said you loved etymology, and that book is brilliant. How the root words spread out and change. It's great, honest."

"I *bellllllllieve* you," Dave slurred.

Slurring now? Oh dear, thought Jane. He flicked through the pages. "Thankyou, I'm going to *enjjjjjjoy* this."

"My pleasure," said Simon.

David closed the book and looked up. His expression was empty.

"Why?"

Jane wondered what had just happened. It had only been a few seconds, but, *hold on, what's this?*

"Why is it your pleasure? To buy me this?"

Oh Dad, thought Jane. *What? I've seen this happen before. After more than a few drinks, it only takes one simple thing to send Dad to a different place. So this time, it was two words, 'my pleasure?' Why? Oh god, no, Dad. Not now.*

"Dad." Jane stared at him, eyes wide, and tried to send a message - *just shut up* - and prayed that suddenly she'd discover they were both telepathic, but, no. Then she realised that while Dad had cleaned, fiddled and re-arranged, there'd been a certain amount of drinking going on.

Over the years, she'd become used to it but now, today of all days, she really wished she hadn't.

"Dad..." She tried again.

Aha, yes, Dad's become his cranky version, in seconds, no less, now he's found some reason to have an issue.

"It's my pleasure," Simon said softly. "Because Jane is your daughter. She doesn't stop talking about you. It's my pleasure because you've helped make her who she is. Without you, she wouldn't be her."

David looked at Simon, then back at the book. He'd become confrontational in moments. Often, the lagers didn't show on the radar at all, but then suddenly- bang - contact, multiple signals.

Cornered in his own home, Jane knew Dad was trying to show *he* was in charge.

"Thankyou for the book," Dave said, flatly.

Simon waited. This had to be done.

"But..."

Then Jane saw- and how could she have missed it? - that Dad was further down this path than she'd realised.

He'd had *Things To Say* for years, to all the boys who'd never got this far. This one act of kindness had filtered through her father's mind - and his beer - to become a threat. Something as simple as a book could herald massive change.

"Yes, thanks for the book." Dave surrendered to the alcohol, which he'd kept at bay all afternoon. "Since you're here, you know, in my home, just a quick question, if that's OK. Is it OK? How many girlfriends have you had?"

"Dad, Dad, god, *girlfriends*? Please. Come on, I'm twenty-nine, it's not..." Jane pleaded, but her words weren't going anywhere.

Dave had turned a corner. There'd had been no real danger with any of the other boyfriends before, but he'd known in moments that this man's appearance meant Jane was going to leave for good this time.

And, fuelled by alcohol, he couldn't let that happen without some kind of fight.

Jane stood between them and hoped.

"Oh, girlfriends? OK, wow. I've had ...since school, what, nineteen-ish years ago? I've had five girlfriends."

"Dad this isn't..." Jane tried again, but she was out of the room.

"Five? Fiiiiive girlfrrrrriends? OK. So why didn't you stick with them?"

"Well. The longest was two years. Jane does know this, by the way."

Two years?" snorted Dad, who'd become a fully different person in minutes. Jane knew this character. He was Lager Dad, his less than Super alter ego.

"Two years? Not exactly committed then, were you, are you?"

Simon held Dave's gaze.

"No, I wasn't actually. Not committed at all, if I'm honest."

Dave huffed, turned away and hissed, "this was probably a *baaad* idea."

"I wasn't committed because none of them were Jane." Simon spoke to Dave's back. "Because none of them were *Jane*. None of them were even close, and I knew it. You get one chance, here, and not one of them was who I was waiting for, then one came along who *was*, and I knew it. So, sorry if that sounds pat, or rehearsed, or whatever, but it's the truth. It happens. You know it does. When you meet that person, you know. So that's why it was pleasure to buy you that book. Because you're her Dad."

David turned round, slowly.

He'd known the truth about Jane's feelings for Simon from the first moment she'd mentioned him. But when faced with the prospect of what's been part of you for so long, when that centre is about to leave, you can fight, or give flight.

Dave had tried to fight the inevitable for that belligerent, brief time, because he was going to lose something and couldn't stop it. This fight was for him, not for his daughter.

It was a tiny struggle, but the battle had already been won months before.

Dave hung his head for a second, and then part of him, the father that loved his daughter more than life, who only wanted her to be happy, re-asserted himself.

His shoulders dropped.

"I'm so sorry."

"It's OK." Simon replied, quietly.

"It's not. It's just…I only want Jane to be happy, and she hasn't been, for so long. It's my job."

"I know. My Dad felt the same. Yours did too, I bet. And Jane's Mum."

"Dad?" Jane tried again, since she'd run out of any other words.

"I'm sorry." Dave repeated.

"Dad?" Jane suddenly knew the only two words that could pull all this back on track, and couldn't be argued with.

"The Roast?"

33 / *Jane Explores, Here*

Somewhen else, Jane stood *Here*, at the door of her Hut, dressed in her green blouse, short black skirt and flat shoes. It was minus-something-awful out there, but she couldn't feel it.

Beyond that door, on patrol - somehow - was a Cold that could freeze you solid in moments, but it had no interest in her. They'd already been acquainted. The Snow, however, was happy to help, and adjusted its temperature to keep things crisp and fresh, rather than frostbitten and deadly.

She looked around, then stepped out.

Jane knew she'd gone for a walk with The Man when she'd first arrived. She remembered that just fine. The rules he'd given seemed hardwired in her mind, *write protected,* she thought, like engaging the little tab on a floppy disc to ensure it couldn't be erased.

But since then…who knew? She may have walked out many times, but Watched The Snow afterward to wipe away any memories of it.

The snow *crrrrunched*, split beneath her feet, and just for a moment, it was so end-of-the-universe cold her blood froze solid. But the Snow knew, and warmed itself in the next few attoseconds, so, no damage done. Fire walkers use the same mechanism- if you expose yourself to the most destructive forces for the shortest possible time, there's no harm. The Snow knew.

Jane stepped into that whiteness, and peered about.

Not much to see. Just a clearing and two Huts, surrounded by the frozen forest. She moved forward, going North.

The sky was bright and blue. Too bright and blue, if she were honest. It hurt her eyes.

No, wrong time, she thought. *It should be…dusk. Dusk in…November.*

And the sky turned itself down, as if she'd taken a TV remote and adjusted the colours. It slid from Sky Blue to Indigo, down to Cobalt.

And…that's enough, she thought, and the sky froze at Cobalt.

Yes.

Jane looked up, pleased. *The ability to control time is a skill very few people are trained up for. I wonder if I could put it on my CV, when - if - I ever leave Here.*

A reversing, popping sound came from behind, as snow re-appeared from no-where to fill in her footprints, a beautiful trick she remembered from that very first day.

Jane stared up at the obliging sky, which had no sun, moon or stars, then back at the other Hut.

Who lives there? She wondered. *Or is it empty? If so, then surely I can go and have a look inside? No. I was Told that in no circumstances should I ever go and look into someone else's Hut, or talk to anyone who didn't wish to be spoken to. But, but,* but...*come on. What could be so bad about talking to someone else who's Here? We don't have to go into specifics, do we? It could just be a little chat. How is it for you, the memory wiping thing? Working out is it? How's your Hut? Just being social.*

She turned and looked left, then right, at the two Paths which disappeared into the Forest, one going North, one South.

Jane walked toward the tree line. *Step, step*, then from behind, *snap, crackle, pop, snap ,crackle, pop.* As she turned, the Snow repaired itself, rebuilt perfection from chaos. The individual snowflakes gathered, then filled in and wiped away every trace of her passing, for now.

She stood at the edge of the Forest, a line between Here and ...*where?*

Oh, I know so many Little Boys And Girls who have foolishly walked into Forests, she thought. *I still remember all those stories. Hansel and Gretel, Red Riding Hood, Snow White, they all stepped into the Forest and no good came of it. Why? Why does the Forest, the woods keep appearing in our stories? Is it a memory, a truth, or something else?*

The trees seemed to gaze back - impossible of course, but why did it feel like somehow they were appraising her?

"So, what have you got then?" she asked. In any other place, she'd have felt ridiculous, talking to the woods, but not Here. *Here,* it felt like they wanted the confrontation.

"I could easily walk between you," she said, louder, but her voice was stolen by the Snow and travelled no further than a few feet.

"I *could*. I could…explore." But the Forest simply stood, waited, and dared her.

She'd been Told that to step into it was damnation. You could wander forever in its darkness, and never know where or who you were ever again.

But she could see gaps between the trees. It would be easy to walk a few steps into those spaces. Just to be somewhere, anywhere, other than Here.

"Am I supposed to be scared of you?" She asked the trees, bolder.

They stayed silent, no wind to rattle their branches, but she imagined their answers whisper into her mind;

Oh yes.

Oh, yes you are.

Please be scared.

That's why we're Here, little girl.

We don't want to hurt you.

But we will stop you.

Because you do not know what happens if you step into us.

We are the Forest.

We have been here Forever.

There are only two paths, Red Riding Hood.

They are the only exits, Goldilocks.

Step onto them without your light and you are lost forever, Gretl.

So please *be scared of us, Hansel.*

Because we love *you, Snow White, and mean you no harm.*

Jane reached forward and pushed a branch. It gave way just for a moment, but the next, became hard as iron.

There was a crackling sound, then the forest rippled and solidified round the circular clearing like a wooden Mexican wave. One after the other, the trees became impenetrable. Crack, crack, *CRACK*, they snapped to attention, became a dense, dark wall.

I could have pushed into that, and it would have surrounded and trapped me. Thought Jane with horror. *Then where would I be? Not Here. But* where*? It's like the brambles and thorns of Sleeping Beauty, winding and binding. Before, The Man Told me this was no fairy tale, but that's* *because Here is the place where all fairy tales began. I know that now. I am scared. Because that was close. The Forest has no sentience, it's not like The Snow, it just closes, like a Venus Fly Trap, no judgement on what it has caught.*

Jane backed off, but still watched the trees as if they were a pack of wild animals that may run at her the moment she turned. So, very carefully she stepped away from that barrier between *Here* and Who Knows Where, Who Knew When.

To her right stood the other Hut. She'd been Told that sometimes there were more Huts, sometimes less. But today - whatever '*today*' meant - there was just Jane's and this one other.

The Huts were wooden, but looked as if they'd grown where they stood. From here, she could see the front door and one of the windows. The curtains weren't closed.

It can't hurt to look. It would only be a quick peek. If anyone's in there, I'll turn away and go straight back to my Hut. But it can't hurt to look.

After all, she was pretty sure she'd only seen the inside of her own - *but hold on, what about Johnson or Janssen's Hut? Was that* this *one? Was this Hut where I'd talked with that old man? Surely I've been in there? Johnson or Janssen had been Here the longest, he had a* feel *for things, I must have been in there, I remember the edges of a conversation.* She frowned. *Yes, surely there was a man called Johnson or Janssen Here once. We sat together at the window. But where is he now?*

She stepped toward that other Hut. *Snap crackle pop!* went the footprints behind her as she reached the window. She stood to one side and glanced quickly round the frame - *like an undercover policeman*, she thought, but didn't know why she'd chosen those words.

The Hut was empty, so she peered in properly.

There was a Larder/Cupboard/Thing, just like hers, slightly open. She could see one of the shelves and amongst other items, there was a tin of Heinz beans (*popular Here, aren't they?*) sausages, Ready Salted Crisps, Rice Krispies and a box of Findus Fish fingers. Obviously no freezer was required, Here.

Food stayed preserved for as long as it was needed.

She looked at the items again and saw they weren't…quite…there.

Opaque in places, foggy and transparent in others, completely missing in parts. As she watched, the beans shimmered, then appeared to gain colour and mass. They reversed from gossamer to solidity. Suddenly, on another shelf, a pack of bourbon biscuits flashed into existence. One moment, nothing, the next, bourbons.

This larder is filling itself. How? More importantly, why?

"Well, well." She laughed out loud at the impossibility of it all. "Whoever you are, we could share shopping lists if we ever met."

She studied the rest of the single room inside. No oven. Weird. Whoever lived there (*or* had *lived there, or* is about *to live there*) wasn't going to burn any words, then. No typewriter, either. No 1941 Royal Companion on the desk.

Ah, yes, Jane remembered - *The Man Told me that everyone who comes Here has a different way of recalling their past. Whoever lived or lives in this Hut obviously used another technique. Interesting.*

How do they even cook? She wondered, but then just knew the food would be hot the moment it touched the plate.

The bed was made, but the pillow still had an indentation. That simple dimple made her shiver, not from the cold, but from the realisation that someone else really had been Here.

This wasn't a Hut waiting to be filled, it was a lived in property. Of course, that didn't mean someone was still Here, but while Jane had *tap, tap, tapped* away at her desk, another person had been sitting just a few yards away.

I wonder why didn't I see them? Oh wait, maybe I did, when I saw the last Aurora.

Had that other person arrived then?

Jane still remembered that night, so obviously hadn't Watched The Snow since to wipe it.

So has this other person left and the larder is preparing for its next "guest?" Or are they coming back? Have they just popped out? Is this their shopping? But if so - she glanced around the emptiness of Here - *where on earth have they popped to?*

Jane walked the short distance round to the front door and turned the handle.

Locked, of course. Not that the Huts *Here* had any locks, but she understood perfectly.

These Huts knew who was meant to be inside, and locked out anyone else, apart from The Man, who seemed to gain entry without the use of old fashioned concepts like doors.

Careful, Goldilocks. You know what happens when you go into strange houses in the woods. Here be Bears. Mummy, Daddy, Baby. With big teeth and psychotically possessive streaks. Houses with mainly uncomfortable beds. Badly made furniture. Probably with porridge in the larder. Chalets made of gingerbread. Tiny homes full of Little People inexplicably provided with glass coffins, should I eat a poisoned apple. Oh, I'm every fairytale character today, aren't I? Then she realised, *and not many of them come out their stories particularly well, do they? Or particularly* alive.

There was nothing else to see, so Jane walked over to the North Path.

It was made of stones arranged into patterns like the spiralling curl of a snail's shell. They seemed to go down and round forever. At a distance they appeared flat, but from up close, descended into themselves. Down, down, always down.

Fractals, she thought.

The Path is fractals.

And I hate Maths.

I know these two facts are true. I hate maths but I know these are fractals. How so?

The North Path stretched into the Forest. It was yellow, of course, since every road in such a ridiculous place had to be a Yellow Brick (fractal) Road, but while solid for the first few feet, it became difficult to see after that.

I could try. I could give it a go, just take a few steps, see what it feels like and then turn round, come back home.

She put a foot on the North Path and…

Have you ever been so drunk you didn't recognise your own house? So lost you couldn't find the street you'd walked in just moments before? So utterly confused you failed to know which floor to stop on, because they all looked the same?

Now imagine all that, amplified. Vertigo, to the power of infinity.

One step, and Jane almost lost herself, completely.

The tiny Jane in her mind that had been the anchor of reason in all this madness shouted, screamed, hit, punched, and hollered -

Get baaaaaaaaack!

She stumbled backward and fell into the Snow, which quickly re-arranged itself with her in it.

Jane hyperventilated, hyper aware she'd just avoided a kind of purgatory by no time or distance at all.

Oh my god, she thought, as her lungs fought to regain control, and the Snow around her warmed up.

I was so close to being Lost forever.

Jane lay in the Snow, and reached up to the little silver snowflake that hung around her neck.

I am still Here, and I can't leave until I have permission to do so.

34 / Jane's Birthday, 27th September, 2003

Jump with me again. In clock time, in life-time, it is Jane's thirtieth birthday, the 27th of September.

As was traditional, her celebration took place in The Hoop And Grapes, a pub that sits on the edge of the City Of London. Leave Aldgate Tube Station, look left, and there it is, slim and dainty, nestled cosily between two other buildings. The Hoop doesn't like to make a fuss of itself, so it's what I'd call *welcomingly reticent*, rather than *reticently welcoming*. There is a distinction.

This place had been part of Jane's life from even before her birth.

As you know, David met Irene in The Hoop way back when everything was young, and shared an evening that led to her being drink-sick. But on the plus side, she also fell in love.

Funny how one too many wines would have such far reaching consequences. Some good, some bad.

The Hoop was Dave's favourite pub and almost Jane's second home. She knew every chip in the bar, every picture, distressed beam and panel. Built in the late 16th century, it had survived the great fire of London by only a few yards. A fixture of the City for generations, one sat with so many ghosts of drinkers, who came from the woodwork to join you.

Conveniently in the very next street, there was a Coach stop that led to the default Dawn weekend destination, Southend On Sea, in Essex. So a weekend afternoon in the pub could easily become a weekend evening *daaaaarn Saaarf*, no bother.

On this afternoon, Jane, Simon and friends sat at the bay window table, heavy with gifts and drinks.

Not a bad haul at all, everyone, good work. Jane smiled round at the people dearest to her. *But am I supposed to feel old now? Doesn't life begin at thirty? Or is it forty? Nah, my life already began again when I met Simon. god, don't say that out loud, though. The Hoop doesn't have enough mops for all the vomit that would follow.*

In no particular order, Jane's 30th birthday presents were;

A 'Best Of The '80s' CD, purchased ironically, since she was now dangerously close to hating '80s music. In fact, she'd developed an almost Pavlovian gagging reaction to, "Do You Really Want To Hurt Me?", Jane now always answered in the affirmative - for that song, she really *did* want to hurt Boy George.

There was some frankly tasteless underwear from the girls at The Reflex - "It's not for you, it's for Simon," they'd giggled. He'd picked up the set and observed that while certainly his colour, it wasn't really his size, and had they kept the receipt?

A green cotton blouse and a short black skirt from an old school friend, which Jane *ooh'd and aah'd* about, as she rarely put that amount of leg on show.

Simon had given her a silver necklace, hung with an intricate snowflake.

"It's very you," he'd explained. "It's completely me," she'd sighed.

When they'd met seven months previously, it was like a resumed conversation between two people who'd never met before.

Oh my god, I am in love, she'd realised, so quickly. *And only because my Mum died. She dies, I go to the Garden Of Remembrance. I meet a man. I am in love. But why did it have to be such a terrible trade off?*

Within weeks, without conscious thought or plan, they'd dropped into their own world, with its own rules.

Simon bought Jane a single rose every fourth of the month, the anniversary of their meeting. "Wow," she'd said. "If any of my exes had tried that, I'd have called the schmaltz police. But then again, that's why they're my exes." Following that, she swooned a little inside every time.

Song titles from electronic band The Human League were suddenly dropped into conversation. If the other party failed to notice, a forfeit was paid, which changed depending on where they were. For example, a drink at the pub, usually something else in private.

They didn't have pet names for each other. Simon once called Jane, "*Jay-Jay,*" by mistake. She'd stood up, said, "oh, this is totally over," and then collapsed into giggles. "Jay-Jay?" She'd finally managed. "*Jay-Jay? Really?*"

"I'm sorry. It just came out."

"Jay- Jay? Where did that come from, *Simey*?"

"Yes, alright, OK."

"No pet names, OK?" she'd sniggered. "I know some people do, but, I mean, look in the mirror, man."

"Yes, I get it, OK."

She'd looked at him with triumph. "'…mirror, man. '*Mirror Man*'? Human League, 1982. Keep your cloth ears open, *Simey*. 'Mirror Man', god, that was obvious. Double vodka, I think, *Sim-Sim*."

"Damn."

They'd invented a game of ten words, creatively titled, 'The Ten Word Game,' which involved describing the essence of something in ten words or less.

So, beer was;

Gold liquid bubbles make increasingly fluid conversation and company.

Television;

Watch as broadcasts make you think or stop you thinking.

Duran Duran;

John Taylor's backing band.

They'd treat themselves to a curry every third Friday, on the understanding it could never come from the same takeaway twice. They deliberately went to see the dumbest film at the multiplex to see who'd crack and leave first. They'd never eat chips on a Thursday *for no reason whatsoever*.

I don't mean for them to sound twee, or smug, so don't begrudge them their own little island, their nation state of Jane and Simon. They did things differently there, and it *worked* because it *worked*, simple as that.

Put it this way; a spontaneous, unexpected party is always more fun than one you've spent months worrying over. Guests enjoy the wedding reception far more than the newlyweds. Why? Because there's delight in finding yourself in a happy situation that's crept up on you unplanned. So it was with Jane and Simon.

In love, as in parties, if you've decided something *must* be perfect, it never works out that way. Jane and Simon were never hunting perfection. It turned out they were just looking for each other.

"Speech! Speech! Speech!" Went the chant round the table. Jane held up her hands, *no, please, I couldn't.*

"Speech! Speech! Speech!" Everyone shouted, and banged their feet on the floor.

Jane stood.

"Ahem." She coughed. "Ahem- hem. Hem. Ahem."

Her friends waited.

"Thankyou." She bowed and sat down again.

Her friends applauded. Simon leant over and kissed her on the cheek.

"Perfect," he whispered. "One for the ages, there."

"Did it feel too *contwived*?" Jane put a finger up to the corner of her mouth, coy pose, Marilyn Monroe voice. Admirably, Simon managed not to gag.

"It hit every beat. The eight hours you spent on it were not wasted."

"Thank heavens for that. My thesaurus is buggered."

As they wandered over to the bar he turned to her with a serious expression.

"I have a confession. And if I don't tell you now, I probably never will."

"A confession? Sounds ominous. I think I need a fag." She pulled out a B&H and lit up.

"Jill, could I have another Foster's please?"

Jill, the Hoops' eternal barmaid, went to fetch his drink.

Ooh, he needs another drink for this, Jane thought. *That's a worry.*

"Go on."

"Right. OK. You know that first day we met?"

Jane furrowed her brow in mock annoyance. "Er, let me think. Yep, just about."

"Right. Ha. Well, do you remember how I said I'd never seen you at the Crematorium before?"

"Yes. But I'd never seen you either, and you work there."

"That's not...entirely true." He took the pint from Jill, handed over a fiver and had a long, strengthening gulp.

"O...K...go on." Jane folded her arms defensively.

"I *had* seen you before. At the Crem. A few times, but you were always in the distance, leaving, or walking somewhere. And I used to watch you and think…" He paused, took another gulp. "I used to think - still do - that you were - are - the most beautiful girl, nah, stuff that, the most beautiful *thing* - if that's even the right word - I'd ever seen."

"You'd seen me before?" Jane was shocked how long she'd believed one version of the truth only to have it re-worked in seconds.

"Aha. And I really, really wanted to talk to you. You even made the garden look dull, like the flowers needed to raise their game." He stopped, thought, then pushed on. "You made a beautiful place more so, just by being in it. I know that if I'd said any of that when we first met, you'd have run. But it's true."

Jane went to speak, but Simon held up a finger. He clearly had to do this in one hit.

"I didn't want to look stalky, or weird, but knew if I didn't at least try to talk to you, I would hate myself."

Jane nodded, and remembered she'd felt the same after that first meeting, and how she'd needed to see that man again, to be sure. Part of her was disappointed the romantic coincidence of their first chat had been revealed as a pre-desired moment, but another part was thrilled. She'd been *chased,* in a really good, non-stalky way.

"Then, suddenly, you were there. Sitting down, I saw you actually sitting, for the first time. In the same place where my Dad's ashes are. It was…right. It was so right, like it had been…"

He struggled to find the words again. "…*Ordained.* It was that moment. If I'd met you earlier, or later, it may not have been the same, but there you were, and there I was." He laughed. "I didn't even need to prune the roses that day. I only did it because you were there and I had to speak to you. I think I've killed them, they've never been the same since."

Jane tried not to smile as he stumbled. *He made this happen, and better than that, I* wanted *it to happen. So what if it wasn't fate, or the Hand Of god, or Cupid? It happened.*

"I didn't know what you'd be like. But then we started chatting, you know, about nothing, and I just thought; *yes.* So, I'm sorry I never told you that before. I kept meaning to, but the time was never right. I wasn't going to let your birthday go without telling you. I saw you, and I just knew. So I waited for the right moment."

"And it was, wasn't it, you great big stalky weirdo." She laughed again, and hugged him, hard. "I was flattered before, I'm even more so now."

"More beautiful than the roses," he said, softly.

*

"Well hel-lo!" bellowed a voice from behind, accompanied by the bang of the pub door thrown open.

"Dad!" cried Jane, and ran to her father. "I was wondering where you were. Please get a phone. For me. god, please."

"I'm not a phone kind of man, you know that," Dave kissed his daughter on the top of the head. "The only texts I like are on paper, or papyrus, at a push."

He wore a shirt and tie, as he always did for Big Events. He held a carrier bag, contents unknown, and, rather strangely, had stood a piece of plywood up against the table.

He'd obviously had some Starter Drinks elsewhere. Jane knew her Dad.

"Where have you been?" She looked pointedly at the piece of plywood, then David followed her gaze. "Ah. In time. But first, let me get my girl a drink."

"I've got one."

"Not from your Dad, you haven't." He pulled her back to the bar. "Vodka and coke for the birthday girl, Jill."

"On the house," Jill shouted back from the till.

"Now, happy birthday Jane, *this* is part of your present. " David handed her an envelope.

"Part? Mysterious. Thanks Dad."

He looked very pleased with himself, eager for her to open it.

Inside was a birthday card. *To The World's Best Daughter.* Dave pointed at the words. "True." A little smile flickered across his lips.

A leaflet fell out onto the floor. Jane retrieved it, but read the message inside the card first.

'A wonderful daughter deserves a wonderful future, with all the love I can possibly give, and more, Dad xxx.'

"Thanks Dad, that's lovely. But what's this, then?" She unfolded the paper, a flyer from a local Estate Agent. Jane turned it over in her hand, confused she may have missed something.

"I'm selling the house," he beamed.

"You're what-ing the what-what?"

"I'm selling up."

"But - it's your house. It's Mum's house. It's our house."

"But sweetheart, Mum's not there, is she?" Dave put his hands on Jane's shoulders and looked at her the same way he'd always done; fondly, with patience and devotion. "And you can't live with me forever, can you? Who lives with their Dad at your age? I'll tell you, only desperate people who don't have a choice. You do. You have Simon now, and really can't live with me anymore."

"But I want to."

"I know, but you don't *need* to. And you shouldn't. I've been looking. The mortgage is done with. For the money we can get from the house, we can get two flats. Two flats! Paid right off! I don't need that house anymore, it's done its job. We can retire it with honour. We still have all the memories, they're transportable, don't even need a removal van for those. But two flats, Jane, one for me, one for you - and Simon, if you wish. Paid off. Do you see what I'm saying? You won't need to work as hard. You can do what you've always wanted. You'll have *time*, Jane. Time to write, make it happen. Which you can't do in that bar, scraping a living. You'll have a flat, and you can write. I'm retiring next year anyway, I'll need somewhere smaller, bit more of a pension. What do you think?"

"I can't...Give me time to think about it," she replied, truthfully. "It's a lot to take in. But I don't want...I couldn't bear you being across town, by yourself and me somewhere else. I don't want you to be alone. I won't do it if you're alone. I'd hate that."

"Well," he smiled. "Neither would I, so I've thought about that. I mean, we could - if you didn't mind, if it wasn't too odd - we could have two separate flats in *the same building*. We'd only be a couple of floors apart. It would be just like being at home, but we'd have our own walls, be right there for each other. Do you think for one moment I'd want to be alone in the city without my girl nearby? No. If it's OK, two flats, one building. Hello in the morning, hello in the evening, come in! Have a cup of tea! It would be almost the same, just a tiny bit different."

He's worked it all out, she thought, *and I love, love,* love *him for it*. Because she knew leaving the family home wasn't going to be as easy as he'd made out. But Dad was doing it for her, as he'd always done.

"It's not leaving the nest. It's building two new nests in the same new tree."

"Thankyou, Dad, thank you, I love you, so so much." They both knew she'd just agreed without actually saying so. He nodded, pleased, and hugged her again.

What a day, she thought, *what a day.* But one thing still played on her mind.

"Dad?" She asked, puzzled. "What's with the bit of plywood?"

"Aha! that's the other part of the present." He nodded sideways, indicated the bay window table. Simon raised an eyebrow at Jane - *what happened?* - but she shook her head and smiled - *tell you later, but it's good.*

"Ladies and Gentlemen," announced Dave, in his best Music Hall voice. "Your indulgence, please. I was trying to think of a way to give Jane the thirtieth birthday she deserved. Many years ago, I told her a story. A thrilling story…a mesmerising story…a bewitching and enthralling story…"

"Oooh," cackled Jane's friends, who'd dropped into their role as Victorian East End Audience with ease.

Dad? What are you doing? She thought.

"Oh yes, good Sirs and Ladies, I told her a story of my youth. Of how a callow lad dreamed a dream, and using the few pennies he had went in search of that dream…"

Jane looked on, totally lost. He turned to her and winked. A big, drunk, pantomime wink. "Do you remember? Do you? One afternoon, back in the eighties, ooh, what a decade, Ladies and Gentlemen!"

"Hear hear," "indeed," "not 'arf!" The audience howled.

"You were cross, that day, Jane, oh, you should have seen her, she was incandescently aggrieved."

"OoOoh!"

"Yes! Yes! Ind-dig-nant, she was, about *logarithms*!"

Oh my god, thought Jane, *I remember and surely this isn't going where I think it is. I wrote about that day in my diary. I remember now. Bloody logarithms. I'd had maths, and didn't see the point of logarithms, and I came home in a sulk and Dad told me a story...*

"She didn't see the point of them, Ladies & Gentlemen. But I, her loving, doting Father, told her that sometimes, you learn things just for the sheer hell of learning them, because you never know where and when they might come in handy, even if they seem pointless at first, am I right?"

"You're right!" squawked the audience.

Jane looked on as her Father went to his plastic bag and pulled out some old shoes.

Fixed to the heels and toes were Blakeys, metal half moons that protect the sole from wear. But of course, they could be something quite different, in a very specific situation.

As David continued, he sat down, took off his shoes and put on the others, with theatrical flourish.

"And that afternoon, I told my daughter, my irate, waspish daughter, that logarithms may be pointless, but then, so is... ta-dah! Ta-ta-ta...Tap Dancing!"

"OOoOoooh," oohed the crowd, delighted. By now, others in the pub had gathered. They knew Dave well, but only as a talker and a drinker, not this vaudevillian.

The plywood, thought Jane. *I've waited twenty-something years for this. My Dad can tap dance. He told me years ago, but I never really believed him. And now I get to find out.*

David reached into the bag again and removed Jane's old cassette player, which had lain unused in the hall cupboard since forever. He placed it on the table, and then, with one dramatic penny dreadful villain's finger, pressed the "Play" key.

The wobbly, hissy sound of Bobby McFerrin's, "Don't Worry Be Happy," filled the air.

Tap, tap, tap danced her Dad, jury-rigged tap shoes doing very nicely, thank you very much. *Tap, tap-tap tap-tap*, his feet got faster, more confident, heel to toe, *tap-tap tap-tap*, machine gun runs of clatters and clicks, that counterpointed the pops and beats of McFerrin, *tap tap tappity tap tap* and the pub looked on. Jane clasped her hands together and let this moment flood over her, *my Dad, my Dad can tap-dance. He can tap dance. He can Tap-dance my DAD CAN BLOODY BLOODY OH MY GOD BLOODY TAP-DANCE.*

Simon clapped, but not in time with the music. Then, because he couldn't help himself, attempted to tap dance too, suddenly lanky, a series of random movements from the outer limits of dancing. Jane watched them as they laughed together, and laughed herself, marvelled at everything that had happened in such a short space of time. *And now this. My two men, tap dancing together. Well, one tap dancing, the other having what could only be described as some kind of seizure.*

But across the pub, another pair of eyes watched them all. And these eyes took in Simon, and hated him, as they'd hated many others for no reason.

Jane gasped, delighted, as Dave swung her round, *tap tap tap*.

"Be happy!" He shouted.

"I am!" She laughed. And she really was, in September 2003.

But we all know that December 2003 is approaching, and there's nothing you or I can do about it.

Here we go.

Again.

35 / Jane Knows, Here

Tap

Silence.

Tap

Silence.

Tap

Silence broken, then resumed.

Jane poked at her 1941 Royal Companion typewriter. She typed, stopped, sighed, tapped again, stopped, exhaled, puffed out her cheeks, looked around the Hut, clacked another key.

Earlier today, if *Here* even had a 'today' let alone an 'earlier,' Jane had explored and very nearly become entangled forever in the Forest. She'd teetered on a precipice but had fallen backwards instead of forwards.

The thought that she'd escaped an awful eternity by just seconds and inches scared the hell out of her.

Jane looked out of the window in front of her. *Here* stared back.

How many times have I explored? Was that the first, or just one of an infinity of repeat performances?

I could be centuries old without even realising. Or maybe just moments older than when I first arrived.

She'd been brought to this place to Watch The Snow, which, by some kind of minus centigrade magic, wiped away memories that could shatter her, never to be repaired.

And, *tap, tap, tap*, writing would filter and declaw those memories, then only allow them back at the exact moment when her mind - and yes, her soul - were strong enough to cope.

That was the theory, anyway, so she'd been Told.

She looked back at what she'd just typed.

It said;

*

"Here I am or, perhaps, I am Snowhere. I prefer "Here," if I'm honest. It's my favourite completely inexplicable name for this place. I'm going to concentrate on this white page instead of the white surroundings and think about snow, rather than look at it.

Snow, then. Unless you actually see snow fall - because you're asleep or busy, or busy sleeping, it's the best magic trick there ever was, or ever will be. Because it wasn't - and then it was. It wasn't - and then it was. If that isn't magic, then what is?

Remember those first seconds when you look out of the window on a frozen, white-out morning, or stare upward at the waves of those endless flakes, your primary emotion is never one of ambivalence, disappointment, or fear. It is always, always, wonder."

*

She sighed.

Hm. Going for the Booker, were you? And how exactly *do you intend to get your manuscript to the judging panel?*

Jane sneered at the page, and pulled it out of the typewriter.

A Burning for you. She crumpled up the paper and threw it into the small oven in the corner.

"'*Snowhere*'? Really?" She asked herself out loud. "When did you leave the sixth form, exactly?"

Jane looked at the empty Royal Companion and sighed again.

After writing, she was supposed to burn the pages if they brought back any memories, feelings, or hunches she wasn't ready for.

Or if the prose was dismal, obviously.

But one thing was clear - *Here* was a frosty clinic and writing was a test that would eventually decide when she was healed and ready to move on.

Aha, but move on where?

Jane reached up to her neck and absently rubbed the silver snowflake that hung there.

What she'd just written was of no help at all. No hints of who she really was, or coded broadcasts from the past. No clues to unravel.

Forget it, she thought, then inwardly laughed. *Oh, I can, can't I? That's why I'm Here. Bingo.*

Forget writing for now. Words aren't getting me anywhere.

So she took her hands from the typewriter and turned her attention to The Box.

How about you, then, Boxy? Anything to add, or just another mystery to add to Here's cavalcade of riddles, hm?

Since its discovery, The Box had sat on the desk next to Jane's Royal Companion, where it continued to un-nerve her for reasons she couldn't fathom.

The Box was just over a foot long and a little under a foot wide, around five inches deep, and made of a deep brown wood. But just like the Huts' odd construction, there were no nails or screws to hold it together. Solid and smooth, but made by no carpenter, or carpenter's son, the Box had two brass hinges on the lid, one tiny keyhole, but no key.

Of course. A key would have been too easy.

It posed her three questions; *Why was it there? Who put it under my bed? And, most importantly, what does it contain?*

But Jane wasn't sure she wanted to know the answers. She had a notion that once she did, things would move very quickly.

She stared at the Box. The Box regarded her.

Go on, girl, open me up, it asked, the same question which had goaded her with since whenever. *Go on, because whatever is inside me is your key to leaving this place, you* do *know that, don't you? I've got your passport in here, your papers, identity card, you can* travel *with what I have, yes, you can travel, they're all in here, just open me up. Go on.*

"I haven't got a key, you bugger," Jane said to The Box, but felt less confident than she sounded. "You know that, so stop winding me up."

Jane picked it up and once again The Box felt like something dangerous that might turn on her. She shook it side to side and felt something insubstantial slide in there. Whatever-that-was had no weight, but oh yes, oh goodness, it had terrible *mass*.

Jane had looked everywhere for the key to The Box, but her Hut wasn't exactly Hide And Seek Central. There weren't many places for concealment. So she'd resigned herself to one of three possibilities, in order of likelihood;

One/ The key to The Box will only be found when I'm supposed *to find it. One day, it'll be there in the lock, as if it had always been there and how did you miss it, Jane?*

Two/ The key is somewhere Here, but out there in the Snow, or in another Hut, both of which would make it impossible to find, even with eternity on my side.

Three/ There is no key and it's just a mistake. The Box was left under my bed accidentally ("lost property") and whoever the cleaners are, they forgot to take it. Ha, oh, the irony.

Options One and Two were likely, but option Three wasn't, not really.

But.

Wait.

Wait…

Oh, wait, now…

Wait, Jane, wait*.*

Hold on, stop. Wait. Think.

She stood up, looked around the Hut, then sat down on the edge of her bed.

Something pulsed in her understanding for a moment. An idea beat its wings, careered without direction, but was still an idea, none the less.

So Jane sat and thought on her single bed. Its clean, freshly pressed sheets were always turned down. Even moments after getting out, she would look back and they would be re-made. The first time, it scared her, but by the second, *ah, well, it's just A Self Making Bed, isn't it? The Three Bears could have done with those. It might have saved Goldilocks a lot of trouble.*

OK, alright. Think. On the day I arrived Here, I met The Man. He Told me the rules of Here and…

No, wait, wait, wait - he said something important in this room. But it didn't seem important at the time, did it? So I missed it, let it pass.

Think, Jane, think. You have kept that *moment for* this *moment. It's in your mind. Remember.*

What did you just think about The Box? Come on, one more time;
The Box is a mistake.

Yes. *That's it.*

But NO.

Why is the statement, "The Box is a mistake," *wrong? Because...*

The Box isn't *the mistake, is it?*

So, that first day, what did I think was *wrong here in this Hut?*

Something shouldn't be here, and I haven't spotted it. But I know it. I've always known it.

Jane thought, and yes, she remembered that very first day, Here.

I remember because I am supposed *to. Whatever happened then was imprinted on my mind. Here knew I would need it. So what did The Man say that was so important?*

The Man had said, amongst so much else...

What had he said?

Think, girl. Remember.

He said...

She spoke out loud. "The Man said, 'there'll be a reason it's Here, though, always is'."

Everything is Here for a reason, Jane thought.

So The Box is not *a mistake because, "everything is Here for a* reason*, always is.'"*

But he wasn't talking about The Box *that day, was he? No.*

What was the Man referring to that seemed like a mistake?

Something that didn't seem right? Something that shouldn't have been in this room?

Jane stood up, slowly. She looked round the Hut again and addressed it. "OK, let's play."

There's an Odd One Out Here, kids, an Odd Thing that shouldn't be in this room, but what is it, Jane? Find the Odd One Out and gold star! - you'll have all your answers.

The desk, typewriter, bed, oven, tap, no. They all have purpose.
The plates, cutlery, cups, no, all used for their function.

She opened the Larder/ Cupboard/Thing, a wondrous cabinet, full of foods Jane had loved since she was a child, never empty, always fully stocked with her favourites. Just as her bed self-made, this cupboard self-filled, from who knew where, or when?

She ran her finger along the shelves.

Baked Beans.

Findus Crispy Beef Pancakes.

Smash Mash.

Blue Top Milk.

Fish Fingers.

Sausages.

White Bread.

Marmite.

Raspberry Jam.

Ready Salted Crisps.

Vesta Curry.

Nesquik Chocolate Milk Powder.

Rice Krispies.

Wait.

Back.

Back, Jane.

There, see it? Where it's always been.

Marmite.

Ah, Marmite.

Jane hated Marmite.

Marmite. Oh dear, Marmite.

Marmite was the mistake.

And she remembered how, on that first day, she'd expressed surprise that Marmite - a foodstuff she despised - was there, and recalled how The Man had picked up the pot and said, "well, that's odd. There'll be a reason it's Here, though, always is."

There'll be a reason it's Here, though, always is.

"Oh," said Jane, softly. "Oh."

It was the, "oh," of someone who has finally seen a truth they should have spotted a long time ago.

The, "oh," of someone berating themselves for not becoming aware of it earlier.

The, "oh," of a woman who'd realised perhaps now she should be a tiny bit scared.

Jane reached in, picked up the pot and turned it over. Just Marmite, a sticky, sickly, brown, yeasty, salty nonsense she couldn't bear.

"Oh, so it's you," Jane said to the pot, which said nothing back, thank heavens.

There'll be a reason it's Here, though, always is, clattered back and forth in her mind.

Jane turned the lid, which resisted at first, but then spun, just three revolutions and loose. She shivered and opened it.

Inside lay the smooth, black surface of her hated vegetable spread. In the middle, like the head of a robot drowning in a sea of oil, a tiny silver dot.

"Oh," Jane repeated. Nothing else seemed appropriate.

She didn't want to, but had no choice, so reached in. Her long nails broke the surface of the Marmite and closed round something solid.

She pulled.

A key, of course, a tiny silver key.

Jane held it up. *Which door of Wonderland does this open, then Alice?* She rubbed the Marmite off onto the bed linen. It didn't matter. Any stain would be gone in seconds, but Jane felt she may not sleep in that bed today.

Or ever.

Part of her needed to open The Box, a lot of her didn't want to.

The key slid smoothly into the lock and there was no resistance, no tumblers fell or pins moved, just a smooth clockwise motion, and one single click.

The Box was open.

Jane waited - for what? - but she waited, certain that whatever was inside would change things.

Finally, she opened the lid and peered in.

Papers.

Of course they were papers, Jane supposed she'd always known, from the *sssh sssh* sound made as they slid inside, but part of her had hoped The Box would reveal something less prosaic. *At least Pandora got a show. All I get is a few papers.*

She pulled them out, stopped and stared at the first page.

On the paper, typewritten, it said;

*

"Let me try this, it may work. I write, I write to remember.

Remember, please try to remember.

Who am I? I am... Janssen (or is it Johnson?) I am <u>so</u> old now and I am Here, in this frozen place where apparently I have come by my own volition, although I do not remember giving such a permission.

But remembering is not encouraged, Here, is it?

Johnson, or Janssen. I'm not quite sure. How peculiar that I don't even remember my name. Johnson, a good English name, or Janssen, a good Scandinavian name?

Stop.

I'm not sure how long this diary will last in one piece. It may burn. It probably will. I think it usually does."

*

Janssen? Thought Jane.

Janssen, the old, old man who once lived Here, in one of the other huts?

She remembered Janssen, sort-of.

She recalled, through a fog, (or was it more like condensation?) of how they'd sat and talked of the Snow, regret and recollection, and wiping memories. *Yes, Janssen had been Here the longest*, she thought. *He had a feel for things.*

She glanced through the writing.

Was this his Diary? Has he written like I have written? To remember? But if it is his, why do I have it?

She looked through more of his pages, and came to this part;

*

"I remember...on old old face and a woman's face, reflected in the window, sitting together in this tiny space. Snow on the window. We watched the snow. Where?

There was talk of Norway? Yes Norway.

The War. Which War? The only War, yes.

We talked of a father, and soup.

Bad Bees? There it is again. Bad Bees and Chimneys.

I should stop.

No. Continue.

I should remember where, when and why and who. It's important."

*

What the hell*?* Thought Jane. *I have Janssen's diary from Here.*

Why have I got Janssen's diary? Why is it in The Box?

Who put them there? Janssen? The Man? But if he did, why hide them in The Box, under my bed?

The Box under my *bed, in* my *Hut?*

Why wasn't it in his *Hut?*

Did Janssen even have a Hut?

I'm scared.

What does this mean?

"What do you think it means, Jane?" Someone spoke from her right. She recognised the voice immediately.

She turned, and there he was, from no-where, ta-dah! Like magic. No, not *like* magic, the real thing. The Man leaned against the wall, still dressed as a North Sea Fisherman. Yellow oilskin, waders, neckerchief, scarf, the full dressing up box's worth. His beard was Jack Frost's, frozen solid. Tiny icy needles hung from his eyebrows and eyelashes. Wherever he'd arrived from had been colder than Here, if that were even possible, since Here was colder than the dark side of the galaxy.

"The Man!" She laughed in greeting, genuinely pleased to see him properly again. "Hello! Wow. Here you are! Good trick, that materialisation... mind reading thing."

He gave a little bow, with an Elizabethan flourish from his right hand. "One does one's best." He straightened up, but wasn't smiling.

And Jane remembered.

On the first day she'd appeared Here, The Man had said they'd meet just once again, when Jane's Aurora came to light her way out of this place.

Oh my god, she thought. *So this is it. Now is when I leave,* she realised. *The Man is here, so I must be going.*

"What do you think it means, Jane? The Box, those papers?"

From their one previous encounter, Jane knew The Man didn't like to spoon feed information. He preferred his...what? *Guests? Pupils? Patients?* to figure it out for themselves.

"I don't know. How could I? I don't know why Janssen's diary would be in The Box, in my Hut."

"Mm." He went over to the Larder/Cupboard/Thing. "Cup of tea?"

"No thanks," Jane replied, airily, as The Man picked out some teabags, mug and a bottle of full fat, blue top milk. As he did, she watched another bottle slide into view like a shadow, coloured itself in, then became solid. *Voila.* Milk replenished.

"You're not looking hard enough. Look harder."

Jane flicked through the pages. There was something about them. But what?

The Man sighed. "Sometimes if you want to find the beginning, you have to look at the end. And vice versa, I suppose."

"Oh good, another puzzle," she huffed. "I would have been really frustrated if you'd just spoken openly."

"It's not a puzzle." He started to boil up a pan of water on the stove. "It's an answer. No tea? Are you sure? English Breakfast?"

"No thanks." She shuffled through the pages.

Jane found the end of Janssen's diary section and read aloud.

*

"The name is Johnson or Janssen and the reflection in that window before says old. How old? The reflection won't say. There I am, in the window.

Reflected. Twisted. There, in the reflection is Johnson. Or Janssen.

That may be vague but it is what I know. I have at least pared the possibilities of a name down to two. That is a victory, Here.

Ah, this isn't good? Why am I writing this? Why am I fixating about whether it is Johnson or Janssen? Maybe I shouldn't bother. Put it away, hide it away, stick to who I really am, whoever that is."

*

Jane looked back at The Man. "Yes? What? I don't see…"

"You don't see because you're not looking."

Something started to uncoil in Jane's mind.

She felt them now, the memories. Not quite in view yet, but they gathered on her horizon, silhouettes that shuffled from side to side and waited to be called forward.

"What do you see?" asked The Man, as he stirred the boiling water idly, unconcerned.

"I see…" Words and phrases on the pages shimmered, focussed and jumped out to her.

*

"Let me try this,"/"why am I writing this?"/"There I am, in the window,"/"put it away, stick to who I AM."

*

Jane felt it, the end, the beginning, the everything, as it approached.

"I can see…Oh god…what can I see?"

"Look at the whole thing, Jane, the whole thing." He poured hot water into the West Ham United Mug.

Jane stared at the pages, riffled them, beginning to end, and back again, not looking at the words this time, not really, but their shape, layout, style, and most importantly, their font.

"These were written on a 1941 Royal Companion. I know the font," she said, quietly, as the blocks began to drop into their pre-arranged places. "*There I am in the window,*" she read, and almost moaned as the origin of those words returned. "'*An old face and a woman's face*'…I see, I think I see, I *can't* see, what do I see? I'm in the window. Oh god. It's me. *It's my reflection.* With an old man? '*Put it away, stick to who I AM*'…I see…" and Jane finally saw herself, as she returned from the blizzard of snow that had encircled her memory.

"I put these papers away, didn't I? I hid them in The Box. Oh, this is the font of a Royal Companion. *My* Royal Companion."

Jane glanced at her typewriter.

Oh, you've been used a lot more than I remember. Oh, Mr Royal, you've been a very busy boy and I've been a very busy girl.

"I wrote these papers in The Box. I did, didn't I?"

The Man nodded, and sipped at his tea.

"But why didn't I burn them? What are they?"

"They are the key, Jane. These pages are the key that will unlock why you are Here. That's why you never burned them. You locked them away, ready for this moment. Because you knew they would set you free. You wrote them the very first day you were Here. But you didn't burn them. They were too important. You knew that, but didn't know why. They scared you, because they were too close. The Box was in this Hut when you arrived, remember now? Right there, on the desk. So you put the papers away and hid the key where you would never ever look and hid the Box, Watched The Snow and wiped away all memory of them. Until you were ready. Until now, this moment."

Memories, like the Aurora, clouded into Jane's head, formed patterns; A man, a tap, a cigarette. The pictures warped, weaved and gained a little clarity. *Cigarettes, snow, a roast dinner, snow, a knife. Snow. I flew. I flew and I killed.*

"But Janssen? The old man Janssen is real. I know it. I didn't make him up. Janssen..or Johnson…was Here. He was an old man, and he was Here."

"No. And …yes… Janssen was real, but he was never Here. Janssen was the last person you spoke to before…when you were…There… Janssen was the last person you spoke with, before you woke up, Here. You knew that. Because the memories of him were still fresh even after you arrived. Covered by the Snow, but there, none the less."

Jane's eyes looked around wildly, not at the room, but inside herself, searching for a man called Janssen, and where she had met him.

The Man continued. "Janssen was never Here. But you knew you'd spent time with him, knew he was important. So you went looking for him in your memory. You wrote his diary, based on fragments of the one conversation you remembered you'd had with him. You wrote and pretended to *be* him, to find him, and in doing so, you would find yourself. But you weren't ready, not then. You had to grow stronger before you could truly recall that meeting. But where was that conversation, Jane?"

Jane searched, and the memories packed together, re-assembled themselves piece by piece. Images built up as the scaffolding of Jane bolted itself back together.

"If you remember exactly where and when you met Janssen, you are truly Jane again."

He put his mug down and stepped forward, then held her in his long, strong arms,

"And you are ready, Jane, trust me, let them come. *Here* has done its work now. You will not crumble or crack, you will face those memories down and see them for what they are. You can see your life again, and why you were put Here, to forget. Look, my dear, look inside yourself. You are ready now. All the Kings Horses, Jane. They did it this time. They put you together again."

Jane looked, she was strong, she was ready and now;

Now

In the time between seconds, in the moment between Planck times, that's all it took.

No lag, no latency, no catching up, all here, all *now*.

She remembered everything.

She remembered the life, day, hours, seconds that put her Here, and exactly where she'd met Janssen.

She folded down onto the bed. The Man went with her too, holding on as she collapsed into herself.

A shifting green and red light filled The Hut.

Jane's Aurora started to dance in the sky, ready to light her way out of Here.

Jane held The Man. She was ready, she remembered, and was strong, but still her eyes ran with tears.

"Remember what I said, Jane?" The Man's voice was soft in her ear as she wept on his shoulder. "Your Aurora would come next time we met. This is that time. It has come and now you are ready to leave, no, you *must* leave. And it is time to decide which path to take, North Or South."

Jane held The Man as the memories, good and bad, ran backward and forward inside her.

"And you know this - the path you take depends on Love. Ready?"

BOOK SEVEN / HERE, THERE, EVERYWHERE / CONVERGENCES

36 / December 22nd, 2003

In a frozen clearing called *Here*, Jane remembered.

The memories arrived, fully formed, in one solid wave. As they crashed through her, she tumbled in their currents and let herself be carried down into the deepest of deep ends.

Now Jane knew why she'd been brought Here to forget, remembered what she'd chosen to wipe from her memory. If she hadn't become strong again, Jane could have spent eternity *Here*, in warm, protective ignorance. But eternity had been put on hold.

One terrible day had returned to her, with ghastly clarity.

Jane couldn't have known everything that happened. Certain events took place outside her life, but still collided with it over a few short hours.

I will now draw the threads together, so you can see the whole picture, rather than just the parts she observed.

So take my hand, trust me, and let's jump in again.

We must be with Jane. She needs us. We've come this far together, so we owe her just one more day.

December 22nd, 2003.

Jump with me again. This is where we are, and this is how it works.

Come. Jane needs us. Come with me, to *now*.

37 / A Flat In Cricklewood, North West London / 7:30 A.M. / 22nd December

Snow had started to fall over London and the South East. The Weather Centre had predicted a light dusting, but they were way off. Today, English snow would rush to ground, like it had a purpose. It rarely visited the South East, but today, snow made up for lost time.

This morning, in Cricklewood, London, a man named Paul Jiggens reached over and turned off his alarm. Last night, he'd had - from what he later recalled through the white light of a nauseating hangover - a no-going-back argument with his girlfriend, Julie Markham.

Accusations had been lobbed, insults fired back and forth. She'd realised he was never going to play for Chelsea, the team. He'd squealed that she'd never be allowed in Chelsea, the *borough*.

Julie stormed out, followed soon after by Paul in search of further alcohol, which he'd found at 'Booze Cruise,' and from there, who knew? Paul Jiggens didn't.

But by 7:30 am, a time that should never exist after that much drink, Paul switched off his alarm, and even though part of him knew he had to be on the road by nine, the rest didn't care.

So he dropped back into the poisoned non-sleep of the morning after, and his body shut down to repair itself.

Paul Jiggens had a job to do, but today, of all days, he failed to get in his van, with its tools, keys and boxes of cigarettes.

Paul claimed to be an 'Engineer,' so he said.

He filled cigarette machines, so the truth said.

He slept.

As Paul rolled over in bed, he had no idea of the consequences of that decision, and never would.

38 / 10:30 A.M. / 22nd December / A Terraced House in Bow, East London

Jane and her father had late breakfasts at weekends, a joyously unapologetic artery-clogging fry up of sausages, bacon, fried bread, mushrooms and black pudding. Dave called them "Kamikaze Breakfasts," and often shouted, "Tora! Tora! Tora!" as he went in for the first banger.

2003 was almost over and it had been a good, no, a *great* year for Jane.

Yes, she still had her dead end job at The Reflex, but change was on the way in 2004, and for the better.

Dad had offered to sell the family home and buy two small flats, one for himself, one for his daughter. That freedom would give Jane time to finally devote herself to writing. It was all she'd ever wanted to do, make words appear from no-where, to see where the *click* and *clatter*, the *tap, tap, tap* would take her.

Jane's very first typewriter, her beloved 1941 Royal companion, still sat on a shelf in their living room. She used it, occasionally. There was something about the Royal her laptop couldn't compete with. The typewriter was warm and avuncular, while her laptop fizzed and crackled. The Companion seemed frozen in the act of laughter, while her computer appeared to be disdainful of anything other than business.

Jane stared out of the window at the snow. It had already settled on roofs and gardens, but hadn't reached an intensity sufficient to overcome traffic and cover roads.

Not yet. That would come.

Dad sat and read The Mirror newspaper over his plate. Jane smiled at him, lost in the pages.

They'd been through a lot together. Despite many failed attempts to move in with many failed boys in many failed relationships, she'd always rebounded back to Bow, Home, Dad.

Previous boyfriends had never really got off the starting blocks - well, they hadn't even put their running shoes on, let alone made it to the track.

But in glorious 2003, Jane had met Simon, and my word, they'd both run from almost that first moment, sprinted together, like nothing she'd ever known before.

*

"WhooOoooooh, look, ghost in Hampton Court." David put on a creepy voice and held up the paper so Jane could see the headline, "COURT ON CAMERA."

It was CCTV footage of what could have been a bunch of branches that approximated a figure, or - perhaps - a man in a thick coat with fur trim.

"I love a ghost story at Christmas. Who doesn't?"

Jane looked at the photo closely. "Weird. You don't believe in ghosts, do you?"

"Hm," he grunted. "I've never said that. I've said I'm not sure ghosts are the dead. Perhaps they're something else."

Jane continued to look at the picture. There was something quite creepy about it. This ghost - or-whatever it was - seemed to stride out of the courtyard door like it was going places.

"So, Mystic Meg, if they're not the dead, what are they?"

"Don't know," he shrugged, and took the paper back. "Echoes? Souls out of time? Reflections of the future? A look at something that's just passing through?"

Something about the way her Dad spoke so matter-of-factly made Jane stop and consider him more carefully.

"Have you ever seen a ghost, Dad?"

"No," he replied, unequivocally. "I've never seen a ghost."

Ah, but you have, you liar, she studied his not-quite-poker face. *You have, and you're not telling me. You're using semantics, you've seen something, Dad of mine, I know you too well. Something you've been keeping.*

"Well. You tell me when you're ready."

He looked up at her again. "Tell you what? Nothing to tell."

"OK." She smiled, thought, *what isn't he telling me and why?* Then changed the subject. "Oh, The Hoop. Yeah. Christmas Menu. Yum-yum. Me and Simon are going to go for a roast at lunchtime."

"Simon and I." He muttered, automatically. "After all that?" He nodded at the almost empty plate of breakfast.

"Well, late lunch, then. Mid-afternoon Lunch. Party hats, streamers. Turkey, Chicken, Beef or some veggie thing. Fancy it?"

"I couldn't eat anything. Well, until teatime, I suppose."

"You love their Christmas Roast, Dad."

"I think their Roast is alright. Mine is better. Crispier potatoes for starters."

David was tempted, of course he was. A few pints, a nice hot roast, his daughter, oh, every box was ticked. But no. He couldn't be at Jane's side every time, although she wasn't easy to refuse, so he made up an excuse on the spot.

As you and I have always known, big changes are often birthed from tiny decisions.

"Actually, I'm going to Southend today."

Until two seconds ago, he'd no intention of going anywhere, let alone Southend On Sea, Essex. But the lie happily tripped off his tongue, and surprised him as it did.

"Southend? By yourself? In this?" She pointed out the back window. "When did you decide that?"

"Oh, I've been thinking about it for a while," he lied. But the lie started to seem tempting as he embellished it. "Yeah. Go back to the old stomping ground. Pint at The Railway, bracing stroll down the prom, quick one at The Cornucopia, then up the pier."

"By yourself, though? Why can't you go next week? After Christmas? We'll come."

"Jane," he sighed, put down his paper. "Be with Simon, by yourselves. I just fancied a trip out for the afternoon. God, it's only forty-five minutes down the road. I'm not going to another planet."

"I'd love to go down - or is it up?- the pier with you, though."

"Next week. We'll go together, maybe for New Years, mm? And trust me, I'll be at The Hoop later. May even eat then. But today, I fancy Southend. I do, actually. There's nothing quite like a seaside town in winter. Seaside towns aren't dressed for snow, that's what makes them so magical when it hits."

"OK." Jane was disappointed. It had been a long time since she'd visited Southend with Dad, and the thought of him going alone felt like - well, not a betrayal, that was too strong - but rather like they should all be together today. It was almost Christmas.

But she let it go.

Jane picked up her empty plate and started toward the kitchen.

"Sure?"

"Postive."

And so it was.

39 / There / 12:15 P.M. / 22nd December / A One Bedroom Flat, Whitechapel

Just after mid-day, a man called Mark Griffiths surfaced, but it took an effort.

Last night, he'd drunk a lot, taken a lot, staggered 'home,' then fallen onto his stained mattress, still fully clothed. In the flat next door, he heard shouting. Below, a TV ran full blast. Above, the steady 120BPM thump of some dark trance.

He hated the DJ who lived upstairs, the people who shouted next door, the deaf old bitch downstairs who couldn't hear her telly. Hating took no effort. Mark Griffiths had an unlimited supply.

As yet, he hadn't acted on any of his hates, apart from a few fights with little *gangstas* who'd puffed themselves up, never backed down, demanded maximum respect. He'd showed them who deserved respect.

Mark Griffiths rose to any occasion that promised trouble, because he simply didn't care. People sensed it, crossed roads to avoid him. He never once considered the consequences of his actions, and that was what made him dangerous. He carried an atmosphere that crackled with negative potential. One day - it was inevitable - Mark Griffiths would do something extremely stupid and very violent.

He sat up on his dirty bed and lit a crumpled cigarette. In the corner stood a half finished litre bottle of cider. He considered it, but wouldn't go there just yet. In half an hour, he'd start the same day over again.

Repeat, repeat, re-*fucking*-peat. I'd like to say Mark had no choice in any of this, that he was a victim of his parents *and* his life, which had conspired to put him on this path, but everyone has choices, however small. You might not be able to choose a bigger bank account or a better job, but you can choose *not* to visit your own bitterness and anger on others. Sadly, that was not a concept Mark entertained.

So, here he was.

Usually, it took Mark some time to reach terminal velocity, but today, he hit the ground locked and loaded.

Last night, there'd been exchanges with *some bloke* which had put him in a vengeful mood. Since he couldn't do anything to that *bloke* - his brothers were well known in the area, there were three of them and he was just one Mark Griffiths - the need to purge that anger had to be sated.

Mark sat on his mattress.

He sat, smoked, and seethed.

Mark would go out today. The snow weaved outside his window, but held no magic for him. He had enough cash to buy a few in a pub somewhere, get something to eat, maybe later steal some booze from the offie.

He started this day in a state of trance and venom. He would end it smashing his head against a wall.

40 / There / 12:30 P.M. / 22nd December / Bow, London.

David had dressed for his afternoon trip to Southend On Sea, in shirt, tie, comfy trousers, sensible shoes and thick coat. He intended to get the bus to Fenchurch Street station, and from there, by two o'clock, straight off the train, down Southend High Street and onto the Prom.

Jane came down the stairs wearing the green cotton blouse and short skirt she'd received for her birthday, a thick black cardigan and black flats. She'd tucked her purse into one cardigan pocket, with a packet of Benson and Hedges wedged into the other.

Dad pulled a face.

"Nice outfit, but have you seen it out there? You're not dressed for snow. You'll die."

"No, I'll be either on the bus, in the Hoop, or in a taxi. I'll be fine. I'm not going *outside*, outside, really. Ooh, you look smart."

"When you have a date with Southend pier, you have to dress up for the old girl."

"Nice."

"You will freeze, Jane. It's December, and snowing like I haven't seen since…"

And when was that *since*? Dave didn't think too long. December 1979. It had snowed like this then, when, well, you know what happened that day.

"I'll be fine, Dad, don't worry. Hot roast and beer, natural insulation."

"Come on, then, Miss Shackleton."

They let themselves out and stood on the step. Dave bent to kiss Jane on the top of her head, as he'd always done since she was so tall.

"Love you," he said.

"Love you, too."

"Be quick, that skirt's really not made for this weather. See you."

Dave looked his daughter up and down again, and took in her inappropriate outfit. He scrunched his eyes up in thought, remembering something, then shook his head to clear it.

He smiled and went one way, as Jane walked the other.

She looked back over her shoulder, but he turned the corner and was gone.

41 / There / 13:10 P.M. / 22nd December / The Hoop & Grapes Pub, Aldgate

Jane walked into The Hoop, shoulders and hair woven with snowflakes. She clocked other regulars, gave a little nod here, little wave there.

A fire burned in the hearth by the bar. There weren't many customers - it was a little early after the revelries of the previous night.

The Hoop & Grapes was where David met Irene. They'd courted and partied here, taken the coach from the next road off on adventures in Southend, spent endless evenings sat at the bay window table, and happy weekends as little Jane ran around the pub like it was her own sticky-floored playground.

As ever, Jill the barmaid waited. Jane thought she may have been there since the dawn of time. She was either a very ruined forty, a well preserved sixty-five, or maybe one thousand. Since Jill always wore a thick mask of make up, Jane couldn't tell.

"Hi Jill, you alright?"

"Been better, been worse," Jill muttered, her standard reply.

"Wonderful. Right then, to business, first, the preliminaries. Merry Christmas." Jane bowed, picked up a party hat from the bar and put it on.

Jill replied with world weary amusement. "Yeah, so here it is, Merry Christmas."

"Thankyou, as ever, for your festive spirit. Noddy Holder would be proud. Lovely. Right, I'm meeting Simon any moment. " She looked over her shoulder at the pub door, which stayed closed. "And we are going to treat ourselves to your famous Christmas Roast. Two turkey, all the trimmings, whatever trimmings are, you know, I've never worked that out and two..." Jane squinted up at the hand drawn sign behind the bar. "Two Festive Pints. Wow. That's new. That's exciting. What's a Festive Pint?"

"It's a pint, of your choice," replied Jill, laconically. "With some tinsel round it."

"Of course it is," laughed Jane. "Brilliant, two of them. Foster's. And the Christmas Roasts."

"Ah," Jill frowned as she poured the first beer. "Bad news there. Kitchen flooded this morning. Tap went all wrong. Sink overflowed. Nasty. No Roasts till tomorrow at least. May even be Tuesday."

"Flood? What? Flood? Roast? Tuesday? No," Jane stammered, reduced to a stream of apparently random words.

Jill had more bad news. "And that's not all," she pointedly looked at Jane's packet of B&H on the bar. "Hope you're stocked up. Paul, the bloke that's supposed to fill the fag machine didn't come today. So, got no fags."

"What?" Jane had become weirdly close to being outraged. "What do you mean he 'didn't turn up'?"

"The company's been calling him since first thing, but he's not answering. So; no Roast, no fags. But…" She tied some tinsel round the pint glasses. "Hooray. Peace on earth, pah-rup-a-pom-pom, two Festive Pints. £4.00."

"That's something, I suppose," Jane conceded, sardonically. "It's the tinsel that really makes them."

"Ooh, nice pair of pints," Simon spoke from behind her, having apparently materialised from no-where.

Jane turned and grabbed him, delighted. "How do you do that, Doctor Who?"

"I bend space and time. Have you ordered the roasts? I am Hank bloody Marvin here."

"No roasts," Jill monotoned, with a worrying amount of relish.

"No *roasts*?" Simon said in the same incredulous tone of voice you'd use for, "what, *war's* broken out?".

"I've been through this," Jane sighed. "Kitchen's flooded."

"Kitchen's flooded?" Simon moaned, aghast.

"Tap went. Kitchen flooded." Jill droned, then offered more unwanted detail. "And the fag machine is empty too. The bloke didn't turn up. Paul, the one who fills the machine. Bloody liberty. He didn't turn up. That's £4.00 for the drinks."

"No roast, no fags," moaned Jane.

"Well, fags aren't exactly a priority," said Simon. "This isn't the middle of no-where. There's a Spar up the road. This is London, remember? There will be cigarettes. Just not in here."

"Gah," squawked Jane. "I'm going to starve. And gasp."

"You can get food from outside and bring it back. You have my permission," Jill said, expansively. "I'll even give you a plate and cutlery."

"Oh, thanks," Jane sulked. "Because I hate using my fingers to eat food off my lap. But I wanted a roast and all those *hundreds* of Christmas Roast Takeaways we have round here are all shut."

"I'll get you a festive kebab," offered Simon. "I'll stick some Paxo on it."

"No roast, no fags," mumbled Jane. "Perfect. Happy bloody Christmas."

42 / There / 14:00 P.M. / 22nd December / Seafront, Southend On Sea

Dave walked up Southend pier.

He could have taken the train, but that would have been missing the point. If you're visiting The Longest Pleasure Pier In The World, you don't cheat, you walk it.

He leaned into the snow, which had become heavier since he'd left the mainland. *This was probably a bad idea*, he thought, *The Hoop seems very welcoming now.* He closed his eyes against the wind.

At over a mile long, Southend pier is an outpost of Essex which extends out into the Thames.

Dave knew that out there somewhere, in the silt and sludge of the Estuary bed, lay the SS Richard Montgomery. Sunk in 1944, it still contained over one thousand tons of high explosive. The Montgomery's back was broken in the sinking, and it rested there, home to a cargo that waited for a combination of factors that could yet send the ship skyward. Collision, erosion, even a shift of the sands and part of World War Two could make a late, unscheduled re-appearance.

Dave looked in the direction of Sheerness, where the Montgomery's masts could still be seen at low tide. For sixty years it had bided its time, a ship full of bombs, ready to see if events would play out with a bang, or a whimper. A little piece of a war that could still resume hostilities.

Funny how the past can rise up and bite you, Dave thought. But then, from long inside and deep away, five words rose into his mind.

She wasn't dressed for snow.

He shook his head as if to clear the thought - *why did Jane's clothes matter?* - but the words wouldn't move.

What have I seen? What have I seen today? What should I remember? Something about Jane. What was it? What have I seen? It is important, so very important.

Something about Jane, not dressed for snow. Yes, I saw she wasn't dressed for snow didn't I, but it didn't mean anything to me, not then. It matters now.

Oh, God. Yes. It was that skirt, that blouse. Oh God.
An outfit for a sunny day, but not for snow. I saw. Yes.
Jane.

Oh, God, Jane.
It happened. It was...
I saw, I remember. That skirt, that blouse. Yes, I saw, that much I know.
I didn't know then *but now I do.*
Oh God, I shouldn't be here.

The realisation came to him fully formed, with no advance warning.
I should not *be here.*

Dave felt the pull and push of something out of his control. He shuddered, but not because of the cold. He shuddered as waves passed through him, white horses that crested on their way to - where?

They rushed through David and he could almost see them, as they spread back along the Essex coast, toward London.

He put his hand on his chest, where those surges pulled and rippled his heart. It beat out of sync for a moment, an unpleasant feeling, as his ticker tried to regain its natural rhythm. It fought against whatever it was that rolled through him.

Dave stared back down the coast, to London, to his daughter.

If he hurried, no, rushed, no, *flew,* he could get back before - what? - but those other waves, the ones that dragged the rolling snow with them, couldn't be outraced. He started back down the pier as fast as could, but his legs and heart wouldn't let him jog.

The pier train passed him, and Dave knew he was over a mile out. But he was further than that. This wasn't just distance, it was also about time, and he was further out than he could have possibly imagined.

He was on solid ground, but also a man overboard.

Jane, he puffed, scared, and heard his heart beat out her name, *Jane-Jane, Jane-Jane, my -Jane.*

43 / There / 14:30 P.M. / 22nd December / The Hoop & Grapes Pub, Aldgate

Jane and Simon started on their third Festive Pints of the day, silly party hats forgotten on their heads.

"I really, *really* want a Christmas roast," she looped round to the subject, again.

"I know, you may have mentioned it, actually. Shall we go looking? It's not like The Hoop is the only pub in the City. We could find a roast, bet you."

"Hmph," Jane actually *hmph'd*. "I wanted one here. It's snowing, perfect for a roast. And besides, other people will be here soon. Dad's probably on his way by now, freezing cold, bored of Southend. If we go somewhere else, then he won't know where. god, I wish he had a phone. Let's wait for our friends. Maybe you can get me a kebab after all. I'll fade away if I don't eat anything."

"OK, in a bit."

Jane reached into her cardigan, hung on the back of the chair. She opened her pack of B&H and then literally wailed. "Oh, aaah, god!" She moaned, drama queen. "I've only got one left. And the bloody machine's empty."

"Come on," Simon put on a deep brown Hollywood voice. "We can beat this, you and I. I swear, if I have to walk this city like Captain Oates, I will hunt down some B&H for you. I will go for a walk. I may be some time."

"And a kebab," Jane reminded him. "A Christmas kebab."

"B&H and a Kebab. A Christmas kebab. What is that? Do you want it in a Yorkshire pudding, or something? With gravy?"

"You know, that actually sounds like a bloody good idea. Write it down. We'll do it next year. Kristmas Kebabs, you know, spelled with crazy K's. Santa Shish!" Jane bounced in her seat as she warmed to the theme. "Ooh, Doner and Blitzen Doners. Chilly Chilli sauce. Chilli spelled 'c.h.i.l.l.y.' you know, 'cos of the snow."

"I may not have done English, *Lit and Lang*, but I did pick up on that."

"And I could dress as an elf with a pitta bread for a hat."

"It's your classiness that makes you so attractive."

She threw the pack at his head.

"Alright, alright, I'll go and get your nasty fags and greasy meat. But only if you rise to a challenge."

Jane put her head face down onto the table. "Oh, blah. What kind of challenge?"

"Your challenge, my dear, is to describe life as simply as you can...In ten words or less, obviously. "

Jane looked up and pulled a sullen six year old's expression. "This? Now? You want to do the ten words now? Wait, what? Describe life? Like, actual *life*? Describe life in ten words? Oh, come on. That's too big."

Simon shook his head. "We had to do it eventually. Come on - life, in ten words, or less. You know the deal."

Jane sat back in her chair and stared at the ceiling, annoyed.

"Oh, easy, then. Life? OK. Wait, give me a moment. OK... 'It started with...' No, wait. 'It began...' ah...Oh, balls."

Simon waited. "Do I have time to get a drink? In fact, do I have time to read Tolstoy? Oh, I need to borrow some money, actually."

Jane tilted her head left to right as she mentally tried out combinations of words before they settled and fitted together in a way she was happy with.

"No. I've got it. Life? Alright, smart arse. Try this. Yes." She counted the words on her fingers,."'*It began, this happened, that happened and then ...it... ended.*' Ta-dah. Back of the net. Dawn scores, some of the crowd are on the pitch, they think it's all over. It is fucking now. There you go. Life. In ten words. Done. That's about as simple as you can get, right? "

"Yes, but it's wrong."

Jane, who normally enjoyed The Ten Word Game, found herself become impatient, thanks to hunger and nicotine addiction.

"Oh, really? What's wrong with, 'it began, this happened, that happened and then it ended'"?

"It's linear!" He laughed.

"Of course it's linear!" She countered. "Life is linear! That's how it works! Life goes from point to point, A to Z! You plant a seed, a flower grows, it doesn't shrink back into a seed! Kids turn into adults, who then don't suddenly decide to lose some *age* and go back to primary school for a laugh. Agh, can I get another drink? Come on, fags, drink and a kebab. That's linear. I'm thirsty, I'm hungry, I'm gasping, soon I won't be. Linear."

"Well, if that's what you think..."

"We can discuss theo-bloody-retical physics all you like when you stick a large greasy disgusting doner in front of me *tout suite.*"

By now, Jane was desperate for chilli sauce and the cool, smooth taste of burning poisons. "So please, enough. Fags, kebab, chop chop."

Simon patted his pockets. "Give us your purse then, I forgot my card."

Jane waved her hands in the air like an angry muppet. "Oh, come *on*! Here, take it, take it all." She threw her purse and cards at him.

She still had £10 in her skirt pocket.

Things would have turned out very different if she'd realised that fact.

Simon picked up the purse and stood.

"OK. While I'm on the kebab and fag run - ten words; death. Death follows life according to you, Miss Linear- so go on, death, described in ten words. Or less. Off you go."

"Oh, for *fuck's* sake. Tell you what, shall I nip home and get my typewriter while we're at it? I can write up a document for you, buy some carbon paper, maybe do it in triplicate, since clearly now I'm your secretary."

"That won't be necessary, Miss Dawn. Just death, in ten words or less. Have it on my desk by four."

She thudded her head back on the table, and gave out a muffled, "gaaah."

Simon winked at her, a wink she never saw, and started to leave.

Far away, a gossamer thought floated through Jane's mind for the briefest of moments.

Stay, Simon. Won't you stay? Just for a while. Not too long. Enough. Just stay with me. Only moments. Moments will do.

But it was too far and too fragile to register.

"Back in a bit, then."

"Yes, yes, course you'll be," replied Jane, but didn't look up. "Everyone's 'back in a bit'."

44 / There / 14:40 P.M. / 22nd December / Abrakebabra Kebab House, Aldgate

A girl, a life, a death, a meeting in a garden, a dripping tap and an empty cigarette machine led Simon to here and now. Yes, let us head into what is known as *real time*. This day, this hour, this moment.

No jumping, no side steps, no bending the clocks, you are about to experience *now* as it happens.

I have no choice. We must see this in the present tense.

*

Simon had taken £20 out of Jane's cashpoint (they know each other's pin numbers, naturally) and bought twenty B&H.

He walks down Aldgate High Street toward the kebab shop, but stops, abruptly. His eyes widen.

A strange thought flickers in his mind, waves at him for attention. It was something Jane had just said, back in The Hoop. Something he'd once seen, back in time.

He frowns. This suddenly feels very important.

What did Jane say? Was it the ten words about life? Or the kebab shop? Christmas?

No, no.

He rubs his eyes, thinks, then it comes to him, all in a rush.

"Shall I nip home and get my typewriter?" She'd asked. Simon pictured it back there, on a shelf in Jane's living room, that very old, much-loved typewriter, a Royal something-or-other.

"No way," he mutters to himself, shakes his head. No *way*.

He remembered that first meeting with Dave, back in March. That particular afternoon was difficult to forget. Jane's Dad had gone extremely weird for the first and only time, but before that, she'd gently tapped the keys of her typewriter and told him it was one of the few Christmas presents she'd kept from when she was a child.

No way.

Simon was studying psychology, in tribute to, and memory of, his Father. He still had many of Dad's more interesting case studies to consult. The names and addresses were redacted, but the content was detailed. One involved a little girl who'd forgotten her parents after an accident, then recalled them one Christmas Day when she'd received a gift of…an old typewriter.

No, no way.

That case dated to the late Seventies. Jane's age worked. She would have been, what, five? Six?

Surely not. The chances of him meeting, and then falling *in love with,* one of his Dad's cases must be astronomical.

Simon looks down the road, back at the pub. He takes a step toward it.

I'll find some casual way to ask about the typewriter, he thinks. *I'll work round to times in hospital, accidents we've had, who wins the Most Hideous Injury Prize, make it seem like another game.*

He takes another step as the snow dances about, pushing him on, pulling him back.

She's never mentioned it. Oh, and Jane would. *She'd never keep a Big Story like that to herself. If that particular case* was *her, of course.*

And then he realises;

If it is *her, oh my God, she doesn't know, does she? Dave never told her. She would have* forgotten *she* forgot. *She forgot her parents, remembered them again, and the grey time in-between was spliced clean out of her memory.*

He takes another step toward The Hoop. Stops again.

If she is that girl, what would happen if I unlocked that part of her life again? What might it do to her? How would she react? What would she think of her Dad, then, if he'd kept such a huge event in her past a secret?

Simon runs a hand through his snow-speckled hair.

I have to find out. But…

Then he turns and heads back in the other direction.

…But if I turn up kebab-less, there will be hell to pay. It can wait. Everything can wait. But if we were *connected, somehow, even before we met, her past and my Dad, then…*

Then what?

...Then we were always *supposed to be together. From even before we knew each other.*

Simon smiles, whiter and brighter than the snow itself, puts his head down and walks on.

*

Now he stands in a surprisingly busy Abrakebabra Takeaway.

Simon's head is reeling. He forces himself to think about kebabs. Sane, safe, predictable kebabs.

Considering it is almost mid afternoon, kebabs are very popular today.

It must be all that Christmas shopping, but no, Simon thought, *we are kebab Customers, we eat sliced greasy meat days before Santa arrives, on an afternoon where the snow is now falling as thick as static on a '70s TV. As Pulp once said, 'This Is Hardcore.' We kebab eaters don't do facile stuff like Christmas Shopping, we drink chilli sauce.*

So he stands and thinks and waits for the next two minutes without even knowing he is waiting.

Because we've established that, in retrospect, big events aren't always given the time they deserve. Not every moment gets fireworks, buzzers, bells and dancing girls when the world - or at least somebody's world - changes. Some momentous moments barely register.

Simon doesn't know it, but one of the biggest events of his life is about to happen. Bigger than meeting Jane, even.

And it happens so quickly, I will barely keep up, so forgive me. I can try to break it down as much as possible, but unless we start heading into the times between time, there's not much else I can say.

Simon is not an aggressive man who enjoys confrontation. In fact, he has an internal, highly tuned radar which could always pick up trouble way before it started. He'd walk into a pub, spot the potential hot spots and hot heads, then leave before they even noticed him. But in the past, he *had* been noticed. He just hadn't realised, that time.

The door of the kebab Shop opens, with a camp ting-a-ling of the bell.

What a ridiculous precursor, no dramatic chords of A Big Entrance, but the *ding, ding-ding* of Tinkerbell, or Noddy.

Mark Griffiths, full of a litre of cider, other substances, and who knows how much hate, falls into the kebab Shop. He staggers, looks around, takes in the potential for violence. Eyes turn to him, but glance away just as quickly. Don't lock with him, don't engage. Punters, without thinking, part from Mark, antelope from lion, and he stares down each of them, daring, challenging. Everyone knows the thoughts that rush behind those seemingly dead eyes.

Come and have a go come and have a fucking go come come come come and have a go go go now now.

"Large doner. Now," he shouts across the queue, pushes through it.

A few customers give out of half hearted, "oy"'s and, "watch it"'s but no-one confronts him with any real commitment. They know they're in a cage with something wild, where the best course of action is to make yourself invisible, then get out.

Mark Griffiths stares round at the other customers, who have found that the walls, floor and ceiling are suddenly fascinating.

Simon, however, has had a few pints and is innately a fair man.

He doesn't know Mark Griffiths, hasn't been introduced as you have, but Simon knows what Mark *is*. He's seen many Mark Griffiths's before, throughout his life. Yes, he's dealt with Mark Griffiths in playgrounds, workplaces, bus queues and bars, and Mark Griffiths is always the same person.

Mark Griffiths is a bully. And you can either let the bullies think they are in charge, or you can call them out.

So Simon decides - as quick as you read the next four words - to call him out.

But this is the wrong decision, at the wrong time, on the wrong day.

Perhaps yesterday, Mark Griffiths may have shouted, then stormed off, but not today. Today, *now*, is when he is finally ready to do something incredibly stupid and extremely violent.

He's been preparing for this moment since he was a child. Perhaps, deep down, he even knew that today was the day. Why else had he picked up the short, serrated blade from the kitchen table, then turned it over in his hand? For a second, he'd even wondered whether to leave it behind.

But maybe history, fate, time or the broken tracks of his life demanded that one, that only decision.

So he'd pocketed the blade, and now here he is.

"Excuse me," says Simon, ever polite. "But there is a queue."

Mark Griffiths turns round, and at that moment, Simon knows he's misjudged this situation badly. This was not someone you said, "excuse me," to, let alone, "but there is a queue".

This was a person who's against the world, and if you dare, *dare,* tell him what to do, then he will take on the entire world rather than do it.

He will not be told, not ever.

Mark Griffiths looks into Simon's eyes and thinks, in a flash;
That's the bloke, the stupid dancing bloke from the pub.

A few months ago, Simon and Jane's father had danced together on her birthday.

Mark Griffiths had also been in The Hoop & Grapes that day. He'd watched them as hate swelled behind his eyes, and he'd thought, *stupid stupid stupid, stupid fuckers, stupid fuckers.* Simon and Dave had laughed together, as one tap danced, and the other flailed about, while people clapped and cheered.

Mark Griffiths had never been clapped and cheered. On life's great report card, he'd never been given a gold star, or any star, for that matter.

Mark Griffiths took himself incredibly seriously, and never wasted time on laughter, unless it was laughing at other people, those who weren't like him. He didn't know the word schadenfreude, but lived by it. Schadenfreude was Mark Griffith's only real grasp of comedy.

Round and round, his eternally outraged mind whirls, perpetual motion hate machine, feeding on its own energy, *stupid dancing bloke, stupid dancing bloke telling me what to do? Stupid fucking dancing bloke, telling me what to do? Telling me what to do? Telling me what to do? Telling me what to* do?

Turning and turning, gyre widening, things fall apart, centres cannot hold, felt rather than thought, in microseconds, then - ta-dah, like magic, the blade is in Mark's hand and then it is in Simon's chest, where it manages to slip between the ribs and into his heart.

As easy as that. It takes seconds of Mark's time to take Simon's life. Seconds.

Simon's brain has no time to register any pain, because the blade pierces his heart and ends his life.

It is terrifying in its banality.

There are no last words, nor great truths to be imparted, just a man, crumpling to the dirty wet floor of a stupid kebab house in Aldgate. There are shouts, shock, Mark Griffiths runs for the door, the whole incident caught on CCTV, between 2:42 and fifteen seconds, and 2: 42 and twenty seconds. Five seconds to take a life's potential and fling it to the four winds.

Simon is gone before his head smacks onto the tiles.

Stop. Please, just stop. Enough context.

I can't take any more of this *real time*. It is too real to endure.

45 / There / 15:02 P.M. / 22nd December / The Hoop & Grapes Pub, Aldgate

Jane looked out of the bay window at the fluttering snow. It felt like she'd sat there her whole life.

She waited for her man. She smoked her last cigarette and waited for her man.

The wait was was curious, because the newsagent was only a few doors down, and Abrakebabra no more than five minutes walk.

Perhaps he's stopped to chat with someone. Maybe they've run out of kebabs. They'd better bloody not.

She hadn't heard the sounds of sirens, nor the ambulance as it raced past the window. This was London, after all, and those wails were a constant soundtrack. You never really heard them unless they were for you.

So Jane waited, unaware that a few hundred yards away and quarter of an hour in the past, her first real love had lain on a Kebab House floor, as paramedics fluttered about him, police took statements and other officers sped to Mark Griffith's flat.

Jane waited, and thought how strange it was.

Strange, but not worrying, not yet.

It takes a little while for strange to become worrying, then worrying to panic-inducing, and from panic inducing, swiftly into unbearable.

Her foot tap, tap, tapped, but she wasn't aware.

Perhaps a quick look. Yes, he may be out there talking with a friend.

In this snow? A tiny, rational, now slightly concerned part of her asked. She ignored it, but that voice wouldn't stop. *He's out there in this, Jane, talking, like it's a summer's day?*

Jane stood, but left her black cardigan hanging on the back of the chair. A frisson of fear flashed over her. Things had started to slide. Jane had become a little unsteady with reality. The flurries of snow were reason enough to wrap up warm, but already, her thought processes had become compromised. Not much, not yet, but soon they would splinter entirely. Her cardigan stayed on the chair.

Jane stood from the table, her old, familiar table, walked out of The Hoop, looked up and down the road.

There were two police vehicles and a crowd. Without thought, her hands went up to her mouth, to try and stifle a whispered, "oh," that had risen there.

"Oh," she said again, because nothing else was appropriate.

So Jane ran.

Her black flat shoes slapped through the slush on the pavement, because Jane knew if she raced, she might be able to stop whatever 'this' was. But part of her screamed that 'this' had already taken place.

As she got nearer to the Kebab Shop, she began to lose any conviction that *this will all turn out just fine.* At that point, Jane hoped she'd never reach those Police cars.

But she did, of course, as she had to.

"Simon?" She looked for his face in the crowd that had gathered.

Where do they come from, the Crowd? How do they know where to meet? Perhaps they are the same Crowd throughout history, drawn to these moments to stand and observe. The Crowd were there when Julius Caesar died on the steps, when Jesus was fixed to the cross, when the twin towers bloomed. The Crowd have always been there to watch.

"Simon?" She shouted again.

A policeman turned to her, expression unreadable.

"Simon?" The officer repeated. "Do you know the…do you know him?"

"He's my boyfriend," Jane answered absently, scanned the area, hoped for him to break through the ranks of the watchers, smiling, arms open, apologetic, *whoops, sorry I took so long, darling. Here's your kebab.*

Jane noticed the policeman had glanced at another officer.

What was that for? She wondered. *Don't you dare, don't you* dare *look at him like that, don't you start* glancing *at each other, because I do not like that expression, I do not like it* one little bit.

The Policeman's expression changed, became softer, an approximation of empathy, and Jane didn't like *that* one little bit, either.

"Come and sit in the car would you, please, Madam?"

Why should I come and sit in the car? Her thoughts had begun to rise in pitch, she felt them squeal like tyres on a wet road, screech as they tried to *stop this*, but were locked in a fatal slide. Deep inside, she knew why she had to sit in the car, but had to question it, because if she didn't, all this… nonsense…would become real.

"Where is Simon?"

"Madam?"

"Where is Simon?"

"You need to come and sit in the car, Madam."

"My. Name. Is. Jane," She tapped out the four syllables of the sentence furiously. "Where is Simon? What's happened?"

"There's been an Incident."

An Incident? Sickened, Jane realised that somehow, the word had gained a capital letter. *Incident? Capital I? What does that mean? Where is Simon?*

"Come and sit in the car." He opened the door.

"Please just tell me where my boyfriend is." Jane tried to assert some control over the conversation, but heard her own voice as if it were a recording from far away.

"He's been… taken away. Please, let's talk in the car, you need to get out of the snow."

Jane allowed herself to be guided to the front seat. She shook, not from the cold, but because she was scared. The words, *he's been taken away*, circled in her mind, but what did that mean?

The Policeman slid into the driver's seat.

"Where is Simon?"

"There was an Incident."

"I know, you told me, where is Simon?"

"I'm sorry, he's been taken by the ambulance."

Jane processed the words, but still discarded what had become horribly apparent to her.

Ignore it, Jane, it will go away. But, oh, he started with the words 'I'm sorry," didn't he? No. No. No. It will go away.

It would never go away.

"Taken where?"

"He was…assaulted. We know who the man is, we're finding him. He was attacked in the kebab shop."

Jane watched as the officer contemplated his next words. "I'm afraid it was with a knife."

In these situations, the police don't start with the bleak, final statement, "your boyfriend is dead."

They edge carefully toward it, one step at a time, let the picture gently fade up.

"With a Knife?" Jane's mind had begun to crumble. It would rather powder away than try to deal with what had become mutely obvious. Dreadfully, "Knife" had also gained itself a capital letter in her mind.

"With a Knife. I'm sorry."

There they were again.

Two words you never wish to hear from a Doctor or an officer of the law. *I'm sorry.*

Jane froze, became ice, colder than the snow, colder than the dark side of the galaxy.

Why was the policeman sorry?

From deep inside her glacier, Jane knew.

All this had taken just seconds. But we always knew that, didn't we? Tectonic shifts don't always need continents of time.

"I'm sorry," he said again, but Jane was already somewhere else. While her body sat in the passenger seat, her mind ran elsewhere, split in every direction, barely hung on to itself.

No no no no he was just here he was just here he cannot be I will not let him be he was just here he is not he is not he is not he is not he cannot be he was just here he cannot be no I will not he is out there somewhere he is lost in the snow that's all he's just lost I need to find him I just need to find him he is just lost he cannot be I will not let him be he was just here there is a mistake there is a mistake they are wrong he is out there he has taken a wrong turn he is just lost I just need to find him.

"Where do you need to go?" The policeman asked from a billion miles away. "Is there someone I can take you to? I'm so sorry. Can I take you to someone? Family? We have people. I just need to let the other officer know. I'm sorry."

He stepped out of the car.

Jane sat, shut down, unable, unwilling to process any more.

As her mind cracked, it sought a safe place.

Dad.

Dad will know. I must find Dad. Dad always knows. He will find Simon. Dad will find Simon, Dad can make it right, yes Dad will know. I must go to Southend. Dad is in Southend. Daddy will find Simon. He will make this right.

*

Context. *Oh, I'm so tired of context, but it is all I have to offer.*

There are points when your brain does not function as it should, when information received can no longer be analysed rationally.

Let's take an example we've all seen, many times.

When Lee Harvey Oswald's third bullet ripped away part of JFK's head, Jackie Kennedy was suddenly in that place, too. Information had been received that she couldn't process in a normal way.

We've watched her, over and over again, as she clambered over the back of the Lincoln Convertible to retrieve part of Jack's skull. Why? Because it was the only action that made any sense to Jackie *at that moment*. She'd just seen her husband's head explode, what else could she do?

If she could fix it, put Jack together again, then everything would be alright.

So, as the Crowd stared, she clawed her way over the Lincoln to fetch some of John that was no longer part of him.

Close your eyes, see, join her in that moment.

Jackie is still there, forever, climbing backward to fix, repair, *reverse* this and make things like they were when the world was normal - just seconds ago would be enough - when John had waved, she'd smiled and Governor Connally had turned to say, "Mr President, you can't say Texas doesn't love you."

Events like that simply can't be understood at first. They are white noise, random, impenetrable. At that moment in Dealey Plaza, Jackie

Kennedy couldn't *deal with*, *cope with*, or *deny* the situation, because she hadn't even perceived it.

A sudden death, catastrophic trauma, disaster, a loss that comes from no-where with no warning and no reason, those kinds of moments are impossible, so beyond our experience, they simply can't exist.

Over time, therapists might describe the emotion as "denial," but at the beginning, it is deeper than that, a re-configuring of your place in the universe itself. When their worlds cracked, Jane and Jackie both moved into an alternate reality, where there was still a chance to put things right.

Jackie grasped for her husband's skull, because at that moment, putting it back, reversing time, was her only option.

Jane walked, because that was hers.

Simon was dead, but that was impossible. Because, in her reality shift, he could not be dead. Jane did not process *dead*, the word suddenly had no meaning to her, was part of a foreign language.

She was like a driver who'd walked away from a terrible car crash, then just carried on walking, resumed their journey on foot. *I was never there, never even in the car. I am simply here now, walking. I am not walking away from anything in* particular, *I am just walking, because I can. Because nothing has happened to me.*

And like that driver, Jane thought, with complete rationality; *I must walk now. I must walk and find my Dad. I must go to where everything makes sense.*

And, alongside;

I tried but I failed and this wasn't supposed to happen.

That odd phrase came from another part of her mind, one so distant, on a frequency so faint, like the faraway cycling song of a star. But it meant nothing to her - like an overheard conversation in a foreign language, she paid it no mind. Not that she had much of a mind by that point. Jane ran on emotional instinct.

I tried but I failed and this wasn't supposed to happen.

I tried but I failed and this wasn't supposed to happen.

Somehow Jane knew she only had one course of action, the only option that made any sense. To make this right, she must get to Southend, and find her father. When your world has become unbearable faster than your mind can keep up, you'll do whatever seems correct, no matter how impossible it may seem to everyone else.

Jane stepped out of the car whilst the policeman talked with his colleague, then became lost in the crowd, lost in Aldgate, invisible in the snow. He never even noticed she'd gone. She walked. She had a purpose.

Yes.

Dad will know. I must find Dad. He will know where Simon is, he always knows. He fixes everything. I want my Dad. He will know. This is what I do. This is how it works.

Jane walked, and the snow powdered her hair. To any casual observer, she looked like a woman who knew where she was going, and she did.

She'd come this way many times before, to St Botolph Street, where the Coach Stop waited. The Coach Jane had taken to Southend On Sea many times, and she knew it would be there, ready to take her again.

Nothing has happened. Simon is not dead. He is not dead because nothing has happened today.

Those were not fully formed thoughts as you read them, but more like instincts.

Jane had just £10 in her skirt pocket, and it was all she needed. £10, one way to Southend On Sea.

As she boarded, Jane was spotted by the Policeman who'd just broken her. He turned the corner and saw her through the coach window as it pulled away. He made a note of the Coach number, but that wouldn't help, because now Jane was on the way to where she'd always been headed.

As she walked down the aisle of the coach everything made sense.

If I'm quick, I'll find Dad, and he'll be with Simon. He must be. If I go now, don't dawdle. Yes. I can find him again, if I rush. Yes. They will be there. In Southend. Yes.

46 / A Coach, Heading East / A127 motorway / 15:52 P.M.

Something else I have learned; do not trust time. It always runs away from you.

Not even one hour ago - or was it decades, Jane didn't know anymore - she'd sat in The Hoop, where the world had behaved exactly as expected.

But then, the strangest thing. Reality had tipped sideways.

The snow wheeled, headed in every direction and no direction at all. Chaos settled everywhere, as a white-out descended on the South East of England.

As she'd walked like an automaton to the coach stop, Jane's mind had spun, but always returned to the same point; *I need to be with my Dad. He can fix this day. But he is in Southend On Sea, so I must go to him. Not far.*

It was perfectly logical, yet totally illogical behaviour, depending on where you stood.

Simon will be there. He must be, because I can't find him here. Perhaps he has been lost in this snow. It happens. Yes, that's what's happened. He has gone out, and the snow has wrapped itself around him, and he is lost. Lost can be found again. Yes. That's it. They are in Southend, and if I am very, very quick, I will find them. But I must run, must rush.

Jane wore a green cotton blouse, a short black skirt and flat shoes.

There'd been a cardigan earlier, way back in history when the world was normal, but that had disappeared, too. She wasn't sure when, or where. It wasn't important.

Despite that, Jane didn't felt the cold, or anything else, for that matter. Her feet led themselves, uncontrolled, to the coach stop in St Botolph Street.

A coach idled there. Of *course* it did.

That made sense. This particular coach wouldn't, couldn't leave without her. In a backroom of her consciousness, Jane thought;

Perhaps it's been there since before I was born, ready for me to alight. Maybe inside, the passengers have sat silently for decades, in their pre-arranged places. The engine's been running forever, the driver has my ticket ready in his hand. Then, when I get on, the passengers will shift, stir, come to life. They've waited for a long time for this particular journey to begin. They've been expecting me.

She'd boarded and all the seats were occupied except for one, next to an old, old man.

Jane said, "is this seat taken?" But it wasn't really her that spoke, just a pre-set question played in from somewhere else. The old, old man smiled, and Jane forged one too, because that's what you were supposed to do, wasn't it?

They said nothing for most of the journey, two strangers who watched the snow as it rushed past the windows, on its way to somewhere. Nowhere.

After a while - seconds, minutes, days, years, Jane didn't know - the coach joined the A127 in Essex, which led to Southend On Sea, Dad, and surely, Simon. Not long now.

Jane was unaware she'd been crying. The tears had spilled silently.

Then the old, old man coughed, and said, "I am Jo/a/oh/anse/on."

Jane was too empty, too past the edge of sanity to ask for clarification, so Johnson OR Janssen he remained.

Snow gathered on the glass. The old man held out a handkerchief which he'd apparently magicked out of thin air.

"Would you?" he offered. For a moment, Jane wondered why this old man held out a hankie, since she didn't need to sneeze, but then felt water on her cheeks.

"It's not used." He smiled, thinly. "I keep it only for the emergencies, of which I must say, yes, this appears very much to be one."

Jane took the hankie, because again, that's what you're supposed to do.

He didn't mention his name again and strangely, never asked for hers.

"Ach." He looked out of the window as the road rumbled beneath them. "Is it heavier than it was a moment ago? I swear it was like dandruff, but now it is like...ach!...cotton wool balls! *Lacherlich, nicht wahr?*"

Jane followed his gaze and yes, it was. Cotton wool balls. Her thumb and forefinger compulsively rubbed away at the silver snowflake round her neck.

"Ha! Would you look at my reflection? I appear older than I even am out there, in the snow. How my molten reflection scolds me, ah? I won't ask why you were leaking, it is not my business, but whatever the reason, or whoever the reason... there must always, always, there must be smiles, yes?"

Jane nodded, automatically, but didn't want this old man to speak any more. She just wanted to fold herself up until she could slip through the cracks between things. Drop out of this place until she couldn't feel herself drop any more. Into the cold and never come back.

The old man continued to talk, and Jane let him. They'd be in Southend soon, and she'd never see him again. As his voice rumbled like the road, one thought rolled over and over.

I have promises to keep and miles to go before I sleep.

I have promises to keep and miles to go before I sleep.

I have promises to keep and miles to go before I sleep.

Unasked, the old man spoke of Norway, his home country, and how he'd lived a life of forgotten, wonderful and terrible moments *und so veiter*, and - ah - how he *still* slipped into German, his second language - how he'd fought in the War, but afterwards had come here, *to this place*, to forget. "So I left Norway, I left Poland *und* Germany, I left them all, and now I live in this place."

He never once called it Britain, just *this place*.

He spoke on, and on, of endless huts, *bad bees* with poisoned pollen. Of soup. Of his father, soup, and chimneys. How he'd watched those chimneys. He'd laughed, and it was dry, like leaves that crackled underfoot. Once old people have an audience, especially a captive, pretty, mute one, they become masters of the monologue. But, suddenly, in amongst his fractured reverie, he turned to Jane and looked her in the eye.

"You know what I have learned? Beware regret." He raised a twig-like finger. "I regret much. The war gave me a history I wish I could paint over. One that has left me with regret, which is both an emotion and a parasite. Regret lives off the 'if only's' and 'could have beens'. It eats you up, until it's all that's left. But if, by a sheer act of will... you could forget the dark stories in your past, you could deny regret its power - but then what else would you lose? If you choose to forget what hurt you, to deliberately discard it, surely you are choosing to lose yourself? Who would do such a thing? Who would take such a course?".

Jane stared at Janssen and managed to distantly think, *Oh my god, that was a speech.*

But after that, there wasn't time for further thought. In seconds, there hadn't seemed enough air in the coach. No, not enough air in the galaxy.

It was 15:52 p.m.

Jane gasped, and clutched at her chest. The old man turned, wide eyed, and asked, "are you fine?" But of course she wasn't.

She stood. Perhaps there was more air higher up, but, no.

No.

No.

n

o

Jane's mind had tried its best to protect her, wrap her in numbness, grasp for impossible hope, but couldn't any longer.

Reality smashed back, hard, and she went into shock. Her heart raced, she grasped at her head. There was suddenly too much information in there.

"Simon, Simon, Dad, Daddy, I can't breathe," she moaned, then staggered up the aisle toward the driver.

People turned and watched. A few stood, unsure what to do.

Is she mad, pregnant or drunk? Is she asthmatic, dangerous or on medication?

No-one stepped forward to help.

The driver heard the noise and took his eyes off the road. Just for a second, but that was all it took. Seconds, always just seconds.

Then; pandemonium.

This particular coach had been serviced a few months ago at a garage in Spring Bridge Road, Ealing, a place of no consequence. The mechanics had done their job, got paid, and moved on to the next M.O.T.

But they'd failed to spot tiny cracks in the rear axle. Even if those breaks had been noticed, they were just wear and tear, too small to be dangerous.

But, as you know, as you always knew from when we first began, it's the cracks you don't see that get you.

The coach driver looked in his mirror and saw Jane stumble toward him. He glanced around, and in doing so, involuntarily swung the wheel to the right.

That movement was fatal. The coach clipped a Mini overtaking in the fast lane. Seconds later or earlier, the car would have been spared. Time and distance, they save, or damn you.

Too fast, it was all too fast.

To overtake today was madness, when the road ran with dark icy promises and visibility was down to just a few metres.

The Mini slammed into, then bounced off the coach. Each vehicle left a dented kiss on the other. It spun a half circle into the central reservation, and crumpled. The windscreen became diamonds as the seatbelt-free driver flew onto his buckled bonnet, where he buckled, too.

At that point the cracks in the rear axle of the coach finally made themselves known.

The collision caused one to widen, then the coach's violent movement tore it in two.

The axle split, which made the rear of the coach slip downward, where it ground on the road surface. The underside slid wildly and screeched a metallic scream. Sparks leapt into the air, fireflies that swarmed upward whilst the passengers were thrown sideways and forward.

Jane was the only person standing, so was launched across the seats and into the coach window, where she collided with a whiplash crack as her head took the impact.

She bounced back into the aisle, but by that point, the coach had spun lengthways across the motorway. Underneath was a display of sparklers, awful crackles and flashes, as metal shredded into white hot shards.

Cars turned and thudded into the side, like cannonballs fired at a ship, *one, two, three, four*, and each passed on their own inertia to the coach, made it buck, shiver and shudder.

Inside, as Jane was thrown again, forward, then sidewards, several bones broke simultaneously. Other passengers crashed into seats, still more spun, pin-balling flesh and bone ripped, twisted, as the coach ripped and twisted.

The cars continued to slide and attack the vehicle.

The coach was pushed further towards the edge of the road, where a natural ditch waited.

All this had taken seconds.

Jane's body, broken now, flipped backward. She was mercifully unconscious, but her brain continued to ricochet off bone, as it bounced inside her skull.

The coach tipped then, roof first. For a moment it resembled a suicide peering over the edge, not sure wether to commit. It swung back and forth, but then seemed to sigh, make the decision to end it all, and *jump*.

It jumped.

The left side windows imploded, then - I see them now, so fast! - tiny needles of safety glass showered upwards.

Jane fell with the coach, down into the broken hole where the window once was. Other passengers fell onto her. Some were thrown further onto the embankment, where snow settled on them as they lay still.

Jane's body tried everything it could to keep her alive, but her breathing grew ever more shallow and her heartbeat weakened.

Jane's body, like yours, is designed to survive, whatever it takes. But strength has to come from somewhere and if it's being used up faster than it can replenish, well, the result is just physics.

The coach died there in that ditch, and took others with it.

For a moment, there was total silence, and then those that could, screamed. They were the lucky ones. They still had the strength to cry out. Jane, however, was silent, her eyes closed, someplace else now.

In the road behind, many mobile phones dialled 999.

As Jane lay dying, Emergency Vehicles converged on the A127, and her father arrived at Fenchurch Street station. His heart beat out a new pattern. Before it had been, *my-Jane, my-Jane, my-Jane*. But now it beat; *Too-late. Too-late. Too-late.*

*

Remember this; snow is made of clouds. They freeze, crack, and fall. David once told his daughter how snow is cold rain which has come to earth for a holiday. A sweet idea, but as anyone who has experienced its ferocity knows, snow is not naturally benign.

Those jealous clouds look down and want to be solid, to feel and touch. So when the temperature plummets, they do, too. Those clouds fell to earth again on December 22nd, 2003. On that day, they kissed many people goodbye.

47 / Here / Fifteen Minutes

Fifteen minutes and counting.

14:59. 14:58. !4:57...

Once upon a time, there was a woman called Jane.

She'd become lost in the middle of a snow-deep forest, surrounded a clearing called, simply, *Here*.

To her surprise, Jane discovered she'd been recast as Red Riding Hood, Hansel and Gretl, Goldilocks, Snow White, and more. But while she remembered those characters, Jane had forgotten herself.

Until now.

14:56. 14:55...

Once upon a time, on *Here's* flexible clock, Jane remembered everything.

Instantaneously, she knew who she was, where she'd been, re-opened every door, re-trod every path of her life.

Even moments she'd lost over time had returned. Previously filed away and forgotten, they were back; childhood toys, smiles on friends faces, school lessons, songs, uneventful bus journeys, kisses, laughs, tears, hours, seconds, long departed, rebuilt with crystal clarity.

When *Here* lets you remember, it does so with the same intensity once deployed to make you forget.

But Jane also remembered the terrible events which led her to this place, the few hours on December 22nd that first cracked, then threatened to destroy her completely.

But Here had done its work. In forgetting, her broken mind and soul had hardened once more, become strong. Jane would need that strength, because alongside her memories, she also had to face Grief.

Capital G, of course.

Grief, as Jane once realised, cannot be negotiated, bargained with, bought off or denied. Some might think they have pushed Grief away, but that is an illusion. It has simply taken up residence somewhere deep and dark inside them, and will return to have its time in the sun.

Grief must be stood up to, ridden and tamed. If allowed to race out of control, it takes the bereaved to a place they will never return from. When Death comes, those who are left behind have a choice; tame Grief, then walk alongside it, or be swept away, gripping its mane, not riding, merely hanging on for dear life.

Jane rode.

Grief bucked, shook, tried to make her fall, but in forgetting, Jane had made herself a saddle, and although harder than anything she'd ever done, she rode Grief, tamed loss, held fast to the reins and would not let go. She'd let go too many times before.

Jane rode.

She grasped the reins and wrapped them about herself, as she raced Grief across her life. All of you will take this ride at some point. Some take it many, many times, but each is like the first. This awful ride never gets easier.

Jane rode.

She sat on her single bed, magically re-made once more, sheets crisp and white, and she rode. Head in hands, she tried to keep the memories that hurtled inside her under control, but it felt like they could crack her mind into pieces.

She moaned. A surprisingly gentle moan, that came from somewhere, *somewhen* inside.

The Man sat with his arm round her shoulders and waited.

He knew neither of them had much time left, although the thought was a paradox, in this place outside of time.

The Man sat as he had done before, and let Jane ride her memories. He couldn't intervene to tame them, she had to hang on by herself. There was nothing he could say or do, not yet. He still had one last rule to tell her, the most important part of being Told.

He stared, eyes wet, as she sat, head bowed.

Jane rode.

She cupped her temples in her hands, pushed at them, attempted to hold in all the memories that had returned in force.

All this took less than a few seconds.

The Man held her just a little tighter, then looked up and round the Hut.

It was lit, from without.

Light streamed in from each of the four windows, glowed at the edges of the door. Waves pulsed and danced out there. The light came like a mist, as reds and yellows - but mostly greens - painted the walls, covered the floor and ceiling, overlaid Jane and The Man.

Jane's Aurora was *Here*, finally.

And yet The Aurora was also outside *Here*.

Remember the rules?

The Aurora appears when you arrive and then dances when you leave.

You may only leave when your Aurora returns, to light your way.

If you try to leave without the Aurora's light, you'll become lost in the forest, never to find your way out, never to find yourself again.

You know this because you too have been Told.

14:54…

Jane's Aurora had come back. *Aurora Janaris*.

The Man never grew tired of seeing it. He watched as the Aurora curled and rippled around the Hut, filled the clearing known as *Here*.

The Man watched, but knew he was on a clock. It was a rare feeling, knowing he must punch out soon.

Because as The Aurora filled Here, it hadn't just brought colour, but time, too. It acted as a doorway that allowed time itself to stream through.

Outside the Hut, hours, minutes, moments, gathered up, a swarm of seconds that buzzed around the too-tiny door. Time was coming back.

Jane and The Man both felt it.

Time was heavy, like the atmosphere before a thunderstorm. Those seconds, minutes, hours, days, months, years, *millennia* were a gigantic wave which would soon break in every direction across *Here*.

Whenever Time returned, The Man always thought it would pulverise everything. But like all waves, Time always settled, found its depth.

As the Aurora shimmered, it birthed Time and the wave broke.

For a moment, the force threatened to collapse the clearing in on itself, make it a superdense quantum sized sphere of almost nothing, the blackest of black holes, but *Here* was built to withstand the assault.

Here was stronger than Time, and protected within it, Jane and The Man felt their bodies squeezed into near-nothingness, then released.

Jane sensed every clock in the universe tick back into life. She felt her internal rhythms begin again.

It's incredible how you only really notice something was missing when it returns.

Time was back, but only passing through. It wouldn't wait, so there was no Time to lose.

*

"Simon," whispered Jane. It was the first word she'd said since her memory had returned. "Oh, Dad," she croaked. "Where am I?" She didn't look up at The Man.

"You're Here. You know you are."

"No," she murmured. "No, that's not what I'm asking. Where am I?"

The Man knew what was coming. That question had been on its way since their very first moment, when he'd gently guided Jane's face away from the window. It was almost the only question left to ask.

"Tell me. Where am I?"

The Man softly took Jane's face in his hand, as he'd done an eternity ago. Her eyes were red, face pale. Grief had not diminished her beauty, but instead made it defiant.

She studied his face, infinitely old now, so tired, and he was crying.

He'd done this so many times before, and it always tore him apart.

Jane gasped. The Man seemed so in control. He didn't cry, he held *you* as tears flowed. But now, tears coursed down his cheeks and lost themselves in his beard. Jane reached up and wiped them away with the back of her hand. He smiled, but it was the sad smile of someone who'd tried to make bad news better, but failed.

"Oh, The Man," she said, gently. "Why are you crying?"

"Because you asked where you were, and now I have to Tell you." His top lip quivered, like a child's. He looked up again at the ceiling.

"Aaa-aah-ah." He exhaled and the sigh caught and stuttered.

"Jane, my darling Jane, you are dying. Your body is in a hospital, and your body is dying. I'm so sorry."

Jane took a moment to think. *But my body is Here, isn't it?*

But no, no it's not, she knew that now. She remembered. *I remember the coach and how as I stood up, unable to breathe, it leapt sidewards, like no vehicle ever should. And I remember…flying? Yes, flying, just for a moment, flying and crashing, and then…Well, then, the next thing I knew was… I was Here.*

But she also knew, with certainty, that she was also back *There*. Somehow, she occupied two places at once.

"You are dying, Jane. You are dying so, so quickly," The Man stared at the colours of the Aurora as they spun around the Hut. "From your Aurora, you have less than fifteen minutes left. Then your body will be dead, and you with it."

"How do you know?" Jane asked. "No. How does The *Aurora* know I have fifteen minutes left?"

The Man smiled and looked at the light tenderly.

"The Aurora is you, Jane. It is the electricity that courses through your body, your brain patterns, your essence, your soul, if that mistaken word helps. It lives while you do, but it is fading, as you are fading. When the Aurora fades and dies, you do, too. Now, you must decide before that happens, or you are lost. When your body dies back *There*, that is it. No more second chances. You are scattered, gone, never to be re-assembled in this or any other universe. You have a choice to make, and you must make it quickly."

He shook his head.

"I'm so sorry. You will be dead soon. Your father is with you."

"Dad?" Jane gasped. She remembered every moment with her father. They'd said goodbye on the steps of their terraced house in Grace Street, Bow, one day in December 2003, and that was the last time she'd seen him.

"My Dad is with me? In the hospital?".

"Yes," murmured The Man "He is about to watch his daughter pass. Something no father should ever see."

Jane slumped again and cried. She cried for her father, alone in a hospital room, waiting for his girl to die. "Oh Daddy," she wept. "I'm so sorry."

The Man could have Told Jane more, but had made a decision. Enough was enough. She had no need to know what else would happen in that hospital room.

"Jane - you must decide what happens next, and you need to decide right now."

He stood.

"I know this is fast, so quick, too quick, but it only takes seconds for a heart to stop, and we must race ahead of that moment. If it gets there before us, you are lost."

"Will I wake up? To see my Dad one more time? In the hospital?"

"No. You are gone, Jane. Your body is about to give up. No final goodbyes, no squeezing of hands. You will just stop. But we have… options. We must rush, Jane, rush to beat death."

48 / There / December 22nd, 2003 / 20:47 P.M.

Jane's body lay in The London Hospital.

Splints, bolts and rods surrounded her like miniature scaffolding. She resembled a broken Gulliver tied down by tiny ropes.

A pipe in Jane's throat breathed for her, with the *tsk-click tsk-click* of the ventilator, as it forced oxygen into her system. Her lungs, which had quietly done their job since her first breath in the Seventies, could no longer work alone.

There was a war going on in this room, and regiment by regiment, Jane was losing.

Her skin was blackened in many places, the bruising so deep she appeared to have been dipped in ink. Cannulas and tubes, hateful analogs of an umbilical cord, dripped medication into her weakening bloodstream. Her blood pressure was dropping - everything was dropping. Even though completely still, Jane was mid-air, falling.

The monitors beeped and flashed, ready to give the slimmest of advance warnings that her body was ready to shut down for good.

Jane lay silent while the concerned machines whispered amongst themselves of her chances.

The lazy observer might even say she looked tranquil, but that was an illusion. She was bound up like Houdini, performing the greatest escape attempt of her life.

Inside, Jane fought for every breath, every heartbeat.

Death reached for her. With every *tsk-click*, with every *beep-beep*, it took hold of Jane just a little tighter.

Unconscious, she felt nothing, but her mind was far from shut down. Faint brain activity sparked and crackled, distantly.

Jane was thinking. Deep away, somewhen far, a decision had to be taken. If it were possible to plot her thoughts visually, they would have resembled a tumbling aurora with colours that slid into each other; reds, golds, yellows and so many shades of green.

Jane's body was static, but her brain was busy. It painted itself anew, re-decorated. Time to move on.

Death was in the room. She just had to out-run him for a few more minutes, but no-one can ever win that race. All one can hope to do is stay a few lengths ahead for as long as you can, but eventually, he'll catch up. He always does.

A doctor and nurse stood in the corridor outside. The doctor leaned against the doorframe.

He was Doctor Stephen Perry, just weeks from retiring and months from dying. Once more, he watched Jane and Dave.

Here you are again, he thought, *and I believe this is the last time. How I wish I could save you both, but I think we know we are all beyond that now.*

*

Inside, David sat by Jane's side and held her hand tightly. But she was off the ledge now, so Dave grasped her hand as if he could pull her back up to safety. In his peripheral vision, he saw two figures in white outside.

Doctors? Angels? David didn't care.

He sat with his blackened, broken daughter, powerless to do anything except hold her hand.

He hadn't stopped weeping since he'd walked into this room no more than fifteen minutes before.

*I should have stayed with her today, instead of (*running away?*) going to Southend On Sea, leaning into a snowstorm on the pier, then realising that something was very,* very *wrong. I should have stayed.*

He'd rushed as fast as his heart and the train had allowed, but on alighting at Fenchurch Street Station, David had known that whatever he'd raced to beat, it had already happened.

He held his daughter's hand, then did something for the first time since he was a child. He pictured a single star in a cobalt sky, and made a wish to it.

There were no other options.

*

On his arrival, the Doctor on duty, an impossibly young man, had been very honest.

"I'm sorry," he'd begun, but wasn't, Dave had known that. They were just two words from a checklist.

"I'm sorry," he'd repeated, then mechanically brought Dave *up to speed* on *where we were* with Jane. "Your daughter has sustained multiple injuries in the crash, many of which are life threatening by themselves. There are many broken bones, including her spine. Her left lung is punctured, as is one of her kidneys. Blood pressure is very low and her heart is weak."

Dave nodded, although his mind had started to fog at *multiple injuries* and *life threatening*.

"If…and I have to tell you it is an, 'if,' I'm so sorry," the Doctor continued, "if she can make it through these first few hours, then her chances go up. Not by a lot, and I don't want to put percentages on this, but with each day she survives, she gets stronger, and, as such, her odds increase. We don't know what the long term damage may be if she does… er…"

If

There it was again. Dave kept hearing that '*if*' dropped carelessly into Jane's life.

He didn't like that conjunction no, not one little bit.

"…But let's deal with all this one step at a time. We're monitoring all her signs and functions, so we'll be ready if there are further complications, problems."

The Doctor had said a few more, "I'm sorry"'s, a few more, "if's", then wandered off to break someone else's heart.

By 20:47 p.m. the A127 Coach Crash was officially confirmed as the most deadly in British history.

Eleven died on the coach itself, with a further nine in the cars that had collided with it.

At 20:47 p.m. the cause was still unknown. Survivors who could talk had told the authorities about a girl who'd distracted the driver just before pandemonium broke out, but it would take many months for the report to emerge.

When it did, that report was basically this observation, distilled;
It's the cracks you can't see that get you.

*

David sat with his shattered daughter as she ebbed away.

How did this happen? He managed to think, *Simon is dead, my daughter is…*

Dying.

Answered his mind, traitorously.

He tried again.

My daughter is…injured, his lying mind answered, and he accepted that word, even as he recognised the lie. *How did we wake up today, have breakfast, like normal, how did Jane go one way and I the other and how did we both end up here, with Simon dead?*

It's not possible, it's not possible, part of his consciousness repeated, but everything was possible given time, and time had been against them both, on that terrible 22nd December, 2003.

My girl, he thought. *My little girl.*

She lay there, barely recognisable beneath the bandages, pipes and wires.

And David remembered. He couldn't help himself, but was hand in hand with his critically injured daughter, and when the present is untenable, the past is desirable. So he remembered;

Jane, *lying in his arms, fresh to the world just moments before.*

Jane, *standing in her cot, waiting for him early in the morning, smiling her tiny smile.*

Jane, *asleep, tightly holding Sugar Lump, the teddy she still has in her room.*

Jane, *face lit by the tiny bulbs of the Christmas tree, entranced, even though the tree is old, plastic and shredded.*

Jane, *lying in a hospital bed, unconscious from a fall of less than a foot.*

Jane, *pulling a 1941 Royal Companion typewriter from a box on Christmas Day, tap, tap, tapping on it as she turns and smiles again, remembering her Mum and Dad.*

Jane, *flying a kite in Victoria Park, "so far away Dad, look!" She shouts, "I'm so far!"*

Jane, *holding his hand as they walked together to the shops, looking up at him with love.*

Jane, *stomping through the living room, furious at having to learn pointless logarithms.*

Jane, *crying over* this *boy, or* that *boy, never seeming to find the right one.*

Jane, *beaming with pride at her exam results.*

Jane, *writing, always writing something, never happier than with a pen in her hand.*

Jane, *jumping up and down in the tiny hallway of their house, clutching an envelope that is her key to Manchester University.*

Jane, *sitting at the end of her Mother's bed, waiting for her to die.*

Jane, *staring, face pale as frost, at her Mother's coffin at the Crematorium.*

Jane, *looking with tenderness at a text message, and Dave knowing at that very moment his daughter's life had changed.*

Jane, *radiant, with Simon.*

Jane, *laughing uncontrollably in The Hoop & Grapes, as her father and boyfriend drunkenly tap dance, her laugh filling the place.*

Jane *saying goodbye on their doorstep, dressed in just a cardigan, green blouse and short skirt, stepping off and away into the coming snow, just hours ago.*

Jane

Jane

My girl Jane.

Take me instead, he thought. *I've done my time, she's hardly started. Take me instead. It's not fair. I'll go in her place. I'll go happily if it saves her. I'll go.* And he meant it, willed a higher power, God, The Universe, whoever was in charge, to play swaps with their lives, to put him in harms way.

But no. Whoever or whatever made the decision wasn't paying attention.

So instead, he looked up at the patchy white ceiling of this terrible room and pictured a single star, far away. A star that wished to be wished upon, one that had never intervened before.

There was no point praying. No point bargaining with Death.

When you wish upon a star, makes no difference who you are, Dave knew. It was a rule every child learned.

So he looked up, saw that star and wished, like he'd done so many years ago.

Star light, star bright, first star I see tonight, wish I may, wish I might, have the wish I wish tonight, and he wished so hard. *Please let Jane come back, please let my daughter come back, whatever it takes, please let her come back.*

49 / Here / Ten Minutes

Ten minutes remain.

No, it's 9:59.

No, 58.

57…

Ah. We try to control things by naming them, but even as we name a time, it has already passed.

Inside her Hut, Jane felt Time begin to swirl away. She sensed it twist around her.

"What do I do? what do I do now?" She quietly asked The Man, who took his arm from round her shoulder and stood.

"You leave." He replied, matter-of-factly. "But you must go before your Aurora fades, and it is dying, Jane, because it is you."

He offered Jane one of his big hands and pulled her up.

She swayed a little, but he caught her.

"It's time. Say goodbye to this Hut."

Jane looked around the four familiar wooden walls. There was nothing to see really, never had been, but it had served as her home for ever, or no time at all. She didn't know.

A peculiar sound came from the larder. It *whooooooshed* and *shifffffffted*, like waves in a shell.

Jane looked toward that sound and smiled. "It's OK, I'm OK. Look. I can stand by myself. See? You don't have to support me. I'm strong enough." She gently took The Man's hands from her arms, stepped forward - still a little unsteady - and opened the larder.

It was almost empty. The '70s foodstuffs that once stacked the shelves were reduced to a few boxes that shimmered and dissolved like clouds on a windy day. Some had already lost their shape and colour, others had almost completely faded away.

"Oh." She was inexplicably sad to see the boxes bid farewell. "My food?"

"You don't need it any more, do you?"

Jane smiled back at him weakly. "The other Hut still had food appearing in the larder. Why not mine?"

"Hm, off spying were you?" Asked The Man, faux stern. He looked around concerned at the Aurora, as the intensity of its colours and shades dropped in and out.

The light appeared to be taking its final breaths.

"I only looked in the Hut next door." Jane huffed like a caught-out schoolgirl. "I wasn't spying. Just looking."

The Man shook his head. "You'd been Told not to. Oh Jane, you could have destroyed everything." He shut his eyes for a moment, exhaled. "Never mind now, it's done, it happened and nothing happened. You were lucky."

"Lucky? Why?"

He evaded the question. He was very good at it.

"You must leave now, Jane. Time has become finite."

Jane took in the Hut one more time.

There, the oven that burned her writing - how many times?

The larder that had magically fed her.

The bed that made itself.

Even The Box, which she'd first considered a threat but now knew was part of her journey.

And there, her precious 1941 Royal Companion Typewriter, the only item in this Hut that came from before. She touched it gently, let her fingertips brush across the keys.

"I don't want to leave it Here, alone." She turned to The Man. "I know that sounds...whatever it sounds...but it's my friend. It's my Royal. I don't want to leave it behind. that would feel like I've let it down."

The Man looked down at the Royal, which sat forlornly on the desk as if it knew what was to come. He shook his head.

"It stays. You can't take anything but yourself on the pathway you choose. Even if you tried, it wouldn't come out of the other side of The Forest. It would remain lost there."

Just for a moment, Jane saw a flash of what The Forest kept for itself. It looked like an Antique Shop had been picked up and rattled. Objects lay strewn amongst the trees, where previous "guests" had once tried to remove them from Here.

Surely everyone knew the rule;

You can't take it with you.

It was a debris field of memories. Scattered like a child would drop their toys, they poked from the Snow beneath the trees. Teddies, books, keys and boxes, seats and tables, clothing, sticks and bottles, paintings, photos and saucepans. Every object unique to one person, the much loved keepsakes they hadn't been able to leave behind, but were now lost for good. It was lovely, dark and deep, that Forest.

Once upon a time, those adored objects all had promises to keep. Jane hoped they'd kept them.

The Man clicked his fingers in front of her face.

"Jane. Please. If you take the typewriter, it will be lost in there. Never seen again."

"But if I don't …what happens to it?"

"It will go back to where it came from," was all he offered, and Jane knew that was as much as she'd ever get.

"Come, come," he said, with urgency. "We must leave. Outside, come."

Jane stared about the four walls again. Part of her didn't want to go. It wanted to Watch The Snow all over again, forget everything, and just live here for always.

The idea was tempting. She wanted for nothing, would be thirty forever. She could sit, write, burn. forget, sit, write, burn, forget, never ever die and wouldn't that be *good*?

The Man saw her thoughts. Jane's expression had telegraphed them.

"No, Jane, no." As he'd done before, he gently took her face and guided it towards his. "If you stay and wipe yourself, there will be a time when there is nothing of you left. Nothing at all. Just an empty person. No love, no desire, no hope, just a vessel, never to be be filled again. You are not an empty vessel, Jane. You have re-filled yourself. We must go."

He didn't give her a chance to argue, just threw the wooden, lockless door open for the last time.

The cold (but not *The Cold*) rushed in, then scattered to every corner of the Hut.

It was a cold that came from the furthest part of the universe, a place never touched by any star's light, let alone heat. That place is out there somewhere, a blackness and bleakness deeper than any ocean, where nothing wanders except the lonely cold.

Jane was ready. For the briefest of times, immeasurably small, her blood froze, the cells of her body cracked and she was effectively frozen dead.

But the cold adjusted, and she lived again. For now.

"Never gets old, that trick," she gasped.

"You're right, it never gets old. Not ever."

They stepped out.

The Snow welcomed Jane's tread, closed around her foot, and somehow insulated her from itself.

She smiled down at it. "I'll miss you, Snow."

The Snow warmed up, just a little more. Jane touched her fingers to her lips, then bent to transfer the kiss to the ground, which shifted, pleased. As she walked forward into the clearing, there was the *rush-pop-rush-crack-pop* as the Snow filled in her footsteps.

"Nothing of me left," she understood, finally. "I was never Here."

"That's what The Snow does." The Man turned and faced her.

They stood around ten feet from the door of the Hut.

Around them, the Aurora silently danced, folded in on itself, slipped and jumped. Its movements gave the impression of laughter, but slow and tired.

"You have a decision to make now." The Man said, formally.

Somehow, Jane knew this was part of a ritual he'd performed many times. She heard it in his old, knowing voice.

"But first, I can give you a Gift."

"A Gift?" She heard the capital G.

Aha, so, this *Gift is no mere end-of term, going away present.*

He checked the Aurora again as it pirouetted about them both. "You came Here to forget. So my Gift is one of remembrance. Wherever you choose to go, North..."

He pointed North, at the Pathway there, which glowed in the Aurora's lights.

"Or South…"

He pointed, again, with a curious formality, as if the gesture was required to be performed that way and that way only.

"…You can still receive this Gift. Jane, you may - only for such a tiny moment - go back to a place in your life. See? To step through, be there, see it again. It will be brief - we can only twist Time so much and it is fragile, despite how it seems - but you will be able to travel, stand outside of yourself and see a point in your life. You will be… There. This is the Gift. Where would you like to go?"

I can go anywhere, *see* anyone, *any* place, *any* time *in my life? But where? When? Who? Whatever I choose, whenever I go, I will sacrifice a billion other precious moments. When do I choose?*

It was not a question that could be answered easily, especially against a clock which was running down and out. Jane's mind rushed through possibilities;

18thbirthdaynomybirthnofirstmetSimonnoholdingmenoDadnoatunivers itynoatschoolno22ndnoChristmasnoidon'tknowtooSimonbedme

She desperately wanted to see Simon's face again, to watch as he'd approached the bench at the Crematorium when they'd first met, to experience those seconds once more.

Or perhaps to sit and glimpse us both laugh on that first, inexplicably comfortable date at that pub, what was it called? Yes, of course, you remember all. The Fox And Eagle.

Then there was Dad, who'd tap danced at her last birthday, which Jane now sadly realised really had been her very last birthday.

Knowinglovingdancingmanytimesthehooppubgrandadnanatoomanytim esSimon

Too many choices. No time to choose.

"Jane," sighed The Man. "I know this is difficult, but you know where you want to go. Who you want to see. You've known for a long time."

Ha, there you are again, making me figure out the riddles for myself.

Yes, Jane needed to see Simon again, but there was another face she hadn't looked on for ten years.

"Mum."

The Man nodded, but then waited for the rest.

He's right. I know exactly where I want to - no, have *to go. It makes sense now. Of course it does. I just hadn't reached this point before.*

"I want to see us on holiday. In Southend On Sea. 1979."

"Yes?"

"Yes."

The Man smiled, and then

she

    was

there

No dramatic dematerialisation effect, no bright lights nor big screen IMAX sequence. The moment was more like a bad film splice, where one scene was butted on to the next without cohesion or continuity.

In one frame, Jane was *Here*.

In the next, she was *There*.

Physically *There*, Southend On Sea, 1979.

The cold of Here was instantly replaced with the heat of There, which wrapped about her. A very long time had passed since Jane had felt real heat, and she staggered a little.

From the empty clearing of Here, she found herself stood on the noisy promenade of Southend On Sea, dressed appropriately - for once - in her green blouse and short black skirt.

She looked up at the blue summer sky of August, 1979.

Oh, hello, Sun, she thought, absently. *My word, that's a Sun, an actual Sun, my Sun, our Sun.*

Jane smiled upward as it welcomed her back to earth.

Oh yes, that Sun has its hat on alright, hip, hip, hip, hooray.

She'd never really registered how blindingly bright it was. She laughed, then shielded her eyes, even though she wanted to look directly into it.

Less, she looked upwards and commanded, automatically. *Less. Sky, turn down the brightness, Make this four in the afternoon.*

Nothing happened, of course.

Oh my god. I can't tell the sky what to do any more. I love *not being able to tell the sky what to do.*

Jane looked down at the shiny heat blasted pavement.

No Snow. How about that? No Snow to grab my ankles. She laughed again. *Ground,* actual *ground!*

She reached up to touch the silver snowflake that hung from her neck, incongruous there in the sunshine, then smiled sadly and remembered the day Simon had given it to her.

I am remembering an event that is twenty four years in the future. I am recollecting something that has yet to happen. My future past exists here, in me.

She stared at all the colours. From a world of white and brown, and a cloudless sky she'd dressed in all the blues, to this.

The sand reflected the light, almost as bright as the sun, and the heat haze weaved its own patterns, made a summer Aurora.

Jane clapped her hands to her mouth with disbelief.

Perhaps Southend is the impossible place and Here makes total sense.

To her right, the pier stretched out to sea, three years after burning down. She could see the funfair at the end, carbonised and blackened. The Bowling Alley stood at the pier-head and Jane could almost hear the snap and thwack of pins, even from this distance.

And then there were all the people.

So many people.

For however long, Jane had sat alone, but now multitudes happily jostled past. They laughed, ate ice creams, sipped weirdly tiny cans of beer. They were dressed in too-short shorts and wonderfully cheap bikinis, but many walked in Sunday Best, (*they had Sunday Best* she marvelled, with joy) suited and booted to come to Southend for the day, in their most expensive floral, curtain fabric dresses for a prom.

She stood in the river of people and watched them flow.

Oh yes, people got right done up *in these days*, Jane smiled to herself. *No-one slummed it. There were only a few 'designer' shops, and yet, these people look more stylish with less effort than anyone in my day. They don't look haunted, like they have things to do, people to see, places to go. They are just here, in this moment,* now.

The girls were fresh faced, the boys cheeky and trying too hard to impress, but it was charming. No-one seemed weary, cynical, buffed up or worked out, because that wasn't how things were in 1979.

I love you, 1979, thought Jane. *I love you so, so much.*

Frying onions and cooking fat were like Southend's own Aurora, the smells weaved everywhere.

Jane turned to look at an amusement arcade behind her called 'Wonderland.' There weren't many video games in 1979, still mainly the *tinkle crish! crash!* of pennies as they fell into one armed bandits, *k-ching, k-ching, whoooowhoooeeooo,* chrome balls bounced on paddles, the stutter of pinball machines, and everywhere at once, it seemed, Ian Dury And The Blockheads blasted from tinny radios, giving everyone *Reasons To Be Cheerful.*

Illuminations were suspended from lampposts.

They'd never give Blackpool sleepless nights, but Jane remembered that once the sun went down, Southend came up. There were simple metal shapes, stars, circles, clowns and smiley faces, but by dusk, the lights turned this stretch of Essex into Regent's Street at Christmas. Further down, she knew, the trees of the embankment also wore lightbulbs, giant snowdrops. And dotted between those trees stood fairytale figures, Goldilocks and her Three Bears, Snow White, gnomes and fairies.

Oh Southend, she thought. *Sometimes, you could be as magical as Here, if you only had the young eyes to see it.*

Jane turned to her left, stopped, then put her hands to her mouth again, breathless.

There.

On the beach sat a tiny Jane with bucket and spade.

Next to little Jane, Irene, in a swimsuit.

Oh my god. Mum. It's me and Mum. Look at her. Mum. *My Mum. How was she ever that young? There they are. We are. Mum and Dad, my young Mum and Dad didn't just exist in our photo album, in stasis. They were here. This happened.* Is *happening,* Jane corrected herself. *Oh my god, she is beautiful.* She finally gazed on Mum as Dad would have first known her. Vital and vibrant, full of potential.

She was still beautiful until the day she died, but this was Irene, distilled into one moment. She looked at her little Jane, then back at someone stood in front of them.

Whoever this person was, he held a small camera, and made the time-eternal gestures that indicated, "move closer", "look up" and "smile". The tiny Jane waved at the camera.

The big Jane's eyes became moist again.

Here we were, the three of us, with so much to do, so much to see and experience, and it was all there, waiting for us to go and find. Living is like exploring a rock pool. You just turn over the stones and see what's there. Look at us, we've barely started. And in fourteen years time, this beautiful smiling woman on this beach will be dead, and that man and his little girl will be lost.

And then, *that man*, her father, David, looked over his right shoulder, directly at Jane.

He stared and his mouth opened in surprise.

But also recognition.

Click went the camera, and froze him.

*

David thought, *wait. Stop. I know that girl.*

Somehow, he knew her, stood alone on the Promenade at Southend On Sea, in a green cotton blouse and short black skirt.

He didn't know how, but it was recognition that went deeper than surface appearance. A connection that drew his gaze to hers. Dave had no idea why he'd chosen to look over his shoulder at that particular second. Something had taken his face and gently guided it round to that one spot.

He stared at Jane, who stared back, in wonder. And David thought, from no-where, for no reason;

Remember this, remember every detail, it's important.

*

Jane was transfixed.

Oh god, oh god. I am standing here *but I am sitting* there *too, oh god please let this moment last. Let it stay inside me forever. Oh god, oh Dad, what must you be thinking, looking at your daughter, all grown up, although this is 1979, and that's impossible. Dad, it's OK, it's OK. See me,* please *see me, know this is real. Oh, but he does. I feel it.* Somehow *he knows this is as real as the sun. His daughter sits in front of him with a bucket and spade, but yet she's also behind him, thirty years old, alone. I was always here, just out of frame in that photograph. It was always me. I was always here.*

Jane tried to say one word, "daddy." But no sound came. Tears coursed down her cheeks.

Across the way, David raised a hand to his daughter, his impossible girl who was in two places at once, infant and adult. He slowly raised his hand, she raised hers back and started to say;

"Dad, oh, Dad, I love…"

But then, in the very next frame, Southend disappeared. The beach, heat, noise, all gone. Her Mother, Father, *herself*, all left behind, happy, in 1979.

Although I hope you now know none of us are ever left behind. Not really.

*

They were still *There*.

Jane was back *Here*.

She crumpled, and The Man took her back in his arms.

"Sssh," he stroked her hair. "Its alright. It's alright."

"He saw me," moaned Jane. "He saw me and he waved. I was always *There*, it was me. In the photograph. He *saw* me but never said, why did he never tell me?"

"Because he never quite believed it himself." The Man held her, rocked side to side, as the Aurora slipped between them, energy dissipating. "And so he kept it inside, wondering, waiting perhaps for …what? Proof? The right time? But the right time rarely comes, does it? Things get in the way."

Jane shook her head within The Man's hold.

"But he knew when it counted, Jane. Yes, I promise he knew when it counted. Come, come. No time now. You must decide." He removed his arms from round her.

"North or South?"

50 / HERE / Five Minutes

5.

    4:59…

    58…

    57…

The seconds were running away from The Man.

"Jane, Jane, my dear." She looked up. The tone of his voice demanded it.

"Your Aurora is leaving. You are leaving. Now, you have two choices. Listen, this is important. You can go North…"

The Man pointed at the North Pathway, no longer the vibrant gold it had been a few minutes before. He was formal again. The ritual had begun.

"This is *Here*." He pointed down at the ground, then gestured South. "That way is *There*. And that," he turned to the North Pathway. "Leads to *Everywhere*. You cannot stay Here. You must go either There, or Everywhere."

Jane nodded, but didn't understand.

The Man saw the confusion, but it was to be expected. He knew this part only too well, because it always shattered him.

"I know. *Here, There, Everywhere*…they seem arbitrary words, but they're not. *Everywhere* has many names," he said slowly, and with great purpose. "You have given it many titles over thousands of years, but it is… the Next Place. It is Everywhere."

"Heaven?" asked Jane.

"No. No, *no*. It is Everywhere," re-iterated The Man. "Its real name, as far as I can translate, is *Everywhere*. It is the next place people go once they leave *Here* or *There*. Call it whatever you like, but it is Everywhere. This is not religion, Jane, forget that. This is not physics, forget that. This is Theophysics. It is how we find the lost. It is how things are."

"If I go…Everywhere…Will they be there? Will I see them again?" Jane turned to look at the North Pathway. She didn't need to say who "they" and "them" were.

The Man nodded. "Yes, but they will be different. You will be different. That's the point of moving on to that next place. It is the difference between the newborn Jane in her cot, where all she saw was the ceiling and the kind faces that appeared over the edge, and the Jane you are now.

You are not the same Jane as the child in the cot. Your perception of the world is different, your priorities different, *you* are different. What you understand as love will be different, just as it is between how Jane in the cot understood love then and how you do now. So yes, *they* will be there, and you will see them, but they'll be different. Once you have chosen to go North, to Everywhere, you will…grow up again, if you like. And what seems important now won't be any more. You won't live the same way you did, before. You will climb out of your cot. You thought you were in a big, big world, but it was just another cot. You will discover that if you go North. To *Everywhere*."

Jane nodded. She understood, but only in the same way an ant understands the concept of a planet. She grasped at the meaning, and held it.

"But I want to love them the same way. How I love them now."

The Man nodded. He pointed. "South. Go South, and you go back, to *There*. Back to your life, again."

"Back? To my life? To what I had?"

"Ah, it's not as easy as that. You'll be put back into your life at an appropriate moment. You won't remember any of this." He cast his arms around the clearing. "But you may have feelings, hunches, *deja vu*, intuitions. Sometimes events will happen that seem pre-ordained, but that's because you've lived them before. You'll feel you know strangers before you meet them, because you *have* met them. You will live your life again. Perhaps, maybe, you'll make different choices, which will lead to different outcomes. You and Simon may live into your eighties, having never experienced December 22nd, 2003. But then again, you might never meet him this time round. Your parents may live longer, or die younger. There are no guarantees. If you go North, you will enter the next place and move on. But if you head South, you are back on the wheel, and seemingly insignificant choices may bless or damn you. I don't know. You won't know. It will seem like living it all for the first time."

The Aurora's colours had faded to intimations of what they once were.

You need a lifetime to prepare for a decision like this, Jane thought, before she realised that's exactly what she'd had.

Her lifetime.

Everything she'd ever done had been in preparation for this moment, for a final, simple choice. *North, or South?* She looked back on her time, and clearly saw all the paths and forks, doors opened and unopened, decisions taken and abandoned, consequences faced.

She saw them all laid end to end and knew what she must do, where she must go.

Surely I can fix this, she thought, *I can fix it, make it right. I can do it all again, but next time round, I'll never see this place. I'll never know what* Here *is, or was. I will die old, and happy, with my grandchildren around me, with Simon. I will have lived, next time. I will have lived and I will* not *be cheated of my life and my love.*

I can fix this, but my god, I am so scared.

What if I get it wrong?

What if I choose the wrong path, open the wrong door?

What if I am damning myself and Simon again, but earlier in our time?

What if I never find him again?

But then she remembered what Dad had said to Mum on her death bed. "I love you. And I'll find you, Irene. I'll find you again, wherever you are, I'll find you again. I love you and I'll find you, Irene, I'll find you again, I promise, I love you."

I will be like my Dad, one more time. I am his daughter, and like him, I will find my love, whatever it takes. Even if we only have one more day together, it will be worth this. Love is worth whatever you risk for it. Even death, again, death over and over, forever times eternity. Until I get it right, that is what it will be.

"I'm so scared." The Man held her tight again. "I think I know where I want to go, but I'm so scared, The Man."

The Aurora had almost drifted away.

"Of course you are."

He held her, but had to let go, as he'd done so many times before and it always ripped him to shreds. "You must leave Here, now. If your body dies, then you are gone. You must beat death, Jane. North or South?"

Jane looked between the two paths.

She chose, then leaned up to The Man and kissed him on the cheek.

"Thank you." She looked him in the eye, thought for a moment, then whispered, "I'm so scared, but I'm ready."

"Yes," he smiled, but sadly. "You're ready. You've been ready a long time, because you're Jane Dawn and this is your story. We all have one, and this is yours. So please, *remember*. One moment is never really the end or even the beginning, but I suppose it can be a start, of sorts. Life is not helpfully arranged into chapters so this is just another moment, that is all. Merely one of many way points. Promise you'll remember that, Jane. It's important. Will you?"

"I will. I promise. This is not the end, or even the beginning, but it is a start. I'll remember." asked Jane, quietly.

"Good. Now go, tell your story, and tell it well. Sometimes all we need is someone to hear it. And you will find them. Go now, Jane. You must go."

Jane nodded, then without hesitation, walked quickly in a straight line to race death toward a Path. For one last time, the Snow sighed, cracked and popped behind her.

She reached the gap in the Forest and looked down at the fractal snail shell shapes beneath her feet. *They twist into forever,* she thought.

Jane took a deep breath, then stepped onto the Path.

She looked back at The Man, silhouetted against the dying embers of her Aurora.

He raised a hand to her, then wiped his eyes. She raised one back. *Hail and farewell.*

Jane stepped into the Forest, and as she did, became darkness.

Goodbye, Jane.

She has infinity now.

51 / There / December 22nd, 2003 / 21:02 P.M.

Hear that? Remember it? A thin sound like the whistle of an old kettle.

It is a machine announcing that Jane's heart had stopped.

She died at exactly 21:02 p.m. in the London Hospital.

Her vital signs flatlined, David looked up at that horizontal path on the screen, managed to gasp, "Jane," then grasped her hand so tightly before the cracks in his heart also broke for the last time.

He died five seconds after his daughter, still sat by her side, still holding on to her hand.

He promised once he'd never let her go.

And he hadn't.

Somewhen / Somewhere / December 22nd / 21:02 P.M.

Hear that? A thin, far off sound, like the whistle of an old kettle. It gains volume and clarity.

It is a machine keening in a nearby ward.

Jane wakes.

She is in a room. It is a white room. The clock on the wall reads 9:02 p.m.

She squints into the light. She can see a friendly looking man and a lady, but doesn't recognise, or rather, doesn't remember them.

There is another man in a white coat.

He must be a doctor.

Her first thoughts, unformed, are;

Was I in a park? Did I see snow? There was a tree. A park, yes. Lots of trees. Snow.

And then they are gone. Wiped.

She opens her eyes fully.

The lady says, "oh."

The friendly looking man smiles, his eyes wet.

The six year old Jane takes in the room and thinks;

"Now where am I?"

/ *Over, Not Out*

Goodbye, for now. You know my name as *Context*.
But once upon a time, long, long ago, in another place, when I was *so* different, my name was Jane.

The Gentle Art Of Forgetting
November 2014- September 2019
For the two who make us all one.

THE SNOW TRILOGY

The Snow Trilogy comprises of three self contained stories; *"The Gentle Art Of Forgetting," "The General Theory Of Haunting"* and*"The Littel* Tale Of Delivering (The Sleigh)"*.

Although the stories can be read independently, and in any order, they are connected. The 22nd of December is a crucial date across the trilogy. They all feature a mysterious box that is the key to secrets. Events from hundreds of years ago impact on every work.

Love, loss, memory and, of course, *snow* weave around all three. Snow is as important a character as the individuals you will meet.

In "The General Theory Of Haunting," snow has a sinister purpose, in "The Little Tale Of Delivering (The Sleigh), snow is an agent of change and in "The Gentle Art Of Forgetting," well, you now know what snow is.

An excerpt from "The General Theory Of Haunting".

Six work colleagues have managed to battle their way through dense snowfall to reach a New Year's Eve party at a remote mansion in Dorset. Isolated there with no phone signal or internet, the guests' secrets and personal demons begin to surface.

But the Hall itself also has a secret built into its walls. A grand and terrible purpose, kept hidden for over two hundred years. One by one, the party-goers begin to experience "events," that may or may not be other visitors.

In the following excerpt, one of the guests, Anne Barker, is first to realise that - just maybe - others have been invited and they've waited a long time for the festivities to begin…

*

Anne Barker sat on the edge of the bed and watched as the snow pushed and jittered against the window. Her eyes flicked to a bag on the floor. It contained her pills.

No, she managed to think distantly. *No, too early. You just had them. You had the pills when you were supposed to have them and you're not taking them again until eleven. You know that.*

But the pills were such a welcome exit. The medication kept her blurred rather than focused and acted as an antibiotic against herself.

She stood, as she should, and tried to do what was expected of her. But what was that? To join her colleagues downstairs and pretend?

Anne walked slowly over to the desk and mirror, where she stared at an emptiness that stared back at her. She tried a smile and it looked real enough. Anne picked up a brush and pulled it through her hair, as if corralling those stray strands would bring order elsewhere.

She took a small bottle of perfume, sprayed it into the air, then watched as the droplets flew and disappeared. They were another non-existent layer to hide behind.

But then, *a*s Anne sat back on the bed, a small creak came from behind her and the mattress shifted downward, just a little more.

It felt as if someone or *something* had also sat down. Someone or something that wanted to join her this evening.

Anne didn't move.

There was no one else here. She'd seen Dan leave, but the bed had *creaked* and the mattress had *rolled*, and she'd felt that movement so many times. It was a simple tilting that said, "you are not the only one sitting here. I am behind you. Look around, see, *I am here.*"

A sharp aroma came from that place. Another fragrance joined Anne in that room, similar to her own perfume, feminine, but not the same. Similar, yes, but filtered of its gentle bouquet, harder, harsher. If it were music, the scent would be *discordant.*

Anne closed her eyes. She'd had moments like this before, 'events' she'd never told Dan about, in case he tried to take the pills away. That could not happen. Anne needed the pills, but occasionally they magicked up these little 'performances', where reality wobbled for a moment.

Moments, seconds, yes, but never like this.

The mattress shifted again behind her, as if that somebody or *something* had changed position.

Anne knew she should just look round and see for herself that her room was empty, that nothing and no one stared at her back, at her vulnerable long white neck, who wanted Anne to sit awhile with them and *see what happened.*

But Anne couldn't. She was frozen. Her chest rose and fell imperceptibly, and she kept her eyes shut. The room was silent, save for her breath and the tiny taps of the snow as it flittered and jumped against the window.

If Anne had opened her eyes and turned her head a little, she could have seen the desk. If she saw the desk, she could see the mirror and, it followed, the reflection of whatever sat behind her. But Anne's mind was more fragile than even she knew, and if something *were* reflected there, it would shatter her.

Slowly, Anne opened her eyes, but couldn't turn her head. It had been fixed in place by fear. She simply stared ahead at the bathroom door. Anne breathed like her lungs were made of paper, would rip if she gulped air down like a drowner. So she inhaled softly in case the sound made whatever was sat there shuffle forward to investigate.

Don't breathe, she told herself, but simultaneously thought, *this is not real. This is the pills, this is the pills made real, nothing more. I must not look round because if I look round, and there is someone sitting there, grinning, I will never come back. I will be lost, my mind will tear, and I will never return. If I look round, and there is a shape under the sheets, a shape that reaches out, I will stop. I will stop being Anne Barker. I will stop being of this place. Just breathe. Be calm. Breathe.*

Quiet and shallow, Anne took in the barest oxygen she needed and continued to stare, unblinking, at the bathroom door. She prayed her peripheral vision wouldn't register movement in the mirror. If something moved there, Anne suspected she'd simply sit paralysed as whatever it was reached for her.

Anne breathed, then realised she was not the only one who did so here.

Yes, she heard it. Faraway, soft, yes, but she heard it. Something that had no need of oxygen behind her inhaled, exhaled. The breaths became deeper, but rolled, almost mechanical, like a respirator in an operating theatre. Human but inhuman, like the other perfume that had filled the air, not quite right somehow, not quite of *here*.

"Oh," she managed to vocalise, but it was a sound with no emotion, it simply escaped like air, dumb in meaning.

No no no, she thought from afar. *I* am *broken. The pills have broken me.*

The breath behind her changed. The mechanical in-out-in-out fluttered and shifted, like a broadcast picked up by a dying transistor radio. This new sound weaved and bent, but was recognisable, none the less.

No, no that cannot be, Anne thought. *It is the sound of crying. Who is crying behind me?*

A tiny part of her took control, the ancient centre of her brain responsible for survival.

Anne Barker slowly stood, put one foot in front of the other and walked toward the bedroom door.

If she could reach the door and turn the handle like an ordinary, normal person, the *world* would return to ordinary and normal, too.

Such a simple thing, to open a door.

Not far now. This 'event' was the pills. The pills that helped her now damned her. The pills had become real.

Anne reached for the handle, but stopped.

She had to look, to know this was just her mind in the throes of a short-circuit. That alone was a terrible enough idea, but preferable to the thought that... something impossible... waited there, just a foot behind her back.

She closed her eyes. She would turn, face the bed, open them, and there would be nothing there apart from what the pills had dreamed up.

Decision taken, Anne turned with her eyes still clamped shut.

Then, from two feet in front, but a billion miles away, from the other side of the universe, but here in the room, a voice suddenly whispered, harshly, "You are *nothing*".

Anne tried to keep her eyes shut but couldn't.

She backed up against the door in terror and looked in the direction of that rasped, hateful statement.

"Do it," that accusing voice grated like metal on metal and went silent.

The bed was empty.

She staggered a little and put her hand out to the wall.

I am lost, she thought and felt faint. She fell against the door, which was still mockingly solid. *I am hearing voices now. I am lost.*

Anne Barker, already buffeted by a storm within her, had become untethered.

COVER STORIES
8 Classic Songs Remixed And Covered As Short Stories

Richard Easter's short story collection, "Cover Stories" offers a *literal* remix of some of the world's greatest pop songs.

The tales answer such questions as; did The Rolling Stones' "Devil" really deserve sympathy? Who was Jimi Hendrix's "Joe" and why did he really shoot his woman down? And where did The Beatles' "Prudence" go out to play? It's a compilation album on paper rather than vinyl, a chance to read songs rather than hear them.

Here's an excerpt from Richard's literary 'cover' of David Bowie's "Space Oddity," which fills in all the details of Major Tom's tragic life that Bowie couldn't fit into the song; who the Major was, how he became an astronaut and why he became lost in space.

In this part of the story, we join David Jones, nickname, *Major Tom,* shortly before take off…

8th January 1947, Heathrow Space Dock

This was it. Showtime. And what a show it was going to be, courtesy of the world's greatest circus. The audience were ready, the drumroll had begun, the spotlight was on him and him alone, as he waited higher than any trapeze act.

No-one could stop the show now. He'd been checked and re-checked, taken protein pills and given cardiograms. He'd put his helmet on, ready to be waved off. David Jones had prepared for this moment forever, it felt, but now Major Tom was ready. Ready for what, though, he still didn't know.

8th January 1947, B.S.N. Ground Control, Brixton.

The children filed into Observation Room Six. There were thirty of them in all, aged between six and fifteen.

O.R.6 resembled a large, white classroom, complete with rows of chairs. Painted across the back wall was the logo of the British Space Navy, a stylised rocket with a Union Jack nosecone. Underneath, three italicised letters, *B.S.N.*

A man in his mid thirties, wearing a tweed suit, stood at the front. He bounced on the spot, excited, eager to begin.

"That's it, children. Welcome! Chop chop, find a desk, quick as you can. Twenty-five minutes until launch!" He clapped his hands together, impatiently, looked through a window behind him and gestured at a room below.

"Down there, children, are the people about to put the first ever human being in space. This is Brixton, Ground Control, today is 8th January, 1947 and you know your job. You are here as witnesses to history."

The children had been specially picked as part of Britain's "Future Legend" programme, that ensured major events within the British Empire were witnessed by the very young, who would then pass on those experiences over their many decades to come. Since the '30 s, British children had been invited to watch most of the Empire's epoch-defining events, to mythologise them into legends for the future.

They watched Ground Control intently. Most of the people down there sat behind ugly control panels comprising equally unwieldy dials and switches. It was *very* British. Dials were politely turned, switches carefully thrown, the occasional cup of tea sipped and biscuits nibbled.

"Busy, isn't it?" asked the man. "But I'm getting ahead of myself. I haven't even told you my name. I am Terence Jones. Terry. I am the brother of David Jones, soon to be the first man in space."

He knew that would get their attention. There were a few gasps and a couple of uncontrolled whoops of excitement. Hands shot up to ask questions.

"Yes. A few miles to the west, at Heathrow Space Dock 1, my brother is sitting on a Jupiter 8 rocket, ready to be the first person in history to leave this planet."

Terry had just jumped several hundred places in the children's estimation. One young boy couldn't help himself. He jittered in his seat and his hand fluttered for attention like a trapped bird.

"Your brother, sir? He is your brother? He is Major David Jones? So why does everyone call him Major *Tom*?"

Terry took a moment.

"Ah yes. Major Tom is the nickname my brother had since…a while back. You see, There is a character called Tom Jones, from a book by an author called *The History Of Tom Jones, A Foundling*. In his younger days, my brother, David Jones, reminded people of this character. He was, er popular with women. So, instead of Major David Jones, they started calling him Major *Tom* Jones, you see?"

Terry looked down at Ground Control and thought; *please take care of my brother. Because I don't think he can take care of himself.*

*

Heathrow Space Dock, 8th January, 1947.

David Jones, "Major Tom," sat in his capsule, alone.

He could only see two small circles of sky through the windows of his capsule. *If something were to go wrong,* he thought, *this would be my last ever view of Planet Earth. Just blue. No trees, no seas, no people. Just this endless blue. Maybe when I get up there I'll see what eternity looks like.*

Jesus, David, calm it down. You don't suit pretentious.

He shook his head. Those kinds of odd thoughts wouldn't do. He often drifted like this, away from the moment, into other realities. He didn't know why. It puzzled him.

It's almost as if there is another David Jones somewhere and we meet in our dreams. David thought. *In other universes, maybe many different versions of me exist. Perhaps, somewhere, I am a leader of men, or, in another reality I'm just a simple singer. Or maybe elsewhere I'm just a clown.*

Perhaps. Probably not. If there are other versions of me, I hope they *are happy.*

"Twenty minutes until launch." said a voice in his headset. It was Pitt, flight director at Brixton Ground Control. "Everything is across the board here. Slight drop in air pressure, nothing in red range. Ah, as you know, your wife is here."

David silently carried on with his checklist.

His headset went dead for a moment. There was a crackling noise and angry squeal of feedback before Pitt's voice came back on line.

"We were on public comms, David. I've switched to private, but I can't do it for long. Just talk to your wife. You agreed. Talk to Angela."

"You know I have nothing to say to her." David grunted.

"It's a British Space Navy order, as you know. She's on in ten seconds. Going back to public comms now."

David sighed. It was showtime - the world was listening and he had no choice but to give this performance.

"*Darling,* " she said, breathlessly. Even now she sounded like she was flirting. David knew she was, with the entire planet.

"Hello, *darling,*" he answered, equally aware of the millions of strangers listening.

"I just wanted to say God speed and how everyone is proud of you. None prouder than me."

"I just hope I live up to everyone's hopes."

"You will."

"Remember, David, this may be one small flight for you, but it is a giant leap for all mankind."

Oh, bravo, David tried not to wince. *That'll be Angie, staking her claim on the history books. She must have sat up late for nights on end thinking of that. I need to do better.*

"I am just one man," he improvised, wildly. "But through me, Man*kind* will fly. To the stars! Farewell for now, my darling!"

A tiny light on the camera above him blinked twice and went out. The camera was blind.

A crackling in his ear told David the radio frequency had changed. Now the rest of the world was deaf for thirty seconds.

David waited for his wife to speak again. He was in no rush. Let the seconds tick away then the world come back into his capsule.

"Oh, well done, David, good line." Her voice was suddenly tinny and small in the headphones. For a moment, his heart fell away from him, aching, beating for what could have been.

He watched the clock count down.

"Where are you watching from?"

"I won't be watching. David. You know that. I still have no wish to see you die."

"Really? That surprises me."

He knew that now was not the time, but couldn't help himself. Successful mission or not, this was it. Goodbye, in thirty seconds.

He had too much to say, and had tried to say it for some time. But it had never come out right.

"Enjoy your life, Angie."

"I will. Whatever happens, you know I will."

"You always did."

"I tried, David."

"You tried for you, Angie. You always did everything for *you*."

She sighed, a long, whooshing sound, a lonely wave crashing on a distant shore.

"Ashley would be proud."

"Goodbye Angie."

"David…"

The comms line crackled again and there was a brief hum before Pitt returned to David's ear.

"Jupiter 8, we're back on public comms, *public* comms, Jupiter 8. We're starting main pumps. Please engage. "

David Jones, Major Tom, sat in his tin can and prepared for blast off. He felt more alone than ever. *I'm about to be the first man in space, but I feel like the last man on earth.*

**COMING DECEMBER 2020 - THE TRILOGY IS
COMPLETED.**

"The Littel Tale Of Delivering"

Nothing happens in the village of Littel Wade. The streets are almost as grey and lifeless as the inhabitants.

But in the days running up to Christmas, fifteen year old Peter Piper and his friend Sally make a puzzling discovery in a local scrapyard.

Despite their cynicism it's possible - just possible - that they've stumbled across something they both stopped believing in a long time ago.

But if *they're* right and the *wrong* people also make the connections, things could become undone, very, very quickly.

Printed in Great Britain
by Amazon